Praise for the novels of Chris Bunch

"Bunch knows how to mold heroes . . .
and how to create exciting scenes
of battlefield mayhem."—*Publishers Weekly*

"Complex plots, intrigue, and great descriptive
narratives of battle and combat."—SF *Site*

"Remarkable."
—*New York Times* bestselling author
Michael A. Stackpole

"Glorious swashbuckling . . . absolutely riveting."
—*Locus*

"Stirring."—*Realms of Fantasy*

"An excellent fantasy adventure."
—*Science Fiction Chronicle*

**Don't miss these other
explosive adventures of Chris Bunch's
The Last Legion!**

THE LAST LEGION

FIREMASK

STORMFORCE

HOMEFALL

Book Four of the Last Legion

Chris Bunch

A ROC BOOK

ROC
Published by New American Library, a division of
Penguin Putnam Inc., 375 Hudson Street,
New York, New York 10014, U.S.A.
Penguin Books Ltd, 27 Wrights Lane,
London W8 5TZ, England
Penguin Books Australia Ltd, Ringwood,
Victoria, Australia
Penguin Books Canada Ltd, 10 Alcorn Avenue,
Toronto, Ontario, Canada M4V 3B2
Penguin Books (N.Z.) Ltd, 182–190 Wairau Road,
Auckland 10, New Zealand

Penguin Books Ltd, Registered Offices:
Harmondsworth, Middlesex, England

First published by Roc, an imprint of New American Library,
a division of Penguin Putnam Inc.

First Printing, August 2001
10 9 8 7 6 5 4 3 2 1

Cover art by Bob Warner
Cover design by Ray Lundgren

R̄OC REGISTERED TRADEMARK—MARCA REGISTRADA

Printed in the United States of America

PUBLISHER'S NOTE
This is a work of fiction. Names, characters, places, and incidents either
are the product of the author's imagination or are used fictitiously,
and any resemblance to actual persons, living or dead, business
establishments, events, or locales is entirely coincidental.

BOOKS ARE AVAILABLE AT QUANTITY DISCOUNTS WHEN USED TO PROMOTE
PRODUCTS OR SERVICES. FOR INFORMATION PLEASE WRITE TO PREMIUM
MARKETING DIVISION, PENGUIN PUTNAM INC., 375 HUDSON STREET, NEW
YORK, NEW YORK 10014.

For
Warren Lapine
and
Angela Kessler

Thanks to Ringling Bros and
Barnum & Bailey Circus for their help . . .
and minor apologies to Bertolt Brecht.

—CRB

CHAPTER
1

There were ten of them, wearing dappled camouflaged uniforms, heavily armed. They were dirty, and smelled like the jungle they'd been living in for the past four days.

Now, they crouched in meter-deep muck at the edge of a swamp, and watched the security patrol move past. The patrol's heatscanners were blocked by the insulated fabric the ten wore, and no one in her right mind would dream anyone would hide out in the reeking swampy goo.

The man on point looked at the team's leader, pointed to half a dozen bubble shelters a hundred yards away, drew a question mark in the air. The woman in charge nodded. The point man held up one finger . . . one sentry? The woman in charge shook her head—two. She pointed, and the point man saw the second, moving stealthily behind the first.

She motioned two others forward, tapped her combat knife. One smiled tightly, drew his blade, and crept forward, his partner behind him . . .

Haut Njangu Yoshitaro picked up his mug of tea, sipped, grimaced at the tepid mixture, then turned back to the holo.

"The problem, boss," he said, "is that they've got antiaircraft here . . . here . . . and I'll bet more missiles right under that finger of land that looks so frigging inviting for an LZ.

"I don't see any way to honk our Griersons into

this LZ over here, either, so we could make a decent attack."

Caud Garvin Jaansma, Commanding Officer, Second Regiment, Strike Force Angara, studied the projection, spun it, spun it again.

"Howsabout we whack 'em with a wave or so of Shrikes on the finger, then put in the combat vehicles through the mess?"

"No can do," Njangu, his Executive Officer, said. "We've got Nan Company right here . . . Rast Company backing them up, too close in to chance a blue-on-blue friendly casualty."

Garvin Jaansma was every centimeter a soldier—tall, muscular, blond-haired, blue-eyed, square-jawed. Everyone agreed he made a perfect recruiting poster. Everyone except Jaansma, which might have been part of his charm. Few people knew the devious mind concealed beneath his straight-arrow appearance.

But almost everyone agreed Njangu Yoshitaro was exactly what he looked like—sneaky and dangerous. Slender, dark-skinned, black-haired, he'd come from the depths of a slum world, forced into the military by a hanging judge.

"Shit," Garvin muttered. "Whose dumb-ass idea was it to put our grunts right on top of the baddies?"

"Uh . . . yours."

"Shit twice. I guess we can't tolerate friendly fire from our own artillery, can we?"

"Not after yesterday," Njangu said. "And all the *aksai* are tied up working for Brigade. Look. Try this. We take a flight of Zhukovs up high . . . above Shadow range, then have 'em come straight down toward—"

He broke off, hearing a soft grunt, as of someone being sapped.

"Aw hell," he said, moving swiftly across the bubble toward his combat harness. He'd barely touched the butt of his pistol when the bug shield was ripped aside, and three dirty men and a woman jumped into the shelter.

He tried for the gun anyway, and two blasters chattered. Njangu grunted, looked at the bloody mess of his chest, fell on his face, and lay still.

Garvin had his blaster up, and the woman in charge of the team shot him in the face. He went backward, through the holo, sending the projector to the ground.

"All right," *Cent* Monique Lir said briskly. "Spread out and take care of the rest of the command group until you get killed. Don't get taken prisoner . . . interrogation is a righteous pain in the ass."

Her Intelligence and Reconnaissance troops went back out, and the sound of blasters thumping came.

Lir sat down in a camp chair, put her feet up on another.

"Nice dying, boss. The new ones love a little realism."

Garvin sat up, wiped sticky red dye off his face.

"Thanks. How thc hcll'd you get through the lines?"

"Just looked for the shittiest part of the world and started crawling," Lir said.

Njangu got to his feet and looked at his uniform distastefully.

"I hope to hell this crap washes out."

"Guaranteed," Lir said. "Now, if you'll excuse me, I've got to go finish wiping out your headquarters."

She left the bubble.

"Fitzgerald is gonna rip my lungs out for getting killed," Garvin said.

"I think she's likely to have her own worries," Njangu said. "Last time I got a sitrep, she was up to her ass in cliffs and Aggressors."

He went to an unmarked cooler, opened it, and took out two beers.

"I guess since we're officially dead, we can have one, eh?"

"Why not?" Garvin said, drinking deeply. "This was about an abortion of a war game, wasn't it?"

"Only goes to show first that a brigade attacking an entrenched brigade takes it up the old koondingie," Njangu said. "Just like in the books.

"Not to mention that well-trained thugs like I&R can always pull a sneaking number on crunchies like we're in charge of."

"As if I ever doubted that," Garvin said. He took another swallow of beer. "You know, it was a lot more fun when *we* got to play Aggressor and do dirty deeds dirt cheap and ruin other people's plans, wasn't it?"

"Maybe," Njangu said. "But when the blaster rounds got real, we also got killed a lot, remember? Which also was real, remember? That was one reason we decided to get ambitious and move upward in the chain of command, like good little heroes.

"More money in that, too."

"But it sure is duller'n shit in peacetime," Garvin said.

"Shut up," Njangu suggested. "Death comes knocking too early in the morning anyway.

"Let's see if we can't wrap this whole mess into one untidy ball, pull the troops out, and go looking for a shower and a drink."

"After," Garvin said gloomily, "we get our asses chewed for losing."

"Ouch," Garvin said, rubbing imaginary wounds. "I keep forgetting that one reason you get promoted to high command is an ability with words. I wish *Caud* Fitzgerald had done the critique instead of *Dant* Angara."

It was late the next afternoon before the Legion's CO had finished his after-game commentary and the troops had been bathed, fed, and turned loose for a deserved two-day pass.

"I bleed, I moan, I sorrow," Njangu said. "What

did he say about me? 'Ineptly planned, carelessly executed, stupidly ended'?"

"I got worse, nanner," Garvin said. " 'Incorrect intelligence, failure to control staff, assumption of a degree of intelligence, deservedly assassinated, generally lazy staff and field work that can only be ascribed to the torpid assumption that peacetime exercises aren't important.' "

"The Man *can* talk some shit," Njangu said, absently returning the salute of an *Aspirant* trotting at the head of his platoon as they went up the steps into the Camp Mahan Officers' Club. "What time's Jasith coming over for you?"

"Eighteen-thirty or so. She said I wasn't supposed to let you get me too drunk."

" 'At's funny," Njangu said. "That's the same thing Maev said about you."

"Great minds, in the same track," Garvin said. "Like sewers." He wriggled. "Sure feels nice to be clean again."

"Gettin' soft, boss," Njangu said. "You ain't much of a field troopie if a mere day or three without a 'fresher gets to you. And you wanted to be out slitherin' through *giptel* doots with Lir? Getting old, grandpa. What are you, almost twenty-six? That's a year up on me."

"Maybe I am turning into a candy ass," Garvin said. "Unlike you younger goons. Hey. Look."

He pointed across the cavernous club to a table in the rear, where a very large, prematurely balding man in a flight suit sat, morosely staring at an almost-empty pitcher of beer.

"What's our Ben brooding about?" Njangu said. "He can't be too broke to drink. We just got paid a week ago."

"Dunno," Garvin said. He went to the bar, got two pitchers and two glasses, and he and Njangu went to *Cent* Been Dill's table.

"Oo looks unhappy," Njangu cooed. "Did oo faw

down getting out of oo's *aksai* and dent oo's ickle nose?"

"Worse," Dill said. "Far, far worse. Mrs. Dill's favorite son got killed today."

"Big frigging deal," Njangu said. "So did we."

"No, I don't mean playing some stupid war game," Dill scowled. "I mean killed killed."

Garvin reached over and poked the pilot.

"You seem pretty solid for a ghost."

"I don't mean killed killed killed," Ben said. "Just killed killed."

"I'm getting confused," Garvin said.

"Here," Njangu said. "Drink beer and tell Aunt Yoshitaro all."

"Can't do it," Dill said. "What's your clearance?"

"Crypto Quex," both officers said smugly. "There ain't no higher," Njangu added.

"Oh yeh?" Dill growled. "What about HOME-FALL?"

Jaansma and Yoshitaro looked at each other blankly.

"Ho-ho," Dill said. "If you ain't heard of it, you ain't got clearance enough, and I can't talk to you."

"I surely understand your caution," Njangu said. "Being here in a nest of spies and all."

"Come on," Garvin said. "Security's important."

"Only for other people," Njangu said. "Now, let us do a little intel analysis while we sit here and work on the beer we just put on Mr. Dill's tab.

"First, we should be aware that, since I've been demoted from my former lofty position as one of *Dant* Angara's intelligence sorts, the quality of Two Section has slipped astoundingly.

"This means that my replacements have slid into the easy grip of giving a certain operation a code name that suggests what it's about.

"We might suspicion that . . ." and Njangu reflexively lowered his voice, looked to make sure the tables around them were empty, ". . . HOMEFALL might just happen to have something to do with the Force starting to investigate why our ever-so-beloved Confederation has vanished and left us out on the far frontiers with a tear in our eye, our dick in our hand, and a hole in our pants."

Dill covered his flinch. "Jeez," he said, "you're getting as wordy as Jaansma."

"There probably has been a certain cross-cultural leveling flow," Njangu admitted.

"More like I've been able to drag him up to our level," Garvin said. "Njangu's doing a good job of guessing, since all of the hot-rod pilots have been detached for a special assignment . . . people like you and Alikhan and Boursier, for instance. And if you get killed killed, but not killed killed killed, maybe you're running pilotless craft out into the wild black yonder.

"But I don't think we ought to get specific if you want to tell us any details."

Dill nodded. "Let's just say I stuck my dick out where it shouldn't've been and got it shortened by about forty centimeters, leaving me with only a ninety-centimeter stub."

The Confederation was a centuries-old federation, sometimes authoritarian enough to be called an Empire, scattering across several galaxies. One of its Strike Forces, the Legion, had been assigned to the mineral-rich Cumbre system, which sat on the edges of "civilization," with the alien, hostile Musth "beyond" and the aggressive systems of Larix and Kura "behind" them.

Garvin and Njangu had been raw recruits on the last transport from the Confederation's capital world of Centrum to support Cumbre, barely escaping a highjacking by Larix and Kura to make it to D-Cumbre.

And then all communications, all transport, ended.

The Force, now isolated, fought first a civil war against the 'Raum, worker-terrorists of Cumbre; then against the Musth; and, not much over an E-year past, a brutal campaign against Larix and Kura.

Now there was peace. But sooner or later everyone knew the Legion, as it was unofficially known, would have to go looking for the Confederation, or its remnants.

And so, very quietly, Force scientists had built drones, with realtime controllers on D-Cumbre "flying" them. The commands to the ship bounced from satellite to satellite as the drone jumped from hyperspace navigation point to nav point, making them ideal for taking a peek at places elsewhere.

"I think we can figure out what happened," Njangu said. "You were out playing with your drone, and somebody or something blew you off. Sorry about that."

"At least we're not sending manned ships out," Garvin said.

"Still, it's damned unsettling, getting killed," Dill said, drinking straight from a pitcher until it was dry, ignoring Garvin's protests. "Shuddup. If I'm buying, it's my beer, so I can drink it if I want.

"Right?"

He glared at Garvin, who nodded hastily. Ben Dill was, thankfully, a cheerful sort of prime mover. Mostly. The problem was that no one in the Force was precisely sure what set his temper off, since it seemed to vary from day to day and mood to mood.

Jaansma waved at a bartender for another round.

"You know," Njangu said thoughtfully, "maybe it's time I put my finely tuned mind to considering things."

"What sort of things?" Dill said, accepting one of the three new pitchers.

"Oh," Njangu said, "like how you got so ugly."

Dill was about to respond when he saw a nightmare entering the club. It was over two meters tall, with many-banded coarse fur in various shades of yellowish brown. It had a small head, on a very long neck, that peered constantly about.

The creature walked upright on large rear legs, and its front legs were clawed. It had a small tail and wore a weapons harness in the Confederation colors of blue and white.

"Hey, Alikhan," Dill bellowed to the Musth mercenary pilot. "Get your fuzzy butt over here and help me deal with a couple of line slime!"

The alien made his way to their table.

"Whassamatter?" Dill asked. "You don't look happy."

He was one of the few who claimed he could decipher Musth expressions.

"I cannot say," Alikhan said. He, unlike most Musth, who had trouble with sibilants, spoke excellent Common Speech. "But if I were where I was not, I would not be here with you."

"Aw," Ben Dill said. "Order up some of your stinky meat and get wasted with us. The whole lot of us have gotten killed."

"Yes," Njangu Yoshitaro said thoughtfully. "Time and past time for me to be thinking about this whole Confederation mess."

CHAPTER
2

Jasith Mellusin considered Garvin Jaansma's skinned nose, and giggled.

"I told you that you've got to be born on D-Cumbre, or maybe some other world with a lot of water, before you can wave-ride."

"Nonsense," Garvin said, eyeing his equally battered chest. "I merely need guidance. You never told me you can fall out of a wave."

"Because I never knew anyone who did it before," Jasith said.

Jasith Mellusin, at twenty-three, was one of the richest women in the Cumbre system, controlling Mellusin Mining and its many ancillary corporations that her grandfather and father had built. She and Garvin had been lovers, ex-lovers, then came together again during the Musth occupation of D-Cumbre.

"I'll just lie here and sunburn a while," Garvin groaned, "then rise up and fight again. Hand me that glass, if you would."

Jasith reached under the umbrella's shade, passing the tumbler sitting atop the small portable bar to him. He gurgled down alcohol. Behind them, on the deserted beach, was Jasith's lim. Beyond, large waves smashed down, slithered up the black sands.

"Ah. I may live." He stretched. "You know, you're doing an extraordinary job of making me forget that tomorrow's a duty day."

"My intent," Jasith purred. "Speaking of which—" She broke off.

"Maybe you want to put your pants back on, and give me that towel. I hear music."

"Naah. You're cracking up." But Garvin obeyed, as two figures hove down the slope toward them. One was Njangu Yoshitaro, the other Maev Stiofan, recently rescued from Larissan service, now the head of *Dant* Angara's bodyguards.

She was turning a handle on a brightly painted box, and Yoshitaro carried a cooler in one hand, something in wrapping paper in the other.

"Ah-yut-dut-dut-dut-dut-dah-doo," Njangu sang as they approached. "We bring gifts of great import, O fearless leader."

"How the hell did you find us?" Garvin demanded. "Thisyere beach is private property, and we didn't tell anyone where we were going."

"Ah," Yoshitaro said, looking mysterious. "Have you not learned by now I know everything?"

"Hey, Jasith," Maev said. "This is all his idea, and I don't have a clue what he's got in mind."

"As usual with these two," Jasith said. "Pull up a towel and have a drink."

"Did I say to stop playing?" Njangu said as he opened his cooler and took out two beers.

Maev obediently began turning the crank, and more tinny music floated out.

"What in God's tattooed butt is that?" Garvin demanded.

"Hah," Njangu said. "And here you claim to be a circus master."

"Ringmaster," Garvin corrected, looking closer at the box. "I'll be dipped," he said. "It's a music box. And it's playing, uh, the 'Elephant Song.' "

"Actually, 'March of the Elephants,' " Njangu said. "Maev found it in some antiquey store, which gave me the idea. Here." He passed the parcel across.

"It's not my birthday," Garvin said suspiciously.

"Nope," Njangu agreed. "Merely my sub-tile way of leading you into yet another of my brilliant schemes."

Garvin tore paper off. Inside was a disk, and on the disk was a tiny figure of a man wearing clothing several sizes too big for him; a dancer standing on the back of a quadruped, another woman wearing tights, and in the center a man in very old-fashioned formal wear. It was made of plas, and the paint or anodizing had worn off here and there.

"I had to get the motor replaced before it'd work," Njangu said. "Hit that button, there."

Garvin did, and the clown in the baggy clothes pranced about, the horse ran around the ring while its rider did a handstand, the woman in tights tumbled back and forth around the ring, and the formally dressed man held out his hands here and there.

"Well, I shall be damned," Garvin said softly. His eyes filled.

"What is it?" Jasith asked.

"It's the center ring of a circus," Jaansma said. "A circus from a very, very long time ago. Thank you, Njangu."

"You see how well my plan's working," Yoshitaro said. "Almost got him blubbing like a babe. Softened the idiot up, I have."

Garvin turned the device off.

"This is quite a buildup."

"This is quite a plan," Njangu agreed.

"First, consider what we've been doing wrong. Back when we were expecting trouble with ol' Protector Redruth, we went and sent a snoopy shit out to see what was whuppin', right? And, thanks to that late and unlamented spy, they wuz lurkin' on us, and we got our butt buzz-sawed, right?

"Now, and ladies, I'll expect you to plug your li'l bitty ears and not listen to what I'm saying, we're now engaged in a certain enterprise, being sneaky once more, and what's happening?"

"You mean those drones we've been losing?" Maev said. "You're not supposed to know anything about Operation HOMEFALL."

Njangu raised several eyelids.

"Neither are you, you common bodyguard."

"Surely am," Maev said smugly. "Who do you think *Dant* Angara uses for his couriers? I got a HOME-FALL clearance about a month ago."

"And never told me?"

"You, my dear, don't have a need to know."

"Zeus on a poop deck," Njangu said. "You see, Jasith, m'dear, why you're best staying well away from the military? Corrupts even the most loving relationship with its insistence on dirty, dark secrets."

"I know," Jasith agreed. "That's why I felt so bad about not telling Garvin here about the Legion contracting to have its drones built by Mellusin Yards."

Both men stared at each other.

"Thank any species of gods we don't believe in there aren't any spies about anymore," Garvin said finally. "This goddamned society leaks like . . . like a noncom with bladder problems."

"How can we have spies if we don't even know who the frigging villains are yet?" Njangu asked reasonably, drained his beer, got another from the cooler.

"Having been thoroughly sidetracked, I might as well stay that way. Jasith, my love, my darling, my bestest friend's delight, could I borrow a ship from you?"

"What sort?"

"Something big and clunky. Some power to it. Interstellar, of course. Doesn't have to be too fast or maneuverable."

"What shape are you going to bring it back in?"

"Damfino," Njangu said. "Maybe perfect. Maybe in a collection of brown paper bags. Maybe not at all, although if that happens, you won't be able to rack my heinie, since I plan on being aboard it."

Jasith grinned.

"I think I've got what you need.

"I happen to have a certain clunker in the yards right now. Commissioned right after the war. Designed to carry and deploy, without a dock, mining machinery . . . I mean *big* mining machinery, like self-contained drilling units, even full mills . . . D- to E-Cumbre and to the outworlds for exploration. It's huge, almost three kilometers long, and gives ugly a hard way to go. Best description I could have is it looks like the universe's biggest nose cone, with landing-support fins that nobody built the rest of the ship for. Lotsa bulges and extrusions. Since it was to be the ultimate pig, and a good tax writeoff, we went ahead and put stardrive in it.

"You could fit a whole handful of patrol ships, plus maybe a couple-four *aksai* in it. Takes a smallish crew to run . . . I don't remember just how many . . . and has living space that can be configured as dorms, cubicles, or even single bedrooms. It'll sleep fifteen hundred or more . . . in comfort and happily, since nobody wants to be around a smelly, angry miner.

"The holds can be sectioned, and, since we sometimes tote delicate stuff around, there's triply redundant antigrav," she added. "I'll lease the *Heavy Hauler VI* to the Force for, oh, ten credits a year, being the sentimental patriotic sort that I am."

"Step one is now accomplished," Njangu announced. "By the way, I admire the romantic names you Mellusins give your spaceships."

"You want to tell me what some lardpig of a spaceship has got to do with a circus?" Garvin asked.

"Why, we'll need a lardpig to haul our circus around in."

"*Our* circus?" Garvin said.

"What a very thick young *caud* you be, *Caud* Jaansma," Njangu said. "What do you think I've been hinting broadly about? And aren't you the one who's always been nattering on, whenever you get drunk and maudlin, about giving all this up and running away and joining the circus, like the ones your family used to run?"

"Mmmh." Garvin considered.

"What we do," Njangu went on, getting more enthusiastic, "is we put together a troupe . . . I went and looked that word up . . . made up of Forcemen, and then we go out, hiding in plain sight, doing a show here, a show there, and all the time we're working our way closer to, maybe the Capella system and Centrum.

"We don't have to be very good, just not visibly anyone interested in anything other than a quick credit.

"We'd best put in some crooked games," he said thoughtfully. "First, nobody'd expect a Confed soldier to be crooked; second, that could be some good coinage for our retirement.

"When we get an eyeful and an earful on what's happening out there in the great beyond, we slide on back home, report, and let *Dant* Angara figure out what to do next. But at least we get an idea of what's out there . . . besides blackness and nothing."

Maev nodded understanding, coming from another system herself. Jasith, who'd known nothing but Cumbre her entire life, shrugged.

"Interesting," Garvin said after being silent for a while. "Very interesting."

"You want to go for it?" Njangu asked.

"Some of it," Garvin said, pretending utter casualness. "I've got a few ideas of my own, you know."

"The last time you tried some of them, you damned near got yourself executed, remember?" Njangu said. "I'm the brains of this operation, right?"

Maev started laughing. "If that's true, boy are you two clowns in trouble."

"Clowns," Garvin said, a bit dreamily. "I've always dreamed of having a center ring full of clowns, so many when they shivaree nobody'll be able to make me out.

"You'll make a good clown, Njangu."

"Me? Uh-uh. I'm gonna be the guy who goes in front, getting the people ready."

"Boss hostler? Dunno if you've got the talent," Garvin said, mock-seriously.

"Wait a minute," Jasith said. "You two are talking about going out, running around, and having fun."

"Oh no," Njangu said piously. "Lotsa big risks out there. We're laughing, ho-ho, in the face of danger."

"Fine," Jasith said. "Change one. You want my ship, you're taking me with you."

"Huh?" Garvin said.

"You're always the ones having adventures," Jasith said. "No more."

"What sort of slot would you want?" he said.

"Are you going to have dancing girls?"

"Sure," Garvin said. "What's a good circus without a little bit of sex around the edges. Most respectable, of course," he added hastily.

"And with me along, it'll be doubly so," Jasith said firmly.

"I have learned," Garvin said to Njangu, "never to argue with Mellusin when she gets that tone of voice to her voice."

" 'Kay," Njangu said. "She goes. That'll keep you straight. Plus she can run payroll and the books, being the business yoink she is."

"And I'll take care of you," Maev said. "Since you said something about recruiting from the Force."

Njangu grinned and kissed her.

"If *Dant* Angara turns you loose, why not?"

"Lions and horses and maybe even bears," Garvin said, lost in his vision.

"Yeh," Njangu said. "Sure. Just where on Cumbre are you gonna find any of them?"

Garvin smiled mysteriously, then came to his feet. "Come on. Let's go tell Angara about your latest craziness."

Dant Grig Angara, the Legion's Commander, stared at the small holo of the *Heavy Hauler VI* as it went through its paces—extruding ramps, opening huge ports, its decks changing— without seeing it.

"My parents took me to a circus once, when I was a kid," he said slowly. "And the prettiest lady in the world, who wore white tights, gave me some candy that was like a pink cloud when you bit into it."

"You see?" Garvin said to Njangu. "Everybody loves a circus. Cotton candy for all."

Angara brought himself back.

"An interesting idea," he mused. "Of course you'd punt out without leaving any tracks so you could be followed back to Cumbre."

"Of course, sir."

"And we could hold a Field Day for the Force, and you could pick any athletes you want."

"Actually," Njangu said, "we could do it for the whole system, since we don't have to worry about this having any kind of security hold."

Angara made a face. "I don't know if I agree. I don't like everybody knowing our business. But maybe you're right."

"If you want to have a mass tryout, sir," Garvin said, "that's fine. But our first stop . . . unless you order otherwise . . . will be at one of the circus worlds."

"Circus worlds?" Angara said, a note of incredulity to his voice.

"Yessir. I know of three. Circus people have to have a place to get away from the flatties . . . the crowd. Even in olden times there were circus towns where the troupers and their animals would go in the off-season.

"That's where they recruit people, practice new tricks, change jobs, catch up on the gossip."

"What will that give you?"

"Animal acts," Garvin said. "Trapeze artists. Flash."

"How will you pay for that?" Angara asked. "It's peacetime, and PlanGov is getting a little tight with the budget. I don't want to have to stand up and say, 'fine, ladies, gentlemen, we're going to put on a show you'll never see.' "

"Mellusin Mining has already agreed to fund us," Garvin said. "Plus I&R's got a ton of money in a discretionary fund that was given us by Mellusin back during the Musth war."

"I am getting very fond of this idea," *Cent* Erik Penwyth, one of Angara's aides said. He was a member of Cumbre's elite, the Rentiers, and ex-member of the elite I&R Company, sometimes considered the most handsome man in the Force.

"And we'd love to have you," Garvin said. "Maybe as advance man."

"Hey," Njangu said. "I thought that was my slot."

"Not a chance," Garvin said. "I wasn't kidding when I said I want clowns. Plus," he added thoughtfully, "I want somebody close at hand for security."

"Oh. Oh," Njangu said in a mollified tone. "That's different."

"Which brings up another problem," Angara said. "This little mission is going to strip the Force clean of some of its best troops. I've got to assume worst case, and you'll have problems. I agree this mission is important—but I don't want it accomplished with the loss of some fine soldiers a long way from home."

Garvin inclined his head in agreement. "First, I plan on bringing everyone back. Second is that some of what I'll call best may not be on your roster."

"A good point," Angara agreed after a bit of thought. "I&R troops don't always make the best line soldiers. I assume you'll be taking a lot of them with you."

"With your permission, sir," Garvin said. "Since we're at peace, that'll give them something to keep out of trouble."

"Bigger trouble generally does," Angara said. "So you'll collect a team . . . a troupe, you called it, and start gathering intelligence. Let's for the sake of argument, and to keep one small measure of security of things, call the operation HOMEFALL, like another, similar one we have running presently. That should thoroughly confuse the issue.

"But back to the matter at hand. What happens if, or when, you run into trouble?"

"We'll have the ship armed to the eyebrows," Garvin said. "With all the goodies out of sight. I'll take some *aksai*, some of the Nana-class patrol boats we took back from Redruth's mob."

"Won't that appear suspicious?"

"If the Confederation has fallen apart," Garvin said, "which seems a little more than logical, considering the drones I know nothing about that have been getting disappeared lately, I'd assume anybody going anywhere off their own homeworlds goes armed these days."

" 'Kay," Angara agreed. "Probably right on that one."

"By the way, we're going to rename the *Hauler*, for good luck," Garvin said. "It'll be *Big Bertha*."

"*Damned* romantic," Penwyth said sarcastically.

"Named after the biggest circus of them all," Garvin said. "Way back on Earth. Ringling Brothers and Bailey and Barnum."

"Whatever you want," Angara said.

"There is one other thing I'd like, sir," Garvin said diffidently. "This whole situation might get a little . . . tense. And I'm just a young trooper. Shouldn't we find some diplomat to go with us? Just to make sure we don't make any mistakes. Soldiers have a, well—"

"Tendency to pull triggers when in question or in doubt," Angara finished.

"Well . . . yessir."

Angara considered for a moment. "Not a bad idea, *Caud*. There's only one problem. I can't think of any politico in this system who qualifies as any kind of subtle peacemaker or -keeper. Cumbre's history over the past few years doesn't exactly suggest any names to me. Do you have any candidates?"

Garvin shook his head, looked at Njangu.

"Other than me," Yoshitaro said, "sorry, sir. My files are empty."

"So I'm afraid," Angara said, "you'll have to play things as best they appear to you. How far do you want to go?"

"As far as I can get, sir," Garvin said firmly. "Hopefully, all the way to the heart of the Confederation, to Centrum itself."

CHAPTER
3

"At the moment," *Caud* Fitzgerald said to Garvin, "you are not one of my favorite Regimental Commanders."

"No, ma'am."

"And you, *Haut* Yoshitaro, are on the same shit list."

"Yes, ma'am," Njangu said. Both Jaansma and Yoshitaro stood at rigid attention in front of their Brigade Commander.

"Once again, I've got to remind both of you. This Force has something called a chain of command. That means when you two thugs have an idea, it is supposed to go to me, then, and only then, assuming I approve, up the chain of command to *Dant* Angara.

"Instead, I find I'm losing both of you to go haring out into the unknown as if you were both still with I&R . . . and the scheme was your idea in the first place."

"Sorry, *Caud*," Garvin tried. "I forgot."

"Old habits die hard," Njangu hurried.

"It's a pity that *Dant* Angara doesn't approve of some field punishments other armies used, such as crucifixion."

Garvin looked into the woman's hard eyes, not sure if she was joking, and said nothing.

"Very well," Fitzgerald said. "Since Angara's already approved, there's nothing I can do but rail at you.

"Don't fail . . . or, if you do, come back dead.

Otherwise, I might have to remember this conversation when it's time for your next fitness reports.

"Now get your asses out of here . . . and, incidentally, the best of luck."

Ben Dill shambled into Garvin's office, something just bigger than a cubicle, with an inspiring view of the Second Regiment's motor pool. He managed a salute, didn't wait for Jaansma to return it, and sat down.

" 'Kay," he growled. "First, I'll listen to you tell me why I can't go on this wildhair trip of yours, then I'll tell you why I'm going."

"Save it, Ben," Garvin advised. "You're already on the roster."

Dill blinked. "Howcum I don't have to threaten you, like usual?"

"I need a good pilot," Garvin said, "but I'll take you. We're bringing along three *aksai*, plus a hangar queen for spare parts, and I understand you know which end of those evil-flying bastards goes first."

"I am only the best *aksai* pilot in the cosmos, including any Musth that might think, just 'cause he invented those evil pigs, he's better than me."

"Which is why I put you down, right after Alikhan and Boursier."

"Alikhan, 'kay," Dill said. "But Boursier? I can fly circles around her butt without power."

"I just wanted to wait to see how long it took you to show up," Garvin said, suppressing a grin. "You want to know your other slot?

"We'll need a strongman."

"You mean, like in the holos, stripped to the waist, all oiled up, with big ol' iron rings on my arms to show off my perfect physique?"

"Plus a corset to hold in your gut."

"Damn," Dill said, oblivious. "I get to show off."

"Within reason."

"Hey," the big man said, "I got a great idea. Since

you're taking Alikhan already, and nobody needs to know he speaks Common Speech, you could use him—"

"As an exhibit," Garvin interrupted. "Meet Man's Deadliest Foe . . . See Him in an Orgy of Decayed Flesh . . . a Cannibal Fiend from a Nightmare Beyond the Stars. And anybody who comes close to his cage will talk freely, not knowing he's got big ears on 'em."

"Aw shit," Dill said. "You went and beat me to it."

"Always," Garvin said.

Dill chortled. "It'll be worth the price of admission just seeing him in a cage."

"Only when the gilly-galloos are around."

" 'At'll be enough. I'll bring . . . what're they . . . nutpeas to throw at him."

"I suppose," Njangu said, "all this is in the noble tradition of I&R volunteering for everything." His hand swept out, indicated the company formation in front of him. "Is there anybody missing?"

"Nossir," *Cent* Monique Lir said briskly. "Other than one man in hospital who won't be discharged before takeoff time."

" 'Kay," Njangu said, then raised his voice. "I'm proud of all you sneaky mud-eaters for courage and general stupidity.

"Now, my flyer mentioned specific talents. Anybody who's got one of them, stay in formation. The rest of you, who're just looking for some cheap adventure like I am, fall out and go back to your barracks."

He waited, and, grudgingly, people began slinking away, until only about sixty of the 130-plus unit remained.

" 'Kay," Njangu said. "Now, we'll start screening."

He eyed the men and women.

"Striker Fleam . . . what are you planning to add to things? Besides your general surly attitude, I mean."

The hard-faced Striker, who always refused promotion but was one of the best field soldiers in I&R, which meant the entire Force, grinned thinly.

"Knots, sir."

"Beg pardon."

"I can tie any knot known. One-handed, off-handed, upside down, in my sleep, on a drunk."

"A knot-tier," Njangu said, beginning to enjoy this, "wasn't on the list."

"Nossir," Fleam agreed. "But I checked around, and went and looked up circuses, and all of them talk about ropes and lines and pulleys and shit like that."

" 'Kay," Njangu said. "You're aboard. What about you, *Cent* Lir?"

"I've been a dancer with an opera company."

" 'Kay. We'll need somebody to ramrod the dance troupe. What about you, *Alt* Montagna?"

"Swimming, sir. High diving too. And I thought I could learn trapeze, since I'm not a bad climber."

"Have either of you thought about what's going to happen to I&R with both the Company Commander and Exec away?"

"Already taken care of, sir," Lir said briskly. "We'll vet Lav Huran up to take over as CO, give him a temp commission that'll go to permanent if we don't come back, Abana Calafo as XO, also with a temporary rank. Already approved by *Caud* Jaansma."

"Mmmh." Njangu turned serious. Of course the incredibly competent Lir would be welcome, although he hadn't heard of her opera experience.

Darod Montagna was another story. Garvin, in spite of his ongoing affair with Jasith Mellusin, had more than a casual interest in the young black-haired sniper/officer. Njangu had caught them kissing when both were drunk during the war with Larix/Kura, but didn't think much further had happened.

It would've been trouble if it had, except Montagna had gotten herself commissioned during the war, so the traditional ban on enlisted/officer relationships wasn't there.

But still . . . Njangu remembered two things. First, that Jasith was going on the expedition and, second and more important, he wasn't Garvin's keeper.

" 'Kay," he grudged. "Now, let's sort the rest of you fools out."

"Send him in," Garvin said. He leaned back in his chair. It had been a very long week, vetting volunteers, listening to the lies of commanders trying to fob off the lame and lazy on him, and to the screeches of other COs who were losing their best. And now this.

Dr. Danfin Froude was one of Cumbre's most respected mathematicians, though his talents led into most areas of applied science. In addition, in spite of his over-sixty years, the rumpled small man was a daredevil and had accompanied the Force on several hazardous missions, getting a reputation for complete fearlessness. During the Larix/Kura war, he'd fallen in love hard with one of the Forcewomen, not uncommon when romance comes late in life. She'd been killed, and Froude's world seemed to have ended. He was still there for the Force for any desired analysis, but he was a bit distant, as if a part of him had died with Ho Kang.

The door came open, and Garvin jumped. The man standing in front of him wore exaggerated stage makeup, the saddest man in the world, with a peculiarly obnoxious long nose. His pants sagged, his shoes were holed, and ridiculously oversize, his vest tattered as much as his archaic hat.

"Hello, Garvin," Froude said. "You're looking very well." He snuffled. "I'm not." He began taking a large handkerchief from a sleeve, and more and more material came out, until he was holding something the size of a bedsheet. There was a flutter in its midst, and a *stobor*, one of the two-legged snakes peculiar to D-Cumbre slithered out, landed on Garvin's desk, hissed, and fled into the outer office.

"Oh, sorry, Garvin," Froude said, still in the same

monotone. A tear dripped from one eye, and he wiped it away. When the handkerchief was gone, his long nose had changed into a red rubber ball. He scratched it, took it off, bounced it against a wall, shrugged.

"I don't guess you're going to let me come with you, are you?"

"You learned all this in two days?"

Froude nodded, and his pants fell down.

"You know there's no way I'd refuse a Willie the Weeper," Garvin said.

Froude snuffled, picked up his pants.

"You're not just saying that to try to make me smile, now are you?"

He lifted his hat, and some species of flying object scrawked and flapped away.

"You're aboard, you're aboard," Garvin said, starting to laugh. "Now get the hell out before you produce some carnivore out of your pants."

"Thank you, sir, thank you, thank you," Froude said, still in the monotone, bowing and scraping. "But I have one more boon, a small favor, just a little service, since Ann Heiser is off getting married to Jon Hedley, and wants to stay home for a while, which means I won't have anyone to bounce my ideas off of."

Garvin noticed the way Froude's face twisted when he said "married," but said nothing.

Froude went to the door, opened it.

Garvin looked suspiciously at the completely undistinguished man who hunched into his office. He was short, a bit over a meter and a half tall, wearing battered clothes that the poorest of poor clerks might disdain.

"This is my colleague, Jabish Ristori," Froude said.

Ristori extended a hand. Garvin reached to take it, and Ristori did a backflip, landing on his feet. He held out his hand again, and as Garvin stepped forward, the man cartwheeled against the wall, then, somehow, up onto Garvin's desk, and against the other wall, once more came down with a graceful bounce, and solemnly shook Garvin's hand.

"Pleased to meetcha, meetcha, meetcha," and Ristori turned another flip to show his pleasure.

"Professor Jabish Ristori," Froude said. "Nice enough guy, a colleague of mine for years, even if he does belong to one of those fields that can hardly be called a discipline."

"Socisocisocisociology," Ristori said, doing a handstand, then lifting one hand off the ground.

"Jabish became curious ten years ago about wandering entertainers, and determined to learn their tricks," Froude went on.

"And I never, ever, ever went back to the univee," Ristori said with an infectious giggle. "Dull, dry, dry, dull."

He pushed off from the ground and landed on his feet.

"Welcome to the circus," Garvin said. "We can always use a tumbler."

"A tumbler, bumbler, stumbler," Ristori said. "Here. I believe this is yours."

He gave Garvin back the identity card that, until a few seconds ago, had been clipped to Jaansma's shirt pocket.

"How'd you . . . oh. Sorry," Garvin said. "I should know, never wise up the mark."

"And this is yours," Ristori said, giving Garvin back his watch ring. "And this." It was Garvin's wallet, which had been most secure in his buttoned rear pocket.

"But you never got within a meter of me!" Garvin blurted.

"I didn't, did I?" Ristori said, in a deep voice full of ominous significance. "If I had, I might have all your credits, which you'll find in your left front pocket."

"You two," Garvin said, knowing without checking,

the money would somehow be there. "Out. Report to Njangu and draw your gear."

"And try to leave him with his pants."

The tall man in greasy coveralls slid out from underneath a Zhukov Aerial Combat Vehicle. He held an unpowered torque wrench about as long as his arm.

Njangu saluted him smartly as he got to his feet.

Mil Taf Liskeard returned the salute, after noting the wings on Yoshitaro's chest.

"Didn't think you flyboys would even recognize my existence these days," he said bitterly.

Njangu didn't respond to that, but said, "Sir, I'd like to speak to you privately."

Liskeard looked across at the two mechanics, who were visibly not paying the slightest attention.

"In that grease trap that passes for my office, then."

Njangu followed him inside, closed the door.

"All right. What do you want, Yoshitaro? Aren't you too busy putting together your latest scheme to be wasting time on a grounded old fart who broke under fire?"

"I want you, sir, as one of the pilots on that scheme."

"Bad joke," Liskeard said shortly. "I say again my last. I broke, remember? I had Angara ground me. Or hadn't you heard? I couldn't take killing people."

"I know," Yoshitaro said. "But I still want you. To fly that Big Ugly Flopper we're going out in. I looked your record up, sir. You had more than two thousand hours in converted civilian transports before you transferred to Griersons. And we're very, very short on people who've got experience moving hogs of steel about."

"I did do that for a while," Liskeard said. "I should have known my limits and kept pushing those BUFs around the sky.

"But that's not the point. I couldn't take it, busting other transports apart like the ones I flew, like gutting fish, and turned my wings in. Angara said he'd make sure I never flew anything military again, and would have my ass out of the Force as soon as he got around to it.

"I guess he forgot about me down here in this motor pool," Liskeard went on. "And I'll be damned if I know why I didn't remind him."

He rubbed his forehead, leaving a greasy smear.

"No, Yoshitaro. You've got something else in mind than rehabilitating a coward. Am I supposed to be the Judas Goat on this new operation? I hear you're famous for nasty little tricks like that."

"I want you," and Njangu paused, trying to hold back his temper, trying to hold to his purpose. But the words didn't come easy, "for personal reasons. A month or so after you . . . grounded yourself, I got in the center of somebody's sights and they dropped a barrage on me. And I broke, too."

"But you came back. Obviously, or you'd be under that Zhukov with me, looking for grease points."

"Yeh," Njangu said. "I did. Maybe because I was too cowardly to tell somebody who saw me go down that I was shattered, that I couldn't keep on keeping on."

Liskeard's manner changed. He eyed Njangu.

"So this is a kind of rehabilitation. You're willing to take a chance on me again?"

"We're not going out in *Big Bertha* to shoot at people," Njangu said. "We're going out to have a look around and get our asses back here to report."

"That doesn't mean I'll be able to hold together if things get sticky."

"Then I'll yank your ass off the controls and break it myself for real. Sir." Njangu growled, his fingers unconsciously curling into a strike hand.

Liskeard saw his hands, then started laughing, very hard.

"Does Angara know you're trying to recruit me?"

"He does," Njangu said. "And he growled something about I better be sure I'm right."

Liskeard looked surprised. "That's the last thing I'd expect that hard-ass old bastard to say."

He took a deep breath.

"Yoshitaro, I'll put the wings back on for you. And if I snap again . . . you won't have to take care of me. I'll do it myself.

"And . . . thanks. I owe you. Very, very large."

Njangu, never happy with sentiment, came to attention, saluted, and turned. Over his shoulder he said:

"Then get over to *Big Bertha*—she comes out of the yards in two hours—and start learning what a pig she is to fly. Sir."

"You're sure that dance is authentic?" Garvin asked doubtfully.

Dec Running Bear, resplendent in breechclout, a rawhide necklace of long teeth, face paint, and a feather sticking sideways out of his braided hair, grinned.

"Just as my mother's mother's mother taught me. Or, if the people I'm dancing for start lookin' like they think I'm shitting them, my father's father's father's father. Hell, I'll tell 'em next performance I'm gonna put bone spikes through my tits, hang in the air, and yodel for the ancient Sun Dance."

"I dunno," Garvin said, still skeptical.

"Look, sir. I could really use some action. I'm bored cross-cocked doing nothing but fly *Dant* Angara around. Great Spirit on a bicycle, I actually found myself wanting a little shooting last week."

Running Bear absently rubbed a scarred arm. He was one of the few living holders of the Confederation Cross, gained in what he called "one ee-holay mad moment."

"So I dance some, tell some stories . . . those are for real from back when, maybe even back to

Earth . . . my gran taught me . . . smoke a peace pipe,
sing some chants, look like a dangerous warrior.

"Isn't that a good way to meet women? Sir?"

"Doesn't sound that bad," Garvin said. "Plus we
can always use another certified crazy besides Ben
Dill. And you can fly."

"Anything short of a Zhukov, right through the eye
of a goddamned needle, sir."

"Well, we're pissing off *Dant* Angara bad enough
already, taking his best. Might as well grab his chauf-
feur as well," Garvin decided.

"Might be fun," Erik Penwyth drawled. "Wandering out there, a day in front of you folks, seeing who
and what can be taken advantage of."

"Just don't get cute on me," Njangu promised. "Remember, you're in the job I wanted."

"Would you stop whining?" Garvin said. "Clown
master you are, and clown master you remain. Pass
the goddamned bottle, would you?"

Njangu pushed it across, just as a tap came on the
door.

"Enter," he said.

The door opened, and a woman wearing hospital
whites came in.

"Well, I'll be goto," Garvin said. "*Alt* Mahim. Sid-
down, Doc. I thought we'd detached you to medical
school."

She sat, on the edge of one of Garvin's chairs.

"I am . . . was, sir. Until three days ago, when the
term finished. I took a long leave."

"Uh-oh," Njangu said meaningfully. "The sy-reen
call of excitement."

"Come on, Jill," Garvin said. "First, knock off the
'sir.' Or have you forgotten I&R tradition, such as
it is?"

"Noss . . . no, boss. I came to see if you need a
good medico aboard."

"Damme," Penwyth said. "What is it about the old

I&R crew? You try to put them in place where they just might not get killed, learn how to do valuable things like deliver babies and do brain surgery that'll give them a slot on the outside, and they come roarin' back to the cannon's mouth, every time."

"I won't even try to argue with you," Garvin said. "Hell yes, we need a good combat medic. Here. Pour yourself a drink."

"Not right now, boss," Mahim said, getting to her feet. "I've got to go steal what medpak supplies I'll need. But thanks."

She saluted, was gone.

Penwyth shook his head.

"We'll never learn, will we?"

Garvin got out of his lifter, started up the long steps to the Mellusin mansion, Hillcrest. He was at the door when he heard a loud crash. He opened the door, heard an obscenity, then another crash.

"Assholes!" Jasith shouted.

There was another smash.

Garvin went carefully toward the sound of the destruction. It was in the remnants of the kitchen.

Jasith Mellusin was glaring at a smashed communicator. Then she went back to the serving cabinet, selected a platter, and threw it the length of the dining room.

"Shitheads!"

She picked up a plate in each hand.

"Uh . . . I'm home, dear," Garvin said.

She looked at him angrily, threw both plates at the wall.

"Sons of bitches!"

"Since you're talking plural," Garvin said, "I can hope you're not sonsabitchin' me."

"Not you!"

"Then can I kiss you?"

Jasith pursed lips. Garvin strode through the ruins

of most of their dinner service, kissed her. After a bit, they broke apart.

"That's a little better," Jasith admitted. "Not that it makes me want to stop cursing."

Garvin lifted an eyebrow.

"My goddamned Board of Directors, my twice-goddamned stockholders, my three-times-screwed executives!"

"Pretty comprehensive list."

"Don't stay so calm, Garvin! They just told me I can't go with you!"

"But . . . you're Mellusin Mining, I mean, the only one," he said bewilderedly. "You can do what you want, can't you?"

"No," she said, starting to steam once again. "Not if it affects the price of the stock, or the confidence of the stockholders if their chief executive happens to be out-system, maybe even in danger and God forbid I go and get killed. The entire goddamned board went and voted they'd resign if I go out with you. Said I didn't have any regard for my own company if I'd go do something dangerous that I didn't have to, that was the job of proper soldiers, not immature little girls like they seem to think I still am!

"Fughpigs!"

A very large crystal dessert tray Garvin had rather liked skimmed across the room and disintegrated in rainbow shards.

"Oh," Garvin said.

"You want to throw something?"

"Uh . . . no."

She gave him a suspicious look.

"Aren't you sorry I'm not going?"

"Of course, sure I am," Garvin said hastily. "So don't go and lob anything my way. Honest, Jasith."

"Dammit, dammit, dammit," she said, and started crying.

Garvin, cautiously, put his arms around her again.

"Why don't they ever let me have any fun?" Jasith said into the hollow of his shoulder.

"I always thought," Garvin said, "the really rich were free."

"Nobody's free, dammit," Jasith said. "Except maybe the dead."

"What do you think?" Maev said, raising her voice to a singsong, "Candy, lifts, chewies, balloons, candy, lifts, chewies, balloons, a prize in every box."

"I think," Njangu said, eyeing her very scanty costume, "nobody's gonna be looking at your goodies. At least not the ones in that tray."

"Sure they will," Maev said. "Little children love me."

"Then what's this about selling lifts?"

"Nothing addictive," Maev said. "A mild mood-enhancer. With about an eight hundred percent profit.

"And if they are ogling m' boobs, that's fine, too. They'll never notice . . ."

And her hand moved under the tray slung around her neck, came out with a smallish, large-barreled projectile weapon.

". . . this. Guaranteed I can put two of these slugs between somebody's eyes at fifteen meters. For less lethal response . . ."

Again, her hand went under the tray, came out with a squat cylinder.

". . . blindspray. Give you convulsions for half an hour, vomiting for an hour, can't see squat for two hours."

"That's if somebody tries to get friendly?"

"Other than you," Maev said. "Or somebody really, really rich." She took off her tray.

"Now, I need a drink. This security operation is sweaty work."

"Already made for you, m'love," Njangu said. "Over on the sideboard."

It wasn't financially convenient, but Njangu had

kept the lease on the apartment across the bay from
Camp Mahan, on the outskirts of D-Cumbre's capital
of Leggett, as a convenient way of getting away from
uniforms when the military made him want to howl at
the moons.

"Pity about poor Jasith," Maev said.

"What? I haven't heard squat."

Maev told him about the near revolt by the officers
of Mellusin Mining.

"So she's out, sulking like a fiend."

"Uh-oh," Njangu said inadvertently, thinking of
Darod Montagna.

"What?"

"Nothing," Njangu said hastily.

"You're holding back."

"I surely am."

"How terribly interesting," Darod Montagna said.
"Poor Miss Mellusin, forced to stay home and count
all her money and not go play with us."

"Dammit," Monique Lir told her XO, "I hope
you're going to be a good girl."

"I'm going to be a *very* good girl," Darod said in
her most sultry voice. "I'm going to be the best girl
that man's ever seen."

"Uh-oh," Lir said.

Finally Stage One—planning; Stage Two—logistics
and personnel; and Stage Three, operations, were finished. There were almost 150 men and women picked,
all volunteers, including a few civilians who'd managed
to penetrate the fairly tight security screen *Dant* Angara had imposed after all.

They filed into *Big Bertha* and found their assigned
compartments. The old soldiers made old jokes that
hadn't been that funny the first time around, the new
women and men wondered why they had tight lumps
in their guts instead of pride.

Garvin Jaansma kissed Jasith Mellusin.

"You better come back," she said fiercely, then looked away.

"I'll go with what she said," Angara said. "But with an addition. Bring me back *something*, Garvin." There was a flash of desperation in his eyes. "Dammit, we can't keep on as we have, not knowing anything!"

"I'll come back," Garvin promised. "With the hot skinny, boss."

He saluted Angara, kissed Jasith again, and went up *Big Bertha*'s ramp. It slid shut, and a speaker blatted: "All personnel. All personnel on ramps. Clear ramps for takeoff. Clear ramps for takeoff. Three minute warning. Clear ramps."

"Come on," Angara said, taking Jasith's arm.

She followed him back into the terminal, went to a window.

The ground trembled, and *Big Bertha*'s antigravs lifted her clear of the ground. Her secondary drive cut in, and the behemoth crawled upward, became graceful, and vanished into the stratosphere and space.

Jasith stood there, watching emptiness for a long time.

CHAPTER
4

N-space

Njangu and Garvin had given themselves more tactical options than just hiding in plain sight if—or, more realistically, when—problems developed.

"I am getting very damned tired of being ambushed every time we come out of hyperspace," Yoshitaro had said, looking pointedly at the three *aksai* pilots. "Which is why I'm going to use your young asses as bait . . . or anyway, some kind of warning system. I just hope you won't slow down and get dead bringing us the word."

The *aksai* was the prime fighting ship of the Musth during the war with Cumbre. Now, with peace looming on all sides and trade flourishing with Man, the *aksai* were being built for the Force, somewhat modified for human pilotage. It was a flying wing, C-shaped, about twenty-five meters from horn to horn, with one, two, or three fighting compartments, capsules, mounted on the concave forward edge of the wing, weapons either encapsulated or just hung below the wing. It was impossibly fast and, as Ben Dill said, "harder to fly than a whore on roller skates."

Jacqueline Boursier, the self-described "shit-hot pilot," tried to put together a fund to hire an athletic prostitute, buy some old-fashioned roller skates, and lock Ben Dill in a gymnasium with her to see what happened. She had no takers.

In-atmosphere, the *aksai* would stall handily and

snaproll into the ground if flying speed wasn't kept up, and transitioning between the standard antigravity lift system to secondary and then stardrives took a most delicate touch.

Out-atmosphere, its instant acceleration and speed were as likely to stuff its pilot into something unpleasantly solid as punt her to the fringes of the system before reaction time could take over.

But those who could fly the ships invariably fell in love with them. They were possibly the most acrobatic craft ever built, with the possible exception of Dawn-age propeller ships.

The procedure Garvin and Njangu had come up with to keep from being mousetrapped was complicatedly simple: *Big Bertha* would set a hyperspace jump to the desired navigational point. However, the navigational instruments were set with a pause feature, rather than the usual, automatic reemergence into N-space.

Hanging in something beyond nothingness, the mother ship would launch an *aksai*. The *aksai* would enter real space and make a preliminary recon for bad guys, surprises, or flower-tossing maidens. It would pass the word back to *Big Bertha*, which could take appropriate measures.

If the system was hostile, the ship would wait as long as she could for the *aksai* to rejoin her. If the mother ship had to flee, the *aksai* was to make a hyperspace jump, to a predetermined nav point, and Mayday in all directions, hoping for rescue before the air ran out.

But this was an option none of the three *aksai* pilots believed would ever happen.

After all, they were *all* shit-hot, not just Boursier . . .

The inship annunciator burped sedately. The synth-voice Garvin hadn't gotten around to replacing, which, unfortunately, 'cast into all compartments, announced

"*Aksai* section . . . *aksai* section . . . ready pilot, report to the bridge."

The man, woman, and alien cut for high card, and Alikhan obeyed the summons, round ears cocked in excitement.

The bridge of *Big Bertha* was as unusual as the rest of the bulbous starship: a self-contained pod at the "top" of the cargo/passenger spaces, with the forward edge, monitors looking like ports, protruding from the hull a bit. Flanking the large bridge area were communication and navigation compartments and, at the rear of the pod, a secondary command center with observation ports looking "down" into the hull's huge cargo spaces.

It would make, Garvin thought, a dandy place for a circus master to crack the whip from. Or possibly, if they kicked out a few of the windows, some sort of high-wire or other flier act.

Alikhan got his briefing, and went along a sealed catwalk through an airlock to the "top" of the ship, where three of the state-of-the-ten-year-old-art Nana boats and the four *aksai* hung, like so many bats in a huge barn.

He wedged himself rear legs first into the *aksai*'s pod on his belly, then closed the clear canopy. He turned power on, checked controls, touched sensors, read the displays on his canopy as the main and secondary drives came alive, then announced he was ready to launch.

"This is Command," Garvin told him. "Your coordinates and flight pattern have been fed into your computer. Launch at will."

A hatch above him slid back, and a steel arm lifted the *aksai* clear of *Big Bertha*. Alikhan watched readouts blink on his canopy, trying to convince himself that the blur of N-space around him wasn't vaguely nauseating, certainly not for a combat-experienced Musth.

Gravity spun, vanished, and he was beyond the

ship's grav field. Alikhan considered what Garvin had told him about the system he was to enter—three worlds, settled over two hundred E-years ago, no data on government, military, peacefulness. It'd been chosen for the first system to enter because it was distant from the nav points "close" to Larix and Kura, and hence, Garvin assumed, hadn't been slandered by Redruth, and, hopefully, wouldn't be that hostile to an intruder.

Alikhan touched a sensor, and the *aksai* dropped out of hyperspace, the swirl around him becoming stars and not-too-distant planets. He went at full drive toward the second planet, reportedly the first colonized, searching all common bands for 'casts.

Within an E-hour, he sent a com back into hyperspace to *Big Bertha*: no hostiles. Safe to enter. Request assistance, nonemergency.

The big ship obeyed, and the two patrol craft, Chaka in command of the flight, were launched, shot toward the homing signal on Alikhan's *aksai*. Behind them came *Big Bertha*.

Dill was riding shotgun on one of the patrol ships.

"What's the problem, little friend?" he asked on a standard voice channel as the two ships closed.

"Your data, to use a phrase of yours, sucketh goats, whatever a goat is."

A louder signal boomed from *Big Bertha*: "Scout One, this is Command. Give details. Over." Garvin didn't sound thrilled at the relaxed com procedure.

"Command, Scout One," Alikhan 'cast. "Details are: There is nothing here, and it appears there never was. No cities, no buildings, no humans. Over."

And so it was. None of the three planets that were supposedly colonized, all within the habitability range, showed any sign of settlement or abandonment.

"This makes no goddamned sense," Njangu snarled. "Howinhell could the Confederation punt some people out with their little shovels and picks and tents . . .

I assume they did that, unless this whole goddamned scheme was some bureaucrat's fiddle to steal something large . . . and then not check on them, not follow up, not send the occasional goddamned checkup team . . . for two hundred goddamned years?"

Garvin shook his head.

"It makes me goddamned wonder," Njangu raved on, "just how much of our goddamned Empire was a goddamned phony. Maybe the whole goddamned thing was some kind of a shadow play."

"That makes little sense," Danfin Froude said mildly.

"Then give me some explanation that does. Goddamit!"

Froude held his palms up, helplessly.

" 'Kay," Garvin decided. "Forget it. We'll pull the recon elements back and try again.

"I don't like this," he finished. "I don't like things that don't have explanations."

Froude looked at him.

"In another life, you could have been a scientist."

"The hell," Garvin said. "In another life, I'm going to be a frigging boulder on a beach somewhere, with nothing to do but watch pretty naked women and slowly turn into sand.

"Get ready for another jump."

Garvin had made one major break with naval tradition. The *Big Bertha* had a club, but it was for all ranks, not just officers. Njangu had agreed with this, since both of them found a noncommissioned officers' club far livelier than anything for upper ranks.

As to the old military policy that these restrictions gave rankers a place to relax and discuss their problems without being around the enlisted sorts, Garvin's answer was short and sweet: "Let those who want to play footsie or whine do it in their own compartments."

He'd found a corner with a beer, and was still wondering about that colony that evidently never had been, when he saw Darod Montagna, mug in hand.

"Greetings, boss," she said. "Are you in deep thought, or can I join you?"

"Grab a chair," Garvin said. "Njangu should be here in a mo, so obviously it's not deep."

She sat, sipped at her beer.

"Thanks for letting me go on this little detail."

"So far, no thanks . . . or blame . . . needed," he said.

They sat in comfortable silence for a few minutes. Garvin realized he didn't feel any particular need to be entertaining or even companionable, somewhat like the peacefulness he felt around Njangu.

He saw his XO enter the rather crowded compartment, make his way toward them.

"I guess I better scoot," Darod said. "Deep, dark secrets and all that."

She got up, just as *Big Bertha* twitched a little, making another jump, and fell into his lap.

"Bastard!" she swore, picking herself up. "I'll never get used to going out of N-space."

Garvin just smiled, thinking how she felt rather nice against him.

"Who does?" Njangu said, taking her seat. "And I'm gonna rip a strip off our damned watch officer, who's supposed to notify us before we hippety-hop in or out of the wild black yonder out yonder."

"Oh . . . maybe I should have said something," Montagna said. "The PA system's down . . . one of the techs is trying to get rid of that old lady in the system."

As she spoke, the overhead speaker crackled into life: "Time to next jump . . . three ship-hours." It was still the weird synthesized voice they were all growing to hate.

"I love technology," Njangu said. "Let's take an ax

to the system and put in voice tubes like the first
starships had. Or uniformed messengers. Or signal
flags."

"Good night, sirs," Darod said, and left. Njangu
watched her leave.

"Not hard on the eyes at all," he said.

"Not at all," Garvin said, pretending casual notice.
"Did she have anything in particular to talk
about . . . being nosy?"

"Other'n what a nosy sort you are," Garvin said,
"nothing much."

"Careful, Garvin," Njangu said.

"Careful about what?"

Njangu waited a moment. "Careful that you don't
spill your beer in your lap. Sir."

"Mother Mary on a bender," Garvin said softly,
staring into the screen.

"Yeh," Njangu said. "Evidently *somebody* didn't
have any qualms about going nuke."

The planet below it, like the twin moons that were
supposed to be fortified, was nothing but desolation.
A counter roared radioactivity at them.

"Any 'casts?" Garvin asked the com officer.

"There's a lot of clutter from the craters, sir," the
man reported. "We've blanked all that come from obvious bomb sources . . . and there's nothing left. We
thought for a minute we were getting some sort of
code from one of the moons, but it's pure random
noise.

"Nothing else, sir."

Njangu scratched his chin.

"The whole goddamned system gone," he mused.
"The book said it had a population of five billion."

He shuddered a little. "Guess there's things worse
than Empire, huh?"

"Maybe," Garvin said. "Unless the Confederation
was the one who decided to break policy first.
Watch officer!"

"Sir!"

"Take us the hell out of here. Next possibility."

"I've got a question," Maev asked.

"I've got an answer," Njangu said, yawning. "Your head is very comfortable on my chest, by the bye."

"I got that notion," Stiofan said, "that you and Garvin had the idea, at one time, of deserting, the first time you hit a world where there'd be some kind of main chance."

"Ah, but that was in the sinful days of our yout'," he said. "Before we became aware of the stellar virtues of serving the Confederation forever and ever or at least until somebody shoots our asses off."

"I don't suppose this whole thing"—and she made a circle in the semidarkness with her hand—"is some elaborate con to get you two to somewhere profitable, at which point you'll exit stage left."

"I'll be a son," Njangu said, sitting up abruptly. "You know, I never even *thought* of that possibility. What a dummy."

Maev also sat up.

"I'm afraid," she said. "You actually sound like you were telling the truth. If I can't tell . . ."

"I *was* telling the truth," Yoshitaro said with an injured tone. "I hardly ever lie, and never ever to the woman wot I adore."

" 'Kay," Maev said briskly. "But assuming you're not lying . . . which is a big assumption . . . let's say we run across somewhere like a nice Eden in our travels, where there's connable marks left and right, and nobody has ever heard of a truth scan. What then?"

"What an *interestin'* possibility," Njangu said. "Naah. Anything like that would've been kicked over in the early days after the Confederation did whatever it did to itself. All those wonderful little sheepies would be shorn bare by now.

"Besides," and he sounded serious, "even if we found such a hog heaven, I've got to assume that there's wolves out there in the darkness, to really screw my analogy up. So we'd sit there makin' credits up the yinger, and sooner or later, probably sooner, given my luck, some baddies with lotsandlots of guns would swoop.

"No, Maev my love, I'm afeared you've cast your lot with an honest dullard. At least for the moment."

"What, the lot, or the dullard?" she asked.

"Probably both. Now, if you'd be good enough to hand me that· knotted cord again, I might find the energy for one more round before my engine runs out, since it's evidently the raw, nekkid trut', honesty, and loyalty of a Confeddie ossifer is wot powers me to new heights."

The next system was still inhabited.

Dill brought his *aksai* out of hyperspace, and his sensors were already buzzing. His briefing had said there were supposed to be four inhabited worlds in this system, called in the star catalogs R897Q33, with an archaic designation of 2345554, and a system name of Carroll.

Three . . . no, five ships were homing on him, two of them sweeping the com bands for a frequency this unknown ship would be on.

He obliged them by opening on the standard Confederation emergency frequency:

"Unknown ships, unknown ships, this is the Scoutship, uh, *Dill*," as he realized nobody ever got around to naming any of the *aksai*, and he wasn't interested in being One, Two, or Three.

Another com beeped, announcing the arrival of a patrol boat from *Big Bertha*, then Boursier in another *aksai*.

"Scoutship *Dill*, this is the destroyer *Lopat*," came a return com. "Be advised you have entered into Confederation space."

Dill's eyes widened, and he broadcast a second message to *Big Bertha*.

A secondary screen that had been added before *Big Bertha* left Cumbre started scrolling:

JANE'S ID positive . . . three ships positive ID . . . Confederation *Diaz*-class . . . the borderline obsolescence at time of final Confederation revision this file . . .

Dill ignored the weapons and crew entry.

Sumbeech, sumbeech, we're home, we're home, he thought gleefully, ignoring the sarcastic part of his mind that asked what and where the hell home was, anyway.

He started to ID himself correctly, stopped, remembering belatedly that anyone could say he was Confederation.

"This is *Dill*," he said. "Understood your last, that we are in Confederation space. Extreme approval on this side."

Another, larger ship blinked into existence.

The ever-watchful *Jane's* told him it was a completely obsolete light cruiser, Daant-class, probably *Quiroga*.

"This is Fleet Commander von Hayn," was the com. "We do not recognize your ship class at all for leading two ships. No linkage shown to Confederation. Third ship identified as standard-manufacture planetary patrol craft. Explain. Over."

"This is the *Dill*," Ben said. "My ship is locally built, and you have correctly ID'd the patrol ship. Over."

"Neither of you look long-range capable," the grating voice said. "Suspect you are outrunners of larger ships. Give system of origin at once."

"Uh . . . Erwhon," Dill said, wishing to hell Garvin was here, or maybe Froude. "And we do have other ships in hyperspace, waiting assessment of the situation."

"That system you named is unknown to us."

"We were just being colonized when we fell out of contact with the Confederation. I guess nobody sent the proper bulletins around. What happened to our Empire, anyway?" Dill couldn't hold back the question.

There was a long time of dead air.

"This is Fleet Commander von Hayn," the voice came reluctantly. "We are not in contact with the Homeworlds, but have sustained order through our own devices for some years, maintaining peace and the rule of law and order."

"As have we," Dill said. "And now we're trying to reestablish contact."

Again, a long silence, and Dill was about to rebroadcast.

"We have communicated with our superiors," von Hayn's voice came. "Permission to enter the Carroll system is denied. Be advised a full launch of our fleet has been made, and any other ships appearing in normal space will be treated as enemy and fire will be opened on them immediately.

"Again, you are refused entry. Leave this system at once, or face immediate attack."

"You paranoid old poop," Dill muttered to himself, not knowing age or sex of the fleet commander, and opened his mike.

"Von Hayn, this is the *Dill*. We come in peace, I say again, meaning no harm, but wishing only supplies . . . and you rotten bug diddler!"

The *Quiroga* had just launched a pair of missiles at the *aksai*.

Ben wanted desperately to make a counterstrike, but remembered his orders and fled back into hyperspace, even as the patrol ship disappeared with him.

He locked aboard *Big Bertha*, and steamed for the bridge.

Garvin, Froude, and Njangu were waiting.

"Thor with an anvil up his ass, but those bastards were unfriendly," he snapped.

"We know," Froude said. "Remember, we were monitoring all 'casts."

"Well what the hell are we going to do?" Dill asked.

"We're going to make another jump, far, far away from here" Garvin said. "Listen. Here's a couple of selections the patrol boat's com picked up. Both came from the homeworld."

He touched a key.

A harsh voice grated:

"Meal hours for all Zed-, Extang-, and Hald-class citizens have been changed by point-one-five tics. Be advised the grace period for change will be four shifts, then penalties may be assessed. Further—"

Static, then a woman's voice said:

"Due to compliance with voluntary work output, issuance of rapture tabs are authorized for the following districts: Alf, Mass—"

"Oy yoy," Ben Dill said. "They tells you when you can eat, get your head ruined. How much you want to bet they let you know when it's 'kay to screw?"

"I don't think we need to trouble ourselves with these people," Froude said. "At least, not until we're prepared to come back in force and discuss this system of peace, law, and order."

The three *aksai* pilots sat in their ready room, waiting for either mess call or another alert.

"I'm starting to think," Ben Dill mused, "this universe might not be that friendly a place."

"When was it ever?" Boursier asked. "Or weren't you paying attention in Astronomy One?"

"I don't mean black holes and wormholes and ghosties and goblins and that," Dill said. "I'm talking about people.

"Not to mention we ain't found squat beside ruination."

"Do not despair," Alikhan said. "For I remember the tale of a great Musth warrior who was once lost in a trackless forest. But he kept on looking, trying different trails, different signals. His belief was 'seek a thousand tracks, and one of them will lead to home."

Dill looked at the alien thoughtfully.

"Be damned. I didn't think you Musth ever said anything reassuring."

"Neither did I," Boursier said. "How long did it take this warrior to reach his home?"

"He never made it," Alikhan said. "They found those words scratched on the outside of a tree, next to which he had starved."

CHAPTER
5

Salamonsky

"Take it in closer, Ben," Garvin said, his voice showing no emotion.

"Yessir," Dill said, and dived into Salamonsky's atmosphere.

Garvin turned away from the projection.

"What sort of lousy bastard would attack a circus world?" he asked no one in particular. "We never did anything to anyone . . . gave them something to laugh at, something to wonder about, sent home with stars in their eyes and a smile on their lips."

The enlisted woman on one of the radars turned. "You ever hear of some people called Jews, sir?"

Garvin looked at her, then away.

Dill was coming in fast a thousand kilometers below—even at his height above land, there was perceptible ground rush.

"Captain Liskeard," Garvin said, "bring it in-atmosphere. We'll have a look, maybe get some idea of who the bad guys could have been. Put two patrol boats out now for top cover."

"Sir."

"As soon as we're below the stratosphere, launch the other *aksai* and the patrol boat. Keep them sweeping, looking for trouble."

Njangu came up to him.

"You got a crawly feeling?"

"Not necessarily," Garvin said. "I'm probably just hoping there's something to shoot at, no more."

Dill flared the *aksai* two hundred meters above the landing field he'd targeted. Small carpet bombs had knocked the tower askew and set fire to hangars and admin buildings. Then strafers must have come in to finish the job. There were remnants of ships scattered around the field, some that would have been modern, others beyond-belief rust buckets that transported small dog-and-pony acts or even sideshows around the region. All of them had been anodized in the most garish colors that were now just beginning to flake.

"I'd guess," Njangu said, "whoever hit them came in less than an E-year ago. There's still cables dangling, looks like some rope that's not rotted hanging from that drive stand, and that old hovercraft cushion's still inflated."

The image on-screen changed as Dill's *aksai* banked over the port's small city. It sprawled for some kilometers, and was mostly separate houses of wildly varying styles and sizes.

"I wonder," Garvin said absently, "if any of those houses belonged to any little people. I remember, when I was a kid, going to one family, and everything was built to scale, and they were smaller than I was, so for the first time I felt like a giant.

"All of them but their daughter," he went on. "She was, oh, maybe thirteen, and as pretty as I'd ever seen. I fell in love with her . . . but of course she didn't know nine-year-olds existed."

The city's business center was a cratered ruin.

"I hope they fought back," Garvin said. "It would've been—"

The watch communications officer came into the bridge.

"Sir. We're getting a transmission, in Common, on a Confederation guard channel. Shall I pipe it through?"

"Now," Garvin ordered. "And get DF finding out where it's coming from."

The transmission quality was wavery, and the woman's voice was flat, tired, as if she'd done the 'cast a thousand thousand times:

"Unknown ship . . . our detectors picked up a disturbance entering atmosphere . . . unknown ship . . . we are refugees in hiding after our world was looted . . . we're only a handful of survivors . . . oh Allah, be a ship, not another damned meteorite. Please."

The emotion stopped, and once more the woman said her plea.

Garvin was reaching for the mike, when Njangu caught his arm.

"Let her run on for a minute. It won't hurt."

"Why?"

"It might not be a bad idea . . . once we find out where she's 'casting from, to drop a drone down before *Big Bertha* wallows over there, don't you think? Since I'm the only me I've got, I'd like to take precautions."

Garvin's lip thinned, then he caught himself.

"You're right. Sorry."

Njangu ordered one of the patrol ships to launch a drone in-atmosphere. Moments later, the direction finders had a location for the plea for help.

"Nap of the earth," Njangu ordered the drone's pilot on the patrol ship. "I want a realtime normal-vision transmit, and metal detection patched to me."

"Sir."

A tech moved a screen down, and it lit up, showing the drone's point of view, approaching the ground.

Njangu told Dill what was going on, ordered him and the other ships to low altitudes.

The drone was flashing over wooded hills, then a lake, a small valley, then more woods.

"That was where she DF'ed from. Nothing to see," Liskeard said. "The poor scared bastards must be hiding."

"Look at *that* display, sir," a technician said.

Garvin looked as well . . . and saw high-zigging lines.

"Nothing but brushes and woodses down there," Njangu said. "And a lot of hidden metal. Like ships under camou nets maybe?"

"Shit!" somebody in the control room swore as ragged black smoke dotted the sky on-screen.

"Most poor scared bastards don't have antiaircraft guns . . . or use 'em on rescuers," Liskeard said wryly.

"No," Garvin said. "No, they don't. Commo, give me an all-channels."

"Sir. You're on."

"All *Bertha* elements. Target Acquisition on our main screen. Indicators show hidden ships . . . and we got fire. Suspect cannon, not missiles. Nana elements, to ten thousand meters, stand off two kilometers. Goddard launch on command.

"*Aksai*, stay clear until we open things up a little, then we'll send you . . . cancel that for the moment."

Garvin hadn't needed the technician's warning. He'd seen a ship lift through trees below.

"Nana Flight . . . take him out."

"Sir," *Alt* Rad Draf said. "Two, do you have that ship?"

"Affirm . . ."

"I'm firing. Two shadows . . . on command . . . FIRE!"

The meter-long Shadow antiship missiles spat from their pods.

"We have a counterlaunch and countermeasures in effect," Draf's ECM officer reported. "Divert one . . . two . . . hit! Hit!"

The seething ball of flame that'd been a small starship spun back toward the ground.

"Nanas . . . proceed with Goddard launch!" Garvin ordered.

"On my command," Draf said, still calm-voiced. "All elements . . . target from flagship . . . one Goddard per Nana . . . FIRE!"

The Goddards were heavy shipkillers, six meters long, sixty centimeters in diameter, with a five hundred-km range. They drove toward the valley at full speed.

AA guns on the ground yammered up, but struck wide.

All four targeted within fifteen meters of each other, and the ground roiled, bucked, and net covering guns and two more ships on the ground burst into flames. Secondary explosions sent flame waves boiling into the air.

"*Aksai*," Garvin said, "if there's anything left to kill . . . go on in."

The fighting ships dived down, swept the small valley. Boursier's chainguns yammered once, again.

"Half a dozen men . . . with guns," she reported. "No more."

"That's it," Garvin said. "All *Bertha* elements . . . recover."

He looked again at the screen showing the destroyed valley, then at Njangu.

"Hope none of the people they captured were down there," Yoshitaro said.

Garvin flushed.

"Goddammit, if they were . . . they were leading us into a trap!"

"True," Njangu said. "Sorry. Boss."

Garvin's face returned to normal.

"No. My turn for the apology. This one got to me a little."

"Forget it," Njangu said. "I suppose you've got another place to look for your elephants."

"I do. Two more, if it comes to that," Garvin said. "But number three is halfway to hell and gone."

"Then . . . unless you want to land, and sift some ashes trying to figure out where those raiders came from, and do a few paybacks . . . I guess we should depart this fair clime."

"Yeh," Garvin said heavily. "There's nothing for us . . . or anyone else . . . here."

Two of the next seven nav points were in inhabited systems. Scouting *aksai* reported those worlds were settled, primarily agricultural and, from detected emissions, were obviously out of contact with the Confederation, slowly working their way back down the energy ladder.

Boursier reported, in rather shocked tones, the second system was even using some nuclear power.

"Obviously," Njangu said, "there's no point in stopping for help when somebody's worse off than we are."

"Nope," Garvin agreed. "Besides, the next jump will be Grimaldi, full of fun, laughter, and life.

"I bleeding well hope."

CHAPTER
6

"This is Grimaldi Control," a woman said. "Link to Channel five-five-four-point-eight-seven . . . you are cleared to land. You will descend vertically from present position, then take course Nan Eleven, as indicated on your Standard Instrument Screen for approximately twenty-two, that is two-two, kilometers. We have clear weather, so you should have visual contact with Joey Field at that point. Use Beam Eleven Teng to guide you to your landing spot."

The voice paused, then said: "Be advised we are a peaceful world, and are welcoming you.

"If, however, you have other intentions, also be advised you are being tracked by various weapons systems we do not want to use. Over."

"This is *Big Bertha*," Liskeard said into a mike. "We are just what we claim to be . . . understand Course Nan Eleven for two-two kilometers, use standard Beam Eleven Teng and visual flight regulations to land on field. Monitoring Channel five-five-four-point-eight-seven. Over."

"Assuming you know what the name of your ship means," the voice said, "welcome home. Grimaldi Control, clear."

Njangu glanced at Garvin, swore that the other man had tears in his eyes. He wondered what would be a home to him, one day, wondered not for the first time

if there was one. Sure as hell not the corrupt sewer
of Ross 248 that he'd been born on.

"Sir," Liskeard said, "we're bringing it in. Do you
want to do the benediction?"

Garvin jolted back to the bridge of the ship.

"Yeh. Yeh, sorry." He took a microphone.

"This is Gaffer Jaansma." He'd decided to start
using the title before they entered the Grimaldi system, figuring it was time to get the troops used to it.

"From here on out, all of you who aren't civilians
are now. For the love of Harriet's Crucifixion, don't
go around in step or counting cadence.

"You've all been briefed on who we are . . . more
or less amateur circus buffs who've fallen into money,
and are trying to give peace a chance by making people happy and laughing, and maybe are curious about
whatever happened to the Confederation.

"You don't have to look moronic when you say
that. The people we'll encounter will already think
you're a skid short of an even landing for looking for
what is obviously big trouble.

"From here on out, things should get interesting."

He keyed the mike off and looked at Njangu, grinning broadly.

"*Damn*, but this is gonna be fun."

Garvin might have been awash in sentiment, but
that didn't make him altogether a fool. The two *aksai*
followed within *Big Bertha*'s radar shadow until the
behemoth landed, then orbited closely overhead. The
Nana boats were ready for an instant launch, and certain unobtrusive compartments, normally kept sealed,
were now open and their 35mm chainguns, firing depleted uranium rounds at 6000rpm, and the smallish
one meter long Shrikes, which could be launched at
anything and guided by anyone, were ready.

But nothing warlike happened, and so Garvin, and
an assemblage of his more impressive people, from

Ben Dill to Njangu to Monique Lir went down the wide gangway after the lock opened.

Waiting were a dozen or more lifters, some circus-colored, others nondescript, two loudly claiming the holo stations they had been dispatched by.

About forty men and women waited, most as excited as Garvin. They were also somewhat unusual in appearance, Lir noticed. Three had elaborate tattoos showing on their bare arms, one was almost as big as Ben Dill, another woman had a rather remarkable beard, and two, including one journoh with a holo recorder, were midgets.

One woman, distinguished-looking, very long-haired, wearing tanned, fringed leathers, came forward.

"We welcome *Big Bertha*," she said formally. "I hope you will find what you're seeking here on Grimaldi. I am Agar-Robertes, and people have given me the title of Gaffer, one of several on this world. That's an ancient term that means—"

"I know what it means," Garvin said. "I'm Gaffer Jaansma."

The woman lifted her eyebrows.

"Of *the* Jaansmas?"

"I am Garvin," Garvin said. "My mother was Clyte, my father Frahnk, my uncle Hahrl. Before that—"

"Stop," the woman said. "You've been kicking sawdust longer than any of us."

Garvin inclined his head.

"Son of a bitch," Njangu managed sotto voce to Dill. "The bastard's for real about this circus stuff!"

"That is quite a ship you own," Agar-Robertes said looking up at the looming behemoth. "Might I ask your cargo?"

"We have little at present," Garvin said. "Which is why we came to Grimaldi. We intend to build a circus, and seek women, men, nonhumans, animals."

"Then the time has come round again," Agar-Robertes said reverently amid a babble from the other

men and women of Grimaldi. "When it is safe for
circuses, it is safe for all."

Garvin made a face.

"I wish I could say you're right. We've had encoun-
ters since we left our native worlds to suggest the time
is not here, not yet."

"Still," Agar-Robertes said. "It might be a beginning.

"And you won't lack for prospective troupers.
We're so stricken we've gone beyond entertaining
each other." She lowered her voice. "Some of us have
even been forced to take flatty *jobs*!"

The people of Grimaldi took the Cumbrians to their
hearts and homes. The *Big Bertha* was given a parking
slot on a corner of the field, the *aksai* and other ships
moved into revetments for maintenance, and the circus itself sprawled out around the ship.

The tent was set up, the midway a long fat finger
in front of the main tent, and the other "tents"—the
mess tent, the clown tent, all actually prefab shelters—
around it.

Some of the crew and troupers decided they could
do without living aboard unless they had to, and made
arrangements with the locals. Garvin didn't care, as
long as everyone was present for his work shift.

It would also be good, he knew, for the Cumbrians
to experience another culture than the one they'd
been born into . . . and the Grimaldians were a bit
unusual.

Some of the population, including the original settlers, were circus workers, as many of them strong-
backs, clerical, or computer sorts as freaks and
performers. Others were retirees, vacationers who'd
been trapped when the Confederation collapsed, circus fans or settlers who seemed to have chosen Grimaldi with a dart and a star chart.

All shared a common belief in individual freedom,
although, as one put it, "Yer rights end at my nose."

Seemingly incongruously, almost all desperately missed the Confederation. But one explained to Njangu, "It's best to have some kind of law and order. Makes travel easier, and keeps you from getting mugged after you've run your con and are trying to get out of town with the snide."

Njangu was starting to understand what Garvin had missed for so many years . . . but still hadn't the foggiest why Jaansma was still with the military.

Nor why he was, either.

"What in the name of God's holiest dildo is *that*?" Njangu asked suspiciously, staring at the huge pile of off-white heavy cloth, leather reinforcements, iron eyes, and heavy line.

"It's a tent," Garvin said. "A real tent."

"Which you use for what?"

"We're going to be the best damned circus ever . . . or, anyway, the best one still flitting around this galaxy," Garvin said. "So, when we can, we'll set up under canvas."

"Why? We've got a perfectly good ship that unfolds like one of those paper sculptures . . . ory . . . eerie . . . you know. Sushimi. All safe and warm, and nice lanes to the cages and quarters."

"Because nothing smells more like a circus than canvas," Garvin said. "And roasting groundnuts and popcorn and . . . and elephant shit."

"I'll be sure to tell Jasith your favorite smells," Njangu said. "It'll thrill her no end and probably spark a new line of perfumes from the Mellusin empire."

Not that Njangu was very successful in maintaining his own usual superciliousness.

Maev came around a corner, and found him buried in a mass of little people, some dwarves, most perfect scale replicas of "normal" humans.

They were shouting something about contract scale,

and he was trying to argue, with a rather beatific look
on his face.

Maev crept back round her corner and never mentioned it to Yoshitaro.

"We've got a serious problem," Garvin said. "Sid-
down, have a drink, and help me out."

"A better invite has seldom been spoke," Njangu
said, and sat down in front of Jaansma's desk. He
pulled the bottle over, poured into a glass, drank.

"Whoo. What's that? Exhaust wash?"

"Close," Garvin said. "Triple-run alcohol our fearless, peerless engine department came up with. Try
another hit. It grows on you."

"Yeh," Njangu said. "Like fungus." But he obeyed.
"Now, what's the problem?"

"Every circus has got to have a theme that everything sort of centers around, from the pretty women
in the spec . . . that's the spectacle, the pageant that
opens things . . . to the blowoff. The costumes should
be designed sorta around that theme."

"Mmmh." Njangu considered.

"It sort of helps if it's kind of wallowy and
sentimental."

"Oh. Easy, then. Refill me," Yoshitaro said.

Garvin obeyed.

"This shit does improve with usage," Njangu admitted. "But I still think it'd be best injected, so your
throat doesn't have to take all the damage.

"You want a theme . . . you got a theme. Even fits
in with our tippy-top secret mission. Call it, oh, Many
Worlds Together.

"You can hit that ol' tocsin of the Confederation
and how we all miss it, put people in any kinda costume you want . . . even look to see if there's ever
been any nudist worlds . . . and go from there."

"Why Njangu Yoshitaro," Garvin said. "Sometimes
I suspect you of genius. Intelligence, even."

"Took you long enough."

                              *   *   *

"Uh, boss, what's going on?" Darod Montagna asked Njangu. They were outside *Big Bertha*, and a high, circular fence had been put up, using one of the ship's fins for a base. Inside the fence were Garvin and Ben Dill.

"Our fearless leader is about to negotiate for a bear."

"A what?"

"Some kind of ancient animal . . . supposedly goes all the way back to Earth," Njangu said. "I looked the creature up, and it was listed as a fine animal who left everybody alone, but if you messed with it, it messed back on an all-out basis. Garvin thinks he's got to have one."

"Why? What do they do? Or is eating people going to be a sideshow?"

"If they're well trained, Garvin told me," Njangu explained, "a bear will ride two-wheelers, dance, do a little tumbling . . . just about anything a rather stupid man can be taught."

"Why do we need one?"

"Because," Njangu said, " a circus just . . ."

And Montagna finished the now shopworn phrase:

". . . isn't a circus without a bear. Or a bunch of tumblers. Or whatever else the gaffer comes up with."

"So, anyway," Njangu went on, "it turns out there's this nuthead back in the hills who raises real bears. Agar-Robertes suggested we buy a couple of robot bears, but not our Garvin. He's gotta have the real thing.

"Look. This has got to be the bear-breeder."

The lifter wandering toward the field looked as if it had been crashed on a weekly basis for some time. In the open back was a large cage, holding a very large, very dark brown, furry animal with very large claws and teeth.

"Yeets," Darod said. "Scares me just looking at him. Anybody bring a blaster?"

"Garvin said the trainer told him the bear was as gentle as a baby."

The animal in the back roared so loudly the cage bars rattled.

"What kind of baby?" she wondered aloud.

"Nobody said."

The lifter grounded, and a rather hairy man got out. He greeted Garvin, introduced himself as Eneas, and limped to the back of the cage.

"This 'ere's Li'l Doni," he said. "Cutest li'l thing I ever did see. Got two more back t' th' ranch just like her, if you want real star power."

Njangu was holding back a snicker.

"Star power?" he muttered.

"You said she was gentle," Garvin said, eyeing a ragged scar down the trainer's arm.

"'At was her mother's doin'," Eneas said. "On'y thing Doni's ever did t' me was break m' leg, an' that was my fault. Mostly.

"Here. Lemme let 'er out, you c'n see for yourself."

Garvin was seeing for himself that Li'l Doni was not only in a cage, but had chains around her upper legs. Eneas opened the cage, and Doni rolled out, snarling, came to her feet, and snapped both chains.

She growled, took a swipe at Eneas, who sensibly dived under the lifter.

Doni saw Ben Dill, and charged after him. Dill followed Eneas. That left Garvin, and Doni went for him. There wasn't room enough under the lift for three, and so Garvin climbed, later swearing he levitated, to the top of the cage.

Doni, in command of the theater, snarled three times around the lift, considered a side window, and smashed it casually.

Njangu was laughing so hard he had to hold himself up against the ship's fin.

Li'l Doni spotted Yoshitaro, and, roaring rampage, charged the fence. She banged off it once, then went up and over it as if it was a ladder.

Njangu Yoshitaro went up *Big Bertha*'s fin as if it also were a ladder.

Darod Montagna found business back inside the ship, closing the lock behind her.

Eventually Eneas came out from under his lift, found more chains, and Li'l Doni vanished from the circus's life.

Three days later, Njangu invoiced for the lease of two robot bears. He insisted on naming one of them Li'l Doni.

The music conductor was named Raf Aterton, and Njangu swore he had to be the reincarnation of at least six generals and two dictators. He was silver-haired, slender, severe in countenance, and brooked no argument from any of the forty musicians the circus had taken on. His voice sounded soft, but somehow carried from one end of the spaceport to the other.

"All of you will now listen very closely. You've got sheet music in front of you. The piece is the 'Confederation Peace March'. You will learn it until you can play it in your sleep, as some of you have been functioning already, I've noticed.

"This is the most important part of being on the show. The 'Peace March' is the sign of trouble. Fire. The cats on a rampage. A big clem, a catastrophe.

"When it's played, all the muscle on the show will start looking to solve the problem, however they can. If we're under canvas, all the animals will get out, right then, as will the kinkers.

"The talent is priceless, and you, my ham-fingered men and women are not. So after everyone's altered, you'll join the roustabouts in solving the problem."

"Question, sir," a synthesizer toggler asked. "What if we're in the ship and something happens?"

"Hit the tune, then get out of the ship. Or follow orders if Gaffer Jaansma's around."

"And if we're in space?"

"Now that," Aterton mused, "could be a bit of a poser."

The woman spun lazily twice high above the net, as a man released the trapeze, and twisted across the open air. Their catcher extended long tentacles, caught them both, sent them flying higher into the air, then had them once more, and they were back at their perch.

" 'Kay," Ben Dill said. "Half the troupe's human or looks it, anyway. What species are those octopot-lookin' types?"

"They call themselves *ra'felan*," Garvin said. "The troupe master says they've got about the same intelligence as a low-normal human."

"Interestin'," Erik Penwyth drawled. "With half a dozen legs to punch buttons with, and no particular intelligence, we ought to recruit 'em as pilots."

"Watchit," Dill warned.

The *ra'felan* had rather tubular bodies, with tentacles dangling at paired intervals. Their eyes bulged ominously from the center body.

"Can they talk?" Dill asked.

"If spoken to politely," Garvin said.

"*Both* you bastards are being cute today," Dill complained.

"I assume you signed them," Penwyth said, ignoring Dill.

The *ra'felan* swung back and forth on his trapeze three times, then jumped straight up, toward a rope that crossed between the two high poles. He . . . or she, or it, for Garvin never found out their sexes, if any, went tentacle over tentacle on the rope across to the other pole, then hooked a trapeze, swung once, and somersaulted down, spinning, into the net.

"Damned straight I did," Garvin said fervently. "You should've been here a couple of minutes ago, when they were throwing ten people around like they were paper aircraft."

"If they were real fishies," Dill said, "y' think they'd be working for scale? See, now I'm getting to your level."

"I say again my last about pilots," Penwyth said. "Except p'raps, I was overly kindly about their intelligence being low-normal."

"Hit it, maestro, it's doors, and the crowd's a turnaway," Garvin shouted. He was resplendent in white formal wear of ancient times, including a tall white hat, black boots, and a black whip.

Aterton obeyed, and music boomed through the hold, and Garvin touched his throat mike.

"Men, women, children of all ages . . . Welcome, welcome, welcome, to the Circus of Galactic Delights. I'm your host for the show. Now, what we'll have first . . ."

Half a dozen clowns tumbled into view, began assaulting Garvin in various ways, some trying to drench him with water, others to push him over a kneeling clown, still others throwing rotten vegetables. But all missed, and he drove them away with his whip.

"Sorry, sorry, but we've got these strange ones who're completely out of control with us . . ." Garvin lowered his voice, cut out of his spiel. "When we get a full complement, we'll have carpet clowns working the stands. Next will come the spec, with all kinds of women on lifts, on horses, on elephants if we get elephants, the candy butchers working the stands, the cats coming through . . .

"Maestro, sorry to put you through this, but we'll need bits for each act as they enter."

"Of course," Aterton said haughtily. "I, at least, know my business and am hardly a first-of-Mayer."

Garvin made a face, decided to let it pass.

"Then, after the spec goes out the back door of the tent, or the hold, or the amphitheater . . . I don't have the foggiest where we'll be playing . . . then we'll have the first act, which'll be something I haven't decided on, maybe some flyers, maybe have some little people working the ground, maybe some pongers, 'though I haven't seen nearly enough acrobats."

He seemed quite at home amid the confusion.

"Earth cats?" Garvin asked.

"At one time," the chubby, rather prissy man with a moustache said, a bit mournfully. "Since then, they've apparently mutated . . . and the perihelion of the species are with Doctor Emton's Phantastic Felines, Who'll Make You Wonder If You're Really Superior and Dazzle You. A Fine Act for the Whole Family."

Garvin looked skeptically at the six lean but well-brushed animals sitting on his desk. They regarded him with equal dispassion.

"Ticonderoga," Emton said. "Insect. On picture. Catch it for him."

He pointed at Garvin, but made no other move.

A cat leapt suddenly from the desk up to the mounted holo of Jasith, caught a bug, bit once, and dropped it daintily in Garvin's lap.

"Interesting," Garvin said. "But more suitable for a sideshow. Which we aren't."

"Pyramid," Emton said, and three cats moved together, two more jumped on their backs, and the third completed the figure.

"Play ball," he said, taking a small red ball from his pocket, and tossing it at them. The pyramid disassembled, the cats formed a ring, and began passing it back and forth.

"Hmm," Garvin said. "We will have projection screens so the audience can see what's going on . . . maybe something with the clowns?"

"Clowns," Emton said, and the six cats stood on their paws, walked about, then sprang cartwheels.

"I'm afraid not," Garvin said.

"Oh. Oh. Very well," Emton said, and got up. His cats sprang back into the two carriers he'd brought in.

"Oh . . . one other thing . . . I, uh, understand that tryouts are welcome at your dukey?"

"Certainly," Garvin said, and noted a slight look of desperation about the man. It must've been his imagination, but it seemed the cats had the same expression. "We're happy to feed you. And your animals."

"Well . . . thank you for your time, anyway," Emton said as he fastened the carrier closers.

Garvin, feeling every bit a saphead, said, "Hang on a second. Can I ask you a personal question?"

Emton's expression was a bit frosty, but he said, "You may."

"Can I ask what your last performance was?"

Emton looked wistful.

"Last time we were on a show . . . just one going back and forth, a mud show really, more to keep from getting rusty . . . actually, was, well, almost an E-year ago."

Garvin nodded.

"I said something about clowns. Do you have any objection to working with them?"

"Of course not," Emton said eagerly.

"Perhaps I'm not seeing your act's full potential, or maybe you could use some new material," Garvin said. "I'll buzz our Professor Ristori to meet you at the main lock in, oh, thirty minutes or so." He hastily added, seeing Emton's expression, "Sorry, an hour. Time enough for you and your troupe to get fed at the cook tent."

"Thank you," Emton said eagerly. "I promise, you won't be sorry."

"I'm sure I won't," Garvin said, thinking that Jasith wouldn't mind spending a little of what had been her money this way.

Besides, the creatures might be useful somehow.

Clowns and more clowns inundated *Big Bertha* until Garvin had more than thirty signed up. He made Ristori clown master, gave Njangu other duties.

* * *

"All right, all right, break," Garvin shouted. The robot bears' handler looked sheepish, and the aerialists overhead went back to their pedestal boards.

"People, we're trying to hit some kind of rhythm here. Let's take it back, to where the bears just come on."

"This much better," the *ra'felan* told Monique Lir. "Used to be, was real rope nets. If a human not land right . . . on back of neck . . . could get hurt. Break leg. Maybe bounce out and no catcher. Bad, very bad."

The circus "net" was composed of a series of antigrav projectors, all pointed up and inward, now set up in the tent's center ring. Anyone falling from a trapeze above would be slowed, then stopped two meters above the ground. The net also had the advantage of being almost invisible. Only a small blur could be seen from the projector mouths, so the audience could get the thrill of thinking the performers were chancing death every time they went aloft.

The being rolled an eye at Lir.

"Why you want to learn iron-jaw act?"

"Why not?"

The *ra'felan* reached up with a tentacle and pulled down the rope with the metal bit at its end.

"Good. You put in mouth, just clamp teeth. Hold firm. Now, we pull off ground. Just little.

"You see how easy? Human jaw strong. Now, we teach how to spin, turn, maybe . . . you look like strong woman . . . do kicks and things."

Njangu eyed the animals skeptically. They looked at him with interest. Not to maybe mention hunger.

There were a round dozen of them, identified by their trainer as lions, tigers, leopards, and panthers.

"You know," he said, "I'd be a lot happier, a whole lot happier, if the bars were between me and your friends."

"Ah, there's nothing to worry about," the tall handsome man with the scarred face said.

Njangu remembered Garvin telling him once, when they thought they were about to die, why he'd ended up joining the Force—the circus he'd been ringmaster for had turned out to be crook, and the locals had realized the hustles and started a riot. Jaansma saw someone about to torch the horses' enclosure, went, as he said, "a little ape shit," and turned the big cats loose on the crowd.

"Yeh," he said doubtfully.

"Not that the diddlies'll ever realize how tame m'pussies are," the slanger—trainer—said. He cracked a big whip, and instantly the inside of the huge enclosure, a huge birdcage almost twenty meters in diameter, was furry chaos, as cats roared, screamed, clawed at the air, sprang from stand to stand, and the trainer was firing blanks from an old-fashioned pistol into the air as he tossed rings through the air, and the animals plummeted through them.

Then all was still again.

The trainer, who said his name was Sir Douglas, grinned, his scar standing out against his near-ebony complexion. "See what I mean?"

"Maybe," Njangu said. "Uh . . . where'd you get the scar, if you don't mind my asking?"

"Muldoon . . . that's the leopard over there . . . gets moody first thing in the mornings. And I was being a little pushy." He gestured. "Accidents do happen, don't they."

"They do," Njangu said, moving toward the cage door. "By the way, what do these fine friends of yours eat?"

"Meat," Sir Douglas said with a ferocious grin. "As much as I'll let 'em have."

"Have they figured out yet, that *we're* meat?"

"No," the trainer said. "But they're working on it."

Njangu noticed Garvin's habits were changing. Now he would sleep all day, waking at nightfall for a light meal, then doing business all night long, breaking frequently to visit various acts around the ship. At dawn, he'd have a big meal and half a bottle of wine, and retire.

Njangu caught him eyeing Darod Montagna, but so far nothing had happened.

So far.

Besides, Njangu had other business to take care of, with two Intelligence Section assistants. He was interviewing, as subtly and thoroughly as he could, everyone who joined the circus about where they'd come from, what they knew of the collapse, and their own personal travels.

A problem was that circus people don't especially like to get personal. They were reluctant to say where they came from, but would say "I was with the Zymecas," or "I came from Butler and Daughter."

Njangu, so far, was amassing confusion. Some worlds or sectors seemed to have made a decision to declare their independence from the Confederation. Nobody seemed to know what happened to the Confederation officials assigned to those areas.

Other worlds, Njangu found, seemed to have lost contact. Their freightliners went out and didn't come back, ordered cargoes never materialized, troops were never replaced, and so forth.

A few troupers had specific stories—of expecting an act or a relative to arrive, and no ship ever appeared in their skies, or contracts had been signed, but the transport never showed up.

There didn't seem to be any single crash, just a series of crumblings.

Njangu had no theories whatsoever.

"Great gods playing feetball," Dill said. "They're goddamned enormous!"

"Nobody really realizes how big an elephant is until they get close to one for the first time," Garvin said. "Isn't that right?"

"We would not know," one of the slim brown-skinned men said.

The other man nodded. "We have been around our friends since . . . since we were born."

One of the men was named Sunya Thanon, the other Phraphas Phanon. They had sixteen elephants, all named, plus two babies, no more than an E-year old, Imp and Loti.

"Do you wish us to display our friends' skills?"

"Not necessary," Garvin said. "I watched the holo you sent me. You are more than welcome."

"Good," Sunya said. "Feeding our friends on our small budget becomes wearisome." He, like Phraphas, spoke careful, unaccented Common as if he were more familiar with another language.

"But we must caution you." Phraphas said. "We are searching for a place, and if, in our travels, we find a way to reach it, we must insist on being allowed to leave the show instantly."

"I suppose that can be arranged," Garvin said cautiously. "And that place is?"

"Have you ever heard of a planet named Coando?" Sunya asked.

"No," Garvin said. "Not that it means much, for I'm not an astrogator."

The two looked disappointed.

"We do not know its location either," Phraphas said. "But we heard of it once, and determined we must make it our life's work to go there with our friends."

"Why is it so special?" Dill asked.

"The legend is," Phraphas said, "that men of our culture left ancient Earth . . . with the elephants they had always worked together with . . . to make their home on a planet that was jungled, hot, like the land they came from.

"But here, no one would hunt their friends for their skins, for the ivory of their tusks, or . . . or just for the monstrous pleasure in killing something bigger than they were.

"The tale is, they found such a world, and named it Coando, and, as they developed this world, being careful to keep it as it was, as their homeland had been before it was despoiled, and then sent expeditions back to Earth, to bring wild elephants to join them.

"That, the tale goes, is why elephants are so rare, with only the friends of the circus, who choose to work with us, and some others around what was the Confederation.

"That is the world we seek, the world we have been seeking, as our parents did before us, and their parents before them."

Dill thought of saying the obvious, then realized he wasn't that much of an asshole. He and Garvin exchanged looks.

"I assume," Garvin asked, "that you've asked since you've been here on Grimaldi?"

"Asked, and consulted star charts," Sunya said. "But without success."

"That's all right," Dill said, surprising both Garvin and himself. "Coando's out there . . . and we'll find it or, anyway, find where it is. Maybe when . . . if . . . we reach Centrum, we can see if the old Confederation master records still exist."

Sunya looked at his partner.

"You see? I knew we had luck when we first saw this ship approach from the skies."

Garvin and Dill turned the beasts and their handlers over to Lir, started back for the ship.

"Anybody ever tell you that you're a sentimental slob?" Garvin asked.

"And, of course, you're not?" Dill asked.

Garvin and Montagna watched the horses pour through the hoops and around the ring like milk, liquid grace, while two long-haired women and an impressively moustached man with equally long hair sat, rolled, tumbled on their mounts' backs as if they were standing still.

"I am going to learn to do that," Montagna said firmly. "No matter how hard it is."

"You'll do fine," Garvin said absently. She smiled at him, reflexively moved a bit closer. They caught themselves, and stepped back.

The man, Rudy Kwiek, leapt from the back of one, did a double roll in midair, and landed in front of the pair.

"Are my vrai not wonderful?"

"They are," Garvin agreed. "What's the gaff?"

Kwiek looked injured.

"There is no gaff. My horses, my vrai, are from a very special, very sleek family, bred only by a few Rom on isolated worlds, and almost never allowed to be seen in public.

"And I have the best of the breed, an attraction so special and so highly trained your circus should not only count itself lucky to have the chance to sign us, but it will double, nay triple your bunce."

"Yeh," Garvin said flatly.

"Maybe," Montagna said, "you wouldn't mind having one of your horses lift a foot?"

"Ah," Kwiek said. "The lady is not only beautiful, but bright."

"No," Montagna said. "I just thought I saw metal gleam when your horse jumped that stand."

"Ah once more," Kwiek said. "I must work with the animal. I must confess that I have made my poor horses' task a bit easier."

"What?" Garvin asked with a grin. "A little anti-grav unit in each shoe?"

Kwiek bowed.

"I can see I will have no secrets with you, Gaffer. Perhaps we should adjourn to your office and taste a bit of the raki I have brought with me, and discuss in what manner my wives and I shall be able to work together."

Garvin nodded.

"Sorry about that dinner invite in town, Darod. It's going to be a hard night's bargaining."

"I am not going to sit on that beast," the young woman stormed.

"And why not, my temperamental little one?" the circus's choreographer, a tiny and somewhat effete man named Knox said. "We've been promised they do not eat people."

"I won't, because . . . because they've got hairy little spikes all over them, and I don't want my bottom to be a pincushion."

Monique Lir, standing near the hull's gangway, muttered to Garvin: "They're all like that. All goddamned thirty of those goddamned showgirls. They won't do this, they won't do that, they don't care what their contracts say, their room's too hot, it's too cold, it's too close to the horses, it's too . . . aargh. Boss, please. Give me all thirty of them for a week, and I promise, those that're left won't be doing any more of this frigging sniveling."

"Now, now," Garvin soothed, hiding a grin. "We must allow for artistic temperament."

"Temperament my left tit," Lir snarled. "All they're supposed to do is wave their pretty little asses about, smile like they've got an idea what day it is, and be frigging foils for the clowns."

"Speaking of which," Garvin said.

"Now, Adele," Knox said, still calm. "I really don't want to put pressure on you . . . but if you won't take that assignment, I'll have to find you another."

"Anything!" the blonde stormed. "Anything but that!"

"Heh . . . heh . . . heh . . . anything?" and suddenly Professor Ristori slunk into view, wearing a long black raincoat and hat. "We have, ho-ho, we have, a little sketch . . ." and extended one leg, with a baggy pair of pants on it. He pulled on the other leg, and the

pants leg was revealed as no more than the cuffs, and
a pair of suspenders going upward.

"A sketch, a sketch," he said, "most funny, perhaps
a little adult, a little adult, a little adult for our
younger sort, where you and I are wedded, wedded
forever, for eternal bliss.

"I roll you onstage, in a wedding bed, and then,
after I make my ablutions, abluting, abluting, then I
climb into bed with you, singing, and we embrace.
Then you discover, somehow, in the bed with us, are
two, perhaps three of my friends . . . little people . . .
who I've invited—"

"Stop," Adele shrilled. "No more. All right, Knox.
I'll ride your dinged elephant!"

"You see," Garvin told Lir. "There's more than one
way to skin a showgirl."

The three men threw things at the woman, Qi Fen
Tan—chairs, a small table, and she caught them,
stacked them atop each other askew, her hands a blur.
Then one man, Jiang Yuan Fong, gave a second leg
up, and he spun up through the air, to the top of the
stack, balancing easily.

The second man went up as well.

Then a very small child, Jia Yin Fong, toddled
toward the man, and she, too, went spinning up to the
top of the pile, and, from nowhere, produced a dozen
sticks and began juggling them.

The thrower nodded, and the acrobats disassembled.

"You, of course, are more than welcome," Garvin
said through the dying traces of a raki hangover.

"Good," the man, Fong, said. "For we have heard
that you will be attempting to reach Centrum, and
from there it should be easy for my family and cousins
to continue our journey."

"To where?" Garvin asked. "We already have some
people who are hitching with us."

Fong looked sad. "Yes. I know who you mean, and

I fear their planet is no more than a dream, although I hope otherwise.

"Our journey is to a quite real place. We are returning to Earth, to our native land called China, as, in the end, all Chinese will do.

"We have been, through a dozen generations, through the galaxy, and now it is time to return home to our village of Tai Sheng and rebuild our souls."

Garvin shook hands with the man, wondered if Ken Fong, back on Cumbre, was any kind of relation, then went back toward his office for a soothing beer and to contemplate the many reasons his troupe had . . . or claimed to have . . . for joining him.

They were almost crewed up, and rehearsing twice a day. Garvin had set their lift date, and tempers were getting short.

The big cats snarled at anyone who came within range of their cages, including their handler, Sir Douglas. The elephants were cranky, and their occasional screeches echoed through the transport. Acrobatic partners snapped at each other, aerialists bit their lips, and roustabouts met behind the ship to settle their differences.

Only a few of the experienced hands were pleased. This was the way it always went before a show was ready to roll . . . and if all had been peaceful and happy, they would've known they were in for trouble.

Garvin picked up the rifle, aimed carefully, and pulled the trigger. The ancient projectile weapon cracked, and the target was motionless.

"Try again, try again, can't win the doll for your lady without you take another chance," the talker chanted.

"The problem with you, Sopi," Njangu said, "is that you think everybody is too dumb to count."

The fat, cheery-looking man tried to look angry, failed, settled on offended.

"Howinhell can you think I'm not a bon homy?" he demanded, his voice high, squeaky.

"For openers, the barrel of that rifle's been tweaked so hard it shoots sideways," he said.

"Same thing with your wheel of fortune," Garvin joined in. "I could see the magnets, and watch the talker's foot kick switches. And we won't even think about your roulette wheel, which barely turns."

"Now, 'at's not good," Sopi Midt agreed. "Have to get them side curtains lowered some."

"And the ball throw was weighted," Garvin went on. "The bottles in the ring toss were too close together, so nothing could land right."

"But whadja think of the jill show?"

"That won't fly at all," Garvin said. "First we've got our showgirls already. And I know sex sells . . . but we're not trying to get in trouble."

"I don't get in trouble," Midt said. "We always play things right up to the wire, and make sure the rozzer's been tipped so there's no arrests.

"Play to the community standards, maybe a meter or so beyond, and you'll never ever, or hardly ever anyway, get in trouble," he said piously.

"You do have a problem," Garvin agreed with Njangu. "You're too quick to go chasing after the credit.

"But I've got a problem, too. I need a midway, I want to be on the road yesterday, and you've got twelve booths, not including the girlie show, and you're not trying to shove freaks at me, although I wouldn't mind a good giant or two."

"Know where I can get 'em, have 'em here by morning," Midt said.

"Shut up for a minute," Garvin said. "Try this for a proposition. Instead of the cut being sixty–forty, like you suggested, let's try seventy–thirty."

"Why're you willing to screw yourself?" Midt asked suspiciously.

" 'Cause I want a straight show . . . or, anyway,

fairly straight. I want you to go through, fix the graft so it isn't too bad a rape, and we have a deal.

"The other condition is you deal straight with me, all the way. Or I'll leave your fat ass, and your crew, in the middle of whatever fix you'll have caused, on whatever miserable world of flatties it happens on."

Midt considered.

"Damn," he said. "If there was any other show goin' . . . I'm not sure I'm real good at bein' honest."

"Then you'd best start learning," Njangu said, finding all this very funny.

Midt stuck out a paw.

" 'Kay. Hard bargaining. But I'll take the deal."

"Then you better get to work, straightening some gun barrels and unwiring your graft," Garvin said curtly, and started back for the ship.

"We sure have a crew," Njangu said. "Crooked sideshows, gypsies, aliens, elephants, and killer cats."

"I know," Garvin said happily. "It really is starting to feel like a circus. And, like you said, back in Cumbre, nobody's gonna think a rooty-tootin' spy mission of heroes is also running some games that are somewhat on the diddly."

It was dress rehearsal.

Garvin, in spite of his romantic lust to do his first show under canvas, had been sensible and performed in *Big Bertha*'s main hold.

He would use exactly the same dimensions whether they were inship or outship: bleachers were set up on either side of the rectangular area, almost half a kilometer in length. The bleachers could be adjusted depending on the crowd they drew, so Circus Jaansma would never look poorly attended.

The horse track ran from the troupers' entrance around the performing area, then back out the entrance on the other side.

Garvin, ever the traditionalist, would run three rings, each about twenty-five meters in diameter. They could be spaced closer or farther apart, depending, again, on the size of the crowd. The crowd came in through the main cargo airlock, whose secondary portal could be stowed on a breathable world.

Overhead was the maze of lines and guy wires for the aerialists, and, high above them was the rear of the command capsule.

Outside the ship was the midway, and at lock's entrance there were spielers, still working on their ballyhoos, drawing the crowd inside.

Garvin had invited anyone on Grimaldi who wanted to attend. The bleachers were full and extra seats, called cattle guards, had been set in front of the general admission seats.

Then it began, and the clowns attacked the pompous ringmaster, and Garvin whipped them away, just as the aerialists, like clouds of satin, dangled by strange monsters, filled the skies.

There were elephants, more clowns, acrobats, big cats, even a finicky man with real Earth cats, constantly harassed by the clowns.

The horses came and went, and more clowns, and the children were starting to yawn, and then it was the blowoff, and the candy butchers swarmed the stands.

"Not bad," Garvin grudged.

"Not bad at all," Njangu agreed. He laughed. "I guess it's time to go to war."

"Sir," Liskeard said. "All compartments report ready to lift, we have hull integrity, no problems reported."

"Then, Mr. Liskeard," Garvin said, "we're trouping!"

Liskeard grinned, touched controls, and *Big Bertha* lifted clear of Grimaldi and waddled toward the stars.

CHAPTER
7

Garvin could have gone straight for Centrum, but he knew better. Njangu's digging indicated that whatever had happened to the Confederation now looked like it had happened in chunks, rather than a total implosion/explosion from the center.

He felt if he went straight for the heart of the matter, he'd most likely get his head rolled, and thought it wiser to skirt the fringes . . . actually well into the heart of the Confederation . . . gathering intelligence before going for broke.

His goal was the multiple systems of Tiborg. That hadn't been his original target, back on Cumbre, but he hadn't planned on having to go all the way to Grimaldi to gather his troupe, either. Tiborg had been one of the secondary options he'd chosen, because a Confederation fiche, fairly classified, said the sector could be "interesting in its approach to diplomacy."

"Which means," Garvin had said, "they're royal pains in the ass . . . or were, anyway, to the Confederation, I'd guess. Well worth talking to."

"Yeh. Right," Njangu said. "This is the old 'enemy of my friend could be worth knowing' routine. It's generally been my experience that somebody who's a good enemy is an all-around pain in the ass to everyone who comes in contact with him.

"But you're the brave leader and all."

Big Bertha jumped through five systems, four inhabited, without landing or contacting the locals. Penwyth, Lir, Dill, and Froude went to Yoshitaro—Garvin having refused to see them, taking advantage of the old military law that an absence of response always means no and go away—to request *Big Bertha* make landings.

"That'll give the planets' peoples *something*," Penwyth said. "The mere assurance that there's folks out there, concerned about the Confederation."

"Touching," Njangu said, not quite sneering. "Truly touching. Especially you, Ben, being one of the petitioners, being a hardened killer of the ether. There are . . . were . . . how many planets in the Confederation at last count? A hundred thousand? A million? Don't you think we might grow old gracefully on such a charming errand of mercy, rather than doing what the hell we're out here for in the first place?"

Penwyth and Dill might've said more, but Froude recognized that Yoshitaro was right. They didn't have time to waste. Lir knew, after the time with him in I&R, better than to argue when the boss got a certain coldness to him.

Njangu asked Monique to stay behind after the others.

"Getting soft?" he asked, and there wasn't a trace of sarcasm in his voice.

She took it as meant, thought for a bit.

"No, boss. I don't think so."

"Good," he said. "We've got soft hearts enough, and I suspect this operation will get sticky before we belly up to the bar at the Shelburne again."

Tiborg

"Boursier One, this is Tiborg Alpha Delta Control," crackled in Boursier's headphones. "You are cleared to land at field, using Channel three-four-three for instrument approach, or under visual flight conditions once in-atmosphere under pilot's discretion. Over."

"This is Boursier One," Jacqueline Boursier said

into her mike—Dill had started something by using his own name for a call sign. "Roger your instructions on Channel three-four-three. Be advised I am forerunner of Transport *Big Bertha*, who will be entering your system shortly."

There was a pause.

"Boursier One, this is Control. *You* should be advised we have patrol ships out . . . but your transport name is certainly disarming."

Boursier, fairly close to being humorless, opened her mike. "Roger your last. We intend no harm. We are a circus ship."

"Say again your last?"

"Circus," Boursier said. "As in entertainment."

A long pause.

"This is Control. I looked the word up. My superior says proceed as before."

"Roger . . . thank you, Control. Switching channels." Boursier touched a sensor, signaled *Big Bertha*.

A few minutes later, one of the patrol ships dropped into normal space. Garvin Jaansma was aboard it.

"Boursier One, this is Jaansma," he said. "No problems?"

"None that I can see."

"Then let's be hung for sheepsies . . . go on down and see what's happening, Boursier One."

"Roger. Switching frequencies." Again, Boursier touched a sensor.

"Tiborg Alpha Delta Control, this is Boursier One. Proceeding to landing. Other two ships will follow me."

The Nana boat went back into hyperspace, and then it returned, followed by *Big Bertha*, and they closed on the planet below.

"Interesting," Garvin said to no one in particular. "Supposedly these systems are democratic, but they've all got names like some soldier named them. Alpha Delta whatever my left nostril!"

"Or else the people only think they've got democracy," a tech murmured.

"That too."

"Purpose of your visit?" the customs officer asked briskly.

"To entertain your people . . . and maybe make a few credits," Garvin said.

The customs officer looked up at *Big Bertha* looming over her, then smiled.

"You know, you're the first person I've ever cleared who wasn't from one of the Tiborg systems. You . . . and your people . . . are truly welcome."

"Ladies and gentlemen, children of all ages, citizens of our Confederation, welcome to Circus Jaansma," Garvin called, and cracked his whip sharply.

The main cargo area of *Big Bertha* was about half-full of people. Garvin had decided for their first real performance, and the first night on an unknown world, it would be safer to keep things close at hand and pitch the tent later.

"We bring you wonders from beyond the stars, from old Earth, from worlds unknown to man, with strange aliens, monsters, deadly beasts, death-defying acrobats high above you, to chill and amaze—"

At this point, the clowns attacked Garvin, as planned. He flailed and whipped them off, the clowns stumbling into each other, their every scheme foiled by idiocy; then one shrieked warning, and pointed off.

Through a portal Alikhan loomed, growling, snarling, "guarded" by Ben Dill, wearing a pair of tights and iron rings about his biceps.

There were screams, especially from the children. Perhaps there were a few adults who knew what a Musth was, but none of them could know whether or not he was friendly.

Behind Alikhan streamed the circus—tumbling acrobats, the aerialists pirouetting on lifters, the cats in their cages, the elephants, the horses, Darod Montagna proudly if a little shakily standing on one of them, and the show began.

They played day-on, day-off for the next four days, honing the routines.

Njangu wasn't around much—he was again scouting libraries for data on the Confederation, looking for possible info sources, but without that much success.

Tiborg had been mostly out of contact with the Confederation for more than ten years, longer than Cumbre. Researching back through the holos of the time, it seemed the break-off hadn't been of much concern.

He wondered what the word "mostly" meant, decided to look further, even though he got the idea the people of Tiborg were perfectly happy to be left alone, content to let the Universe roll on by.

He made some attempts to size up the local military, found, in common with many worlds, curiosity wasn't encouraged. He did discover there was an Armed Forces Club in the capital, and considered if there might be something there.

Running Bear paced back and forth, stepping carefully, chanting as he did, moving steadily down the sawdust around the three main rings.

It was coming back to him, he thought, wishing he'd had a grandfather or father he was sure actually had remembered the rituals.

He only half believed in racial memory, but was trying desperately under the face paint and body paint.

He tried to remember a time before the whites, when his people ruled the plains of a distant world, warrior lords of the prairies.

He came back, realized there was a small girl staring solemnly at him, who'd come out of her seat in the stands.

"Are you real?" she asked.

"Nope," Running Bear said. "I'm a ghost. A ghost dancer."

"Oh. What are you doing?" she asked.

"A rain dance of my people," Running Bear intoned, trying to keep from laughing.

"Oh." The little girl nodded, started back for her seat, then turned back.

"It's a good dance," she said. "It just started raining when we got here."

Running Bear grunted like a good AmerInd should; felt, inside, a tiny ripple of fear for messing about in the territory of the gods.

"We certainly seem," Ristori said to Froude, "to have arrived in interesting times. I assume you've noted there's a campaign going on for Planetary Premier?"

"I've seen something on a holo," Froude said. "Unfortunately, I was trying to learn that damned forward roll you think my old bones are capable of."

"Shame, Doctor," Ristori said. "Wolves should always attend on the doings of the sheep. Otherwise, they might miss the hiring of a new and dangerous shepherd. Or a flock of sheepdogs."

"I'm worse than that," Froude confessed. "I don't even know how the damned system works."

"Most simple, simple, simple," Ristori said, reverting to his chosen clamor. "Sorry. You have a supposedly freely elected Premier and Vice Premier, plus their various appointed secretaries. They, in turn, help rule all of Tiborg's twenty-odd worlds through four systems."

"Interesting device," Froude said. "Sounds like it might be fairly representative."

"Perhaps," Ristori said doubtfully. "However, I also noted there are some thirty members of what's known as a Directorate. There's very little on the holos about them, but they seem to be former planetary politicians, who, and I am quoting here, advise the Premiers, bringing their years of experience to bear."

"Mmmh," Froude said. "How much real power do they have?"

"No one says, which suggests a lot."

"Indeed. So the Premiers are puppets, then."

"In a manner of speaking . . . except that it seems to me that one of them who's properly cooperative and understanding will have his name set down as a potential Director."

"Ah, humans," Froude said. "We do come up with strange ways of doing things."

"Especially this election here on Delta. It would seem that the government is a shade on the corrupt side, and has held power for some eight years. Gaming, whoring . . . whatever. Delta seems wide-open, which we haven't seen, not having gone downtown nearly enough, for other citizens of Tiborg to find this an exciting place to vacation.

"But now there's a young reformer named Dorn Fili who's a candidate for Premier, swearing he's going to throw the rascals out, bring honesty, truth, and justice to government, rule hands-on and such. He's very pretty, according to the holos I've seen."

"Ah?"

"The interesting thing that I've discovered," Ristori said, "is that Mr. Fili's father was Premier some years back, thrown out of office by outraged reformers."

"Oh."

"Precisely. Let's tear the old crooks away from the trough so new crooks can have their turn to come in and fatten."

"You know," Garvin said contentedly, "I could get into this habit of making money."

"You mean we're actually in profits?" Njangu said.

"Well, if you ignore the initial outlay from Jasith . . . and the cost of the ship . . . we're making credits hand over fist."

"Always easy to show a profit if you blow off the overhead," Njangu said. "That's why being a thief attracted me so much.

"Speaking of which, I've got the angle on this Armed Forces Club thing. It's got a big building near the center of the capital, provides rooms for its members, has a bar, meeting halls, some kind of museum, serves meals . . . I'd guess the usual private club menu of gray vegetables and boiled meat.

"However, they're very proud of their charities."

"Ah-hah."

"Exackle," Njangu said. "I'm gonna roll Penwyth in, and say the circus would be delighted to sail some Annie Oakleys . . . that's the term, right, for freebies? . . . for their gimpy kids or something."

"Which'll give us what?"

"Which'll give us maybe a temporary membership for Erik."

"Which'll give us . . . besides having to listen to Penwyth whine about the food . . . what?"

"Soldiers love other soldiers," Njangu explained carefully. "They really suck up to bigger militaries."

"I wouldn't know," Garvin said. "Never having been around a bigger one . . . but maybe you would, given your fondness for the late Larissan military."

"Screw off," Njangu said. "So, assuming there might've been some kind of contact beyond this break-off ten years gone, we might be able to pick up some data of interest about the Confeds and what happened.

"Maybe."

"Thin, my little brownish brother. Very thin indeed," Garvin said. "But I agree. We should—"

There was a tap at the cabin door.

"It's open," Garvin said, and the door slid open and one of the gangway sentries stood there. With him was a handsome man in his early thirties, and a heavyset, satisfied-looking companion in his late middle age. Both men wore business wear that Njangu, even though he knew nothing of the planetary style, decided looked expensive.

The younger man was very handsome, in a rugged sort of way, his face open, exuding confidence and trust.

Njangu decided that he hated him.

"Good evening, gents," the middle-aged man said. "I'd like you to meet Dorn Fili, soon to be Premier of Delta, and possibly we can discuss some matters of mutual benefice."

"Now, now," Fili said with a smile, "we've yet to win the election, Sam'l."

"We have the people behind us, Dorn," the older man said. "They're tired of corruption and dirt in public office."

"I hope so," Fili said. "But we don't have to campaign in front of these people, who we hope will do us some good. My friend here, is Sam'l Brek. He's advising me, which he's been doing since I was born, and before that was one of my father's most trusted men."

"Thank you," Brek said.

"You said we might do you some good," Garvin said carefully. "In what way?"

"I'll explain . . . may I sit down?" Fili said. Garvin waved him to a chair—the cabin was crowded with more than two people in it. Brek stood against the wall, looking interested at whatever idea Fili was going to propose, as if he'd never heard it before.

Njangu watched both men very carefully.

"As Sam'l said, I'm running for Premier," Fili went on. "I'm fortunate enough to have been left quite a bit of credits by my family, which I've dedicated to defeating the machine that's been holding Delta back for eight years now.

"I'm doing what used to be referred to as a full press, hitting the Constitutionalists high, low, here, and there.

"One of the means I'd like to use is your circus,

which I was lucky enough to see tonight. What a show! What an amazing show!"

"Thank you," Garvin said.

"I would like to put your resources to work on my team, for which you'll be well paid during the campaign, and, if I'm elected, you and your team would be considered good friends."

"Thank you for your offer," Garvin said. "Unfortunately, we're not wealthy, and can't afford to volunteer to help anyone."

"Plus we're outsiders," Njangu put in. "I've never noticed folks are real fond of strangers coming in and helping them with their business."

"I think you misunderstand me," Fili said, frowning, his expression echoed by Brek. "I don't want you to starve in my service . . . nor to be widely known for helping me."

"What I need, I pay for. I'd guess, for instance, that your performance tonight probably grossed about thirty thousand credits."

Garvin covered his surprise. In fact, that was only seven thousand credits below the actual gate.

"I would want to hire your entire show for two, perhaps three, benefits, for which I'd pay fifty thousand per show."

Both Garvin and Njangu looked very interested.

"Plus there are certain charities and good works I support, such as crusades against crippling diseases, against birth defects, and such, and I would want to hire certain of your specialists, perhaps the elephants and perhaps the horses to perform outside hospitals three or four times in the next few weeks."

"How would this be tied in with your campaign?" Njangu said skeptically. "The elephants will carry banners in their trunks?"

"Nothing so crass," Brek broke in. "The posters would merely mention that your circus is performing under the auspices of one or another of Dorn's committees. We'd leave it to the voters to make the obvious association."

Garvin considered. He could see no problems, and it would certainly be good for some of the acts to get away and work on their own.

"We wouldn't be able to cut any of our people free on show days," he said.

"Of course not," Fili said heartily. "And we'll provide volunteer workers for anything you might need beyond your normal functions."

"Security, for instance," Brek said.

Garvin looked at Njangu, who moved his head microscopically up and down.

"I think something could well be arranged," Jaansma said.

Fili was on his feet.

"Good, good. That's wonderful news. And you'll never regret your decision, and I'm sure you'll enjoy being part of my campaign."

There was more glad-handing, exchange of com numbers for the working out of the details, and Fili and Brek left.

"Free money," Garvin gloated, cackling, rubbing his hands together in his most miserly imitation.

"Looks like," Njangu agreed. "I just wish I liked Fili."

"What's the matter with him?"

"Handsome bastards always grate on my spine."

"Then why're you my friend?" Garvin asked blandly.

Njangu snorted. "Maybe because you take instruction well."

Njangu and Maev rolled out of bed, pistols in hand, to the scream of sirens and the synthed voice:

"Emergency! Emergency! In the . . . cat area. In the . . . cat area!"

Njangu found time for a pair of pants, Maev for a robe, and they went out of their cabin, pelted down the corridors and two companionways into the hold, others behind them.

They pushed past a throng into the cat compartment, into horror.

Muldoon the leopard crouched, growling, over a bloody, torn body. Against one cage wall lay Sir Douglas, moaning, barely conscious.

"What the hell?" Njangu snapped.

A tiny acrobat answered: "I . . . I heard commotion, opened the door, just as Sir Douglas arrived. That black monster had this man down, and the cage door was ajar.

"Other cats were coming out of their sleeping cage. Sir Douglas went into the main cage . . . he didn't even have his whip . . . slammed it closed behind him.

"One of the striped cats got behind him, and he was shouting for it to get back. The animal got scared and hit him . . . I think more by accident than anything else . . ." and the woman started crying.

"Who's the man?" Njangu demanded.

No one knew. Njangu thought of shooting Muldoon, but with his small pistol didn't know if he'd do more than make the leopard angrier.

Garvin, bare naked, ran into the compartment, caught the situation up.

"Get blasters," he ordered. "We'll have to kill the cat."

"Not yet," someone said. It was Alikhan, and behind him was Ben Dill, carrying a meter-long bar of steel as thick as his forearm. "Let me try to get the animal away."

Garvin shook his head, realized Alikhan's intent and jumped for him, but was too late as Alikhan opened the cage, went inside. Dill knocked Jaansma out of the way and went after him, muttering, "God-damned fool of a dumb-ass frigging alien bastard!"

Muldoon growled a warning, but Alikhan paid no mind, moving toward the animal steadily, calmly, waving his arms. Muldoon crouched, about to spring, and

Dill braced for the charge. Then the leopard, evidently, caught the alien's scent.

He growled once more, slid back from his barely moving victim, then scampered into his sleeping area.

The other cats, still half-asleep, also scented the alien and sulkily went back into their own quarters.

Alikhan banged shut the doors between the cages.

"Now," he started, but the main cage entrance was already open, and Jill Mahim was kneeling over the man, medikit at her side.

"Hell if I know who he is . . . phew, he's been drinking a storm," she said. "Some fool drunk maybe who hid out when the show broke up and wanted to play with the kitties."

Someone shouted, "I've got a medic flight on the way."

"Good," Mahim said, her fingers moving easily through her kit, punching a trach tube through the man's ruined throat, feeling the man's pulse, hitting him with three painkillers and an anticoagulant, tapping blood substitute into a vein. "Get one of the stretchers from the corridor." Crewmen ran to obey.

The moaning man was taken out of the cage, just as Sir Douglas stumbled to his feet, shaking his head.

"I did not see who hit me," he said. "Was it that bad Muldoon?"

"One of the tigers," someone said.

"I was careless," Sir Douglas said. "I thought they were my calm friends. I should have allowed for the excitement."

"Not you," someone cracked, "but that idiot on the stretcher."

"Who," Mahim said, "is probably going to live, and father many idiots. There's no justice."

"All right, everyone," Garvin said. "The excitement's over."

"Uh, boss," Njangu said, trying not to laugh. "Maybe you want to be the first to leave?"

Garvin looked down at himself, realized his naked-

ness, and reddened, especially when he saw Darod
Montagna eyeing him thoughtfully.

"Not bad at all," she murmured, and Jaansma fled
for his quarters.

"Ain't that the thing about circus life," Njangu said.
"Never a dull moment."

"You wished?" Phraphas Phanon asked Sir Douglas

"I was wondering if you have any interest in ex-
panding your gaff," the animal trainer said.

"We are always interested in the new," Sunya Thanon said. "What do you have in mind?"

"Combining my Deadly Dangerous Beasts with
your Monsters of the Midway."

"Ah," Phanon said. "Your large cats and our
friends. An interesting thought."

"I don't know if you've ever worked with cats," Sir
Douglas said. "I've never done anything with elephants. If their hides aren't as thick as they look, we
could maybe use pads."

"What sort of tricks would you have in mind?"

"Oh, leaping from one elephant to another," Sir
Douglas said, a bit vaguely. "Posing next to them."

"Hmm," Phanon said. "Perhaps we could come up
with something more spectacular."

Njangu stood at the side of the mess line in the
compartment known as the cook tent. Running Bear,
plate laden, came past him.

"Better grub than some we've known," he said.

"Careful," Njangu warned.

"I meant, in some of the circuses we've trouped in,"
the AmerInd said innocently, went on, found a seat.

The conversation was a buzz of various languages,
some translated into Common, others between men
and women from the same planet. Garvin sat at the
head of one table, chattering away like one of the
Earth monkeys he despised.

It felt happy, Njangu decided. Maybe like a family.

And how would you know what a family really is, he thought wryly. *No. Maybe I do. Maybe the Force. And isn't that a helluva thought?*

"You wished to see me?" Garvin said. He was sweating gently, having just come out of the ring on the break, the clowns cavorting to keep the crowd's interest.

The man waiting for him was elderly, every man's beloved grandfather, richly and conservatively dressed. "I did indeed."

"Perhaps my office, though we'll have to hurry, since I'm back on in half an hour," Jaansma suggested.

"Perhaps so, Gaffer Jaansma," the man said. He had a gentle yet firm voice, and followed Garvin through the managed chaos of backstage. Garvin saw Njangu, made a slight gesture.

In Garvin's office, the man declined a drink, sat down.

"If you don't mind . . . I think my mind's as spry as ever, but these bones thank you for a bit of relaxation."

"I'll only take a minute of your time. I'm Director Fen Bertl, by the way, and happened to be here on Delta on business to do with Dorn Fili's campaign.

"First, let me say how much I'm enjoying your show. Fantastic. You're certainly right when you say it's for children of all ages, for it certainly took me back to much younger days, when we were all innocent." He smiled beatifically.

"I thought the very least I could do in return is offer a bit of advice, although I'm certainly aware of what most people think of unsolicited suggestions."

"Sir, I'm always willing to listen to any suggestions," Garvin said truthfully. "I keep an open door, and always have."

"Many people say they do just that, but don't really mean it. If you do, I'm most impressed. Perhaps you were in the military once?"

"No, no," Garvin said. "I've been circus all my life."

Bertl nodded.

"My advice has to do with your involvement with the Fili campaign. No, don't look angry or upset that I've learned about it. There are very few secrets to a Director, particularly one who's decided to back Dorn, just as I backed his father years ago.

"My advice is this: People love to wallow in their vices for a time, then loudly want redemption. This is the crest Dorn Fili is riding, hopefully to the highest office, as his father did, who also had the intellect to realize when to back off his crusade.

"Something you should be aware of is that elections throughout the Tiborg system are, shall we say, most freewheeling, particularly when there appears to be a radical change in the direction of government proposed.

"Our elections can get bloody, I'm ashamed to admit."

"All I agreed was to do a few shows for Fili," Garvin said. "For hire, not as a believing volunteer."

"Unfortunately the opposition frequently takes small things like that and magnifies them out of all importance. This is one reason I think they will lose the election, for they've lost the sense of perspective all of us in politics must maintain. Because of this, it's now the turn of the loyal opposition to take office."

"You have, if you'll forgive me, for I'm hardly interested in politics," Garvin said, "quite a system. First, it's Set A, then Set B, then Set A again. Aren't you worried that the people are, sooner or later, going to ask for a real change?"

"No," Bertl said calmly. "No, my romantic friend, I'm not. Our system has worked well for almost five hundred years, in spite of Confederation meddling . . . not for an honest election, I assure you, but because they wanted Set C, their own handpicked fellows, to take office.

"Besides, we have certain . . . control measures to keep matters from getting out of hand in an emergency.

"My own personal belief is that we absolutely should have real free elections one of these years, when the time is right and the populace is sufficiently educated and mature for such an event.

"But until then . . . matters should stay as they are." He got up. "To return to the reason for my visit, I thought I should tell you, as, perhaps, thanks for your job of entertaining me . . . and the people of Delta . . . that you may have made a mistake, no matter how well paid you'll be for your services."

"I don't see any way to undo my agreement," Garvin said.

"Neither do I," Bertl admitted, "since you're more than evidently an honest man. I, on the other hand, would cheerfully find a way to loudly abrogate the agreement. But you are what you are. At least I thought I might give you the chance to be on your guard.

"As I said, all I can offer is a bit of a warning."

He smiled in a most fatherly manner, bowed, and was gone.

Garvin waited a minute, and Njangu came into his office.

"Not an election this year, nor next year, but by gum your grandchildren will be happy as snot," Njangu snarled. "Why is it shitheels like that never think it's the right time for the people to have squat in the way of power?"

"I dunno," Garvin said. "And howcum there's wars?"

"What makes me worry," Njangu said, "are these emergency measures. Like martial law, maybe, which we surely don't want to get caught up in."

Garvin poured drinks from a decanter, gave one to Njangu, shot his own back.

"I'm starting to wonder if we might have made a slight error," he said quietly.

Director Fen Bertl got into his lim.

"Back to our ship," he ordered, and the lifter silently came off the ground.

"Well, sir?" his supposed driver asked.

"An interesting young man. Most subtle for his years. He only looked twice at where I assume some sort of pickup was hidden in the wall spaces," Bertl said.

"A very nice young man, who's playing politics and has men looking for data on the Confederation.

"I think it might be wise to find out a bit more about him and his circus."

"I know our cooks are the best recyclers in the universe," Darod Montagna said. "But it sure is nice to get out and eat something that isn't seasoned with what used to be your own sweat."

"How genteel. How ladylike. How guaranteed to spoil my appetite," Garvin said. He poured what remained of the bottle of wine between their glasses, and, unobtrusively, the busboy was there to take it away and the sommelier to provide another.

"Oh, I'm just so sorry," Darod said, staring pointedly at the bony remains of a fish on Garvin's well-polished plate.

"I kept eating just for politeness," he explained.

"I thought I'd never get another chance at that dinner you promised," Montagna said.

"I'm always a man of my word," Garvin said. "Sometimes the word is just a tiddly slow."

He looked around the restaurant. It was quite a place, a polished wooden ocean ship that had somehow been transported to the lake near the field *Big Bertha* was parked on. Its waiters wore white gloves, liquids were served in real crystal, and there were actual tablecloths.

"It is nice to get out," he said. "I was starting to think everything smelled like elephant."

"Speaking of being indelicate," Darod said. She put a hand on Garvin's, and he let it stay there. "I was most impressed by your command presence the other morning."

Garvin held back laughter. "You just said that to make me blush."

"Oh no," Darod said. "I already saw you blush, and I must say you do a very thorough job of it."

She giggled.

Garvin yawned as he took the lifter off from the lot beside the moored restaurant ship.

"And so back to grim reality."

"I guess so," Darod said, then pointed. "Not yet . . . unless we have to. See that point, way up there? And there's two . . . no, three moons out. Can you land up there?"

"With a bottle of that wine in me, I could land on the head of a pin and dance."

"Just put us down on the big rock," Darod said. "Dancing might be for later."

Garvin brought it in skillfully, surprising himself, and set it down.

They sat in silence for a few minutes, contentedly looking at the moons, the silver lake below, the lights of the ship.

"For some reason," Garvin said, a bit surprised that his voice was a bit hoarse, "I feel like kissing you."

"That can be arranged," Darod said, turning to him, and her mouth opened under his.

Some time later, her formal dress slid down about her waist, she found herself in the lifter's huge rear seat, looking up at Garvin.

"Perhaps you'd lift your hips?" Garvin said.

She obeyed.

"You'll notice," she said, "no underwear, meaning

I was hoping something like this or maybe just this was going to happen." Then she gasped.

"I hope you know what you think you're doing," was Monique Lir's only comment when Darod Montagna bleared into her compartment the next morning just after dawn.

"*You* hope," was Darod's only reply.

"Well, well, well," Njangu said, pushing the holo screen to Garvin. "Guess who's a man of his word, a worthy candidate for public office."

Garvin ignored the pics, scanned the readout. Candidate for Premier Dorn Fili was pleased to announce that Circus Jaansma had joined his campaign, at least so to speak, for they'd be doing benefits and charitable appearances for various worthy causes.

"So much for letting the votes make the correct assumptions," Njangu said.

"Problem?"

"Flip the page," Njangu suggested, "and read the top two stories."

Garvin did. One was of a bombing by "unknown terrorists" of one of Fili's campaign headquarters, the other was the savage beating of three of his precinct walkers.

"Not good," Garvin said. "I think, between that moron wandering loose inside *Big Bertha* who wanted to play with our pussies . . . he is, by the way, indeed going to live, unfortunately, as Jill predicted . . . and this, we better start being a little more concerned about security. Ideas?"

"Yeh," Njangu said. "Pull everybody in I&R who's not a kinker onto security. Double the gangway guards . . . no, triple 'em. Put a roving patrol out around the ship.

"Cancel your idea of putting up that smelly tent for the show. Only let the midway outside the ship, and keep roving patrols through it. If Sopi loses a few of his crooked grafters, that's tough titty for him.

"Have either an *aksai* or Nana boat ready to launch on short notice if they try a heavy hit.

"From now on nobody goes into town or anywhere alone, and if there's enough of them going to make a target, they'll have to have a security tail gunner.

"Other than that," he finished, "it's just lovely life as usual."

That night, there was a bit of a clem on the midway, set up just outside *Big Bertha*, and all but two of the gangway sentries were drawn into it, to Njangu's later wrath.

Then those two guards were distracted by four happy drunks who wanted to serenade them.

No one noticed the unobtrusive figure slip up to one of the ship's fins, take a chest-size centimeter-thick pad, anodized to exactly match the ship's skin color, from his coat, and hold it against *Big Bertha*. The epoxy bonded the pad to the ship's fin instantly, and the man went away, as anonymously as he'd come.

Monique Lir muttered obscenities as she tracked the dozen squealing women through the shopping district. She swore this had been either Garvin or Njangu's idea of a joke.

Guarding the showgirls indeed. As if anyone . . . other than a brain surgeon studying vacuums or a lech who didn't believe in conversation would bother any of them, on their promised shopping expedition into the capital.

If someone had told Monique the only reason she went unnoticed was because of the brazen display of the showgirls, she would've most likely spat in their eye, or perhaps broken an arm or two.

As it was, she concentrated on her duty, eyes moving back and forth constantly behind very dark wraparounds, watching for anything, one hand on the grip of the heavy blaster hanging from a sling under her very stylish, very useful, long coat.

The dozen had just stopped to admire the holos swaying through the air outside a boutique when Monique saw the man, small, shabbily dressed, dash from a recess, saw the gun in his hand come up, and fire once.

Lir heard a woman scream in agony, but paid no mind to whoever was hit. She shed the coat, had her blaster up, safety off.

The man spun, about to run, and saw Lir and her gun.

"Stop!" she shouted. "Freeze!" knowing assassins must be taken alive.

But the man's gun was lifting, aiming, and she pulled the trigger.

The bolt took the man in the middle of the chest, spinning him back across a concrete bench.

The crowds were screaming, running, women and men going flat, and there were alarms howling.

Lir paid no mind, quickly went thorough the corpse's pouch, took everything, then was up and running, leaving the blaster across the body.

"Thanks," Njangu said, shutting off the com and turning to Garvin. "The showgirl . . . her name was Chapu, by the way . . . just died."

"Bastards," Garvin said, sorting through the contents of the shooter's pouch.

The com buzzed again, and Njangu took it, spoke briefly.

"That was Fili," he said. "Expressing his sympathies, even though he's sure it had nothing to do with politics or him, just some mental case."

"Yeh," Garvin said, flatly.

Njangu picked up the com, told the ship's com center to hold all outside calls, but log them, joined Garvin in examining the meager contents of the pouch.

"Too much money," he murmured. "Nice crisp

credit bills, nonconsecutive numbers. A for-hire job. Ho. What's this. A com number?

"Maybe his bosses forgot to shake him before he went out, eh?"

He went back to the com, told the center to connect him with that number.

"It's NG," he reported, said into the mike, "try the old code of adding one or subtracting one number." He waited. "Nothing connects going down one. Try up one." Again, he waited, then swiftly broke contact. "Here we go. Add one number, and we just happen to get a voice that says 'Constitutionalist District Four, Maya speaking.'

"Sloppy, sloppy work."

"Yeh," Garvin said.

"You know," Njangu said, "in a properly run democracy, that wouldn't be anything more than minor evidence."

"Which is why I'm damned glad I'm not running a democracy," Garvin said grimly.

CHAPTER
8

"Sorry to hear about your casualty," the slender man with the carefully trimmed moustache said to Erik Penwyth. He wore an expensive but somewhat shabby civilian suit like a uniform.

"We circus people don't think like you soldiers," Erik drawled. "We don't take what I suppose you call calculated risk into account. P'raps we should, though," he softened his response, burying his flash of anger. "Considering some of the risks taken."

"But I gather the woman who that madman shot was no more than a decoration," the man said. "Hardly someone who gets in a cage with monsters."

"I guess we all die, sooner or later," Erik said. "Here. Stand you a drink?"

"Thanks," the man said, and motioned to the human barkeep. "Whiskey. And a glass of charged water."

Penwyth nodded to the bartender to refill his brandy and ginger, although he was still getting used to the local brandy, better than anything native to Cumbre, and the mix, far gingerier than expected.

The man took his drink, lifted it to Erik.

"As we used to say . . . here's to a nice, neat war, with quick promotions."

Erik smiled, drank.

"Although," the man said, "none of us in the Club have ever seen a real war."

The Armed Forces Club's walls were decorated with

old weaponry, regimental banners, holos of stiff men looking proud.

"Just riots, a few raiders, every now and then a district or a world deciding it can go on its own and needs-reminding about the proper order of things," the man said. "Oh, by the way, I'm Kuprin Freron. Retired *T'ousan*, last duty assignment with the General Staff."

"Erik Penwyth. I'm one of the publicity hounds."

"I know," the man said, started to go on, changed the subject. "What will your people do about the tragedy?"

"What *should* we do?" Penwyth said carefully. "The killer was some lunatic who killed our trouper, then got shot down by an unknown civilian. That's what your holos say, anyway."

Freron raised an eyebrow. "I wonder about that quote unknown civilian end quote. We have very stringent gun laws here on Delta . . . although it certainly never seems to stop a criminal or one of our political thugs from arming himself with anything he wishes for his villainy."

"Crooks everywhere generally don't worry about breaking small laws," Penwyth said. "But I still don't understand what you're saying."

"I just thought that you offworlders might have your own . . . resources . . . when trouble happens, which is good, since I doubt if our authorities will do anything about searching for the people everyone knows are behind this bloodshed."

"Perhaps we do," Penwyth said. "If so, they've never told me about anything like that. By the way, you said you know me, but I don't remember us having met."

"We haven't," Jabish said. "I heard about your show, and the largesse your circus has extended to some of the charities the Club supports." He glanced to either side, saw no one was close, dropped his voice.

"I've also heard that you've been inquiring about the Confederation."

"Surely," Penwyth said, alarms going off. "We're loyal citizens . . . although it's certainly been a long time since we've been able to show our loyalty. Traveling people like order. And, speaking personally, I'm most curious how something that huge can vanish, seemingly overnight."

"Soldiers also like order," Freron said. "You know, I was lucky enough to do an intelligence course on Centrum itself a long time ago.

"And one of my jobs on the Staff, before the damned politicians decided there was more profit going our own way, was liasing with the Confederation attachés."

"Interesting," Erik said.

"I thought so at the time," Freron said. "And think so now, as I'm considering writing my memoirs.

"Because I kept thorough records. *Very* thorough records of everything I encountered dealing with the Confederation. But right now, it seems that no one is terribly interested in these anecdotes of the past."

"I always was, as a kid," Erik lied. "Somehow adults always had better things to talk about than us lads did." He wondered where the word "lads" had come from, decided that was the kind of word Freron would use. "But you said something about keeping records?"

"I did, and I suppose that was illegal, then, since a lot of the Confederation material I have was fairly classified then.

"Now it's just dusty fiches, although some might find it interesting."

"Such as?" Penwyth said, wishing to hell he had a bug detector in his pocket to see if Freron was Tiborg counterintelligence, trolling.

"Oh . . . historians, perhaps. People who're making the Confederation a subject of study, for whatever reasons. People who're well funded, since my pension hardly extends as far as I'd like."

"*T'ousan* Freron," Erik said, waving to the bartender. "You interest me greatly. Perhaps we should find a table and discuss this matter."

"Call me Kuprin."

Garvin was rather pleased that about half of his circus quietly came up and asked if he was going to do something about Chapu's murder, and if so, could they help.

He was, but he only needed nineteen, all chosen from I&R. They boarded one of the circus lifters in the late afternoon and flew into the capital, landing very quietly, on the roof of a building overlooking Constitutionalist District Four headquarters. High above, two *aksai* were flying cover, Dill and Alikhan as pilots.

Four soldiers, the best Shrike gunners in the Force, their modified missiles hidden in innocuous-looking cases, plus their gun guards, went down from the roof and found firing positions in alcoves and alleys.

Six others, lugging Squad Support Weapons, the tripod-mounted blasters, and their assistant gunners went to firing locations near the three entrances to the precinct building, under Lir's direction.

Then they waited, ducking into cover anytime any of the planetary police lifters came past.

Garvin and Njangu had chosen to land just after normal quitting time.

"That'll let the innocent, which means the small-scale sorts, get out before the fun starts," Garvin had said.

"What, just to be cynical, about the secretary whose boss ordered her to work late?" Njangu said.

Garvin looked at him coldly.

"Sorry," Yoshitaro said. "I didn't mean to throw shit in the game."

It was just dusk, and about a third of the windows

across the way were still lit when Garvin opened the com to his troops.

"Shrike element . . . fire as instructed."

Two of the missiles were aimed at the fourth story of the five-story building, the other two at its midsection.

Launchers whooshed, and the missiles arrived before their sound. The explosions sent shock waves across the capital, shattering windows for blocks. The building rocked, and its façade cracked, fell toward the street, forcing one SSW team to run.

Flames flickered from three floors of the building.

There were screams, shouts, and men and women ran downstairs into the street.

"SSW, clear to fire."

Perhaps politics on Delta was a young man's occupation, but Garvin doubted it. He'd given orders for the SSW teams to pick out anyone middle-aged, anyone who looked expensive, and especially anyone who looked like a Constitutionalist goon.

A police lifter rounded a corner, and a gunner put a burst into its engine. It bounced off a parked lifter, crashed. The cops piled out and, no fools against autoblasters, ran like hell.

Dill's voice came into one of Garvin's earpieces.

"Boss. Time to scoot. I've got some things that look like fire engines and maybe some military lifters in the air headed yours."

Garvin thumbed to the *aksai* channel.

"We're pulling out. Stay in the air until we're gone, then go on home." Then, without waiting for acknowledgment, he went to the grunt channel.

" 'Kay, troops. We're gone."

The women and men cascaded back up the stairs to the roof, piled in the lifter as Njangu took it up a few centimeters, dancing against the rooftop, then at full power down an avenue, below the roofs, and away.

In minutes, they were back at the field and *Big Bertha*.

"Any idea on casualties?" Montagna asked, a bit angry for not having been chosen, as they landed.

"Not nearly enough, whatever it was," Lir said harshly.

Garvin swallowed half a liter of sport drink.

"All right, friends," he told Liskeard, Lir, and Yoshitaro. "That's evened things up a little. Now, recall anybody that's in the city back home, get the troops to start packing and the midway struck aboard. We'll be gone by midnight, and Tiborg Alpha Delta can find its own path to hell."

"Hang on a second, boss," Njangu said. "Could you maybe gimme a moment of solitude?"

Garvin hesitated, then nodded. The others filed out.

"We just got a spanner up our asses, I think, as far as beating feet," Njangu said. "Erik just wandered back, a little buzzed, with something interesting."

Yoshitaro told him about Penwyth's evening with Freron, the retired staff officer. Garvin started to open another sport drink, curled his nose.

"This calls for alcohol."

" 'Deed it do," Njangu agreed, found two beers in Garvin's cooler, and opened them.

Garvin drank mightily.

"Why do I ever consider putting anything healthy inside me," he wondered, "when the evil stuff tastes so much better? 'Kay. So we've got somebody with . . . maybe . . . some good intel, high-level or fairly high anyway, on the Confederation. Ten years old, though."

"Older than ours, but surely at a higher level than anything the Force has, isn't it?" Njangu said.

Garvin nodded.

"But that'll also mean we'll still be targets for those assholes," he said.

"Which set?"

"Does it matter?" Garvin said. "A Constitutionalist bolt'll do you just as dead as one from . . . what's our boy's party . . . the Social Democrats, right?"

The com buzzed, and Njangu fielded it, listened, hung up.

"Speaking of which," he said, "we've got our pet candidate, ol' Dorn the Mouth and his aide pounding on the gangway. Shall we let 'em in?"

"Why not?" Garvin said, draining the beer and tossing it into the cycler. "I don't guess we can just up our hooks and scamper, now can we?"

"Not until we find out if this guy we're suborning is honest and subornable, or some kind of goddamned counteragent," Njangu said. "Though I'm not much more fond of the idea of hanging around than you are."

There was a knock at the door, Garvin touched the sensor, and a wide-eyed Dorn Fili, flanked by Brek, hurried in.

"Great gods," Fili said. "You people are dangerous!"

"I beg your pardon?"

"Dangerous and careful," Brek said. "I suppose you haven't heard about somebody blowing up a Constitutionalist headquarters an hour or so ago."

" 'Fraid not," Garvin said. "We've been concentrating on our own right now, and getting ready for poor Chapu's funeral."

"They're saying over a hundred and twenty-five Constitutionalist workers were killed, and the attackers used rockets and fully automatic blasters, like the army has," Fili said. "I've heard of ten for one . . . but . . ." He let his voice trail off.

"Sounds like," Njangu said to Garvin, "there must've been some kind of industrial explosion, hmm?"

"Is that it?" Garvin asked innocently.

"This evening we were discussing whether or not we'd lose you," Brek said, "which we could easily understand, and were wondering if we could convince you to stay if we provided some of the security elements of our party."

"Your circus has added a new note to the campaign," Fili said. "Adding holo bits of your various benefits has raised viewership on what otherwise might be considered nothing but political natterings, and we'd hate to have you leave before the victory celebration."

"We're not leaving yet," Garvin said. "We made a deal, and we'll hold to it."

"Good, good," Fili said heartily. "Especially the final rally for our party workers. That'll give them a huge morale boost for the last week of the campaign."

"And, as I've said," Brek added, "you'll have full security cooperation from us."

"We'll use you," Njangu said. "Outside the ship. No outsider with guns inside. Period."

"You're certainly confident enough about being able to defend yourselves . . . and my workers . . ." Fili said doubtfully.

"We are," Njangu said. "Especially since if everyone's thinking that unfortunate accident had anything to do with us, that should calm the waters."

"Don't be too sure," Brek said. "The Constitutionalists have been in office for a while, and they'll take some convincing to change their ways."

Garvin remembered what Director Bertl had said about their having lost a sense of proportion . . . and then about the possible trail, so far the best they'd come across, toward Cumbre.

"No," he said again. "We're staying. Although there'll have to be a discussion about our fees."

"Migods," Darod Montagna said weakly, "you certainly get passionate after action."

She unwound her legs from Garvin's thighs, and he rolled on his side.

"Do I?" he said, running a thumbnail down her breasts and across her stomach.

She drew in her breath sharply.

"Can I say something? And then I've got a question."

"Talk."

"I won't be able to unless you stop kissing my nipples," she said. "First, is something I want you to know, that I'm not going to think that what we're doing has anything to do with anything other than what we're dong, 'kay?"

"Odin's birdhouse, but I'm glad you went and joined the army, so you could learn to express yourself clearly," Garvin said.

"You know what I mean," Darod said. "Now, let me change the subject before you turn on the lights and see that I can blush better'n you.

"What're we going to do about these idiots here?"

"Nothing," Garvin said. "Finish our contract and go on our way."

"I don't know what you and Njangu have got running . . . it's none of my business. But I think it blows *giptels* for the people of Delta to have nothing better than these two parties, who seem to pass the looting back and forth."

"I figure it's pretty much the people's business to change things when they want," Garvin said. "Soldiers trying to play God end up getting themselves all screwed up."

"Even if, say, Lir and I just happened to build this thingie that just happens to go bang? And we just happen to plant it in the capital building for next inauguration, which is a known time and date, and it's easy to set up a thingie with a long det fuse? And just when the old scum are giving things over to this Fili and his new scum, there's a real loud bang? Wouldn't that help?"

"You're forgetting about the Directors, who seem to be the power behind the throne," Garvin said. "And I really sound like I know squat from politics, don't I?"

"We could figure *something* out and get them, too," Montagna said stubbornly.

"First one bang, then another, then we'll have to

find a third bomb . . . like I said, here we'd go, playing holy redeemer," Garvin said.

"Garvin, I'm trying to think, and while that feels good, especially there, I'll . . ."

"You'll what?" Garvin said muffledly.

"Try not to make as much noise coming this time," Darod said, and moaned.

"We may have erred," Director Bertl told his aide. "All that little transmitter does is tell us about the ship's location.

"I would like to have better data about people as . . . immediate . . . as these circus people. They seem much more than happy wanderers from a distant planet."

"I wondered about that as well," the aide said. "And have something . . . or, rather, someone, ready to go."

"As usual, you anticipate my thinking," Bertl purred.

"Now, here's the hot setup," Njangu told the assembled women and men. "The Social Democrats, who we shouldn't have gotten in bed with in the first place, but it's too late to cry over spilt drugs, are giving us security out the gump stump.

"I've seen their assembled legions, and they're about what you'd expect from a bunch of politicos— mostly big apes with glowers and hair growing out of their ears. If they've got any smooth suckers, they're keeping them around the throne.

"But that's fine with us," he said, winking at Maev, in the front row. "Let them swirl about and attract any baddies' attention.

"You pros, you shooters, are going to stay invisible.

"Until the shit comes down," he said, his good humor vanishing. "Then we obliterate the bastards."

* * *

"Here," Garvin said, handing Njangu a tiny button.

"You shouldn't have. What is it?"

"Something that'll tell me of your every doing, your every nefarious move."

"Mmmph."

"Everybody who's a shaker, aboard, including me, gets one."

"You're anticipating more trouble?"

"Maybe . . . or maybe I'm just trying to cover my ass in all directions," Garvin said.

"But that's *my* job."

"That's what cross-training is for."

"I'm not sure I like anyone knowing where I am," Njangu complained.

"Tough."

"Where am I supposed to wear this?" Njangu inquired.

"In a pocket. Glued in your frigging navel. Up your ass for all I care."

"These fiches here are very interesting," Freron told Penwyth, standing in the middle of his apartment, which, if an ex-military sort hadn't fussed about it every once in a while, would've been a motherless clutter. Instead, it was a well-categorized mess.

"Ah?"

"This was one of my pet projects. I was ordered to begin it when I attended that intelligence course, as I've told you, and after that I added to the file.

"It is, I think, absolutely current as of ten years ago."

Penwyth waited.

"It is the listing, I think very close to complete, of all mechanical warning and security devices that the Confederation posted around Centrum, the three other habitable worlds in the Capella system, and all nav points approaching it.

"Also, there's a listing of where the Confederation

guard points were around Capella. I should think that would interest any historian."

Penwyth noted Freron put ostentatious verbal quote marks around the word "historian."

"A historian, no doubt, would be interested. What would you be asking for your material?"

"My asking . . . and selling price is one hundred and fifty thousand credits."

Penwyth covered a minor choke.

"I think that's reasonable," Freron said, sounding a bit injured. "Not only for the historian, but conceivably for someone concerned about current affairs. All of these mechanical devices were built on a single world, and they were self-modifying.

"It should be simple for someone to visit that manufacturing world, perhaps institute a relationship with the builders of these devices, and be given the program for the auto-upgrades, wouldn't it?"

Penwyth scratched his nose, had another snifter of the brandy he'd brought with him.

"You have an interesting mind, Kuprin. I'm amazed you didn't reach a higher rank than *T'ousan*."

Freron smiled, a little bitterly.

"In those days, I was a bit more interested in gaming than was healthy. Star rank in Tiborg is given only to those who have no flaws. Visible ones, at any rate.

"Another thing a historian of the final days of the Confederation might value is this complete map of Centrum itself, focusing on the various military installations.

"That would be on the market for . . . oh, I don't know. Another hundred thousand credits.

"Or, perhaps, if I encountered a well-to-do collector, I might release the map and the data on the security systems for two hundred thousand.

"As long as we're thinking large," he went on, "I'd be happy to donate my entire collection of material on the Confederation for, oh, half a million."

* * *

"What does the son of a bitch think we are, kagillionaires?" Garvin complained.

"I don't guess he knows about Jasith, now does he?" Njangu said.

"Sharrup," Garvin said. "Erik, can we bargain?"

"Don't think so, boss," Erik said, enjoying Jaansma's reaction. "He had a certain air of firmness to him. Oh yeh. He's also a cagey bastard. The fiches he was waving about are only partial files. The rest is nice and secure in a deposit box in a largish bank, whose name he wouldn't give out."

"Why that duplicitous bastard!" Garvin snarled. "What does he think we are? Burglars?"

"Untrusting sort," Njangu agreed. "And I was just about to ask Erik for the floor plan of his flat. Oh well."

"At least," Garvin said, "I had the sense to jack our price way up to Fili and company."

He put his head in his hands.

"First we got a circus in the middle of politics, which my family would disown me for doing, then we've got an antiquated traitor with too high a price tag . . . nobody knows the troubles I've seen."

"Cheer up," Njangu said unsympathetically. "You know it's bound to get worse."

Kekri Katun didn't have a voice so much as a purr, Garvin thought. She was also the loveliest creature he'd ever seen, from her platinum hair, which seemed natural, to her perfect face, smooth skin, generous bust, and waist that was improbably thin.

He wondered how many credits and plastic surgeons had been spent making her what she was.

"Oh yes," she said. "I've been trained as a tumbler and acrobat for half my life . . . and I do believe in staying in shape."

Without effort, she fell sideways, out of her chair, onto one arm, and hoisted herself up into a one-hand stand. Her light tan dress slid over her thighs, and

Garvin thought, alarmed, that she might not be wearing anything under it.

"Now I could tell a funny story, recite a poem, sing a song from right here," she said. "I know a lot of songs, for I was on the road with a small troupe for five years."

Very slowly, she put another hand down, opened her legs into a Y, did a pushup, then sprang up, landing on her feet, not a hair out of place, not a breath louder than normal.

"I also, since I understand you people of the circus work at other things besides your main talents, am an excellent bookkeeper, office manager, and, if it's needed, can do poses as well."

"Poses?"

"That's something the clubs of Delta like," she explained. "Especially the older gentlemen, who won't admit they'd like to see a woman just take off her clothes."

She touched fasteners, and the dress fell away. She *wasn't* wearing underclothes.

Garvin's mouth was very dry.

Katun struck a pose.

"This is Director Randulf, one of our heroines, as she appeared on her wedding night."

"Uh . . ."

"This is *T'ousan* Merrist, when she fled the rebels. I know several dozen more."

"Uh . . . yes. Very interesting," Garvin said. "You can put your clothes back on. We don't do anything like that."

"Oh. I thought, coming up past the attractions outside—"

"That's called the midway."

"The midway, and I saw all those banners with ladies not wearing much of anything . . ."

"That's Sopi Midt's operation," Garvin said. "He believes in going for the lowest common denominator, and, by the way, he isn't ashamed to cheat a little. All of the girls in his shows never get down to their underwear.

"At least they better not, or I'll slaughter him."

"And what's the matter with a little nudity? Especially among friends?" Katun said, sliding back into her dress, and half smiling at him, lips parted.

Garvin chose to change the subject.

"We're hiring all the time," he said. "Right now, we need a showgirl. And I'm sure the acrobats and the showgirls would be interested in your . . . talents."

"I saw that murder on the holos. Poor girl."

"But the problem is, we might not be coming back this way for a while."

Katun shrugged.

"My father was a salesman with a big territory, and I really don't remember my mother. I'm used to being on the road." Again she smiled her sultry smile. "And I've never been offworld. Besides, for a girl like me, there's always a way to get back home.

"Or I can find a new one."

"Uh . . . right . . . your com number's here on the application," Garvin said. "I'll . . . we'll be in touch within a day or so."

Kekri Katun got up, slunk to the door, turned back, and looked at him.

"I think performing . . . with you . . . with your circus . . . is just about the most exciting idea I've ever known," she breathed, and the compartment door slid closed behind her.

"Phew," Garvin muttered, went for a beer, decided he needed something stronger and got out the brandy decanter. The door slid open again, and he jumped.

"Phew indeed," Njangu said. "She keeps herself nicely shaved, doesn't she?"

He found and opened a beer.

"So what are we going to do about her?"

"I'm just the security man," Njangu grinned. "Of course, you're going to hire her."

"Why of course?"

"Because it's always good to have a spy right under your eyes." Njangu snickered. "Or thighs as the case may be."

"Aren't we being a little hard on her? What's this spy business?"

"Not as hard as she'd like it to be," Njangu said. "Come on, Garvin. Get your head out of your crotch and back in gear. Women like her don't blow in your ear . . . or mine, either . . . because they think we're the best-hung items since the elephants."

Garvin slumped down in his chair.

"Yeh. You're right. I was being dumb. You got any idea who she might be reporting to?"

"I could make a guess," Njangu said. "Since she didn't object to offplaneting, that'd suggest to me she's working for somebody with longer-range views than either Fili or who's that guy running for the Constitutionalists."

"And the folks who've got long-range views would be—"

"The Directors?"

"Perzackly."

"So why shouldn't we just tell her the position's filled?"

"Because they'll try again . . . whoever they are . . . maybe buying one of our roustabouts, maybe filtering another agent in," Njangu explained. "If they already haven't. We've had twenty-three people quit—all citizens, naturally, who decided they like Tiborg so far, and added, uh, about thirty of the locals. Not counting ol' Cooin' Kekri.

"Hire her, then . . . oh yeh, do you have a tendency to talk in your sleep?"

"Not as far as I know."

"Then turn her into our agent. Screw her black-and-blue, and get her singing our tune.

"Or else I can pop a shot in her pretty little ass, and have her singing like a buzzard, telling us everything including what, specifically, that Director Bertl wants, and never realize it when she wakes up. Remember how they screened us when we joined the Force?"

"Yeh."

"The first way's a lot more fun, by the way."

"Uh . . ."

"I'll never tell Jasith," Njangu said. "And there's surely no other reason for you not to sacrifice your virtue for the Force, now is there?"

He smiled, evilly.

Garvin glowered, realized that he must know about Darod, probably the whole damned circus knew.

"She signs on," Njangu said, "and I'll have all her gear shaken, and make sure if she's got a com it won't work very well . . . and whatever she transmits goes straight into my security trap.

"Come on, Garvin. Where's your fighting spirit? And weren't you the guy who was bragging, back in Grimaldi, what with all the midgets and freaks and Chinese acrobats, that this was starting to feel a lot like a real circus?"

"Circuses don't generally have spies," Garvin said feebly.

"Then be innovative! Start a new tradition! You owe it to yourself!

"Besides, think of ol' Randulf on her wedding night."

"It's all done with lights," the little boy insisted.

"Of course," Jiang Fong agreed.

"And . . . and mirrors," the boy said.

"How clever," Fong said. "You must have a closer look."

He picked the boy up from his lift and tossed him, spinning, shrieking, up to his wife, Qi Tan, balancing on her hands three meters in the air on a weaving forked pole. She caught him with her feet, tumbled him about, tickling him with a finger until he stopped screaming and started laughing, then tossed him from one hand to another as she swayed, then dropped him back down to Gang.

Gang set him breathless, back in his lift, and Jia Yin, just a meter high, walked up to him, balancing a tray with four bowls, another tray with glasses atop that, four other clear trays with tiny budvases and flowers in them, and, on top of everything, a huge vase almost as big as she held on her chin.

"Lights and mirrors, you said," she piped. "Would you like me to jump, and all these glasses will land in your lap? You and your liftchair will be very wet."

"No, no," the boy protested.

"But I am going to do it anyway," and she jumped, and glassware cascaded, but somehow was caught, juggled, hurled back into the air and, in somewhat reversed order, balanced again.

The boy watched, fascinated.

"I wish I could juggle," he said in a low voice.

Jia Yin heard him, leaned closer, still without spilling anything.

"After the show," she promised, "I will show you how easy it is."

"Even for somebody who can't walk, like me?"

"Especially for someone like you, 'cause you'll pay closer attention."

A thousand meters above the hospital, a Nana-class patrol ship orbited.

"All units," *Haut* Chaka, who'd taken a three-rank reduction in rank to go with the circus, "I've got me a good possible. Illuminating him . . . now!"

The other Nana boat and two *aksai* watched screens and the laser indicator flashing across them.

"He's been circling the hospital since we got here," Chaka went on. "No ID, no big journoh markings, so I put a viewer on him. Zoomed on in, and what we've got is a lim full of gunnies. One of the stupid bastards even waved his blaster or whatever it is around a little, enough for me to see. Over."

"All Safety elements," Njangu said into his com. "This is Safety Leader. Suspect he's gonna go strafin' when this breaks up. Try for us, and if he gets some of the ankle biters we're being nice to, that won't matter.

"We'll take him out now. Lir . . . hit him. Gently. You *aksai* hot rods, track him. I want more than just a handful of dead punks. *Big Bertha,* get the third *aksai* in the air and homing on the other birds."

Mikes clicked assent.

Below, hidden behind a clump of brush, Lir checked the sights on her Shrike launcher, set the missile's fuse to proximity detonate, turned the homing device off, aimed well off the lim, and fired.

The Shrike exploded twenty meters from the goon-wagon, and it spun, almost pinwheeled, then the pilot gave it full power, gunning away in panic.

"Tracking," Chaka said, and the *aksai* followed at altitude, above the clouds.

The lim sped around the city, on north, to a spattering of islands.

"It's coming in for a landing," Chaka said, and swept the area ahead first with radar, then with infrared.

"Looks like there's something down there," he reported. "Maybe a nice little landing field."

All three of the *aksai* were orbiting below the Nana boat.

"This is Boursier One. I've got a visual flash through the clouds. It's a field, with, oh, ten or twelve lifters. A couple of them looked like they were armored, or anyway set up for some kind of police or military use."

"This is Safety Six," Njangu 'cast. "Arm 'em up, troops. I'd like a nice clean billiard table down there. Take out all buildings and anybody you happen to want to shoot at. Clear."

The *aksai* inverted, and dived, pilots' fingers/claws blurring across sensors as the attack ships shot downward.

Boursier, firing lead, toggled half a dozen Shrikes.

The missiles blasted across the field as Dill and Alikhan swept in low, chainguns roaring. Lifters exploded, and one of the three hangars burst into flames.

Men ran out, across the field, toward the safety of the jungle or water. Few made it.

Boursier came back in, a solid wave of shells sweeping the field, and the last scattered small antipersonnel firebombs from two hundred meters.

Chaka brought his patrol ship down low and slow, thought two lifters were insufficiently damaged, donated a pair of Shrikes to the cause, then climbed.

"I don't see anything left to break, Safety elements. Let's go on home."

Both Garvin and Njangu thought it was very interesting that there were no holo reports of the destruction of the airport.

"I guess it's not in anybody's best interests," Njangu said.

"Which says something about this whole damned power structure, doesn't it?" Garvin said, a bit disgustedly. "I should've given Darod and Lir the go-ahead."

"To do what?"

"Never mind."

"Men are nothing but hard dicks and no brains!" Darod Montagna stormed to Monique Lir.

"So what else is new?" Lir said, grinning. "And what has the boss done to piss you off this time?"

"I just saw him walking outside the ship with that . . . that popsy he went and hired!"

"Isn't he entitled to walk anywhere with anybody he wants?"

"Not with her!"

"Hoboy," Lir said. "Darod, my young former Executive Officer, you are getting, like they say, your tit in a wringer. If you're all jealous that he's just walking with this Katun, what are you going to do when we get back to Cumbre, and you've got to realize he's sleeping with Jasith Mellusin?"

"That's different! She was ahead of me in line! She outranks me!"

"Hoboy twice," Lir said.

"This Circus Jaansma has certainly paid for itself," Dorn Fili said. "I know the big rally night after this will get our workers to pour in their last bit of energy. Not to mention how it'll look on the holos."

"The offworlders *have* done well for us," Sam'l Brek agreed. "But we're getting close to election day, and I keep thinking of all those credits we're giving them, and how I'd like to have them for a last-minute blitzkrieg."

"Use the after-campaign funds we've got set aside for our supporters," Fili said.

"I could do that," Brek agreed. "But that would leave our friends a bit angry. If only we had a way to recoup some of that circus money . . . mmh.

"You know, I think I've got the beginnings of an idea."

"Could it get back to us?" Fili asked.

"Very doubtful, at least if I set it up right, with the correct people."

"Don't tell me any more," Fili said. "Just do it."

"Something interesting," Njangu told Garvin. "We did a thorough shake on your bimbolina's gear, and guess what we found?"

"A nifty little sender?"

"Nawp."

"A serious interstellar com?"

"Nawp."

"What did you get?"

"Nothing . . . except that your Kekri Katun has too much in the way of cosmetics, and interesting taste in lingerie."

"Nothing?" Garvin said, a bit incredulously. "What does that mean? She isn't a spy?"

"Don't get your hopes up," Njangu advised. "It just means that she's been trained a little better than I thought."

Penwyth passed the com across to Freron, who heard the automated teller say he now had somewhere over half a million credits to his account.

Freron smiled pleasantly, took keys from his pocket, and gave them to Erik.

"The box is nine-eight-five-four, at the Military Banking Institute. It's quite large, so you might think of taking a confrere with you." He gave the address, added that no one would bother anyone carrying the keys.

Penwyth went to the apartment door, opened it, and gave the keys, and where they were to be used, to Ben Dill. Two hulking roustabouts were behind him.

"Now," Penwyth said, coming back and sitting down, "we'll just wait here until my friend Ben says he's back at the ship safely."

Freron sighed.

"I suppose, in this dirty business, no one trusts anyone else."

"I trust you implicitly, Kuprin," Erik drawled. "I'd just like to hear a couple more stories about how it was, serving in a planetary force under the Confederation before I leave."

"Everybody's on an Annie Oakley tonight," Garvin told Sopi Midt. "All political sorts, so don't rape them too badly."

"Hadn't a thought of it. Naw," Midt said, "I'm lyin'. Always hated those bastards who think, 'cause they know which end of a ballot box to stuff, they're somethin' special.

"Still can't figure why you let them put us in their pocket."

Garvin made a face. "Maybe I was worried about the gate, this first time out for real. Sure as blazes not something I'd be doing over again."

"Ah well," Midt sympathized. "So far, outside of that poor showgirl, nothing's gone awry. I'll tell you, I'm glad we've got their buckos doing security. My people've taken a dozen or more guns off floppies in the midway."

"Any idea who they were working for?" Garvin asked.

"Di'n't ask. Somebody with a gun on my midway who ain't workin' for me is nothin' but trouble, so we disarmed them, give 'em a thick ear, sent 'em on their way."

Midt leaned closer to Garvin.

"Got a suggestion, Gaffer, if you don't mind. Are you plannin' to stick around until election day?"

"I don't know," Garvin said. "I'm inclined to think not a chance."

"Good. Good. Very good," Sopi approved. " 'Cause the minute the tab's taken, one side'll be thinkin' about revenge, believing we somehow turned the tide, and the other'll be trying to get out of paying us."

"I've had the Social Democrats pay in front."

" 'At's good," Midt approved. "Guess you *are* your father's kid."

By dusk, the Social Democrats were thronging in from across the planet, and several ships had come in from other planets in the system. Garvin, looking out from the nose of *Big Bertha,* dimly hearing the band in the great hold below, was thankful for the outer screen of Fili's security people. This crowd, which promised to be a solid turnaway, was burying the ducat grabbers and circus security.

He looked at himself in a mirror, adjusted his white top hat, curled his whip under his arm, and, the picture of youthful dignity, went to the lift taking him to the center ring.

Overhead, several acrobats were tossing each other around, the *ra'felan* catching them. He saw Lir among them, doing a spinning twist, almost missing her catcher, and being swung back up to the trapeze.

The man was tall, skeletal, with short hair and neat beard. He wore a shirt blazoned FILI FOR PREMIER, as did most of the other entrants. The shirt was too large for him, which helped hide the gun and shoulder stock in his belt. That wasn't intended for the task he'd hired on for, but to ensure his own escape amid the hoped-for debacle.

There was a metal detector at the gangway, but there was a press around it, and it was easy for the man to sidestep the device and enter the ship's hold with the happy throng.

Phraphas Phanon hadn't exaggerated when he said he might be able to come up with something more spectacular than Sir Douglas could envision.

After much rehearsal, they had a number.

A lion menaced Imp, one of the babies. Imp didn't see the trunk that took him around the waist, lifted him to safety on the top of another elephant. The lion reared, roaring.

On a howdah on a third bull, Sir Douglas cracked a whip, as two tigers leapt onto the howdah with him. His pistol cracked, and they cowered back, jumped to the back of another elephant, just as three bulls reared, paws together, and a fourth lifted Imp to safety as other cats darted around the center ring.

The audience was agape in amazement.

And that was just the opening.

Njangu Yoshitaro was prowling the midway, looking for any signs of trouble, when it found him.

He'd ducked behind a wheel of fortune stand, intending to cut back to *Big Bertha* through the back, avoiding the crowd.

Njangu had only a moment to notice a woman had followed him, turning to see what she wanted. The anesthetic dart snapped into his neck before he could draw his gun.

Two men followed the woman, carrying a long canvas roll that looked as if it belonged somewhere in the circus.

Njangu was rolled into the middle of it, and the men picked it up, and, moving without haste, went back down the rear of the midway, into the parking area, and slid the roll into a lifter.

Seconds later, the three were aboard and the lifter was airborne, heading for the capital.

CHAPTER
9

"Welcome, welcome, Social Democrats of all ages," Garvin chanted, "to the finest show in the galaxy. We've got clowns and bears and lions and tigers and beautiful women, and men stronger than oxen . . . all brought to you by the good graces of Dorn Fili."

The crowd cheered, and Garvin snapped his whip twice. As the clowns mobbed him, he tried to concentrate on the routine, but kept thinking that now, with Penwyth back with the loot from Freron . . . or what he hoped was loot, awaiting analysis . . . they could pull in their horns and get away from this mess.

"Unroll him," the woman ordered, and one of the two men in the lifter obeyed. He turned on a small sensor, ran it around Njangu's neck, held it in front of his open mouth.

"Sleepin' like a babe," he reported. "Vital signs just fine."

"He'd better be," the woman said. "The man said alive only. And that there'd be paybacks if we screwed up and killed him."

"Who is he?"

The woman shrugged. "One of the offworld mucketies."

"So why'd these guys want him grabbed?"

"Hell if I know," the woman said. "Blackmail, I guess."

"You got any idea who we're working for?"

"Yeh," the woman said. "That's why I went double

on the price. Political types. The ones who're doing the campaign right now."

"But that don't make sense," the man behind the controls of the lim complained. "I thought this *auzlan* circus was hired out by them."

"Nothin' nobody does in politics *ever* makes sense," the man crouched over Njangu's unconscious body said. "How long we gotta be nannyin' him?"

"There'll be somebody come get him as soon as we get to the dropoff point."

"With the other half of our credits, I hope."

"You think I'm some kind of virgin?" the woman growled.

"Groundnuts, popcorn, candy as soft as your dreams, poppers, everything for the young and old," Maev chanted, moving through the stands, eyes constantly moving.

An old man waved a bill at her, and she pitched him a bag of nuts, and bill and change went back and forth down the line.

There were other butchers working the crowd—a few real candy salesmen, more security.

The bear operator turned as the thin man entered his tiny booth, near one of the entrances. He had time to gape before the man's blade went into his heart. The other operator had been waylaid earlier on the midway, his body dragged out of sight.

The man pushed the body under the console, examined the sensors. He'd come to the circus for eight nights running, watching only the robots, spending his days learning how to operate remote machinery.

This setup, he decided, pulling on the helmet that gave him perspective through the "bear's" eyes, wasn't that different from what he learned. He would have no trouble carrying out his mission.

He touched sensors, and a small screen showed him

the two bears in their unnecessary cage, just offstage. One, then another, stirred as he moved the controls.

One stood, waved its arms, walked back and forth. The man was ready.

Danfin Froude, in his Kelly makeup, looked longingly at Kekri Katun, who smiled. He came closer, and, expression filled with the world's woes, started to take her hand, did a pratfall, rolled back to his feet.

Katun didn't notice Ristori, who tumbled into view from nowhere, came up from behind, leering ostentatiously, eyebrows waggling insanely.

He started to touch her bottom, and she spun, caught him by his collar . . . actually the harness under his ragged clothes . . . and tossed him high up into the safety gravs.

Froude, looking even more unhappy, was slouched on the bench. Katun went to him, sat beside him, started stroking his hand.

Ristori sank down through the layered antigravs, crept back up on the pair.

This time, Froude moved first, grabbed Ristori, and they had a knockdown battle, hitting each other with fists, padded clubs, a huge ball, anything that came to hand.

Around them other clowns were bedeviling, and being bedeviled, by the other showgirls.

Kekri saw Ben Dill trot past, in his muscleman's outfit, considered him speculatively, then saw Garvin looking at her from center ring. She slowly, deliberately, smiled at him, and licked her finger. Garvin looked hastily away, and Katun laughed to herself.

These were nice people, she thought. But they weren't very efficient. Her control had said she would be searched, and so she'd taken nothing aboard *Big Bertha.* She'd used dusting powder, sprinkled here and there, as a giveaway, and found marks that confirmed her baggage had been searched.

This night she'd gone into the midway, as she'd

been instructed, and been given a small, compact case by a man who approached her and whispered the code words she'd been given.

The case held a small, powerful com, capable of in-system communication. She wasn't sure how useful it would be, but assumed she would be signaled at a certain time by the pickup team she'd been promised would be trailing the ship, and given instructions on what she was to report on, besides any information about the circus's intent and mission she would be able to get from Garvin. There had to be a secret intention, since innocents would hardly have searched her gear.

Kekri Katun turned that part of her mind off, concentrated on cartwheeling and cheering for her champion, Froude.

At last Ristori was down, and Froude, after jumping up and down on his chest, picked up the tall woman, aided by a dropper he had hidden under his baggy coat, and carried her off in his arms, to cheers from the audience.

On the bridge of *Big Bertha,* a technician glanced at a screen, reacted. One of the tiny locators was moving steadily away, almost off the screen.

He bent over its controls, started tracking the locator, called for the watch officer.

"Have an ID on that?" the woman asked.

The tech keyed a sensor.

"Yes, ma'am. Yoshitaro."

"Allat in a supporter! I better let the boss know . . . assuming that sneaky bastard isn't doing something nobody's supposed to know about."

The officer went to another tech, had him key the emergency com that fed into Garvin's tiny earpiece.

"Can he lift it? No one has ever been able to press a thousand kilos, and Mighty Ben is going to attempt it here, now, for your amazement," the talker brayed.

"Let's cheer for him, wish for him, put all our energies behind Dill the Human Powerhouse."

Dill, wearing pink leotards, a half shirt, and chrome rings around his biceps, leaned over, took a breath, made sure the droppers hidden inside the enormous weights were on, then heaved. He got a couple of centimeters off the ground before the weights smashed down. Again he tried, and again, the crowd moaning in sympathy.

At last, every muscle bulging, he heaved the weights aloft, staggered back and forth, then, turning the droppers off, got out from under.

The weights crashed down, and the noise from this side ring buried the yips from the risley act in center ring.

Dill was about to bow, move into the finale of his act, when his earpiece burped, said, "Post. Emergency!"

The talker gaped as Dill jumped out of the ring and went, at a dead run, toward one of the corridors into the ship, then he recovered and began improvising another spiel on the acrobats in the center ring bouncing each other about on their feet.

Other select I&R people suddenly quit their tasks or performance around the circus and went after Dill.

Security people throughout the ship stood by, waiting to find out what was going on.

Darod Montagna concentrated on staying on the back of her horses as the animals poured out of the ring, to thundering applause, wondering what the hell was happening.

She reflexively waved to the bear operator in his booth, a nice one who'd helped her curry some of the horses, a bit surprised to see him with his helmeted head in the open instead of glued to the screen in his booth. She was momentarily puzzled she got no return greeting, but guessed he was concentrating on the bears' turn, which came next.

*   *   *

"And now, the man who's brought you all here, the man of the hour, the week, the year, Dorn Fili, soon to be your next Premier," Garvin shouted, and the workers in the stands were on their feet, cheering. He suddenly froze and cocked his head, eyes going wide as the transmission about Njangu came in.

Fili, beaming, waved to his campaign workers, let the cheers build.

The thin man touched sensors, and the robot that Njangu had named Li'l Doni got up, pulled his cage open, and ambled through the entrance, then dropped to his four paws, and started toward the center ring, where Garvin and Fili stood.

"My friends," Fili said, and his voice rolled around the hold, "and you are my friends. Tonight we're celebrating, maybe some say a bit in advance, but I say . . ."

High above, swinging back and forth, waiting for the acrobats' second turn, Lir yawned, then saw the robot bear, moving at a run toward Garvin and the politician.

Something wasn't right, and Lir was cursing that she couldn't hide a gun in her skimpy tights. She dropped off the perch, fell, tucking, toward the safety gravs below, knowing she was far too late.

A little girl was looking through Maev's tray, trying to decide what she wanted, when Maev saw Li'l Doni.

"Here, kid," she said, pulling the tray's sling off her neck. "Take everything and have fun."

Gun in hand, she hurried back to the aisle, and ran down it, toward the circus floor.

". . . a little premature, but I'm confident that we'll see victory, only a week distant, and—"

The bear was ten meters away when Garvin, about

to bow away and head for the emergency post, saw him. It came to its feet and shambled toward Fili, arms open for a crushing embrace.

Garvin's hand slid into his coat, came out with a small pistol. He shot Li'l Doni twice in the head to no effect, then tackled the bear from the side, knocking it down.

Raf Aterton, the music director, heard the beginning screams and shots, cursed and grabbed a trumpet from a musician, and blasted into "Peace March."

The other musicians goggled for an instant, then got it, and the ragged music swelled.

And everywhere on the ship the women and men of the circus went to full alert.

Li'l Doni rolled to its feet and went for Fili, who ran for a trapeze mast, found climbing rings, started up. Then Doni had him in its paws, and was pulling him down. Fili was screaming, and there were roustabouts there, with benches, poles, smashing at the robot.

Maev was behind the bears' operators' booth, pistol out. She snapshot, blowing most of the bear operator's helmet and head off.

The skeletal man convulsed, fell dead.

Li'l Doni went suddenly limp and fell, almost on one of the roustabouts, and Fili dropped on top of him.

Garvin checked the robot, saw no signs of activity, pulled Fili to his feet, and made sure the politician's throat mike was still live.

"Keep talking," he shouted. "Keep them calm. We don't need a panic."

Fili, eyes wide, opened his mouth, then closed it, then opened it again, nothing coming out.

*　　*　　*

Erik Penwyth, dragging on a white formal jacket over the dark pants he'd worn to Freron's apartment, ran into the hold, clipping a mike to his throat.

"Clowns, clowns, clowns, we've got 'em, and we don't want them," he shouted.

Behind him ran every clown in the circus, and behind them the tumblers. The clowns ran the length of the ring, then back, peeling off into the stands, the tumblers end-over-ending along the ring banks.

The audience was trying to see what had happened, if Fili was hurt, and finally his voice came back.

"Everything's . . . fine," he said, his voice somewhat squeaky, then steadying. "That was a little stunt that didn't work out right . . . I guess I should've known I'm not cut out for the circus, but look at my friends around me, who are."

His laughter sounded almost real, and the crowd settled back a little. A clown lifter zoomed toward Fili, and he was buried in joeys as two men muscled the Li'l Doni's "corpse" into it, lifted away. Another lifter was bundling the corpse of the thin man into it, unnoticed.

"Clowns," Penwyth said, as Aterton batted his baton and the "Peace March" died away. "I promised 'em, you got 'em. Take one or two home with you, please. Next we've got the high-wire artists, and artists they are, braver women and men than I surely am."

A flyer launched herself out, was passed by another, and a *ra'felan* at each pole caught them, spun them, sent them back the way they came.

Lir, climbing up, grabbed a trapeze, and started swinging, each time higher, pulling herself into a bird's nest, and the show was back to normal.

"I have them," Boursier reported, her *aksai* banking high above the capital's center. "Landing on the roof of a high-rise. Looks like an apartment building. They're carrying a bundle, and there's somebody waiting for them.

"They're inside. The guard's still on the roof, though."

"Maintain patrol," came the orders. "There's a civvie lifter on the way with the alert team in it, blue-white, open top, who'll get close and case things."

The ship's compartment was packed with I&R troops.

"All right," Garvin said. "We'll keep this short. Somebody . . . I don't know if it's the same somebody who tried to ice Fili or not . . . has just grabbed Njangu. We've got a location, will have details in a moment, and we're going after him, right now."

He looked around the room.

"For starters I want you, Ben, Monique, not you, Alikhan . . . no, wait, I do want you on this, Jill—we might need a medic." He hesitated, seeing Darod's eyes on him, didn't want to, but knew better:

"You, Montagna, you're in. And me. As for—"

A speaker crackled.

"Boss, I've got that lifter with the alert team patched through."

"Go ahead."

The lifter went noisily down the street, well below roofline. Faces stared out from the apartment building as the drunks inside yahooed and toasted anyone in sight.

"Got Njangu," one of the drunks, part of the normal standby I&R team, in the lifter reported. "Or his locator, anyway. The building's sixty stories high, he's down five from the top. Stationary, so I'd guess that's where they want him to stay for a while."

"Received," *Big Bertha*'s com center sent back. "Take it up to five-zero, stand by for further orders. Chaka, if anyone from outside tries to interfere, take them out. Repeat, anyone."

The mike clicked twice, and the lifter climbed away, toward the orbiting Nana boat.

*   *   *

" 'Kay," Garvin said. "He's close to the top of the building, and there's a sentry. We'll have to land on the roof, take that guard out, plus anyone who's with him, and then—"

"Excuse me," a polite voice said, and Garvin wondered who the hell let Jiang Yuan Fong, a civilian, into the compartment.

"I've been listening, and if Mr. Yoshitaro is being held in a high-rise, as that transmission indicates, and you evidently plan to rescue him, rather than possibly alert that sentry on the roof, would it not be wiser to make the initial entry through, perhaps, one of the windows on the side of the building with someone who has certain acrobatic skills? Such as me, and perhaps one of the *ra'felan*?"

Garvin thought for an instant, then nodded.

"Good. Have you ever used a gun, Mr. Fong?"

"A few times I have found it necessary to defend my family, so yes."

"Fine. Somebody issue him a blaster, and somebody grab the nearest octopus. We'll deploy from one of our cargo lifters. Let's move!"

The last elephant trumpeted out the Back Door, and the lights came up.

"All out and over," Penwyth shouted, "and it's a wonderful evening, and we've never had a better audience."

The band was playing for the blowoff, and all the remaining butchers were working the crowd hard.

A little girl's mother stopped an usher.

"Excuse?"

"Yeh," the man said, then remembered his manners. "Sorry, I meant yes, ma'am?"

"One of your salesmen left Mara with her entire tray of sweetmeats, and told her to take whatever she wanted. But we can't do that, and the woman never came back.

"What am I supposed to do?"

"Why," the usher said, "you've just been gifted with the entire tray." He forced a smile down at the girl. "Remember our circus always."

"Oh, thank you," the woman said. "You're wonderful, all of you. I hope nobody was hurt in that accident."

"No, ma'am," the usher said. "Everyone's fine."

The girl, eyes wider than any *ra'felan's*, was borne away, and the security man, one hand close to the gun under his jacket, went back to watching the crowd.

The cargo lifter's hatch was open, and the team climbed inside. The huge *ra'felan* swung in easily, found a seat next to Alikhan. The alien wore the Musth combat harness.

Garvin, buckling his fighting belt on, climbed in front.

"Haul it on out," he ordered, and Running Bear nodded. The hatches closed, the upper hatch on *Big Bertha* opened, and the lifter sped toward the capital.

"The game might be getting interesting," Chaka reported. "Another lifter, this one a posh sort of lim, came in on the roof, and the same guard greeted them.

"Two people out, went inside."

Garvin turned down the lift's speaker.

"You heard what the man said. That's got to be either an interrogation team, or else they're pickup for Njangu. So we'll have to get in quick."

"Three minutes out," Running Bear said.

The cargo lifter orbited the high building below.

" 'Kay," Chaka reported. "Stand by for transmit of what I've got on the building to your screen."

"Got it," Garvin said.

"Two lifters on the roof. Two drivers per vehicle, plus the sentry. Our man's in the fourth apartment in—there's a gap between units you can make out from here."

" 'Kay."

"Your plan, sir?"

Garvin saw, on one side of the building, through heavy glass that ran the height of the structure, emergency stairs.

"You stand by and take out the lifters and their crew when I give you the word. We'll go in from the side, a story high so any noise we make doesn't carry."

"Yessir."

Garvin leaned over to Running Bear.

"Can you put it right next to that wall with the emergency exit, fifty-sixth floor, with our doors open?"

"One-handed," Running Bear said, "picking my nose. Depending on the updrafts."

"Use both hands, and take us in now."

The AmerInd nodded, and the lifter dropped to a hover, its doors clamshelling up.

Garvin took a small tube from his belt pack, tore it open, and unrolled it. It was a thin, small, flat, shaped charge, about fifteen centimeters on a die.

"Mr. Fong, can you get across to that window and hang there long enough to stick this right in the middle of that window? It's self-adhesive."

"I can do that."

Garvin gave hasty orders as the lifter closed on the building, rocking as the rising night currents sent it swaying.

"Closer," Garvin said, and Running Bear, teeth gnawing lower lip, obeyed.

Fong braced on the lifter's hatch sill.

"Now!"

Fong sailed across, landed on the tiny window ledge, slipped, knelt, had a hold with his free hand, and was steady. The patch went on the window center. Fong looked over his shoulder at the lifter, readied, and pushed off.

He missed the lifter, but a tentacle was waiting and swooped him back aboard.

"Do not tell my wife that happened," he said, taking a deep breath. "I need more rehearsal time, it is evident."

Garvin, breathing harder than the acrobat, touched the charge's detonator, and it blew with a muffled thud. Glass cascaded in a silver shower down toward the street.

"Go!" Garvin ordered the *ra'felan*. The alien swung out; keeping a firm hold on the lifter, he had the shattered window ledge in two others, a sentient grapnel, then reached with his other two legs for the team members, passing them into the stairwell.

Dill and Alikhan, not waiting for the full team, went down one flight. The door was locked, but only for an instant as Dill grabbed the knob and tore it away. He muttered, fingers inside the slot, then the door came open.

By then, the others were around him, and they went down the corridor.

"Still out," the distinguished-looking man in the gray coat said. Njangu Yoshitaro lay on the lavish apartment's couch, eyes closed, breathing easily, a gentle smile on his face.

"He'll be waking up any second," the woman who headed the kidnap team said. "I know my dosages. We do this for a living, you know, and corpses don't generally pay ransoms."

"We'll wait until he comes to, if you don't mind." He took a thick leather envelope from under his arm. Guns were in his, and his companion's, hand.

The woman's two partners moved to the side, their hands motionless, but near their pockets.

"You can count the money while we wait," the distinguished man said.

"We'll do that," the woman said. "And you can

put the artillery away. We're not people who go back on—"

The outer door crashed open, and horror was in the room, a furred monster bigger than a man, head sweeping back and forth, eyes red, a strange-looking pistol in one hand. It fired, and a huge bullet took the distinguished man in the center of his chest, blowing a head-size hole in it, the edges around the hole moving as strange gray insects swarmed, eating, in the wound.

Behind the monster came a woman wearing tights, a blaster in her arms. She fired, and the man's companion spun, went down. She fired again, and the woman's head was missing.

One of her partners turned to run, but there was nowhere to go, and a huge, balding man, growling rage, had him by the back of his clothes and hurled him against the wall, headfirst. There was a crack, and he fell, lay still.

The last man in the kidnap team had his hands up, babbling surrender. Garvin shot him twice in the chest.

Explosions crashed from above as Chaka strafed the lifters on the roof.

Mahim knelt over Njangu, felt for a pulse as other members of the team started rapidly searching the corpses and room.

"He's alive. I'd guess—"

Njangu's eyes came up.

"Of course I'm alive," he said in a furry voice, then looked about, yawning.

"What kind of a party are we having, anyway?"

CHAPTER
10

Garvin took Darod aside as they got out of the lifter. Dill and Alikhan carried the stretcher with Njangu on it, Mahim beside it, toward *Big Bertha*'s dispensary.

He'd spent much of the flight going through the documents taken from the distinguished man and his companion's corpses.

"You said something once that you and Lir had an idea of a fiendish thingie that'd deal with matters in a rather drastic manner. Were you pulling my chain?"

"I don't kid about things like that," Montagna said indignantly. "Lir is the one who looked everything up, with my help. I think this whole frigging planet needs a little demolition."

"That guy who looked like he was the boss of this little caper just happened to have a membership card in the Social Democrat party."

"Nice world, like I said," Darod said, trying to pretend she wasn't shocked. "The guys who hire us try to screw us. Very nifty."

"Yeh," Garvin said. "You also said something about knowing where to plant said fiendish thingie and the precise date it should come to life."

"Certainly. A piece of cake."

"Go to it. I've had enough of these idiots. Now and forever more."

By dawn, the midway was broken down, and all of the circus's gear was loaded.

Big Bertha sat on the landing pad all that day, locks

sealed, making no response to any com. All three
aksai orbited ominously overhead, diving close to the
two holo lifters that tried approaching.

At midnight, a small lifter came out of the ship, and
flew at speed, nap of the earth, below any radar horizon, toward the capital.

It hovered for an instant over a great white building
on a hill, and two women in black, with heavy packs,
rappelled down to the roof of one of the buildings.
They pried open a window and vanished inside.

An hour later, they came back out, and the lifter
came in for a pickup, flashed back to *Big Bertha.*

The watchmen on the grounds of the Civic Palace
never noticed a thing.

An hour before dawn, without clearance or notify-
ing port authorities, *Big Bertha* lifted clear of the
ground and left the Tiborg system forever.

CHAPTER
11

Cayle/Cayle IV

The Cayle system, once a prime Confederation ship-builder, felt to Garvin like an abandoned factory.

Three of the outer worlds were supposed to be mines for Cayle IV, the most habitable and the ship-yard center, but *Big Bertha* detected activity on only one, and that slight.

Cayle IV was a gray world, Garvin thought, corrected himself: gray-green.

Great forests climbed snowy mountains, and the valleys were green, welcoming, in a wintry way. Most of the cities, gray stonework, were located along the planet's wide rivers.

Landing fields on the planet were lined with finished or half-completed star craft of various Confederation types, some flecked with rust in spite of anticorrosion coating.

Njangu found some ancient lines coming as *Big Bertha* closed on the planet, didn't remember where he'd heard or read them, nor the poet's name:

> *"My mother took me to the cities while I lay
> Inside her. And the coldness of the forests
> Will be with me till my dying day."*

"What're you muttering?" Garvin asked.
"Poetry."

"Didn't sound like it rhymed," Garvin said suspiciously. "Couldn't be very good."

"Probably not."

Big Bertha made three orbits around Cayle IV, broadcasting, on all open and approved frequencies, circus music, the roaring of the big cats, the trumpeting of elephants, and the ballyhooing of talkers, until only the deaf and reclusive didn't know that the circus was in town.

The Nana boats swept over the main thoroughfares of the major cities, scattering broadsides in all directions. Garvin cheerfully took complaint coms from city officials, promising to pay any fines levied for pollution, preferably in free passes.

Aksai compounded the felony, to the greater rage of politicians and the glee of children, low-flying the cities with long banners that, as the day turned into night across the planet, self-illuminated, flashing:

LIONS!! BEARS!! TIGERS!! ELEPHANTS!! EARTH
HORSES!! BEAUTIFUL LADIES!! STRANGE
ALIENS!! ACROBATS!! STRONGMEN!! CLOWNS!!
DEATH-DEFYING FEATS!!

Announcing their intentions on the last circumnavigation, *Big Bertha* orbited the capital city of Pendu three times, then, on secondary drive, slowly flew to the nearby field and settled in for a landing.

Crowds swarmed in, and spotlights caught the monstrous ship as it grounded.

Civilian lifts overflew the ship, to Captain Liskeard's mutterings.

The main lock's ramp slid out, and clowns and little people tumbled out. Garvin, in white formal, accompanied by Kekri Katun, wearing a white outfit that cast flashing, multicolored lights and covered no more than absolutely necessary, came out to meet the hastily assembled dignitaries, including the planet's ruler,

Graav Ganeel, a mournful-looking middle-aged man with a bit of a belly. Garvin thought it interesting the head honcho himself would appear, suggesting just how much interstellar travel was current these days. Njangu, on the other hand, noted Ganeel showed up with only one aide and one driver/bodyguard. Either he wasn't an autocrat, or else everything was a lot more under control than Tiborg.

Everyone welcomed everyone, and Garvin said how thrilled they all were, and they would make sure this was an event for the ages.

Before dawn, Erik Penwyth had rented a huge open area on Pendu's outskirts and the heavy lifters, carrying canvas, the midway booths and the flying squadron, shuttled back and forth, and roustabouts set to.

Early risers—lot lice—began gathering, and if it was a school day—Garvin had forgotten to check—officials would have been frothing at the mouth. If, of course, they weren't lining the streets together with what seemed to be every kid on Cayle, as lifters swept back and forth, proclaiming the Parade Is Imminent.

It was.

Animals in their lifter cages, elephants on foot, horses prancing, with Montagna, Kwiek, and his pair of wives, not to mention a scattering of midgets, clowns afoot, in lifters, in strange, old-fashioned wheeled vehicles, tossing candy as they went, Aterton's band in a pair of lifters, Dill the strongman, the showgirls posing, acrobats rolling, tumbling amid the procession, and Garvin in front, standing in an open black lim, face utterly blissful.

In the backseat was Njangu, and, crouched out of sight, two marksmen—just in case.

They reached the lot without incident, as the tents were being guyed out.

Garvin stepped out of the lim as it grounded, bowed to the flatties watching, in some awe, and sniffed.

"I love the smell of canvas in the morning," he said happily.

The circus was, indeed, in town.

By late afternoon the circus was sold out for a week, with more ticket orders avalanching in.

"It appears as if there's nothing much to do around these parts," Njangu said, looking at numbers flash across screens in the "red wagon," actually a compartment aboard *Big Bertha,* but "wagon" was traditionally the name for a circus's money center.

Sopi Midt grinned. "It looks that way, indeed. Look at all that alfalfa roll in. Damn, but I wish Jaansma would let me run my games wide open. I could really show the gilly-galloos a good time.

"Do you know how rich we'd be?" He looked hopefully at Yoshitaro.

"Sorry, Sopi," Njangu said. "Into each life some honesty must fall."

"And now, our aerialists of acclaim, known galaxywide, flyers and their strange alien companions, who train secretly on dark worlds far from Man's reign," Garvin intoned. The band played, and the flyers soared across the roof of the tent, *ra'felan* catching them, and the trapeze artists and cloud-swingers went back and forth as holo images flashed here and there just above the crowd.

Garvin bowed, himself off to spray his throat, wishing he didn't get as excited as all those kids in the hastily erected cattle-guard seats in front of the general admission bleachers. A little calmness would be easier on his vocal cords.

Darod was waiting for him outside the center ring.

"Better stick around, Garvin," she said, handing him a jug of energy drink. "Monique's trying a new one, and it's gonna be radical. If it flies, she's gonna want an intro next time."

"How dangerous?"

"A lot more than it looks," Darod said.

"Wonderful." He knew there was no stopping Lir, however. He drank deeply from the jug, put his arm around Montagna, who snuggled closer.

The band segued into a *galop,* as Monique trotted into the center ring. Fleam grabbed a line that ran down from fifty meters up the center pole, another worker sledge-smashed an iron stake into the ground, and two others pulled the rope taut, hitched it to the pole.

Aterton waved the band to silence, except for a snare drum's snarl, and the tent lights went down as a pinspot picked out Lir.

"I wish she'd told me she was planning something," Garvin whispered. "I do like to be kept up on things."

"She didn't want to bother anybody until she'd got it down," Darod said.

"I love this," Garvin said, a bit grimly. "She's outside the damned safety grabbers. What's she got in mind, anyway?"

Monique answered his questions by picking up a long balance pole and starting up the angled rope, gripping with her toes through the slippers she wore.

Garvin found his lips were getting dry, drank again.

The pole flailed, and Lir wavered, then caught her balance, continued on, getting closer and closer to the center pole. Then she was a meter away, bounced twice, flipped the pole away, and backflipped clear of the rope.

The crowd shrieked, and then a long tentacle swept down, and one of the *ra'felan* had her, flung her toward the top of the tent, and another alien caught her, and pitched her to a catcher whose bar was at the top of its swing, Lir spinning, knees up in a ball, as she went.

Monique had the catcher by the hands, let go, flipped again, had the catcher once more, and was safely on the bar.

Garvin realized he hadn't been breathing for a while. He sucked in air.

"That," he said, "is some trick. But I wish she'd told me about it so I could spiel it."

Or, he thought, *break her lovely little goddamned thumbs for considering it.*

"As I said, she didn't want to make a big thing out of it if it went awry," Darod said.

"Supposing it had," Garvin asked, not really wanting to know. "What would she have done? Quietly eaten sawdust?"

"If you look over there, back of the bandstand, next to where the bear handlers are supposed to be, if we ever get them trained," Darod pointed, "she's got a man with an antigrav projector.

"She thought he'd have time to get her lined up before she hit."

"Thought," Garvin snarled. " 'Kay. We got a star turn here. But we're gonna put in the safety gravs before she does that one again. Hide 'em under one of the elephant stands maybe. But I am not going to have me a flattened flyer, period. No more 'I think it'll work.'

"And you can tell her from me that's an order. She's still in the goddamned Legion. And I still outrank her sorry ass. You might want to remind her of that."

Garvin was strolling the midway quite happily early the next morning. Let Njangu worry about security, he had decided. It did everybody good to get out of that damned ship and its recycled air. So the canvas smelled a little stuffy—that'd wear off in a week.

He passed the cat cages. Muldoon, the killer leopard, was lying on his back, playfully pawing at some kind of flying insect two meters over his head.

Montagna, who'd spent the night in Garvin's arms, was earnestly working on some new routine with two horses, while Ristori had a dozen clowns sweating, try-

ing to fit into a barrel that logically would only take
one.

He rounded a corner, and saw a medium-size man
with a potbelly scratching Loti, the baby elephant with
a stick, and deep in conversation with Phraphas Phanon, one of the elephant handlers, while Sunya Thanon had six others in a corral, crumbing them up with
a bucket of soap and a long-handled brush. Garvin,
as he approached, recognized the tubby man as *Graav*
Ganeel, Cayle's ruler.

He wasn't sure how to greet the man, settling for a
quick bob of the head.

"No, no," Ganeel said. "I'm the one who should be
kowtowing. Fascinating, listening to my friend Phraphas talk about the world he's seeking, this Coando.
Unfortunately, it's not one I've heard of.

"I will, however, talk to some of our savants, and
see if they can help."

"Speaking of help," Garvin said, "I would like to
ask a favor of Your Highness. I suppose that's the
correct title."

"It is, if you wish," Ganeel said, looking a bit
alarmed. "You've got to remember I'm a constitu-
tional monarch, only the third in succession, and really
don't have much authority.

"So if you want someone executed, or put in an
iron maiden, whatever they were, you'll have to go
through Parliament."

Garvin, assuming he was making a joke, laughed,
then cut it short seeing Ganeel's serious expression.

"No, no," he said, "nothing like that."

"If you'll excuse me," Phraphas said, "I go to help
my partner wash our friends." He bustled away,
clearly not wanting to hear gaffer's business.

Jaansma and Garvin strolled away.

"The favor I need," Garvin said, "is your help with
our navigational files. I would like for our tour to
finish on Centrum."

"Ambitious," Ganeel said, sounding impressed.

"Perhaps," Garvin said. "But I . . . and the rest of my troupe . . . would like to find out what happened, why our worlds are out of contact with the Confederation."

"You, too," Ganeel said. "Have you seen our thriving starship 'industry,' for want of a weaker word? And all the ships contracted for by the Confederation, but never picked up or paid for."

"I've seen them," Garvin said. "Why haven't you sent salesmen out looking for new customers?"

"Our contracts were almost always with the Confederation," Ganeel said. "We've sent a few ships out, with but one returning from an outer system, and that one reported chaos, with no one having the Confederation credits to do business with us."

"That's pretty much what we've found," Garvin said. "And we'd like to do what we can to maybe start opening communications again."

"A circus?" Ganeel said, with a bit of incredulity. "Admirable, but isn't that a bit romantic?"

"When I said 'we,' " Garvin explained, "I meant some of the worlds we come from, or have visited. If people knew what had happened, why the sudden collapse, perhaps there's something that could be done to prevent a total interregnum."

"I can explain one part of the fall," Ganeel said, "being a bit of a historian before my father died early and gave me the throne.

"The collapse didn't happen as quickly as most think. Rather, the Confederation was held up long past its time by force of arms . . . the remarkably efficient military the Empire had . . . plus the fact many planetary governments could lay off their problems on the distant Confederation.

"But the final, real reason was that all too many of the Confederation's citizens wanted the Confederation to be there, even while they were unwilling to participate in its government, reluctant to pay taxes or provide service. Because they imagined it was immortal, the Confederation was able to stumble on for years, decades, perhaps a century even, a walking corpse.

"And then, one day, something happened, and the corpse stumbled over a twig and fell."

"What?" Garvin asked.

"I wish I knew," Ganeel said. "Because then, as you suggest, it might be possible to reanimate the body."

He shrugged. "I do not know. I simply do not know."

They admired the Chinese acrobats for a moment, walked on.

"I don't either," Garvin said. "Which is what I'm trying to end. I want to find out what happened. Which is why I need a favor of you."

"You may ask."

"I've found out that Cayle provided many of the security apparati of the Confederation."

"We did," Ganeel said reluctantly.

"If the Confederation has collapsed, some of those machines and posts may be still manned and dangerous, or roboticized and even more deadly. I would like to borrow . . . or purchase if I must . . . your files, so I can access these machines and convince them I'm friendly when, or rather if, we're able to reach the Capella system."

"They were highly classified," Ganeel said.

"They were. Ten years or more gone."

Ganeel looked vaguely frightened.

"I don't know," he said, then brightened. "But in any event, I wouldn't be able to provide them, since those data were not state secrets, but rather held by the manufacturer.

"That would be Berta Industries," he said. "Some say," and he faked a laugh, "that, at their peak, they were the real rulers of Cayle. Perhaps so, perhaps no."

"Would you be willing," Garvin asked, "to forward my request, perhaps with your approval, to whoever heads Berta Industries? In return, if I reach Centrum, I'll happily provide you with what I've found out, as I return."

"Berta Industries," Ganeel said, and a look of mild fright crossed his face, then he firmed his lips.

"Yes," he said. "Yes, I'll do that. *That* woman can't kill me, after all."

Garvin noted the emphasis. Ganeel changed the subject, asked why there were no primates—other than human. Garvin explained that he'd always hated the smelly, flea-bitten, dangerous apes that seemed to echo all the worst habits of man.

"Indeed," Ganeel said. "I've always been interested in them, although I admit I've seen nothing but holos. The last Earth monkey died almost four hundred years ago in our zoo, and somehow was never replaced."

"Look at this," Monique stormed, pointing to a boxed poem on the inside page of a holo.

> *"There's a legend about*
> *That her legs, arms, hands*
> *Are wrought iron*
> *Like we build ships from*
> *She's a woman of miracles*
> *Of strength and skill*
> *Our Monique, our Monique."*

"Damn," Ben Dill chortled, "it surely is nice to be around someone famous."

"Famous my left tit," Lir growled. "You show up tonight, and see what kind of famous I am."

Ben did.

One entire stand, directly in front of center ring, where Monique did her rope walk, was packed with women, all cheering for Lir.

Monique tried to ignore them, couldn't, especially when Garvin made her do a curtain call directly in front of those women. Dill saw that many of them were dressed in fashions more characteristic of the men of Cayle.

He thought the matter exceedingly funny, suggested that Lir should start associating with her fan club more.

Monique told him, quite explicitly and obscenely, to shut his yap.

"I don't see why you're taking that attitude," Njangu said reasonably. "Look at it this way. You always had admirers who were men, right? Now you've just doubled the available talent who want to kookookachoo you under the chin."

Monique growled incoherently, climbed high into the big top, and worked out her discomfort doing endless planges, swinging over and over, one hand and wrist in a loop.

"I could stand a beer," Maev said. She and Njangu had gone into Pendu with a couple of quartermasters on a larder-restocking run.

"As well as not," Yoshitaro agreed. "They'll be haggling over flour prices for another two hours in there. 'Sides, investigating them barrooms is a big part of our exciting life as intelligence operatives, right?"

Two blocks down, they found a store that, from its signs, would sell something in bottles.

From the midday sun they went in, blinking into the darkness inside. Maev's eyes adjusted first.

"Uh-oh."

Then Njangu could see.

"Indeed uh-oh."

There were only two or three men of the thirty or so people in the bar. The women all wore costumes, various changes on ancient schoolgirl uniforms.

And all of them were smiling their most inviting best.

"I think," Njangu said, backing toward the door, "I just found out what a slab of meat feels like when Sir Douglas tosses it into the cats' cage."

"Strange planet, this," Darod managed.

"Yeh," Njangu agreed, breathing a sigh of relief as

they went back outside. "Looks 'kay on the outside, but . . ."

"Maybe a little strange?" Maev suggested. "Or do all men have the secret desire to boff kids?"

"Not one of my kinks," Njangu said. "Maybe it's something peculiar to Cayle. Look. There's a bar with tables outside. That'll give us running room in case we mess up again."

Njangu inquired, found out from a local they'd just wandered into the Rot District, one of the larger ones in Pendu. "Anything, I mean anything, can be found there," the Caylean said enthusiastically. "Or, since you seem interested, you can also com and they'll come to you.

"Some of us were wondering why your circus hasn't offered such entertainment."

"Uh . . . 'cause we're shy folks," Njangu managed.

The pair of midgets caught Darod as she came off the hidden antigravs and spun her up just as her horse trotted by.

The band changed tempo, and the horse began dancing, quick little steps in time to the music.

The faces in the seats beyond were blurred as she concentrated on keeping balance and moving with the animal. She felt the world, whatever was going on with Garvin, swirl away, and let herself be lost in the moment.

YOU AND A COMPANION ARE INVITED TO DINNER AND, ON THE FOLLOWING DAY, A TOUR OF HER ESTATE AND WORKS, BY LADY LIBNAH BERTA, SIX DAYS HENCE. TRANSPORTATION WILL BE PROVIDED. REPLY COM 34532

"*Graav* Ganeel came through. So I abase myself, and beg access to her records, right?" Garvin asked.

"Exactly," Njangu said. "About time we got some

real Intel work out of you, instead of you just prancing about in your formal and snapping that stupid whip."

"I guess Darod'll be thrilled," Garvin said.

"Uh, no," Njangu said. "I want you to take Kekri Katun."

"Why?"

"We shook her once," Njangu said, "and found *giptel* shit. I want to do it again, and have her out of the picture long enough to do a thorough job," Njangu said.

"You aren't making my life any easier," Garvin said.

"If that's true," Yoshitaro said, "why are you smiling? Masochism?"

"Guess that's what it must be," Garvin said.

"I am never going out on this stupid planet again without a bodyguard," Monique Lir snarled. "Two bodyguards. Both hairy and male."

"Why?" Darod asked. "What happened?"

"I accept an invitation to be interviewed by this journoh, or anyway I thought she was a journoh. Turns out, she's the one who wrote that stupid goddamned poem about me."

"Oh," Darod said.

"Yeh," Monique said. "Name was Lan Dell. Wore a leather jacket and smoked this big tube of some kind of weed or something that stank up the whole lift.

"She says she's more comfortable in a club than an office, and so we end up in this bar. Filled with nothing but women, and this woman says they're my fan club.

"Fan club, in the name of Loki's pizzle! And so instead of being interviewed, I'm given this mike, and everybody's throwing questions at me.

"And the questions get real personal.

"And Dell starts stroking my knee, under the table."

"What're you so upset by?" Montagna said. "Can't

be the first time someone as pretty as you got hit on by another woman."

Monique looked perplexed.

"Yeh. 'Course you're right. Hell, I can even think of a couple of female officers in the Force who've been concerned about me sleeping alone. And I surely know how to handle men.

"I dunno. It can't be because we're in a strange place . . . I grew up all over."

She thought about it for a bit.

"Maybe," she said slowly, "maybe it's because I felt, with that Dell woman, like I was in a zoo. Or a circus."

"You are," Darod said.

"I know, douche! Not that kind of circus. It was like everybody was waiting for something, for me to be the entertainment, and if I'd gone off with this Lan Dell that would've been some kind of victory for them.

"I dunno," Lir said again, and lapsed into silence.

The circus was half-empty that night. Njangu made a few com calls, and found out there'd been a riot in the city, and transport was screwed up.

"Remember," he asked Garvin, "there were riots on Centrum when we were passing through, back when we were ree-cruits?"

"I do, and damned if I don't wish you hadn't re-minded me."

Froude came to Garvin the next day, with a stack of printouts.

"How long," he asked, "do you anticipate our being here?"

"Not long," Garvin said. "I've got a meeting to-night, and hopefully I can find a way to start feeding you the Centrum data we came here for."

"Good," Froude said. "This world is not a healthy one, and I'd just as soon be gone.

"I happened to check the books, and things are not at all well.

"We take local currency, like we did back on Tiborg, and then convert it into Confederation credits. Failing that, we'll take interstellar credit transfers, right?"

"Of course," Garvin said.

"The bookkeepers had a wad of the local money, and went to change it. No can do, the answer came back," Froude said. "They don't seem to have any credits . . . or, what they do have is being kept out of circulation."

"By whom?"

"Some say the government. Some say this big industrial firm that's run by the Berta family."

"Which I'm seeing tonight," Garvin said.

"Maybe you ought to try to get the key to their vaults, then."

"We aren't on this mission to make money," Garvin said.

"I'm aware of that," Froude said irritably. "But I'm also aware we'd just as soon play nice, stable worlds.

"You want some other statistics? I did a little cheap research. Planetary employment is about thirty-five percent. A lot of people have flat given up looking for work and ride on the dole. The government doesn't seem to have any kind of restraining or any other plan, other than keeping its fingers crossed and hoping, one day, someday, the Confederation is going to reappear, buy all those parked starships, and whoopie do, it'll be pink clouds and happiness again.

"Not good," Froude finished. "As I said, let's get our business done here and get on our way."

Garvin looked out the lim window as it climbed over a mountain. Below was a wide valley, with a large town in its center and factories spread out along the river.

He remembered the poem Njangu had quoted as they approached, said, "Surely looks cold out there."

"But it's nice and warm in here," Kekri Katun said. She was absolutely perfect in a gray traveling suit and knee boots, although Garvin thought, purely for propriety's sake, she could have done up a couple of the blouse buttons.

"Landing in five minutes, sir," the lim driver's voice said through the-intercom.

"A question," Garvin said into the mike. "All these factories are part of Berta's holdings?"

"This valley, including the towns, and four other towns downriver that can't be seen in this haze," the driver replied, "are indeed *part* of the family's possessions."

"It must be nice to be that rich," Kekri said. "I've always wanted to be rich. Then there's nothing to worry about, is there?"

"I wouldn't know," Garvin said. "All I know is whether you're rich or poor, it's nice to have money."

He checked his appearance carefully. He hadn't thought, if Lady Berta was the muckety he'd been told, she would likely approve of his white-on-white-on-white ringmaster garb, and had chosen a conservative dark blue jacket, white shirt, and dark brown pants.

The lim braked, banked left.

Atop a low plateau, just where the town ended, a great mansion rose. It was ugly, a huge, seven-story rectangular box with a flat roof, no attempt being made with architectural niceties. Atop the roof were various antennae and, Garvin was fairly sure, a standard electronics suite for an antiaircraft missile site. Gardens spread around it, all carefully designed and manicured.

The lim grounded in front of the mansion's steps, the clamshell roof lifted, and the driver was out, offering Kekri a hand.

The mansion's arched doors opened, and a woman

who could only be Lady Libnah Berta came out, unaccompanied by any servants, to Garvin's surprise.

Berta was a big woman, big all over, easily two meters tall. She was, Garvin guessed, in her eighties. Her face was lined with the marks of power, and her lips easily pursed in anger. Her hair was pure white, drawn back in a bun, and she wore a long green skirt with red piping and a matching long-sleeved jacket, a frothy white blouse under it.

"Good evening, Gaffer Jaansma . . . and Miss Katun."

She looked Kekri up and down once, then turned her full attention to Garvin.

"Please be welcome to my home."

"I'm grateful for the invitation."

A wintry smile came, went on Berta's face.

"*Graav* Ganeel and I go back some years," she said. "In fact, I remember . . . or claim to remember, at any rate, dandling him on my knee when he was a toddler, while I talked to his father, the king.

"When I remind him of that," she went on, her smile getting a touch broader, "it seems to put him off his stride a bit."

She didn't need to add, and therefore easier to do business with.

"Come in," she said. "There's a chill in the air. I'll have someone bring your bags in, and escort you to your chambers. After you refresh yourselves, perhaps you'd join me in the library for a predinner drink."

As they entered the huge house, Garvin noticed that somehow Kekri's blouse buttons had been done up.

The rooms they were shown into on the sixth floor were enormous, and rococo in their decoration.

"I feel like I've just dropped back in time," Kekri said. "Maybe a hundred years."

"Maybe a thousand for all of me," Garvin said.

The paintings on the walls were realistic, heroic, soldiers posing bravely in ancient suits, armored and

space; there were horned animals at bay, wistful maidens watching their heroes go off to war, the colors
starting to brown to match the fading archaic wall-
paper. The chairs were soft, overpadded, with tassels
at their ends. The tables were dark, highly polished
wood, and the wall mirrors trimmed in gold.

The bed . . .

Kekri giggled.

"What did you tell them when you responded to
the invitation?"

"I didn't tell them anything," Garvin said truthfully.
"They said a companion, and I thought—"

"One bed? Shame on you, Gaffer Jaansma," Kekri
said. "Bringing me out here in this howling wilderness,
planning to take advantage of me, no doubt."

"No, no. Honestly," Garvin said, feeling about fifteen years old. "Let me get ahold of that old fart who
brought us up here, and see about getting you another
room that—"

Kekri came up to Garvin, put her hands on his
elbows.

"I really don't mind," she said in that purr. "I'm
sure you're a man of high moral resolve. Certainly
two people can share a common bed without anything
happening. And if not . . ." She broke off, giggled. "I
guess we should be glad you didn't come here with
Mr. Yoshitaro. I wonder if Lady Berta is *that* broad-
minded."

Garvin began to step back.

"As long as we're here," Kekri murmured, lifting
her head, eyes closed, lips parted.

Jaansma would have been somewhat less than mor-
tal if he hadn't kissed her. Her tongue went in his
mouth, curled back and forth for a time.

When she slowly broke away, Garvin felt a little
dizzy.

"Speaking of your friend," Kekri said, "I've got to
be honest and say that he frankly scares me a lot. His
eyes seem to look quite through you."

"You want to know something even scarier?" Garvin said. "If you told him that, he'd probably take it as a compliment."

Kekri grimaced, sat on the bed, bounced.

"Changing the subject . . . Real feathers," she said. "That might be interesting."

Garvin took a step toward her.

"No, no," Kekri said. "You take your bag, and go into that bathroom there and change. I don't think Lady Berta would like being kept waiting . . . at least not for very long."

She giggled again.

"Besides, this will give you something to look forward to. Maybe."

Garvin changed into ankle boots, slightly flared black slacks, a white shirt with black studs under a black monkey jacket.

Kekri came out of her bathroom wearing a sheath gown, with a jacket over it, both in sequined white.

"And aren't we both beautiful," she said, holding out her arm.

He took it and they went out, down cavernous corridors, to the lift, down to the enormous hall that led to the library.

Inside there were holos, reels, shelves of ancient real books, maps of other worlds, portraits of stiff, dedicated-looking men and their noble wives, no doubt the lineage of the Bertas.

Libnah Berta greeted them, and a waiter took their drink orders. Kekri asked for pale wine, Garvin for a brandy with a glass of ice water that he planned to nurse forever, and Berta, without asking, got a tall glass full of multicolored liqueurs.

She asked them, as if she really cared, what they thought of Cayle, and was pleased they liked it so much.

Berta had two more of the spectacular drinks, Kekri

another wine, and Garvin no more before they went in to dinner.

"I know it is considered rude to talk business over a meal," Berta announced. "But I have almost no other life, so forgive me.

"Also, I'm fascinated with various aspects of your most unusual profession."

Her questions were penetrating, and it seemed she actually was interested in circus life—at least the financial aspects of it.

The meal was spectacular, in a very old-fashioned way—a consommé to begin, an assortment of grilled, breaded small fish, a roast in a rich, cream-looking sauce with sautéed vegetables, a mixed salad, and finally a dessert, flaming on the outside, frozen on the inside.

"I certainly hope you don't eat like this every night," Kekri said. "If you do, I want your fitness regime."

"Of course I don't," Berta said, with a laugh that sounded programmed. "In fact, my advisors are generally unhappy with me for not eating at all when I'm working on a specific project."

With each course came a different wine that Garvin barely tasted, and Kekri, to Jaansma's approval, took no more than a sip of. Berta drank heartily from each bottle and was completely unaffected.

Meal finished, she led the way back into the library, settled Garvin with another brandy, Kekri with a liqueur, and had another of her multicolored drinks.

"Now then," she said as she settled back, "why, exactly, did you want *Graav* Ganeel to set up a meeting between us?"

Garvin thought of various subterfuges, decided on the semihonest one, explaining that his circus was heading toward Centrum, and would appreciate any help Berta Industries could provide about the various security devices they'd provided the Confederation around Centrum. He added, without giving details, that they already had charts, serial numbers, and descriptions of these devices and outposts.

Berta raised an imperious eyebrow.

"Well, I cannot say you're evasive, young man. But one thing you should know is that Berta Industries prides itself on its integrity. Once our services are contracted for, no one else has ever been given any details."

"I can appreciate that," Garvin said. "But it's been ten years since you provided those devices, and at least five years since the Confederation has dropped out of contact with everyone, it seems."

"True."

"I'm not arrogant enough to say that a circus can do anything to restore what once was, but I'd like to try."

"Frankly, I don't care much about your enterprises, Gaffer Jaansma. But there is this justification for my interest: Cayle is, perhaps not quite helpless, but certainly floundering without its Confederation business. We've not been able to establish new avenues of trade to compensate for the loss.

"Perhaps you've noticed the huge unemployment. I've tried to keep as many of my employees on as possible, but, of course, I'm not a charity.

"I'm afraid that the people out there, if they begin to lose faith in our government, may seek a more radical solution. Simple people will seek simple solutions.

"A man . . . or woman . . . who can offer easy answers would be very appealing.

"And, to be brutally honest with you, a good number of this system's magnates would support such a person, if for no other reason than they fear to lose what they have. And I could well be one of them, if there's a sufficiently large social disruption.

"No, I do not think your circus can do any good, could help us solve our problems, any more than the

momentary relief of taking the people's minds away
from their concerns.

"But something is always better than nothing.

"I shall think on this matter overnight, and give you
my answer tomorrow."

"Well hold me and kiss me where the sun don't
shine," Njangu muttered as he looked at the small
case he'd found in Kekri's compartment. "Either
we're complete dunderbrains, or else this wasn't here
the first time we searched her."

"It wasn't here, boss," one of the security techs said.
"I made thorough notes of the last time we went
through her gear. The third thing we checked was in
her cosmetics case, and I'm not blind enough to have
missed that case."

"A com of some sort," Njangu mused. "Run this
up to your shop and disclose me its secrets."

" 'Kay, sir," a tech said.

"Be a little careful," Yoshitaro added. "Just in case
there's something stupid inside like a suicide charge."

"We could always keep with the idea that accidents
happen," Kekri said, kicking her shoes off.

"We could," Garvin said, who suddenly decided he
was going to seize the moment just for a change, and
the hell with the consequences, for which thought he
knew he'd unquestionably pay. "Or I could light this
candle . . . old-fashioned sort, that Berta here, plus
the one on the other side of the bed."

"You could do that," Kekri said. "And then what?"

"And then I cut the main lights like this, come over
here, and kiss you."

"And then what?"

"Then," Garvin said, "I take your jacket off, and
slide your gown down to your waist like that. Then I
kiss your neck, and some . . . other places a few times.

"Yes, you can be taking off my jacket, and unfasten-
ing my pants if you want."

"Oh," Kekri breathed. "Yes."

"Thank you. Now I'll find a way to kick these god-damned boots off, and push your gown down around your feet like this.

"Tsk. You're not wearing anything under it."

"I don't like last-minute details to get in the way," Kekri breathed.

"An excellent idea," Garvin said, carrying her to the bed. She lay, eyes half-closed, looking up at him as he took off his shirt.

"Now, if you'll lift your legs up so I can take hold of your ankles . . ."

Moments later, he ran out of words.

Garvin drank a cup of stimulant tea the cook had recommended, smiled politely at Berta across the table.

He thought of Njangu's advice: "Screw her black-and-blue and get her singing our tune." Not only was the bastard sexist, but he obviously thought too highly of somebody's capabilities. Not Katun's. Feeling very black-and-blue, he wondered if he'd be able to walk un-spraddle-legged on this inspection tour, put on his best face, and determined to tough it out.

He was a little disgusted to see Kekri, quite bouncy, making cheerful talk with Libnah Berta, and tried to find the energy to pour himself more tea.

The electronics security technician yawned and rubbed sleepy eyes.

"What we've got here, boss," he told Njangu, "is a neat little transceiver. In-system only, unless some-body is dogging us. And, so far, we haven't found anybody on our tail.

"The entire back is a light-sensitive charging system, not even needing UV light, which is fairly sexy. The set remains on at all times, so somebody . . . say a nice spyship . . . could enter whatever system we're in, activate the com with a set signal, then our spy can find out somebody's waiting to chat with her and take it from there. Naturally, it's got a record-and-blurt capability so she wouldn't hang herself out for too long."

Njangu thought, poured himself another stim.

"I think," he said, "it would be very nice to put the com right back where we found it, except maybe, if there's room in the box, you can put a secondary circuit in that'll tip us if somebody rings Kekri up."

"Already set up the circuitry, boss. Thought you might like something like that. Also piggybacked another circuit so we can static-up her transmission, and whoever's on the other end will have the devil's time making sense out of it.

"Now, all we need is what data she's after."

Njangu grinned, drained his tea, touched his inside breast pocket where a copy of Kekri Katun's notes, kept in a simple substitution code, sat. Another copy, mostly broken, was with a crypto tech.

"Now that, my fine feathered friend, is what they call beyond your need to know."

He rose.

"C'mon. Let's go down to the dukey and I'll buy breakfast. Garvin'll have some interesting things to listen to when he gets back."

Berta's works ran on forever and a half kilometer. Garvin very quickly got tired of admiring huge extrusion machinery, engine-casting plants, lathes that could turn out something the size of a Nana boat, programming divisions, and all the rest. He moved just a little awkwardly, not used to using his body to aim the pinhole camera in his lapel.

There were workmen about, but not many, and Garvin noticed most of them occupied their time polishing and maintaining, not building.

They ended up in a huge, stone building, very archaic in design, with webbed glass skylights, an open center, and row after row of terminals and operators along the walls. Outside were armed guards that Garvin rated as fairly alert.

"These are our archives," Lady Berta said proudly. "Going all the way back to the first tender the first Berta built . . . and used as a personal runabout."

She came a little closer, lowered her voice.

"In these records is the information you asked me about, and it is as good a place as any to tell you I cannot permit you to access what you want.

"I'm sorry, but, as I have said before, there is a bond between Berta and its customers, a bond that's been unbroken for more than three hundred Earth-years."

Garvin looked into her eyes, saw nothing but stern resolve, and knew better than to argue.

"Then," he said, "I suppose we'll just have to take our chances with whatever security devices remain around Centrum."

"I am sorry," Berta said, and just a bit of a smile came and went.

Now why, Garvin thought, and felt Njangu would be proud of him, *would she have taken the trouble to show me where the secrets are, and then tell me to bugger off? Let alone grin at me? Interesting. I think I'll have to consider this.*

Ristori crawled carefully toward the bowl, where six Earth cats lapped milk. He inserted himself between two, started to take a drink, leapt back as a cat slapped him across the nose.

The children in the stands roared.

Again Ristori tried, again was batted away.

He got up, sat in thought for a while, then visibly brightened.

He got back down on his hands and knees, and suddenly he was moving like a cat, sinuously, slinking toward the bowl. The cats moved aside, evidently fooled, and Ristori began lapping milk like they did.

Damned glad, Garvin thought, watching from outside the ring as the applause began, *I changed my mind about Emton and his act.*

The cats were, surprisingly, one of the bigger hits. Garvin guessed it was because the cat wasn't an unknown pet, but no one in his right mind imagined they could ever be trained to do tricks.

Ristori got up and schlumpfed away, and five of the cats licked themselves twice, then rolled on their backs, paws in the air, and, seemingly without any direction from Emton, who lounged nearby, the sixth leapt on top of the lifted paws, and was bounced from cat to cat, a perfect tiny parody of the risley act in the second ring.

"Did we have fun with our Kekri?" Darod Montagna hissed, a smile on her face to fool the crowd.

"It was work," Garvin tried.

"Of *course*," Montagna said in utter disbelief. "I hope you two made yourselves very happy. You can move her into your compartment if you want. I, certainly, won't be objecting."

Garvin tried to think of something to say, managed a feeble "but . . ." as Montagna stalked away.

The last thing he would do was move Kekri in with him. He certainly hadn't the energy, and Katun had shown no particular desire to press matters, although she'd been fairly affectionate on the flight back. It seemed obvious, Garvin thought with a bit of misery, not only had he failed to impress Katun, but he'd evidently blown what he did have with Montagna.

He'd barely had time to report his failure to Njangu, and learn Kekri was, indeed, a spy, before it was time for the evening show.

Sunk in self-pity, he almost missed the cats' scampering offstage, and the growl outside the tent of the big animals, waiting their cue.

Roustabouts muscled a huge cage down into position over the center ring, shut off its lifters, lashed it firmly in place.

Garvin snapped his whip three times.

"You can hear them, you can smell them, now they'll be coming in, fangs bared, claws ready. Watch your children, ladies and gentlemen, for these voracious, vicious beasts of the wild are barely under control.

"I myself wouldn't enter their cage on a challenge. Only their master, the impossibly brave Sir Douglas, dares that, and now, let's welcome him and his mankillers!"

Monique Lir wasn't paying much attention to the dancers on the stage of the Pendu club, either the clothed or the naked ones, listening to Darod Montagna snap out her anger.

"Are you sure you meant to cut everything off?"

"I'd like to have cut his futtering cock off," Darod stormed. "Preferably at the elbows."

"Did you ever consider why the boss took that tits-and-ass wonder along with him?"

"Why . . . because he wanted to screw her! And . . . and because she's a lot prettier than I am!"

"Maybe on the first, so what on the second. That Mellusin woman he's involved with back on Cumbre might be a bit prettier than you as well. Did you maybe consider there was another reason?"

"Like what? What could there be?" Montagna demanded.

"Oh, say, maybe that somebody wanted Katun out of town for the night. Maybe somebody wanted to search her dunnage."

"*Giptel* doots!" Montagna snapped. "How could you know that?"

"Because my . . . our, now again . . . compartment's on the same level as hers. And because I'm a very light sleeper. And because I saw Njangu, looking innocent, wandering around with a couple of his goons after people settled down for the night."

"Oh," Montagna said in a small voice.

"Now, if he *keeps* boffing her," Monique said, "all

you can do is shrug, walk away, and forget about it. It wasn't as if you weren't warned."

"No," Darod said in a dull voice, and sipped her drink. "Maybe I am being stupid. But it still doesn't set right."

"No shiteedah," Lir said. "That's 'cause men, basically, blow *giptels*."

"So what should I do . . . just hold in place?"

Monique, without answering her, looked up at the various male and female impedimenta being enthusiastically waved about by the dancers.

"I'll be glad when we lift off this frigging planet," she muttered. "The whole damned world smells of sperm. Sperm and cold, rusting iron."

"Odd and odder," Njangu mused. "Hokay. Let's try one. Berta wants to go along with us . . . maybe . . . or maybe not even consciously. She wants order, law, and the rest of that bullshit people think is so goddamned important back in her life, and the only thing she can think of is the Confederation.

"She won't give us the data . . . but that doesn't mean it's sealed beyond recovery. 'Kay. I think me, and maybe a couple of friends, can help her conscience out."

"Yeh," Garvin said. "I just wish somebody'd help mine."

"Well," Njangu said, "it does look like you maybe weren't everything Katun dreams of . . . or maybe she was just curious, and that was part of her investigation, since the notes she took are all over the map.

"She might as well be some kind of ologist, doing a holo on circus folk. Go buy some flowers for Darod. Maybe that'll help, and she'll get over her piss-off, you betrayin' bastard, in an aeon or epoch or two."

"Thanks," Garvin muttered. "So now you're going to make a run at making yourself into her honey-trap?"

"Not me, brother," Njangu said. "First there's Maev,

who's one mean piece of work. Second, I'm hardly a superman, which maybe is what our Kekri is looking for. Third is, unlike some tall, blond sorts, who pose nobly in charges and circus rings, I know my limitations."

"B . . . but . . . but you're the one who told me to do this," Garvin sputtered.

"Ah well," Njangu said. "I've learned to move on from my triumphs. What I'm looking for right now, after examining your fuzzy, out-of-focus holos of the Berta plants, is a nice, reliable midget."

CHAPTER
12

"Thank you enormously for inviting me out," Kekri Katun said.

"Thank *you* for coming with me," Ben Dill said. "It's nice, taking the prettiest woman in the ship out to help you buy maybe a painting or something with my ill-gotten wages."

Kekri smiled wryly.

"I don't seem to get asked anywhere much. I feel like some kind of pariah, sometimes. Maybe because I'm from another world than the rest of you."

"Aw balls," Dill said rudely. "Nobody's pariahing you," he lied. "We're from as many worlds as you can think of, so that doesn't matter. More likely, it's 'cause you're so pretty. Notice that a lot of the showgirls don't get taken anywhere? Don't think you're anything special in the way of a martyr."

Kekri grinned, squeezed Dill's arm.

"Careful, lady," he said. "Don't go messin' with the pilot, even if he is the best in six systems and it is only a stinkin' lifter."

"What're those weird-looking ships you usually fly?"

"The *aksai*," Dill said. "Built by the Musth . . . like Alikhan. They flew in combat . . ." and Ben suddenly remembered Njangu's warning, and his cover story, ". . . against some Confederation ships, just before the collapse.

"We know some people who know some people, and bought some of them."

"You get along with the Musth?"

"Circus people get along with everyone," Ben said.

Kekri seemed to feel a warning, for she found another topic.

"So what, exactly, am I supposed to do?"

"I prob'ly have the taste of a water buffalo as far as art goes," Dill said. "But my compartment looks pretty damn' bare. They told me about this art thing they do every weeks-end, along the river that runs through Pendu, and I thought maybe you could help me find something that isn't too atrocious."

"A pilot," Kekri mused. "You want something with flying, or space in it?"

"Not a chance," Ben said. "I do it, and don't much want to look at it. Something abstract's more my line."

Kekri looked at him with a bit of respect.

"So you have advanced taste in art, can lift a ton of weights, can fly *aksai*—"

"And just about anything else," Ben said. "No boasting."

"And anything else," Kekri said. "What other talents do you have?"

"I'm a balding secret sex maniac, and modest as a sumbitch to boot."

Kekri laughed, reached over, and patted him on the upper thigh.

" 'Kay, Mr. Modest. Isn't that a landing field down there?"

"Surely is, lady. Now watch this, and hang on to your stomach."

Dill flipped the lifter on its side and dived straight down for the small field. He flared at the last minute and set it down, with never a scrape from its skids.

"And here we be," he said. "The river's right over there, so let's go see if there's anything worth buying."

They climbed out, and an attendant approached, a bit wide-eyed at the woman and the monster of a man.

"Here," Dill said, spinning a credit through the air.

"Don't let anybody put their initials on the pig, and keep it easy for me to get out!"

"Sir," the attendant said, bowing repeatedly. "Yes, sir! Would you like me to wash and polish it, as well?"

"Naah," Dill said. "It'd on'y get dusty all over again."

As they walked away, he said, "What'd I do wrong? Throw him the wrong coin or something? I thought he was gonna propose marriage."

"One Confederation credit converts, somebody told me, if you can find a place to convert it," Kekri said, "to about a week's wages in local currency."

"Be damned! The hell with art," Dill said. "Let's go find us a temple and set up as money changers."

The midget's name was Felip Mand'l, and he frequently referred to himself as "Lucky Felip."

"Of course Lucky Felip is delighted to help the circus, for doesn't my contract call for me to be 'generally useful,' besides my act? And I do know how to keep silent, and will admit I thought our troupe has some dark secrets, especially considering how we are now dressed, which is certainly not the norm for most troupes," he said, a little adrenalined.

"But how did you come to pick Lucky Felip? There are over a dozen little people with Circus Jaansma."

"I did a little asking about," Njangu said. "About people's pasts."

"Ah! All that was a mistake," Mand'l said. "I was very young, and she was very pretty, and she swore those jewels had been taken from her by a jealous lover, and I was the only one who could climb up into the man's penthouse, and I *almost* got away with it."

"Relax," Njangu said. "Back some time ago there were things *I* almost got away with, too."

Mand'l looked at the other three in the back of the lifter. Like him and Njangu, Penwyth, Lir, and an electronics technician named Limodo wore black from head to toe, with roll-down watch caps on their heads, amplified light goggles on their foreheads, throat mikes in place. All wore small patrol packs.

"I, uh, notice that the four of you are carrying guns. Why was I not offered one?" Felip asked, trying to sound indignant.

"Do you know how to use a blaster?" Lir asked.

"Unfortunately, not. Not one of the talents I've been able to cultivate. But I am deadly with an old-timey projectile weapon, and can't think there's that much difference."

"There is," Monique said. "We don't want you shooting yourself in the foot. Or me, either."

"Ah," the midget said, and subsided into his seat as the lifter low-flew into the mountains.

"Good farpadoodle," Dill muttered, staring at a semiactive holo/painting almost as tall as he was. "I didn't know there were that many shades of red, or that many ways of looking stupid waving a blaster about."

"Sssh," Kekri nudged. "I think that's the artist over there."

"Introduce me," Ben said, "and Mrs. Dill's favorite son'll pitch him right over that embankment into the river. He's too lousy to live."

Artists, maybe two hundred, maybe more, had their works strung along a wide sidewalk, some leaning against the stone wall. On the other side was a three-meter drop to the gray, wintry river, with an occasional boat tied up along the wall.

"Come on," Kekri said, tugging at his arm. "We've barely begun."

"Isn't there a bar somewhere? My taste seems connected to my taste buds, and maybe if I had a beer or six, some of this crap might look better."

"Never buy art when you're blasted," Kekri said. "That's an old saying of my grandmother's."

"Oh yeh? What'd she do to earn her keep to be so wise?"

"I think she ran a bordello."

"By the Sun God's suppository, I better hang on to you," Ben said. "A whorehouse is just what I want to retire into."

He snorted laughter.

"All right," Kekri said. "You're obviously in no frame of mind to look at any more art."

"Especially not this shit. Why anybody thinks there's something mournful about a stupid painting of a stupid busted-up starship, its ribs showing through, at sunset is way beyond me," Dill said. "Maybe I better stick to finger painting. My own."

"That, I think, is one of their public houses," Katun said, pointing.

"Awright! Now, we'll just wait for this convoy to float on past, and—"

The convoy was half a dozen heavy lifters, with covered camion backs. The canvas came away, and men with guns piled out.

"Ohboy," Dill said, grabbing Kekri's arm, and pulling her back toward the art booths. "What the hell are we in the middle of?"

"Over there," Kekri pointed, and ten or more lifters were crossing the river on a low bridge.

The men behind Dill started shooting at the second convoy, and men leapt from those lifters and returned fire. Heavy blasters atop the lifters slammed rounds at each other, and there were screams of fear, of pain.

Dill was flat on the pavement, half-atop Kekri, and the artist whose work he'd hated was beside him.

"What the hell is going on?"

The artist shook his head rapidly.

"Probably the anarchists are shooting each other up again. They can't agree as to the form of their organization."

He screamed, flopped as bolts chattered along the walk, and through his back.

"This isn't safe," Dill said, glanced around, then grabbed Kekri, who screeched in surprise. He ran backward, kicking over easels, cursing that he was un-armed, and someone saw him, fired, and missed.

Dill went over the embankment wall, and dropped into the river, going under, still with one hand firmly on Kekri's leg.

The two came up, Kekri sputtering.

"You better know how to swim," Dill said.

"I do," she said. "Your little jumping act took me by surprise."

" 'Kay," Ben said. "We'll go for that little boat over there, cut it loose, stay in the water on the far side, and let it take us downstream for a while."

"Good," Kekri said, starting to swim, then rolling on her back. "You think fast."

"A man my size has got to. Now shaddup and keep stroking."

They swam hard for a few meters, then Dill spat water like a sounding whale.

"Shit," Dill said. "Anarchists fighting each other. What a *truly* screwed-up world this is."

"Lucky Felip could dance the gavotte on this slab of steel," Mand'l said into his mike as he went quickly up the webbed glass of Beta Industry Archives. "I could do it on my hands."

"Sharrup and bust us in," Njangu answered.

Mand'l knelt, and there was a tiny flare as his torch lit. He took half-melted glass out with asbestos-gloved fingers, reached inside, found the catch, and opened the skylight.

"Enter voose," he said.

"Toss the rope down first," Limodo said. "I'm no goddamned acrobat."

Mand'l tied the rope off on something sturdy inside the archive building and threw it down to her. She went quickly up, hand over hand, and the other three followed.

Inside, they were on an iron platform, high above Berta's records.

They held for a moment in silence, scanning the dark inside of the building. All of the Legion troops held up circled thumbs and forefingers.

No watchmen. At least, none seen so far.

Njangu pointed down, and they crept down stairways to the main floor.

Limodo checked terminals, turned one on. For long minutes she stared at the blue light, occasionally touching sensors. Finally, she nodded.

"I think I've got it," and began her search, checking against a tiny screen she'd taken from her patrol pack with the serial numbers gotten on Tiborg.

An hour passed, then another as she wove her way into the bowels of the archives.

"At least there aren't any booby traps or firewalls," she reported. "Seems fairly straightforward."

"FREEZE!" was Njangu's response, and they obeyed, seeing two men outside the main door, shining normal lights inside. No one moved, the men went away, and the search went on.

"And here we are," Dill said, guiding the small boat in to a dock, jumping out with a painter, and tying the craft up.

"You impress me," Kekri said.

Dill hopped back in the boat. It rocked and he caught himself against the roof of the tiny cabin.

"Then you might reward me, m'lady, with a kiss. Then we'll call for a liftout, let somebody come back for that damned lifter, and the hell with my artistic sensibilities ever again."

Kekri lifted her lips to his, mouth opening. The kiss lasted, then got a little more intense. Her arms slid down from around his neck down his back, and then around and down his stomach.

Katun suddenly broke from the kiss.

"Ohm'gods!" she breathed.

"Uh . . . you knew I was a pretty big guy," Dill said, slightly embarrassed. "That includes—"

"Shut up," Kekri ordered. "Is that cabin unlocked?"

"Uh . . . yeh."

"Then inside. Hurry!"

"Uh . . . 'kay."

"Got it," Limodo reported, attaching a small vampire recorder to the side of the terminal.

"Five, maybe ten minutes, and we'll have everything. Another five for me to clean up my tracks."

Lucky Felip stirred from where he was hiding, just inside a lectern.

"You make things easy. I was expecting excitement."

"Quiet," Penwyth whispered into his com. He and Lir were on either side of the entrance, guns ready against intruders. "It's bad luck to be confident."

"Remember those jewels you went after," Lir echoed. "Almost ain't is."

"Tails up, tails up," Thanon and Phanon chanted, and the elephants obeyed, even the small Imp and Loti, linking trunks and tails, and the line swayed out of the tent as the lights came up.

"And that's all there is, ladies, gentlemen, children," Garvin chanted. "It's all out and over," and the butchers swarmed the crowd.

"Don't forget your souvenir programs, a real memento of Circus Jaansma, something for you to keep for your memories until we come back this way again."

"Early in the next frigging century," Montagna muttered to herself. "Or the one after that."

She saw, in a front row seat, *Graav* Ganeel, staring after the elephants, face most wistful.

Big Bertha lifted two hours before dawn.

Monique Lir was on the bridge, looking down as the lights of Pendu vanished into the cloud cover.

"This frigging planet," she observed to no one in

particular, not knowing she was echoing Lady Libnah Berta, "damned well needs the Confederation back. Or they're gonna end up marching in lockstep to some real fool and all end up dead or worse."

CHAPTER
13

"Probably most of you have an idea of what was going on," Njangu told the Legion officers assembled on the bridge of *Big Bertha*, "but here's the real skinny. I'll let Dr. Froude explain."

"We've made some interesting progress so far," Froude said. "We now have . . . or think we have . . . a skeleton key of sorts to the Confederation, which hopefully will keep us from being killed by our own people or robots," Froude said. "From the nav points we're close to now, there's a six-jump sequence that will put us in the Capella system.

"However, I favor an eight-jump series, for one reason: This second set of navpoints, and I indicate them here on a greatly simplified chart holo, are 'nearer' to the systems around Capella.

"I would like to nose around a bit, as close to Centrum as we dare, before committing ourselves.

"Comments? Questions? Additions?"

There were none, and so *Big Bertha* jumped again into N-space.

"This is most interestin'," Njangu observed as he checked several screens. "This system, W-R-whocares, was supposedly empty. No listing on settlements, no listing on fortification, carried as UNOCCUPIED.

"Yet over on that world the detectors picked up a big chunk of metal."

He keyed a mike.

"Ben, what do you have?.," not bothering with formal call signs.

Silence for a moment, then:

"On my second orbit. What we've got is damned weird, Njangu. The detectors picked up what looks to me like a big goddamned fortress, modern, most of it underground. I'm transmitting pictures and realtime data for you to eyeball.

"But what's interesting is the thing's abandoned."

"What do you mean?"

"I mean, my detectors pick up nothin' on no waves from nobody. Nothing on IR, nothing on radar, nothing on heat imaging, not even residue. On visual, there are hangar bays, nit and cleverly camouflaged, but the doors are hangin' open like the seat of my pants when I was poor day before yestidday," Dill went on. "I see what I think are weapons launchers, but with no missiles on the mounts. I've got me some scanners and some antennae. I chanced a low sweep, and nothin' went BINGO at me.

"It looks to me like people just got bored and up and left."

"Could you bring *Big Bertha* in closer?" Froude asked the ship captain.

"Affirm," Liskeard said, and the planet blurred, the screen showed the whorl of N-space, and then the planet filled the main screen.

"Sorry, Ben," Njangu said. "Forgot to tell you we were jumping in closer."

"Oh, 'at's all right," Dill said. "I just saw you guys pull out on me, and now somebody's gonna have to clean up this here *aksai* cabin. This is not the place I want to grow old gracefully in all by myself."

Froude was paying no attention to the chatter, but watching screens.

"I think Big Ben is maybe right," he said. "The Confederation . . . I'm assuming this was some kind of a secret base for something, since it looks like it's

been there for a while, and who else but the Confederation would've spent who knows how many years
building this . . . just up and left. Leaving the barn
door wide-open.

"Very strange indeed."

"Why," Kekri said, "did we spend so much time in
that dead system today?"

"Damfino," Ben lied. "I was in the ready room
playing with myself. Alikhan was the duty pilot."

"Wasn't that weird to be just hanging out there
without anything happening? Didn't Garvin give you
some kind of clue?"

"Nawp," Dill said. "What's weird is that I've been
out of my flight suit, wandering around nekkid and
all, with a nicely worked up me in me hand, and I
haven't leapt on you yet."

"Wait a minute," Kekri protested. "We can't screw
all the time! And we were talking . . ." and then
she squealed, and for a time the conversation in their
compartment was somewhat fragmented.

The next jump was through a dead system, with
no surprises.

Sabyn/Sabyn I

The next jump was more interesting. There were supposedly three inhabited planets of the six in the system
of Sabyn. They were listed as settled, with light manufacturing, mostly agriculture, no details on culture.

The *aksai* sweep reported life on all three worlds,
no observable armament, no threats.

Garvin had *Big Bertha* brought out of N-space, and
sent a cast for landing instructions.

There was no response to the first or the third com.
Other coms were sent to the other worlds, with zed
results.

Garvin, feeling his skin prickle a bit, put out all his combat ships, looking for trouble.

None materialized.

"All right," he said. "We'll do it the dumb way."

As on Cayle, they snowballed the three populated worlds with 'casts, in-atmosphere fireworks. Again, nothing.

"Now, here is something a bit out of the ordinary," Alikhan sent from his *aksai* close to the first planet's surface. "Transmitting pictures. What you are looking at is a landing field, but you will note it has been rather completely destroyed. The towers have been knocked down and the maintenance buildings bombed, as on Salamonsky. It would appear to me that the damage was done some time ago . . . a planetary year or more.

"However, the world is *not* abandoned. I sighted a small lifter, overflew it. It ducked away into a forest byway, and I lost it, not having my infrared pickup turned on at the time."

The watch officer brought *Big Bertha* closer to the planet, and they waited some more.

"We were swept twice with radar from the planet's surface, but the band wasn't anything the computer said was used by target acquisition," the electronics watch reported. "Then nothing."

Everyone looked at Garvin for his decision.

"Let's wiggle our fannies and see what happens," he said. "Put it down on that open patch of land near that torn-up field, and we'll set up canvas."

"You are being a daredevil," Njangu murmured.

"I'll want full air cover while we do," Garvin said.

"Why're we putting the tents up, if I might ask?" Penwyth said.

"I can't think of any better way to signal that we're friendly."

Their first customer was a tough-looking subteen farm boy, who walked up, listened, stone-faced to the

spiel of one of the midway barkers to her solitary
audience, waited until the chant broke for an instant,
then demanded, "Whatsit take to get in?"

"Only half a Confederate credit for the circus," the
barker said. "Dunno what it'd be in your currency,
but we're flexible, son, mighty flexible. The midway's
free, but the attractions and the games require a small
contribution."

The boy nodded, went down the midway, looking
curiously about.

Garvin was watching from the bridge of *Big Bertha*.

"Damned spooky to be the only flattie around," he
said, "and you'll note everybody's working him, just
for practice, no doubt."

"Maybe you best slide on down and find out what's
going on," Njangu said.

"What, me, the ringmaster?"

"Yes, you, the ringmaster. Move out."

Garvin obeyed.

The boy, in spite of his best efforts, couldn't help
but goggle a little at the tall, white-clad blond man
standing in front of him.

"Welcome to the circus," Garvin said. "My name's
Garvin. Yours?"

"Jorma," the boy said.

"Enjoying yourself?"

"Dunno yet."

"Here," Garvin said, taking a ticket from his
pocket. "Free admission to my circus. Better," and he
brought out more tickets, "bring your whole family."

"Don't need that many," Jorma said. "There ain't
but me and Ma, and one baby sister left."

"Left?"

"Since the damned Confederation come and gone."
Jorma spat on the ground.

Garvin recovered.

"What did the Confederation want? Don't mind my

dumb questions, Jorma, but we're from way offworld, and haven't heard any news lately."

"Bastards come every couple years," Jorma said. "Grab whatever's worth taking. Quick-butcher whatever cattle they can come on, freeze-dry our vegetables." Jorma paused, and his face twisted, and he fought back, found control. "They take anybody who wants to go with 'em.

"Sometimes people who don't. Like my sister."

He scrubbed across his eyes with the back of his sleeve.

"That's not right," Garvin said.

Jorma gave him a look of infinite scorn.

"And how're we supposed to fight back? No guns, and they've got rockets and ships."

He pointed at the nearby field.

"They done that last time. Said they didn't want us messing around in space. Some peddler came through, said they shot up some of our cities pretty bad. I wouldn't know. Most of us live in little villages. Get in cities, you're a target. My dad went off, looking for work, and he never came back."

"All of these raiders call themselves Confederation?"

"Yeh," the boy said. "And we got all these holos talkin' about how good the Confederation was for all of us. Lyin' sonsabitches!"

He caught himself.

"Sorry, mister. My ma says I'm not supposed to use language like that."

"Doesn't bother me," Garvin said. "If I was in your shoes, I'd probably use worse myself."

The boy smiled, very faintly.

"Maybe you're not a trap."

"Trap?"

"Ma said the only ships that've come here in the last four years have been raiders. Before that, she said, there wasn't anybody for six, seven years.

"Before that, she swears there were *other* Confeder-

ation ships, but those were bringing things in, and not
stealing everything we've got. All kinds of ships, not just
warships, but transports, even liners. She said you could
get on one, if you had credits, and it'd take you anywhere in the Universe.

"Anyway, Ma figured, when we heard your speakers
in those weird-looking ships that you were just another way for us to get stolen."

"Look," Garvin said. "If I wanted to steal you . . .
or your mother . . . or your little sister, you think I'd
go to the trouble of bringing in all those elephants?"

"Is that what they are? Like from Earth?"

"Maybe, a long time ago," Garvin said. "That herd
goes through a ton of dried grass a day, maybe more.
Plus they've got to have vitamins, and treats from the
hydroponics area, or from our freeze-dried stocks."

"Doesn't seem to make much sense just to grab me
and my family," Jorma agreed.

"Look," Garvin said. "I'll get a whole roll of tickets.
You sell them for whatever you can get, keep half
the credits."

"Why me?"

"Because you were the first to show up, which
means you've got some courage. Plus nobody'll get
near any of us, 'til we've proved we're not the Confederation. Most likely, they'd take a shot, or wing us
with a rock," Garvin said.

"That's prob'ly true," Jorma said.

Garvin took him over to a spieler's booth, took a
roll of tickets about the size of the boy's chest, and
gave it to him.

"You make money, we make money."

Jorma nodded, considered, then, possibly afraid
Garvin would renege, pelted back down the midway
and disappeared into brush.

"I've got a tracer on him," the speaker in Garvin's
ear said. "Want him tracked?"

"Yeh," Garvin said. "But nobody takes any action
except by my permission. Period."

That night there were ten people, including Jorma and his skeptical family. The next night, fifty.

Garvin kept the *aksai* and patrol boats in the air, constantly 'casting. Some of the cities had taken some damage from the air, but nothing was as shattered as Jorma's peddler had claimed.

The fourth night, there were three hundred people, some of whom had arrived by decrepit lifter or ground vehicles.

Clowns and butchers were augmented with Njangu's Intelligence analysts.

"The kid was telling the truth," Njangu reported. "Some folks who call themselves Confederation are milking this planet every year or so. But they're not dumb. They don't steal enough so people starve or can't keep the economy limping along.

"A lot of the people go with them willingly. But there's some . . . Jorma's sister, I'd guess . . . somebody gets the hots for and she's theirs."

"Wonderful," Garvin said. "This'll be a nice reputation to live down. Wonder how many other worlds these phony Confeds loot?"

"Damfino," Njangu said. "But you want a really nasty thought? You ever think maybe this *is* the real Confederation?"

Garvin gnawed a lip, didn't answer.

"Another interesting bit of info," Njangu went on. "Nobody from whatever government exists has shown up to check out the circus."

"That's damned unlikely."

"Sure is," Yoshitaro agreed. "The only officials that've materialized are bureaucrats or village elders or whatever they call themselves. So this means the mucketies either are hiding in the bushes, scared shitless that we're somehow tied in with the kidnappers, or else they really don't have any government beyond the local yokels and the guys who keep the power and water running.

"That, I think, is impossible. Humans aren't that in love with anarchy.

"But it does give another fact. We've been prodding gently, and nobody, and I mean nobody, down to little kids, is willing to point to somebody and say, 'Yeh, he's the prime minister's bootlicker' or such."

"Nice tight discipline," Garvin offered.

"Or fear, more likely."

"Nobody ought to live that scared," Garvin said.

"No shiteedah," Njangu said. "But there's a lot of us who grow up like that."

"Us?"

"Hell yeh," Njangu said bitterly. "Remember, I didn't know there was anything other than run or get beat on, big dog chews on little dog until I got shoved in the military.

"And ain't that a bastard," he added. "You gotta put on a uniform to find out you've got anything called basic rights? This goddamned cosmos sucks a big fat one.

"Maybe we ought to just go on back home and vegetate, since we've beat the butt of all the local baddies, and let the frigging Universe go to hell in a handbasket."

Garvin just looked at him, and Njangu forced a grin and shrugged.

"Sorry. I've been pissy-headed lately. Oh yeh," Njangu said. "Something else. People've been asking me how much longer we're going to keep playing this world, since we've found out what there is to be found out, and nobody's got any money to make it worthwhile to hang on, and counting the take in rutabagas is making Sopi even balder."

"Another four, five days," Garvin said. "I'm a soft heart, but it's nice to see people come in all hangdog and walk out smiling."

"Yeh," Njangu agreed. "Nice. You ain't got a soft heart, but a soft head."

Mais

The next jump was to a nav point between systems,
the one after that into the Mais system, with two settled planets, each with half a dozen moons, other
worlds far out from the G-type sun listed as "suitable
for mineral exploitation."

Preliminary reconnaissance by a pair of scoutships
produced nothing, either positive or negative, other
than both planets were still populated, and *Big Bertha*
left hyperspace, the nav point, in the gap between inhabited and uninhabited planets.

She closed on the nearest world, and was neatly
mousetrapped by two ships. *Jane's* listed them as
"Langnes-class light cruisers, currently second-line
Confederation fleet service, moderately armed, exten-
sive electronics suites, lightly armored, superior in ma-
neuvering and reliability."

Captain Liskeard looked at a blank screen, listened
again to the unseen voice demanding they maintain
present orbit and stand by for boarding, looked at
Garvin for a response, got none.

"This is the Circus Ship *Big Bertha*," he sent back.
"Intend planetfall on Mais II."

"Make no attempt to land on any planet until you
are clearanced," the voice replied. "And bring your
two survey craft inboard, or they will be fired on."

"Well, hmpty hmpty hmp," Njangu said.

"Sir?" a tech moved a projection into Liskeard's
view. It was of the closest planet and its moons, with
various swirling readouts below each world.

"I think," Liskeard said, "they can hmpty hmp all
they want. Look." His finger reached out to a moon,
through it, then touched another. "Both of these
moonlets are fortified. If the cruisers weren't dogging us,
they could launch, and odds on the missiles would have
enough sophistication to follow us back into N-space and
go bang."

"Mmmh," Njangu said.

"Yeh," Liskeard agreed. "Especially since they didn't think they needed to bother to mention those fortifications. The bastards are cocky." He looked worried. "How are we going to handle this boarding?"

Garvin smiled wryly. "That's one thing we won't have to worry about very much. There's never been a circus that isn't ready for the rozzers to do a shake-down day or night."

"I just wonder what's going to come *after* the inspection," Njangu said. "Oh well."

Garvin motioned the on-watch talker over, with her mike ready. "Put out an all stations that we're being boarded, and no one is to offer any resistance without a signal."

"Hide the women and the good towels," Njangu added. "Here comes trouble."

One cruiser's lock opened, and a small boat shot out, arcing to intersect with *Big Bertha*'s yawning loading bay. The boat didn't enter, but mag-grapneled to the ship's skin, and suited, blaster-armed men floated out, and inside. Their suits were armored, and the helmets blank, with only a pickup instead of a viewport.

The boat unhooked and floated a few meters away from the lock, no doubt with weapons ready.

"Cycle the lock closed, sir?" the watch officer asked.

"Go ahead," Garvin said. "If they don't want us to proceed, they'll shoot you for a warning."

But none of the weapons was lifted as the great lock closed, air pumped back in, and the inner portal opened. The half dozen suited men came into the main cargo area.

Garvin walked forward, flanked by Njangu and Penwyth.

"Welcome to *Big Bertha*," he said. "Inbound to Mais Two."

A voice came from a suit speaker:

"Your planet of origin?"

"Grimaldi."

Silence, then:

"We have no listing for such a world. Your last planetfall?"

"Sabyn."

"Purpose of visit there?"

"To make a credit, do some shows, have some fun," Garvin said. "The same reason we want to land on Mais Two."

"Length of intended visit?"

"Perhaps two local weeks," Garvin said. "Less if we don't draw a crowd."

"Under the Confederation Act three-one-six-one, as proper officials of the Confederation, we are authorized to search your ship for illegal materials and contraband."

"You're Confederation?" Garvin said, covering, thinking these bastards were the raiders, and maybe Njangu had been right, worrying about what would happen after the search.

"We are," the voice said. "Do you have any legal objections to our proposed search?"

"It wouldn't matter if we did," Garvin said, "since you're the one holding the high cards and guns."

The figure turned, spoke to the men behind her, and they began to fan out.

"It might be better if I called certain of my men, and let them escort you around," Garvin said, trying to sound amiable. "*Big Bertha*'s kind of complicated."

The suited figure looked up, around.

"You could be right," the voice said, sounding almost human. "However, I don't think you should attempt any deception."

"What you see is what there is," Garvin said, and opened another channel. "Dill, Montagna, Froude, Lir, report to the hold's main lock area immediately." He went back to the general channel.

"If you and your men want to unsuit, it'll be a lot more comfortable."

There was a pause, then the figure reached up, touched seals around its neck, and lifted the helmet clear. The figure became a woman, close-cropped brown hair, a not unattractive face that was very businesslike.

The other men and women did the same.

"We'll not unsuit completely," she said. "It's safer like that."

"As you wish," Garvin said. "By the way, I'm Garvin Jaansma. Gaffer's my title, if you want one."

"Commander Betna Israfel, Thirty-fourth Division, Eighth Confederation Guard," she said.

Garvin introduced Erik and Njangu, as the summoned men and women of the Legion arrived, then went off with the Mais.

"Would you care to visit our bridge?" he asked.

Israfel considered, then nodded.

"Surely. You don't appear to be anyone with anything to hide, I must say."

"The only secrets we have are those of the midway, those of strange worlds and stranger games and magics," Garvin intoned.

Israfel looked at him closely, decided Garvin was being humorous, granted him a smile. Garvin thought she didn't seem to have much of a sense of humor.

On the bridge, Israfel was offered refreshments, refused them, looked about the large room, its gleaming equipment and neatly dressed watch.

"You keep a very taut ship, sir," she told Garvin.

"Thank you. My parents taught me any fool can be a pig," Garvin said, hoping to be thought a trifle simplistic.

"I had to look up what a circus was, before I came aboard," Israfel said. "Are there many like you?"

"There were many circus ships, even convoys," Garvin said. "But that was before the Confederation, meaning no offense, vanished."

"Frankly, for you, and us as well," Israfel asked.

"But you're Confederation!"

"We are a detachment," she said. "Charged with providing security for the Mais system, no more. As far as what lies beyond the system . . . you know far more than we do, although that's something we of the garrison here don't like to broadcast, although you'd certainly find that out by yourself before long. It doesn't exactly increase the faith the locals have in us."

Garvin chanced a comment, feeling a sudden warmth for these soldiers, no different than the Strike Force, even though they were far closer to the heart of the vanished Empire.

"In the Sabyn system, we were told they'd had raw materials and manufactured goods seized, on a regular basis, by ships claiming to be from the Confederation."

"Yes," Israfel said. "Those pirates have tried three times to attack us. Each time, they've been driven off. But—" she broke off.

She didn't need to finish. Garvin could imagine trying to maintain a highly technological unit in a system without heavy manufacturing.

The Force had been lucky, even though cast to the frontiers, that Cumbre was as developed as it was.

"Do you have any idea where these self-styled Confederation troops are based from?"

Israfel shook her head, looked away, and Garvin realized he'd found out as much as he could from her.

But it was quite enough.

He regretted the week's commitment to playing Mais, because there didn't appear to be that much more to learn.

Mais/Mais II

Six days later, his opinion was confirmed. No one knew where these false Confederation units were

from, only that they'd come three times, and been
driven off, with fairly heavy casualties. The wounded
and dead had been replaced by local recruits from
Mais I and II, and a factory had been tooled up to
replace the expended missiles. But the ships that had
been lost were irreplaceable.

That was also why they'd only made one attempt
to reach Centrum. The cruiser and its two destroyer
escorts had simply vanished, and the Guard was reluctant to waste any more starships.

"Were we not required to keep the law in spirit as
well as letter," Commander Israfel told Penwyth, "I'd
surely like to commandeer those patrol boats and light
survey ships you have."

"It would take a while to learn to pilot an *aksai*,"
Penwyth said truthfully. "But we appreciate your
honesty."

Erik and Israfel had become a twosome, although
Penwyth swore that nothing more than light handhold-
ing was going on.

The circus was a raving success, and the Confederation garrison had Garvin, Njangu, and other officers
to dinner twice. Garvin made a point of inviting Dill,
not so much to awe the soldiers as to his strength, but
because he'd bring Kekri along.

The younger male, and a couple of the female, officers fell in love with her, to Garvin's amusement. But
she clung to Dill as she had ever since the ship had
left Cayle IV. He also brought along some of the
showgirls and a scattering of performers.

Garvin was mightily impressed with the detachment's
commander. She kept rigid discipline in the unit, and
never let on to anyone that she was the only authority
known. Rather, her orders were always signed FOR THE
CONFEDERATION, and her dealings with the civilians
were as if she was reporting daily to Centrum, with the
stern Parliament vetting her every decision.

Garvin almost took notes, thinking that one of these
years he might be in the same place himself, and need

to know how to handle matters. But after due consideration, he decided he didn't have the woman's basic moral courage, and if he ever got stuck in a situation like this, the first thing he'd do would be to tuck for the tall timber.

One nice thing that happened to Garvin—Darod Montagna had been closely watching the relationship, if that was what it was, between Kekri Katun and Ben Dill. One night she tapped at Garvin's compartment, asked if he was interested in company. Mightily thrilled, he invited her in, and she stayed the night. Garvin figured, or hoped, anyway, he was forgiven for his indiscretion.

A bit cheered after the week on Mais that at least they weren't the only fools in the universe interested in keeping the Confederation alive, they made another jump.

This one was into Paradise.

Or so it appeared for a time.

CHAPTER
14

Nelumbo II was a beautiful planet, with small, mountained continents, mostly in the higher and lower temperate zones.

There was no information available whether or nor Nelumbo had been colonized, yet the first *aksai* in-system picked up radiation on the standard bands of a populated planet.

The recon sweep gave no reason for alarm, and so *Big Bertha* closed for a landing.

Garvin was beginning to enjoy the landing control dialogue: reporting presence of *Big Bertha,* then a few moments of rather stunned silence while someone found out what the blazes a circus ship might be. Then a frenzy.

They were given landing clearance, and, as usual, settled down on the outskirts of the planet's capital. This was a smallish city, built on the hills of a narrow peninsula, extending from a forested continent.

The promotional sweeps reported there didn't seem to be any slums in the city, only light industrial areas, and most of the housing looked palatial, great estates carefully built to give maximum privacy.

A crowd had assembled by the time Garvin ordered *Big Bertha*'s ramp dropped.

"Nice-lookin' folks," Sopi Midt observed, rubbing his hands together in anticipation. "Healthy sorts, look to be the type with credits.

"Heh," he added, possibly inadvertently.

Midt was right—the people were nice-looking, of many colors, and well dressed. The lifters they arrived in were all of ten- to twenty-year-old Confederation design, and none was ramshackle.

Here and there Njangu spotted light blue uniformed men and women, but only a scattering.

Again, Garvin ordered the show out under canvas, and Fleam's roustabouts set to work.

By now, the troupe had fallen into its routine, the acts moving smoothly into the three rings, doing their acts, then off, and the performers helping other acts if they had time and no animals to feed.

Here they had their first real fright: a child, only three, wandered away from his mother. The hue and cry went out, and they finally found the boy. He'd managed to open the cage of Muldoon, the killer black leopard, and was sitting just inside, watching Muldoon watch him.

Sir Douglas went in before anyone had time to decide if Muldoon was being friendly, or if he was calculating how many mouthfuls the boy would provide.

Everyone involved got an enormous ass-chewing from Jaansma, and Njangu was ordered to put two of his security thugs on safety patrol, making sure nothing like that would ever, could ever, happen again.

But that was the only problem.

Sort of.

Njangu found out why Nelumbo wasn't in any of the data banks. Before the Collapse, it had been the chosen vacation home for the Confederation higher-ups, which was why the mansions, why the ecological sensitivity, why the carefully scattered population. Of course Confederation officials wouldn't particularly care to let the outside world know where their nearest and dearest could be found.

When the Confederation collapsed, it left more than two million vacationing men, women, and children abandoned on Nelumbo, plus the planet's necessary

technicians and workers, and, of course, the families'
blue-uniformed security teams.

Some of the people mourned their missing, but
more began new lives. Women outnumbered the men
about six to four.

"An easy damned life," Garvin said. "Not enough
people to have screwed the world up, and lots of
money so almost everything's automated."

"Yeh," Njangu said. "Heaven itself."

"What's the matter with that?" Garvin said. "Isn't
there someplace that's got to be perfect?"

"Probably," Yoshitaro agreed. "But I'll give you
odds that we'll never be the bastards to run across it."

The show went on for a week. Garvin made no signs
of wanting to make the next jump toward Centrum,
but spent his time in his office, working up new routines, or exploring the nearby city.

Njangu thought Garvin was maybe running some
kind of investigation he wasn't ready to talk about,
also thought Jaansma was being more than somewhat
of a flake.

Garvin stood outside *Big Bertha,* listening to the
rope caller as the crew guyed out the big tent, taking
up the slack in the canvas:

"Speak your latin, speak it now."

The ten men and women pulling on the rope
chanted: "Ah, heebie, hebby, hobby, hole, golong"
once, then again in unison, then the crew moved to
the next guyline.

He smelled the evening air, and the wonderful
scents from the pop-up buildings around the big tent:
lion piss, manure, cooking steak from the dukey; other
smells from the midway: corn popping, vehatna coming off the grill, real sawdust.

He dreamed of this life being all time, not a moment
away from the fine art of killing people, seeing strange
constellations overhead he couldn't identify. He
thought of naming them as the circus roamed the gal-

axy—"The Big Tent," "Horsedancer," "Strongman," which brought him abruptly back to something resembling reality as the idea came of Ben Dill actually having stars named after him.

Fleam, boss canvas man, the unpromotable combat thug and knot expert, saw the first mote.

He was steering a small lifter, a gilly wagon loaded with freshly painted splashboards down the midway, and he moved aside for a young, but very well-dressed mother, her twin girls about twelve, and two of the blue-clad bodyguards.

For some unknown reason, he looked back, and saw one of the bodyguards slide his hand down into the waistband of one little girl's shorts caressingly. The girl's shoulders twitched, but she didn't pull away or say anything.

He gaped, then wider as the mother turned, obviously saw what the guard was doing, and quickly looked away.

Fleam, whose only soft spot might have been for little girls, felt his stomach roil, wondered if he should tell anybody about this, decided maybe it was none of his, or anybody else with the circus's business, then thought Njangu might find it interesting.

"Sometimes," Garvin said, staring out at the lights over the ocean, "sometimes, Njangu my friend, when we find a place like this, I really want to tell everybody to shove it.

"Sideways."

"Which would accomplish what?" Njangu asked.

They sat, both a little drunk, on the balcony of a mansion they'd been invited to after a performance, a half-empty bottle of extraordinary brandy between them.

"Just going on," Garvin said dreamily. "We've got the circus going strong, and we could go until we die of old age, ducking baddies and playing places like this."

"You don't think we'd hear from Froude, or Dill, or, God with a wooden leg forbid, Monique Lir?" Njangu asked. "She's got a damned strong sense of duty and might want us to get our asses back in tune with the mission."

Garvin muttered, drank brandy.

"Still," he said. "I remember, when we first joined up, the whole idea was to stick with the uniform bit until we got a good running shot at freedom and then the Confederation, the Force, and working for somebody else could pack their ass with salt and piddle up a rope.

"Now we've got it, and what're we going to do?"

"Go on to Centrum and get our asses shot off, because we are gods-fearing patriotic morons," Njangu said.

"Yeh. I suppose so," Garvin said heavily. "But still, be thinking about living on a world like this . . . worlds like this.

"And how we could sweet-talk Lir into deserting."

Darod saw the second sign. She was outside, after a show, cooling off, and saw a rather luxurious lim ground, and a pair of women start to get in, assisted by their blue-clad driver.

One said something to him, and Darod saw him frown. The second woman said something else. Darod couldn't tell what it was, but her voice was angry.

The driver backhanded the second woman, pushed both of them into the lim, slammed the door down. He started toward the driver's compartment, saw Montagna watching, and hard-eyed her.

Montagna, feeling the adrenaline rise, stepped toward him, automatically in a combat stance.

The driver hesitated, got in the lim, and took off.

Darod thought about what she'd seen, decided she'd tell it to Garvin. Garvin also found the behavior of the security man more than slightly odd, passed the word to Yoshitaro.

"We're certainly delighted to have you people visit us," the man who'd introduced himself to Njangu as Chauda said. He was middle-aged, hard-faced, and wore light blue, but with golden emblems on his epaulettes. Njangu had spotted him as a top cop even before Chauda said he was the head of Nelumbo's security.

"Thank you," Njangu said, wondering why he still felt a little nervous around a policeman, any policeman.

"It's a bit of a pity that you couldn't be persuaded to stay on for, oh, an E-year or thereabouts," Chauda said.

"I think you'd get bored with us before then, and we'd be losing credits."

"Maybe, or maybe not," Chauda said. "One problem we have here is a certain airlessness. You've given us fresh air."

"People lived for a lot of centuries on just one world," Yoshitaro said. "They seemed to get along all right."

"Did they? I remember reading about things like wars, riots, civil uprisings, and such," Chauda said. "But even so, that was in the days when they didn't know there was anything different.

"Show the flock a nice, new valley, let 'em feed and water in it, then tell them they can't go back there anymore . . ." Chauda shook his head. "That might cause problems."

"I still don't see how us staying a year would do any good, and, by the way, I haven't noticed space travel seeming to have cut down the amount of head-banging that goes on."

"Well," Chauda said, "first, you've got a lot of talents in your circus that could train interested people to perform after you've gone on. For pay, I mean.

Then, since you're experienced voyagers, we could possibly hire you to visit other worlds, and perhaps bring back other talents to keep us entertained."

"Interesting idea," Njangu said. "I'll talk to the gaffer about it. If we were interested, what sort of officials would we be talking to? We've had some of your politicians come to the circus, but we haven't really made friends with them."

"Don't worry about it," Chauda said easily. "I can handle everything on our end. There wouldn't be any problems."

That, too, was reported to Garvin.

Emton's house cats were the great hit on Nelumbo. They now had a whole new bag of tricks, from rolling balls while standing atop them, to doing a wire act (a meter above the ground, wearing specially sewn slippers), to letting birds land on their backs and preen.

Garvin had asked Emton about that one, and he said it'd only taken two or three brace of birds for the cats to learn what was and wasn't dinner.

The big cats had their own fans—there was always a knot of the security men around their cages, quietly admiring.

Sir Douglas complained quietly to Garvin that he really didn't like rozzers hanging about. "Their faces, gaffer, are too much like my cats when they feed.

"No, I insult my animals. There is greater intelligence on Muldoon's face when he eats than on theirs at any time at all."

Alikhan saw the next sign. He was out with an *aksai,* flying along the coast, when, about two kilometers ahead, he saw moving dots along the cliffs. For some reason, he climbed, and put a screen on them.

The dots were a dozen or so men, light chains around their waists. In front and behind were four blue-clad guards, carrying blasters.

He banked back to sea, cutting his drive, not wanting to be heard or seen.

This, too, was reported to Garvin.

"Perhaps," Sunya Thanon said, most sadly, "we have been fooling ourselves all these years, and there is no such place as Coando, and we, and our families before us, have created this lie so we do not give up hope, surrounded by evil and blood."

"No," Phraphas Phanon said, putting his arms around Thanon. "It is out there. We just have to keep seeking."

"Are you sure?"

"I am very sure," Phanon said, hiding his own doubts.

Njangu walked up beside the man in coveralls, who had been busily running a small street sweeper, pretending not to notice Yoshitaro's obviously foreign clothes.

"Good evening, sir," the man said tonelessly. "Might I offer you some assistance if you've lost your way?"

"Matter of fact, you can. I'd like to have a chat with you, somewhere people in blue might not see."

Njangu showed him a bill. The man pretended he didn't see it. Yoshitaro added a bill, then another, then a fourth.

"The fifth note got him," Njangu said. "I figured, go to the bottom rung with money, and you'll get somebody who won't mind talking. People at the top, people at the bottom have a lot in common—things are either so good or so bad they can afford a little honesty.

"This guy laid it out. He used to be a univee instructor. Then the collapse came, and things were a little rocky for a while. I'll write up a full report, but I thought you might want to know a little, right now, about your frigging Paradise.

"There were some riots, some people going crazy, and the security apparat took charge. This guy, Chauda, who's been chewing on my earlobe, seems to be the muckety.

"The deal was real simple, and never talked about. Things would be put back the way they were before the Confederation vanished, the wives and kiddies and such could pretend it was business as usual, and everything would be perfect.

"All they had to do was do whatever the boys in blue wanted. And I mean whatever.

"I guess Chauda's smooth enough so he doesn't let things get too far out of hand—if you're one of his goons, and want somebody, you can have them. But only for a while.

"The people go along with the program 'cause they know the exploitation . . . or at least the heel they're under at the moment . . . won't last forever, and the thugs like it, because they get variety with their villainy.

"Disagree, think maybe you'd just as soon somebody not grab your house or your wife or your son or daughter like Fleam saw, and they bust your ass down to streetsweeper or put you out in the forests, quote improving the parks end quote, or maybe there's other chain gangs that have other jobs that aren't as pretty.

"Or maybe they just take you out a few kilometers at sea, and invite you overboard for swimming lessons."

Garvin slumped at his desk. "Man, man. And things looked so nice here."

"Don't they mostly everywhere?" Njangu said bitterly. "Nobody likes to look at the crapper direct and have to admit they're living in it.

"But sort of smooth over the surface so the turds

don't float up too close, and maybe spraypaint things purple and use a deodorant . . ."

Yoshitaro let his voice trail off.

"So," Garvin said, "I guess the brightest thing is we fold our tents after the show tonight. I feel like a goddamned fool, and there's nothing but a worn patch in the greenery where we used to be, come sunrise."

"You got a better idea?" Njangu asked. "Sure as hell there's no way we can change this damned world. Even if I heard any whisper of anybody out there in the bushes with a gun trying to change it, we don't have time to hang around to build some kind of revolutionary movement.

"Nope. We just vanish and hope that if there's ever a Confederation again, there'll be paybacks."

CHAPTER
15

N-space

"I've got something interesting, boss," the electronics tech said to his superior.

"Go."

"I was checking the monitors, to make sure we don't have any stray electronics leakage. And I found, just before we made this last jump, a bleat.

"I checked it out, and I can't trace it to any of our gear."

"That's strange."

"Stranger," the technician went on. "I ran a search all the way back, and found that damned bleat again, every time we made a jump after Cayle IV.

"We get it just as we jump, and also when we come out of N-space.

"I've spent most of two shifts trying to track it down, with zero-zed results."

"I don't like this," the officer said. "I think I better make a report. And you put a bug on that frequency, and try to record the next transmission."

"I've been thinking," Maev Stiofan said.

"Yeh?" Njangu said cautiously.

"About when we get back."

"Yeh?" Even more cautiously advanced.

"About all these screwed worlds we've been on . . . not to mention Cumbre and where we both came from. Howcum?"

"Uh . . . people are basically screwed-up?" Njangu offered.

"Sure . . . but that doesn't explain why . . . well, there used to be kinds of government that seemed to work. Or, anyway, that's what the disks say."

"And of course, nobody'd ever lie to somebody as cute as you," Njangu said.

"Come on!" Maev said. "They can't lie like they were counting frigging cadence!"

" 'At's true."

"So then comes this thing called the Confederation, and everybody sort of joins up, or gets joined up, and things hammer on for a thousand years or so."

"More like so. A lot more so, in fact."

"Then the Confederation gets invisible, and what we get are all these goat-screwed people, running amok in all directions, nobody seeming to have much of a government that works except maybe Grimaldi, and they don't seem to have much of anything, so that doesn't count."

" 'Kay, I'm tracking," Njangu said. "But I don't see your point."

"When we get back, assuming we survive Centrum and all," Maev said patiently, "then we grab all the guns and start trying to put things back together, right?"

"That's our hee-roic intent."

"Maybe somebody ought to be looking at what kind of government comes back?"

"Not us," Njangu said hastily. "Soldiers make crappy governors. Everybody knows that."

"But somebody's got to start thinking about what comes next," Maev said stubbornly. "Maybe by studying all the ways we've screwed ourselves might give somebody some ideas."

"Like you?"

"Why not me?"

Njangu wanted to bleat out the reasons, then caught himself. Neither one of them had made any commitment beyond the moment, and had no claims on the other's future.

CHAPTER
16

Garvin glared at the battleship hanging not five kilometers distant on a *Jane's* screen. He tried to ignore the data scrolling past on how modern and heavily armed and state-of-the-Confederation it had been eight years ago, the most recent edition of *Jane's* the Legion had.

The battleship didn't get any smaller, nor did its two sisters flanking *Big Bertha*. Garvin might have convinced himself that the circus ship was huge, but these three warships dwarfed it, twice as long and half again as fat, but lethally curved instead of just obese.

They were well and truly trapped, four jumps from Centrum by these three ships and the swarm of accompanying escorts. Alikhan had entered this system, reported no ships within range of his detectors, and that four of the system's ten planets, as their data said, were still inhabited.

Big Bertha had left N-space, and, seconds later, the warships had jumped it. Either the circus had gotten careless, or these warships had sensors better than anything aboard *Big Bertha* and its smaller craft.

"I have a com on the Confederation standard watch freq, sir," the watch radio officer reported.

"Plug it through," Liskeard ordered.

"Unknown ship, unknown ship, this is the Confederation Protectorate Battlefleet Kin. Respond immediately or be destroyed."

"This is the Circus Ship *Big Bertha*, inbound for Desman II, purpose, entertainment."

"This is Kin," the response came. "Correct your records. The Desman system is now the Mohi system. You will be escorted to landing, and then you will be searched and determination will be made of your fate. Make no resistance, or—"

Njangu finished the phrase. "Or you will be destroyed. Boss, I think we may have found the raiders."

"Confederation Protectorate, eh?" Garvin said. "Now I *really* wish we had a diplomat on board."

Liskeard requested an orbital approach, for economic reasons, actually to give observers a chance to see as much of Mohi II as they could. The answer came back:

"Refused. Make direct approach to spaceport. Or you will be destroyed."

"Varied in their approach to problems, aren't they?" Njangu asked.

"At least they don't seem to be taking us seriously," Garvin said. "They've only peeled off one battlewagon and half a dozen escorts to get us safely to ground, deadly rep-tiles that we are."

Njangu called the watch officer over: "I want every eyeball on every scope we've got as we come in, to give me some idea of how deep the shit is gonna be, since we ain't gonna get the pleasure of peering about as we low'n'slow it down."

The news was not good—Desman II, now Mohi II, was a garrison world. Huge landing fields, most freshly built, dotted the landscape. Nearby were barracks complexes and factories.

"I suppose they're worried about trouble," Dill said.

"Getting into, or out of?" Boursier asked.

Dill pointed to the screen showing the enormous battleship hovering above them as they made their final approach, didn't need to answer the question.

*   *   *

Lifters with chainguns in open mounts surrounded *Big Bertha* as its drive shut down, and troops doubled toward the ship, took positions around it.

"Damn, but we're dangerous," Ben Dill said.

"Now all we have to do is convince 'em we're little pink pussycats," Monique Lir said with a tight smile. "Then, when they relax, we'll kill 'em all."

Big Bertha was searched, very efficiently, in teams of five, taking more than a ship day and a half. As before, Garvin and his officers "helped," ensuring that no one found anything, at least anything important in the way of weaponry. These men and women of the Protectorate were realists, recognized the need for some weapons in these times, which simplified what had to be hidden.

One officer stopped, looking in some dismay at Alikhan, who was sprawled on a bulkhead, under which were some of the Legion's crew-served heavy weapons. She fingered her blaster.

"Is that creature dangerous? Should it not be caged?"

"It is of no real danger," Garvin said. "In so long as its handlers are careful."

"If it were mine," the officer said, "I would have it penned up."

Garvin smiled, and the search went on. Alikhan glowered after the party, ears cocked in mild anger.

"Handlers indeed," he growled to himself. "Little do these humans realize who is the handler and who the handled."

The soldier peered around the bridge.

"Everything works," he said.

"Of course everything works," Froude said mildly. "If it didn't, it would have no place." Then what the man had said stopped him.

"When something breaks aboard one of your ships, what do you do?"

"We replace it, of course, with a new unit from the Confederation days."

"But if you don't have a replacement?"

"Then we rely on other, redundant systems, and hope there are still sealed units in the warehouses back at our base to install when we return."

"But you cannot fix what is broken?"

The soldier looked as if he thought he'd said too much, clamped his lips shut, went on.

Muldoon lay, very much at ease, in his cage, purring loudly.

The search team nervously admired his sleekness, passed on.

Muldoon stared after them, still purring. His claws were working rhythmically in and out of the matting on his cage's floor.

"We have found your ship to be free of forbidden materials and contraband," the young officer welcomed. "Remain in your ship until you are advised what stages we intend next for you."

A half day later, the summons came: The commander of this circus ship, together with his high-ranking officers, and representatives of this so-called circus, were to present themselves to the *Kuril*'s presence on the next E-day. Transport would be provided.

Garvin picked his team carefully: he and Njangu of course; Alikhan, who could wear his combat harness carrying a Musth devourer-weapon and wasp grenades that wouldn't be recognized for what they were; Dr. Froude in his clown suit; Sir Douglas and a completely tame and unchained cheetah; Monique Lir; and Ben Dill for his ostentatious muscles and the hope he wouldn't have to use them.

Kekri Katun pouted to Ben that she hadn't been chosen. "I would've thought Garvin would have taken at least one of the showgirls to, well, show off. And I certainly do that well, and tumble, and things like that."

"Probably exactly why he didn't pick you," Ben said. "Supposing this *Kuril* took a fancy to you?"

"Oh. I guess . . ." Kekri's voice trailed off. "Then what about Monique Lir? She's awful pretty."

Ben thought of explaining just how lethal a package Monique was, thought better of it.

"Dunno," he said. "Which is why I ain't the gaffer."

He still was having trouble calling Garvin anything other than "boss" at best and "*giptel*-brained asshole" or "my rotten-crotch former gunner" at worst.

Froude looked about as the troupe shambled up the steps between rows of soldiers at rigid attention, blasters at the salute. Behind them were the military lifters that had brought them into this city from *Big Bertha*.

"I suppose this says everything about the Protectorate," he whispered to Njangu.

"Maybe. But think good thoughts."

The enormous building, stone, columned, in the style of an ancient temple, had been, according to an only half-obliterated sign: THE EISBERG CENTER OF MODERN ART.

"Wonder what they did with the paintings?" Ben Dill said.

"Probably used 'em for bumfodder," Monique replied.

The officer leading them into the *Kuril*'s presence turned back and scowled. Evidently the troupe was not showing sufficient respect.

At least, Njangu thought, *Kuril* Jagasti looked like a proper dictator, just as Garvin looked the proper leader. After the late, unmourned Protector of Larix/Kura, Alena Redruth, who had resembled a medium-level bureaucrat rather than a ruler, he was ready for a goon who looked his part.

Jagasti was tall, lean, with a scarred neck and a

beaked nose, his graying hair worn straight and long.
He had the hard, predator's stare of an Earth eagle
Njangu had seen in a holo. Or else he badly needed
vision correction.

His throne was in the biggest room in the former
museum, and was skillfully made of polished steel,
weld beads deliberately not ground down, and dark
leathers.

His entourage dripped weaponry from many eras,
from contemporary blasters to ugly-looking fighting
knives and close-combat tools.

Jagasti took his time looking over the troupe, then,
without greeting them, asked their business. He
looked puzzled at the reply.

"Entertainment? I am not sure I know what that is,
other than seeing the destruction of a foe, the pain of
an enemy, the delight in hearing his cities burn, his
starships explode, his women scream, his warriors
moan."

Garvin nodded to Sir Douglas, who tossed a ball to
his cheetah. Froude instantly started contesting the cat
for the ball, mimicking the cheetah's motions.

Jagasti watched, stony-faced.

Garvin motioned to Ben Dill, who took a stance,
and Monique Lir struck off from him, spun high in
the air in a triple somersault, landed on her feet.

"Ah," Jagasti grunted. "You mean tricks."

"I mean tricks such as the galaxy has never seen
before," Garvin said. "With real Earth horses, elephants, fearsome beasts, strange aliens, men and
women flying high above your head, games of chance
and skill, clowns to make you helpless with—"

"Enough!" Jagasti snapped. "I am not a prospective
purchaser of your circus."

Njangu was thinking that Jagasti might be the very
model of a major waste-layer, but his navigation
bridge might not be in that close a communication
with his stardrive.

A man, heavily bearded, stepped out of the throng.

"I am hardly superstitious, as you know, *Kuril,*" he said. "Might not the arrival of these strangers be a sign, be something we can use to send around to our various troop encampments to lift their morale?"

"Their morale will be raised sufficiently by the sight of my brother lying dead in the dust," Jagasti said, but he didn't sound that certain.

"A better idea," another warrior said, a man in his forties, hard body just starting to paunch out. "We should take what we will from these people, for surely they are not strong.

"Their men could become laborers, their beasts either slaughtered if they prove dangerous or caged for our education, and their women . . ." He let his voice trail off, staring at Lir.

"That could be an option," Jagasti agreed.

Garvin held back anger. "I would think that anyone who claims to be the Protectorate of the Confederation would welcome innocent wanderers, especially those who have vowed, as we have, to do all in our power to bring the return of order and law."

"The Confederation will return," Jagasti agreed, "as my late father swore."

Interestingly, at the mention of Jagasti's father, everyone in the room bowed their heads for an instant. Garvin hastily followed suit, as did the others, except for Alikhan, who kept cold, reddening eyes locked on Jagasti.

"It will return," Jagasti repeated. "On my terms. My brother and I have sworn the same oath as my father, and were it not for certain . . . unforeseen developments of late, we would surely be making plans for our conquest of Centrum."

Garvin glanced about to see if anyone preened at the word "brother," saw a thin, intense man, about ten years younger than Jagasti, purse his lips and nod hurriedly. Garvin noticed the man's eyes remained on his brother, his expression unreadable.

Njangu noted the look as well, filed it as possibly interesting.

"Of course this will happen," the heavyset man said. "No one doubts that, just as we don't doubt your traitor of a brother will be destroyed soon enough.

"But that doesn't answer the question of these intruders. We . . . all of us . . . believe that from power all else falls.

"I, for instance, am interested in this woman trickster. She, no doubt, with her muscles, could provide me with interesting evenings, and I don't doubt there are others like her in this so-called circus."

He smiled unpleasantly, started toward Monique Lir.

Garvin stepped between them, and there was a blaster in the man's hand.

"Move aside," the man ordered.

Garvin looked at the throne.

"Do you allow this mistreatment to your guests, Jagasti?"

"I have not yet determined if you are my guests," Jagasti answered. "Or my prisoners. But I would suggest you obey Toba. He has a very short temper, and has killed more than his share."

Garvin hesitated, then obeyed.

"My sympathies, sir," he murmured.

Toba, grinning, came forward, reached out with his free hand to tweak one of Lir's nipples.

Flat-footed, Lir kicked, and the pistol spun up and out of Toba's grip. Before he could react, Lir's foot was back on the ground, and she spun, back-kicked with her other foot into Toba's face. He screeched in agony, staggered back, fell.

Lir was back in a stance as Toba sat up. He lifted a hand to his mouth, saw the gouting blood, spat teeth, sighed, and fell back, unconscious.

Alikhan's paw was on a wasp-grenade, ready to claw it into life and pitch it into Jagasti's lap, where the insectlike killers would come alive and deal the man a terrible death. Dill stepped wide, to give himself fighting room.

Njangu decided there didn't seem to be any other options other than running, wasn't up for it, and got ready to die.

To everyone in the troupe's surprise, Jagasti, after recovering from his astonishment, roared in laughter.

"Good! That was very good! Toba has always thought he could do anything he wished. I now rename him Gummy, and welcome you strangers as guests, for there is clearly more to you than is visible, and I suspect at least some of you of being warriors, not merely the despised servants we batten on.

"Perhaps your shows will, indeed, build the morale of my fighters."

CHAPTER
17

"Uh, boss?"

"What's the problem, Ben?" Garvin asked.

"Kekri and I . . . actually, just Kekri . . . we need to have a talk with you."

"Sure," Garvin said.

"Private? And it'll take a while?"

"Come on in," Garvin said, leading the two into his office. He noticed Kekri was carrying a small case.

"So what's the problem?" he said after the door closed.

"I'm . . . I'm a spy!" Kekri said, and burst into tears.

"Well I shall be dipped," Njangu said. "Full confession, she's an agent for—"

"Director Fan Bertl, back on Tiborg," Garvin said. "Just like you thought."

"Hmm," Njangu said. "I'd been thinking about her, figuring we'd have to do cleanup before . . . how much longer before that thing Lir and Montagna planted wreaks havoc?"

"*You're* supposed to be the one keeping track of things like that. But I looked it up. About two E-months, which means two and a week here."

"And she's given us everything she's got?"

"She's still being debriefed. But it looks like it."

"What was she looking for?"

"Bertl didn't tell her . . . he just said report anything interesting, particularly about where these people are really coming from, and what their real intentions are.

Guess he didn't trust her all the way, which is the only way to treat HUMINT.

"And there's an interesting little side note. She was supposed to transmit this diary when her little sender got a signal saying somebody was listening.

"Also, Bertl promised that she wasn't on a one-way trip. At a suitable moment, she'd be rescued. I don't know if Bertl was stroking her or not, but she surely believed someone would be there with a rope ladder.

"I don't like that at all," Garvin went on. "Especially since there's no way that I can figure out that Bertl could be tracking us."

"*Damn,*" Njangu muttered. "Wheels within cartwheels. Would've been better if she didn't confess, so we could grab when that transmitter went off . . . if it ever did. Ben Dill went and did too good a job. What the hell good's an agent when she's all the way out of the chill?"

"That's another thing," Garvin said. "He's decided he's in love, and really hopes that neither of us set this whole thing up as any kind of a joke."

"Oh."

"He said he'd be really, really, really assed if we had."

"I don't think I've ever seen Ben more than really, really, assed," Njangu said thoughtfully.

"Me either," Garvin said. "Maybe we ought to send Kekri's whole file to the shredder? Especially the parts that might ah-hem have anything on your thoughts about me and Kekri."

"I'll shred it twice," Njangu said. "Dill scares me snotless.

"But let's keep that nifty little notebook/locator of hers handy. We still might need it someday."

He sat shaking his head.

"*Damn,* but it's sour when a plan goes just the way it's supposed to, and you're still sucking wind."

"Back to our device on Tiborg," Garvin said. "Did we screw up?"

Njangu began to say something, thought about it.

"You want a gut response . . . no. Goddamned politicians and their tradesy-ing power back and forth, and busting it off in people like you and me . . . good to see the whole damned lot of them in a thin spray on the walls."

Garvin started to respond, but Njangu held up his hand.

"That's the gut feeling. But now that we're a bit away, and my head's out of me bung . . . maybe. A very large maybe, starting with the position that people who kill things and break people ought to stay the hell out of politics. Plus the idiots on Tiborg went and got themselves in this shitter, and they should be the ones to dig themselves out.

"We can't go around playing Saint John the Rescuer to everybody."

"But isn't that what we're doing right now with this chasing about after the Confederation?"

"Goddamit, Garvin, don't confuse me any more than I can already confuse myself.

"In answer to your question . . . if I had it to do all over again, back on Delta, I don't think I would've done it. Or, rather, that I encouraged you to do it."

"You think that way bad enough that we should think about going back when we get free of these idiots, and turn off the machine?"

"That'll be a good trick in itself," Njangu said. "Naw. I don't think so. They were all a bunch of shitheels, and deserve a little maiming around the edges.

"Not to mention they'll sure as hell try to blow our ass up around our shoulder blades if we ever get within range of them again.

"Forget it," he said. "We've got enough problems, and that'll sure as hell never rebound back on us, especially now that we've got Kekri and her little direction finder all neutralized."

CHAPTER
18

"Thank you, ladies, for taking the time to listen to this parlari," Njangu said. "Does everyone have a drink or an inhaler?"

Ten of the circus showgirls, carefully selected by Yoshitaro for seeming lack of moral turpitude, were gathered in one of *Big Bertha*'s rec rooms.

"Perhaps you've noticed that the people we're among now are, shall we say, a little more direct than some of the other townies we've appeared before?"

"Damned straight," one of the women said. "I turned my back on two of the bastards last show, and they tried to rip my gown off for a laugh! Damned glad we're playing in the ship instead of under canvas.

"Direct hell," she went on. "Goons and rapists, if they think they can get away with it."

"I think the technical term is 'barbarians,' " another woman said.

Njangu scratched his chin, waited until the laughter stopped.

"What we want, what Gaffer Jaansma wants," he said, "is to play a few dates here and there in this system, then proceed on our course toward Centrum.

"The Protectorate isn't keen on that idea."

"Why not?" a woman asked.

"Because, I suspect, they've got designs on whatever remains of the Confederation themselves."

"And we're a threat?"

Njangu held out his hands.

"It seems so."

"Idiots!" another woman snapped.

"Quite possibly," Njangu said. "Which is where my proposal stands. I'm looking for volunteers who wouldn't mind making friends with some of these Protectorate sorts."

"You mean, officers, high-ranking types?"

"I certainly don't think your average deck ape might be able to talk about things we might be interested in hearing."

One of the women, a Delot Eibar, whom Njangu had pegged as somewhat quicker than others, looked at him skeptically. "You mean pillow talk."

"Not necessarily," Yoshitaro said carefully, feeling the tiny bit he had of what he guessed other people called "morality" squirm. "Just . . . talk."

"But not *not* necessarily, either," Eibar said.

Njangu didn't answer.

"What other kinds of spying are you doing?"

Njangu smiled blandly.

"Oh. I get it. If one of us goes and falls in love, instead of the other way around, she won't have any pillow talk of her own?"

"You are a clever woman," Yoshitaro said.

"Maybe," Eibar said. "If . . . *if* I go for a proposition like that, it would have to be my choice. I don't want to get rammed into the sack with some thug who hasn't taken a bath in a year or so."

"Agreed," Njangu said.

"Now, since this is way outside being 'generally useful,' might I ask what this bit of cherry pie will pay?"

"If any of you agree, you can double your contract price," Njangu said.

There was a murmur from the showgirls. Njangu got up.

"Talk about it with each other. I promise no risk, and if anything seems a little shaky, we'll have you wired, with security backing you, and we'll break anything up that looks like it's getting troublesome."

"Security," a girl murmured. "Like that Ben Dill?"

"I'm sorry," Njangu said. "Ben's a big man, but he's no more than that."

"Yeh," Eibar said skeptically. "Yeh, sure. Not that it matters, since Kekri Katun's got his chastity belt keys.

"At any rate," she went on, "I think I understand what you're looking for very, very well."

"And *I* think," Njangu said, "that scares me a little."

Monique Lir swayed, looked seductive, and beckoned to the sad-faced Froude. He looked down from his perch, swayed, flailed his hands, recovered his balance.

Again, Monique beckoned, and this time, Froude saw a balance pole, which just happened to have a midget at each end. He picked it up, seemingly not noticing the little people, and stepped out onto the wire toward Lir.

He dipped, almost fell, the midgets flailed with him, and the audience bayed amusement.

Monique, as secure on her wire as if she were bolted on, looked down at the packed stands. It was what used to be called a sawdust crowd, she knew, with all the stands full and people sitting on the deck. It'd been that way for seven shows, and she didn't like it any better now than before.

There was nobody in the crowd except men and women, all in uniform. No children, no old people, no civilians at all, not even government officials, since Jagasti believed anyone connected with the Protectorate should be part of the military.

Froude overbalanced, and fell, still holding on to the balance pole. But somehow he didn't come off the wire, but spun through a full circle, still holding the pole and little people, and was back on top again, to thundering applause. Froude looked a bit shaken—this gag, heavy on antigravity devices, even though there was a *ra'felan* catcher hanging overhead, was a little new. This was only the third time they'd done it since Froude had the idea and rehearsed it endlessly, a meter off the deck into a trampoline.

Lir wondered how they'd get through these bastards and on about their business toward Centrum. This circus stuff was interesting, but the thrill was starting to fade.

She really wanted to put her uniform back on, assemble the troops, and go out and beat the butts of some of the yoinks she'd endured over the past months.

Lir was more than willing to start with the morons below who called themselves the Protectorate.

Njangu, Dalet Eibar, and Bayanti, Jagasti's younger brother, sat in a closed skybox, watching the caracoles of the circus below them. Bayanti, Yoshitaro was pleased to note, kept flicking looks at Eibar when he thought Njangu wasn't looking.

"You actually have a life like this?" Bayanti asked. "Just traveling about, doing these shows?"

"It's what we've chosen," Njangu said.

"We like . . . excitement," Dalet put in suggestively.

"These are dangerous times for wanderers without support," Bayanti said.

"Which," Dalet added, "is why we like to get along with everyone." She smiled.

Njangu thought that was about enough, so he triggered a sensor on his belt com. It buzzed, and he answered the false summons to the bridge. He apologized to Bayanti, asked Dalet if she'd mind escorting him about and show him whatever he wanted, left.

He left it to Eibar to explain that she and Njangu weren't companying each other, that she had no one special and, in fact, hoped she'd meet someone to show her about this fascinating system the circus had landed on.

He also made a note to adjust Dalet's contract.

* * *

"You were a soldier, once, I think," Phraphas Phanon asked Alikhan.

The Musth considered, decided there was no harm in speaking the truth. "I was."

"We would like to hire you to teach us something," Phanon said, and Thanon nodded eagerly.

"If I know something of worth, you have but to ask," Alikhan said. "It will help pass the time. I am bored being stared at by these short-haired idiots and thought a horrible monster."

"We want you to teach us how to use weapons."

Alikhan's head darted back and forth, lifted his paws in surprise.

"Why do you wish to learn such?" he asked.

"These are troubled times," Phanon said. "We feel vulnerable, needing to be able to protect our gray friends."

"That is not hard to understand," Alikhan agreed. "But why have you come to me?"

"First," Thanon said, "you are the one we have decided most clearly was, perhaps even is, a soldier, although there are those such as Mr. Yoshitaro or Mr. Dill we suspect of having once had such a trade."

"I didn't know that," Alikhan said. "I thought Ben Dill was too fat to be a soldier." He was proud of himself for making a human joke, couldn't wait to tell this to Dill.

"You see? We are not sure."

"The problem will be," Alikhan said, "the actual firing of the weapons. I assume you do not mean to learn the tools I carry with me on occasion, since I have but two sets of them with me, and they would be very difficult for a human to use.

"I doubt if these Protectors would be impressed should we take some of the ship's blasters outside and start banging away at targets."

"We thought of that. Could you not teach us the working of these weapons, how to load, aim, fire them, and then, at a better time, perhaps we could shoot for real?"

Alikhan thought.

"Yes. Yes, I could do that. And, in return, I would ask a favor?"

"Whatever we have is yours."

"I would like you to introduce me to one of your elephants and perhaps, if he learns I am no threat, to give me a ride?"

Njangu sent out agents, some openly to what remained of the planet's libraries, some more covertly. A bit at a time, cautiously, skeptically, he was building a history of this Protectorate. All data were, of course, categorized in the aeons-old classification:

A: A participant in the reported events.
B: A witness.
C: Accurate source.
D: Not dependable.

To this was added the evaluation of the information:

1: Information verified through two additional B- or C-level sources.
2. Information probably accurate, but no high-level verification.
3. Information not verified, but fairly logical.
4. Rumor.

Muldoon leapt out from his perch on an elephant stand toward the waiting lion, who boomed a roar at him. The leopard tucked, and the lion caught him on his paws, bounced him to a tiger, who risleyed him on to the next, waiting cat, almost throwing him into Sir Douglas, who cracked his whip menacingly, then back to the lion and to rest.

The crowd was silent in awe for an instant, then boomed approval.

Muldoon yawned complacently at the recognition, licked his paw.

"Very damned good," Garvin said. "I like the way that everybody's looking at everybody else's act—"

"You mean stealing," Sir Douglas grinned.

"I never use words like that. Congratulations. You make it look dangerous."

"Around me, there is never danger," Sir Douglas said loftily. Garvin grinned, went back to Ring #1 as the cats were cleared out of the center cage.

"I'll not tell the gaffer your fingers were crossed when you said that about no danger," Darod Montagna said.

"I thank you," Sir Douglas said.

"Maev, if you'll take the door," Njangu said.

She nodded and, pistol half-hidden, stepped out of the small conference room, buried in the middle of *Big Bertha*'s command module.

Inside were the ranking members of the Legion, plus Doctors Froude and Ristori.

"What we're going to get here," Garvin said, "is a short history lesson on who these Protectorate sorts seem to be, which may help us figure out what to do next.

"Since Dr. Froude is probably the best of us at syncretic thinking, I've asked him to do the lecture, which is based on almost all of Froude's, Njangu's, and his staff's digging and delving. Doctor?"

Froude leaned back in his chair and started talking.

About twenty E-years earlier, the Confederation had begun hiring entire population groups, those considered warrior-types, for security, and keeping them as integral units, rather than relying on the more conventional military like the Navy or the Legions.

No one in the audience had heard of this practice having been done before, nor did anyone have any idea why something this primitive and dangerous was begun.

"I wish," Garvin said, "that we had a few of the old soldiers with us. Maybe *Caud* Williams or Rao knew of such units, and why the Confederation chose such a step."

"I'll make a guess," Yoshitaro said. "They got paid in loot and worked cheaper."

There was a murmur of laughter.

"I wasn't being funny," Njangu said, and the laughter stopped.

"Monique," Garvin went on, "you're the closest thing to an old soldier around. Did you ever hear of anything like this?"

"No," Monique said, then stopped, thinking. "Wait a sec. Before I joined up, when I was an opera dancer, somebody said something once about being damned glad that the local soldiers were regulars, since she was getting tired of chasing off shag artists.

"I don't remember her saying any more."

"Interesting," Froude said, and went on.

"These people now calling themselves the Protectorate had been moved closer and closer to Centrum, evidently as problems on the homeworld worsened.

"Then the Confederation fell out of contact with everyone, including these charmers.

"The father of these three brothers who now are running things got the interesting idea that he was strong enough to take Capella and Centrum and then dictate what should come next.

"The Confederation should dissolve Parliament after 'electing' a strong leader to put things back together, allowing no systems to declare independence, and to destroy any worlds attacking Confederation members.

"He seems to have been a very cautious man, for his first steps were away from Centrum, taking control of other systems like Sabyn, turning systems like Mais into puppets, and so on. We are sure they control at least twenty systems now, maybe more.

"The way the Protectorate operates is to skim only

the cream from these systems, leaving enough for the worlds to keep functioning, not hurting them badly enough to tempt them to revolt, and, evidently, instantly coming down with an iron heel on anyone who dissents. I've heard of at least two worlds that didn't listen to reason and got the nuclear treatment.

"I haven't been able to find out just how long Jagasti's father thought it would be before the Protectorate was ready to make a hard move on Centrum, although I did get a couple of hints that recon units were sent out, never to return. They were probably destroyed by whatever war fleets the Confederation still has operational, backed by the mechanical security devices around Centrum."

"Things were going well," he continued. "And then the old man had the lack of grace to die. A surfeit of eels or some such. I couldn't tell, through the holos' purple hosannas at the funeral.

"I don't think any of his sons did the usual junior tyrant act, and slipped a shot of radioactive bilgewater in the old bastard's nightcap, or piss poison in the porches of his ears.

"Regardless, he's dead, and so Jagasti, who has a reputation of being a most noble warrior, although what real war he's fought doesn't get mentioned, takes over as *Kuril*.

"He has nowhere near the ability of his father at keeping all of these thugs somewhat under control, and so the number two son, who evidently fancies himself a Greater Leader, stomped off, with his supporters, and now holds two systems, Degasten and Khon, and keeps saying that he's the rightful *Kuril*."

"What about the third son?" Garvin asked. "He was at the circus the other night."

"I'm developing certain areas of interest with him," Njangu said, trying to sound pompous. "Bayanti is ambitious, but it doesn't seem, so far, that he's thinking about striking out on his own.

"However, I'm thinking of ways of encouraging his ambition."

"That's a very fast précis of this Protectorate," Froude said. "I've got far more details for anyone interested.

"The question now is what do we do? It doesn't seem that the Protectorate, for their own paranoiac reasons, will encourage or even allow us to make the next four jumps to Centrum."

"I get the idea," Njangu put in, "that we're increasingly well thought of by Jagasti and crew. Which is good in one way, but makes it very hard for us to tiptoe out the back door without Jagasti getting a lethal—for us—case of the pouts."

"What we need," Garvin said thoughtfully, "is a way to put some shit in the game, without us getting brownish in the process."

The people in the room looked at each other.

No one's expression suggested she or he had the slightest idea.

Njangu's lips were moving up Maev's inner thigh when he sat bolt upright.

"I'll be a sunnuvabitch!"

"You damned sure are if you don't go back to what you're doing," Maev managed, with a sharp intake of breath.

But Yoshitaro paid no mind, was sitting up, and touching com buttons.

"This," Garvin's voice came, "had better be goddamned important, Njangu. There is a time and a place for everything, especially for using this number." He appeared to be breathing hard.

"Boss," Njangu said proudly, "I have a scheme."

CHAPTER
19

"I propose," Njangu said, "to make the situation worse."

"For whom?" Froude asked, amused. Garvin yawned sleepily, said nothing. The three were gathered in Garvin's cabin office, waiting for a stim.

"Certainly not for us," Yoshitaro said. "At least, I hope not.

"Look at what we've got. Three brothers, barbarians, two of 'em at least not getting along. They're plotting on grabbing all the gold, but, like their father, don't appear quite ready to make the big jump and go after Centrum. I'd guess if this Gegen, who's floated over to Degasten with everyone he can subvert, wouldn't mind at all if Big Brother Jagasti happens to trip and fall on his saber."

"Your points are undebateable," Froude said.

"Therefore, I propose to throw some shit in the game, as they used to say," Njangu said.

"What species of doots?" Garvin broke off as a mess attendant came in with a tray, then, after he'd left, waited for an answer.

"Suspicion will lie on every hand. And foot," Njangu said. "I'm going to convince these three yahoos they're about to get assassinated."

"Good," Garvin said. "Who's going to be the head of the plot?"

"Why, me, of course."

"For all three?"

"Can I juggle, or what?" Njangu said, slurping caff.

*   *   *

Jagasti's idea of fine sport was equipping lifters with probes, and hanging a cloth of a given color from one of them. The others . . . ten to a side, two men to a lifter . . . tried to take the cloth away or protect the flag-carrier until he reached a goal.

As far as Njangu could tell, there weren't any especial rules, except all lifters should withdraw to their end of the field while an ambulance rescued the survivors of a crash.

At least blasters didn't seem to be permitted.

"Interesting sport, *Kuril,*" Yoshitaro said.

"Yes! It is the sport of men. Real men! Supposedly we first played it, riding animals, back on our homeworlds. But now it is much faster," Jagasti said.

"And kills even more of our best fighters," Bayanti said.

"Life is just a waiting for death," Jagasti said impatiently. "Men get weak, become like women, unless they test themselves."

Bayanti was about to say something when two lifters soared high, then dived on the flag-bearer. The first slammed into the flag-carrier, sending it spinning, the flag carried away by the slight breeze. The second lifter speared it, and, at full drive, jinked right, then left, then through the goal.

Jagasti was on his feet, bellowing praise, promising rewards to the scorers and the screen.

Bayanti looked at Njangu strangely, then away.

Jagasti returned to his seat, a metal vee with canvas strung across the metal.

"You, Bayanti," he said. "Go praise those pilots, and give them . . . give them permission to join my First Imperials. This alien has said he wants to discuss something with me that is private."

"And your brother isn't entitled to hear that?"

"I shall decide that," Jagasti said. "Later."

Bayanti got up, then stamped from the prefab enclosure.

"Brothers!" Jagasti said, shaking his head. "Do you have any, Yoshitaro?"

"I wasn't that lucky," Njangu said.

"No, you are the lucky one," Jagasti said. "It must be wonderful, growing up, not having to watch your back or to be able to run without someone trying to trip you.

"Then, when you have finally seen clear to the goal, to have one of your own blood call you a fool, say you are not entitled to what you've won, and declare himself your enemy.

"You are young yet, and do not know what it is to have your own flesh a traitor, betraying what he knows is right."

Njangu waited.

"Never mind that," Jagasti said. "My problems are my problems. Tell me why you wished to see me in secret."

"I want," Njangu said carefully, "to make your problems mine."

"What does that mean?"

"As you've no doubt figured out, Circus Jaansma is a bit more than it appears."

"I knew it! I knew it!" Jagasti exulted. "No one but a fool goes about in bloody times such as these doing no more than swinging through the air and hoping to be rewarded for it.

"Tell me. What else do you do?"

"It depends," Njangu said. "Sometimes we do no more than we offer at first. But sometimes, when we deal with the right kind of people, and the reward is great, we provide certain services."

"You are still being vague."

"I'll be specific, then," Njangu said. "For a fee, which we'll negotiate in advance, I think we can rid you of your brother, Gegen, and leave the way clear for you to continue your conquest of Centrum."

Njangu thought Jagasti's eyes glowed yellow, like

those of Muldoon the leopard before he tried to rip someone's face off.

"This is a *long* damned shot," Darod Montagna complained. "Plus this is one shitty platform to shoot from."

Montagna lay behind a rather skeletal weapon, a still-experimental sniper rifle. It looked like something a child had built from a construction set, all struts and bolts. Rather than use a conventional blaster bolt, the weapon fired an old-fashioned solid projectile.

The caliber was shockingly large—almost 18mm. The projectile was shielded from gravity and winds with a miniscule antigravity dropper in its nose that would keep the round on a flat trajectory for as far as six kilometers.

The magazine held three rounds, the bullet weighing about 170 grams, and traveling at just under 2,000 m/sec. Above the action was an ugly stabilized sight, giving a variable magnification of from 2x to over 200X.

It was deliberately weighted, for stability and to reduce recoil, to over eighteen kilos, and, of course not being shoulder-fireable, had a shocked, rear-pointing bipod up front and an equally angled monopod at the rear. It still would have kicked the marksman's shoulder into next week without two heavy springs in the stock against the action's rear, giving it almost ten centimeters of recoil, like an ancient cannon. Not that the piece could ever be considered fun to fire.

Montagna was right about the firing platform's stability—she lay on the deck of a lifter hovering at about two-thousand meters, the weapon sticking out its lowered rear ramp.

"Stop sniveling, Nimrod," Lir said as she ratcheted rounds half as long as her forearm into the rifle's box magazine. "And you're supposed to miss the bastard, remember?"

"Yeh," Montagna said, squirming. "But I gotta get

at least close enough to make him think he's a target, right?"

Montagna wore a very tight shooter's jacket, and the rifle sling with an automatic tensioner ran from the weapon over her back, down between her legs, and back up to the gun's stock. She couldn't have wiggled if she'd tried.

The lifter swayed in the breeze, and Lir muttered "Stop that," to the autopilot, trying to keep the lifter dead stable, using three points—the nose of *Big Bertha,* a dozen kilometers away, barely visible, Mohi II's second moon overhead, and a distant mountain.

Montagna sighed, peered through her sight at the mansion, five kilometers distant, its stone façade glittering in the rising sun. She found the steps, swept over the waiting lim, moved up to the main entrance. She ran it up to full magnification, decided this was the best it was going to get, backed the wheel down a turn.

Lir had a pair of stabilized glasses on the mansion's entrance as well.

They waited. Montagna felt the dawn breeze, brisk in her nostrils.

"The driver just popped to," Lir warned. "He's got to be on the way."

Montagna saw the door of the mansion come open, breathed in . . . out . . . held it . . . touched the first of the very old-fashioned set triggers. A heavy breath on the second trigger would set the rifle off.

A man . . . clearly Bayanti . . . came into sight, talking animatedly to someone.

Montagna touched the trigger, and the rifle, in spite of its flash/sound suppressor at its muzzle, slammed the Last Trump.

Montagna, ignoring her mind saying, *You flinched, you dumb-ass bitch,* forced the behemoth back on target, waiting to see what happened while the bullet went on its way. By the time she had her sights back, the huge bullet had made a decent-size hole in the

stonework about a meter above Bayanti's head, and
he was flattened on the stairs, his companion bravely
lying atop him, shielding him from another shot from
the assassin.

"I think you signified," Lir said.

"Guess so," Darod said, unstrapping herself, and
rubbing her shoulder. "Damn, but this sumbitch
kicks."

"Decent shot," Lir said. "Now let's go home and
see how much of Njangu's shit this stirred up."

It was considerable.

Jagasti summoned Njangu within the day.

"Someone," he said icily, "tried to kill my young
brother this morning."

Njangu pretended surprise.

"That was all the commotion this morning. We were
turned back from the city twice."

"You were lucky you were not fired on," Jagasti
said. "My men were in shock, and most trigger-happy.
Now, you are officially given the commission to take
care of my brother Gegen, as you said you could do."

"I said I could try to do."

"You *will* do it," Jagasti said. "I do not respect
failure, particularly when someone not familiar to me
volunteers for a task, then does not succeed.

"You can have any resources you need, any amount
of credits.

"Now go, accomplish your mission!"

Degasten/Ogdai

Njangu wished they'd had room in *Big Bertha* to
conceal a small destroyer, or, better, one of the Musth
velv. But covert operations is exactly like hiking—
there's never room enough in the pack for everything
that might be needed. So they took a Nana boat, and
had one of the Protectorate's battleships transport it

two of the three jumps to the Degasten system, where Gegen and his dissidents headquartered.

Njangu took four with him: Ben Dill as pilot, Monique Lir; Alikhan because an alien with big ears might be useful, and Danfin Froude as his "handler."

Ogdai was Degasten's most settled world, and Dill set an open orbit toward the planet as soon as they came out of N-space, after leaving a small object just beyond the nav point.

Unsurprisingly, they'd only been in normal space a ship-hour or two before a pair of heavy cruisers dropped on them, ordered them to stand by for boarding, and performed the usual search. As usual, they missed various items Njangu had well hidden about the ship. He was starting to realize Garvin was right when he said a professional smuggler always stole the march on customs.

Njangu declared his intent as "forward man for a circus." Their ship was escorted to a distant, barren field, and he was told to stand by.

Four officials of increasing rank came, were told of Circus Jaansma and its desire to play Ogdai and Degasten's other worlds, and here was an example of their artists, looked startled when Njangu said the circus was currently appearing on Mohi II. The last, and highest-ranking, was also told that Yoshitaro wished an audience, if that was what it was called, with *Kuril* Gegen.

The officer looked at Njangu haughtily. "The *Kuril* hardly needs to be involved in deciding whether to allow a group of entertainers to appear in our system."

"Of course not," Njangu agreed. "But he could be interested in something involving his brother."

"Jagasti? What? You can tell me. I report to *Kuril* Gegen myself."

Njangu smiled, didn't answer. The officer stared at him for a while, then left.

Two days later, the summons came: Njangu to be ready at dawn the next day, alone.

"I don't suppose," he asked Maev, "if there's any way I can put a secret gun up my wahoonie or something."

"You can shove a frigging howitzer up there for having this idea of yours that surely sounds like you're gonna end up at the bottom of somebody's dungeon," Dill said. "But no. There's never been a weapon made that wouldn't show up on at least a density detector. If you feel murderous, bite him to death."

"Mmmh," Njangu said, and at dawn was pacing back and forth outside the Nana boat's lock.

A rather bulky lifter settled down, with two destroyers floating overhead, and Njangu was ushered aboard and told, unceremoniously, to strip. He pretended indignation, actually felt none, and was escorted into a room by two obvious medical types, and told to wait.

I just hope, he thought, *they aren't into laxatives and vomitoriums. Never can tell when these damned barbarians run out of peep-bo machinery in the walls and start using the good ol' soapy water.*

But evidently the machines still worked, for Yoshitaro was told to get dressed, and his treatment became noticeably less chilly. But Njangu wasn't given access to a compartment with a screen or porthole.

They landed after about two hours estimated flight time, and Yoshitaro was ushered out and greeted by four men in uniform-like gray, and a smiling young man who introduced himself as *Maj* Kars. Njangu noticed the smile never touched the man's eyes, but then, he'd been accused of having the same chill look himself.

"Forgive the care," Kars said, "but it seemed worthwhile, since you said you had something about the Kuril's brother to discuss, and we hardly consider Jagasti someone to take casually."

"No," Njangu said. "He certainly is not."

The landing platform was atop a huge stone fortress that must have been a thousand years old, standing above a large city. The fortification might have been a monument until recently, but had been brought up to contemporary requirements, with little consideration for niceties such as architecture or historical importance. Stone gun turrets had been cut off flat, and various antennae mounted on steel decks. Domes had been rebuilt so missile launchers protruded through them. Here and there along the walls and roofs blisters with chainguns sat like boils, and on the once-gardened grounds were entrenchments and pillboxes.

Kars motioned Njangu to an open door, and the six went into an elevator, which dropped precipitately for quite a long time. Yoshitaro guessed they must've been a hundred feet or more underground before his stomach returned and the elevator stopped, and he was taken down a long corridor.

There were no guards in the corridor, which impressed Njangu that perhaps Gegen kept his security where it was most important—very close at hand.

Kars opened a double door, bowed, and Njangu entered the presence of *Kuril* Gegen of Degasten and Kohn, as he would no doubt style himself.

This Gegen was also a model of a modern barbarian: He was not that tall, but very solidly built, a man who'd seriously lifted weights for a time, but, now in his thirties, had gotten a bit lazy. He had a neatly combed, short beard and close-cropped hair, just beginning to gray.

Unlike Jagasti, he'd learned the virtue of simplicity, and wore plain gray, with a Sam Browne belt with holstered pistol, knife, and pouch. The only concession he made to barbaric excess was the Squad Support Weapon leaning against his chair—the Confederation-issue blaster, this one configured with a long barrel, laser sight, and bipod.

Njangu noted something interesting, and added it to his datafile: there were clear plastic walls between the door and *Kuril* Gegen, no doubt blaster- and grenade-and bulletproof. A very careful man.

Kars made a quiveringly correct salute, and Njangu

touched his forehead with a respectful civilian knuckle.

"I understand you have arrived here with two requests," Gegen said without preamble, in a nice barbarically growly voice.

"You are correct, *Kuril*."

"Do you actually think my brother will give you leave for your . . . circus, it is, correct? . . . to come here and perform?"

"Possibly yes, possibly no."

"And what, exactly, did you wish to see me, personally, about Jagasti?"

"About the possibility of his no longer being your enemy."

Gegen snorted. "Ask the solar wind to stop blowing. Ask men to stop lusting after what their neighbor has. Ask entropy to reverse itself."

"I didn't say anything about *asking* Jagasti," Njangu said.

"Perhaps I misunderstood what you meant by circus," Gegen said. "I looked it up in the encyclopedia, and there was no suggestion of your group having might enough to sway Jagasti in anything."

"All that it takes to sway any man is a tiny bit of steel, correctly applied," Njangu said. "Which your brother well realizes, for he's commissioned me to remove you."

Kars hissed, reached for his gun. Njangu ignored him. Gegen motioned, and Kars froze.

"So you thought you could come to me and get a higher price for Jagasti's death?" Gegen sounded amused.

"Exactly," Njangu said, giving Gegen his best see my steel teeth and realize what a killer I am look.

"He bought your approach without requiring any proof of ability?"

"Why not?" Njangu said. "He has nothing to lose. If I fail, I fail, and his vaults remain full. If I succeed . . ." Njangu held out his hands.

"You mean you asked for no payment in front?"

"I did not."

"Hmmp. You are confident."

"No, sir. Just competent."

Gegen smiled briefly.

"How would you go about such a task?"

Njangu shook his head.

"One of the people in our circus is a magician. He told me once he showed how his tricks were done, after a show, and the people were terribly disillusioned and disappointed."

"What would you require of me?" Gegen said. "I cannot believe that you would sell out my brother without any credits changing hands."

"I am confident in the quality of my work," Njangu said.

"I must think on this." Gegen frowned.

"While you do," Njangu said, "perhaps you would give permission for the handful of troupers I brought with me to show their abilities to however many of your upper echelon you wish."

"No," Gegen said. "I trust you not, Yoshitaro. So I'll hardly play the fool and give your associates a chance to decimate my staff.

"But you may perform if you will. My *junior* officers will be quite amused, I think."

Njangu made a hasty readjustment to his plan, decided it'd still work, got up, bowed.

"You are careful, indeed, *Kuril*."

"That," Gegen said, "is how I survived growing up with a monster for an elder brother."

The show wasn't much, but the small crowd, less than half a hundred, seemed to enjoy it. Njangu decided the most likely crowd on this first night would come from Gegen's bodyguard and headquarters, since those closest to the throne normally scarf up the first goodies.

His plan, therefore, might indeed work.

At least it would put some shit in the system.

Dill did his strongman act, then Monique used him as a sawhorse and thrower for tumbling and acrobatics. Froude brought the dreaded Alikhan from his cage, and had him do some basic tricks.

The soldiers eyed the monster warily, and the Musth did his best to appear completely crazed.

Froude bashed him back into his cage, and used Njangu as a straight man for some card tricks and simple magic.

Evidently prestidigitators weren't common with these people, for the officers were utterly enthralled.

The four aliens, less, of course, the monster, were in sight the entire evening.

Alikhan went out the back of his cage, using the hinged secret door, took a small parcel from its hiding place near the Nana boat's emergency lock, barely crowded through that lock into the open air. The parcel's timer had already been set, and it was mag-clipped to one of the patrol ships that'd brought Gegen's officers.

The show ended, to roars of approval, and the soldiers dispersed.

The timer on the parcel had ticked down fifteen minutes . . .

An hour and three-quarters later, the first timer clicked, and the magnetic timer shut off. The parcel tumbled down through the air, into a dense forest, not far from Gegen's great fortress.

"It is working," Alikhan reported from a control panel on the Nana boat. It was indeed, the pieces of the parcel breaking away, and thin metal legs unfolding. At the top of the tripod was a long tube, which glowed, and started emitting various radiations on various wave bands.

"Our package is on its way," Dill said, noting a flashing readout on his heads up display.

Just beyond the nav point the boat had used to enter the Degasten system, the first package Njangu had left came alive. It was a Shrike missile, given an auxiliary fuel tank, set to home initially on the drive of the Nana boat.

"Now, let's get our target rearranged," Njangu said. "Makes me nervous that sucker's homing on my roof."

Froude tapped fingernails against his teeth. "Let us see . . . assuming our homer came off the Protectorate boat when it should . . . that would put it down about here," he said, looking at a screen. "Gegen's headquarters are over here . . . so I'll target the Shrike . . . here. Close enough to wake the cooks up early."

"Less talk, more setting," Monique urged. "I'm with Njangu, and don't appreciate incoming."

"A touch . . . a slide . . . another touch . . . and there you have it, m'lady," Froude bowed. "It should wander in-atmosphere in a bit."

The Shrike did, searing past the atmospheric patrol craft at near lightspeed, a searing comet in Ogdai's upper atmosphere, then a smashing explosion not three kilometers from Gegen's castle.

At that speed, the missile, even with its small explosive charge, made quite a large, radioactive crater. It woke up the cooks and everyone else around Gegen.

The device on the tripod a couple of kilometers away flashed, then fell over. The destruct charge on the laser sight "unfortunately" didn't completely destroy the device, and its power supply was more than enough to be found by searchers just after dawn, enough to explain that some monster had used the device to guide the Shrike in on its target, but without clues as to who operated the device.

Njangu Yoshitaro stirred in his sleep, perhaps feeling the explosion through the kilometers of rock, and the boat's hull, then, smiling, returning to his dream of money.

"Might I ask, *Kuril,* what has made up your mind so firmly to hire me?" Njangu asked.

"No," Gegen said. "And if I had not had your ship

watched continuously, I might think what I know to be impossible.

"Let us just say you've proven your point, and that my brother is accelerating his plans for my destruction.

"I bid you carry the war home to him, and, when you have succeeded, you can name your fee.

"Within reason, of course."

Njangu and company, still gloating gently at the success of their phony laser-guided missile attack, were picked up, as arranged, by Jagasti's waiting battleship for the jumps back to Mohi II.

Jagasti's lim, with two battleships overhead, lowered toward the desecrated museum. As it passed below a thousand meters, a sensor clicked, and the left half of the lim blew off.

The explosion pinwheeled guards into the air. Jagasti grabbed his seat cushion, jumped clear of the tumbling wreckage, had time to pull the straps on and activate the dropper.

The antigravity mechanism clicked on, and slowed his fall, so his only injury was a broken ankle, making a bad landing on one of the statues he'd had ripped out of the museum.

"Somebody did what?" Njangu asked.

"Went after Jagasti's lim with a bomb," Garvin said. "Dunno how they missed him."

"Son of a bitch," Njangu said slowly.

"I assume that wasn't one of your fiendish thingies, given the sincerity of your response," Jaansma said.

"There's more than me putting shit in the game," Yoshitaro said, then, still reverently:

"Son of a bitch!"

CHAPTER
20

The Civic Palace was packed. In minutes, according to custom, as the year changed, the Constitutionalists would hand over power to Dorn Fili and his Social Democrats.

Fen Bertl sat with the other Directors above the central podium, looking about beatifically.

Things would change a bit now, with the new regime, but they would essentially remain the same, and Tiborg would be run as it always had been: carefully, economically, reasonably, with power remaining in the hands of those who deserved it.

Thank the God he didn't believe in, Bertl thought, the flurry of trouble with Fili's ambition, that damned circus, and the Constitutionalists' intransigence had ended long before the citizens went to the polls and voted as they'd been taught.

He looked down, at the podium packed with the elite of both parties and the outgoing Premier, then at the floor, at the party workers, happily working themselves up. As soon as Fili shook hands with his opponent, and uttered the time-honored words of "I succeed you, sir," they'd go into a mild frenzy and snake-dance around the stadium until dawn, chanting the slogans that, tomorrow morning, would be dust like the campaign itself, and Tiborg would go on as it had for another six years.

Bertl took a moment to consider old business, par-

ticularly that circus, now long gone. He thought of his
spy, that woman, whatever her name was.

He thought, ruefully, that he'd possibly overreacted
with everyone else, first with the locator to follow
them to the Capella system, if that was indeed their
destination, and then adding . . . Kekri, that was her
name.

It would be just as well, he decided, to drop the
whole matter, abandon the tracker probes they'd been
sending out every time they were notified the circus
made another jump, and not waste credits or energy
launching more.

There didn't seem to be much point in dispatching
any expedition after the circus ship.

Capella and Centrum could wait for another few
years, and they could mount their own expedition if
it seemed necessary.

As for the spy . . . Bertl smiled. It was unlikely
she'd come to harm, either remaining with the circus
or wherever they decided to abandon her, if she was
exposed. She was certainly a survivor type. And if
they decided to take extreme measures . . .

No. It didn't matter.

The band built to a crescendo.

The Constitutionalist Premier stood, smiling, and
the smile looked almost real, waiting for Dorn Fili.

Fili, flanked by Sam'l Brek, his aide, came up the
podium steps. Bertl frowned. Brek should not, no matter how important he was to Fili, be sharing this
spotlight.

He could get his rewards, like the rest of the SD,
in tomorrow's clear daylight.

The Premier turned, holding out his hand.

Fili took it.

They waited for a moment, eyes on the cesium clock
high overhead.

"I succeed—"

Lir and Montagna's bomb went off at that moment,
just as it'd been set to do. A hundred kilos of Telex

had been carefully fitted under the podium, formed to look like one of the supports, and color-matched by the two women.

A shaped charge, it blew straight up, and Fili, Brek, and the outgoing Premier became no more than a reddish haze, as did almost all of the parties' hierarchies.

Stonework fragmented, shotgunning up and out, decimating the Directors and then the faithful below.

Bertl was sent tumbling backward, body cushioned by other Directors behind him, crashing through chairs, but landing on his back.

Deafened by the blast, in shock, he pulled himself up to a sitting position, not realizing his right arm was broken in two places, looked in horror at the smiling head of another Director in his lap, pulsing gore.

He knew, he knew who'd done this, who had to have done this, and the hell with forgiveness, the hell with forgetting about those aliens.

Before anything else, Fen Bertl, in the end as human as anyone, now wanted revenge. For himself, for his party, for his fellow Directors, for Tiborg itself!

CHAPTER
21

Mohi/Mohi II

Njangu Yoshitaro was going quietly nuts, especially since he realized he'd caused his own insanity.

Kuril Jagasti had been hounding him near daily since his return from Degasten, almost an E-month earlier. When would he make his move against Gegen? What would it be? He had promised much, and so far had delivered nothing.

Jagasti was right.

Njangu thought at first he'd accomplished a deal with the phony missile attack on Gegen. But all that it seemed to have done, Jagasti's handful of agents on Degasten reported, was drive Gegen into the depths of his fortress, where he did nothing, as far as external events indicated.

Njangu wondered if Gegen had more than one string to his bow, and had been responsible for the sabotage on Jagasti's lim.

Without hinting anything to Njangu?

That would make him a really subtle sort of barbarian, having two sets of killers in the field.

The other likely candidate for the sabotage had to be Jagasti's little brother, Bayanti. And what would have set him off? The phony long-distance shooter, making him believe it was Jagasti behind the trigger men?

But there seemed to be nothing amiss with Bayanti's relationship with Jagasti. At least he said and showed nothing to Delot Eibar, who was definitely earning her bonus.

Besides, what would Jagasti's death get him? Bayanti didn't seem to have much interest in Jagasti's constant military maneuvers and evolutions, or, at any rate, said nothing publicly.

Njangu didn't discard little brother entirely, but thought him not a likely candidate for this completely unknown Master Schemer.

A local lad? Or lass? Somebody who'd decided enough of tyranny, now was the time to make a stand? But the scarce populace Njangu encountered were completely terrorized and worn down, and so he discarded that option.

What made matters a little worse was Jagasti's habit of weekly banquets, like any decent techno-savage, at which he would praise the few who pleased him, and castigate the failures. Those, of course, included Njangu, and it didn't help that Jagasti couldn't be specific about Njangu's failures, but merely rail on at him for being an ignorant, boastful alien, whose only talent appeared to be fripperies and con games.

A couple of Jagasti's goons thought that meant Jagasti was calling Njangu a womanish sort, and decided to lie in wait for him after a banquet.

Yoshitaro handily demolished both of them, not bothering to pull any punches, and, when questioned, shortly admitted to Jagasti he'd killed both of them, and why couldn't the *Kuril* control his own court?

But that got little accomplished, except to raise the general hostility level.

Meantime, the circus continued performing for the soldiery, even more popular than before.

Especially popular was the tiny Jia Yin Fong, whose mother had made a small Protectorate uniform for her. She cannonballed around the top of the tent, from her parents' teeterboard to *ra'felan* high above to Lir, swinging from a trapeze, giggling happily. The soldiers thought she was their mascot.

Njangu gloomed over maps of Gegen's fortress. Dammit, Angara should have let them take a nuke along . . . assuming he had some stashed somewhere in a secret armory. Maybe he could put a force atop Gegen's fortress, slide the nuke into an elevator, send it down, and . . .

Gegen's quarters were probably shielded.

And besides, he didn't have a nuke in *Big Bertha*.

Njangu thought maybe the late Confederation wasn't quite as dumb as he'd thought.

He checked military holidays, thinking that Gegen might come out to review his troops, and he could get Montagna and her hellshooter in range.

But Jagasti's younger brother seemed content to sit far underground and wait.

For what, Njangu knew: the assassination of his brother, Jagasti.

Njangu considered that briefly. It would be fairly easy to smuggle some sort of gun in and give Jagasti a third eye. And then what? He wasn't about to mount a suicide mission.

A bomb suggested itself, but after the incident with the lim, Jagasti had all rooms swept twice before he entered them.

The worst of it was all of these complications were caused by Njangu Yoshitaro being a terribly, terribly clever intelligence operative.

Garvin couldn't decide whether to worry or think the whole mess funny. He compromised by keeping the Legion members ready for any eventuality, and spent many hours plotting with Yoshitaro, trying to figure a way to the next stage.

It came of itself.

Maev, who'd taken to going to the banquets with Njangu more out of pity than thinking he needed bodyguarding or because she'd developed a taste for the overcooked game animals Jagasti served, automatically cased the situation as they went up the aisle to their assigned table. Jagasti's table ran across the large hall,

once the museum cafeteria, and long tables ran down
the room at ninety degrees from it.

"Back door's not locked," she whispered to Njangu
as she'd been trained. "Stairs look open, only one
guard. There's an exit behind Jagasti, as always, but
guarded."

Njangu nodded, not needing to reply. He was wondering what, if anything, he could do to get out from
under the inevitable harassment.

He sat down, and the room filled. He winked at
Delot Eibar as she entered with Bayanti, sat at the
head table.

Jagasti, flanked by four guards, came in almost last,
as was his custom.

He took his place at the head of the table, unbuck-
led his combat harness, and hung it from his chair.
Then he poured a glass of ice water and drained it.

He banged it down, and picked up a pitcher of the
very light, almost nonalcoholic wine he favored, filled
another glass. So far, very much according to custom.

"I greet you, guests, friends, and warriors," he
called. Again by custom, everyone at the table filled
glasses from their own pitchers, held them ready.

"To the Protectorate, and to the Confederation we
all serve, and to the oath that we shall restore it
soon!"

He drank, and so did everyone else.

Next, he would set the glass down, call out introduc-
tions of people who hadn't been there before, sit
down, and wait for the first course.

Instead, Jagasti lowered his glass, and coughed. At
first it was experimentally, then harder and harder.

The glass spun from his fingers, shattered, unnoticed, on the floor.

Njangu noted Jagasti was turning several interesting
shades of purple.

His mouth flapped open, shut as his eyes bulged.

Both hands reached for his throat, and he spun, fell
into the table, knocking it skidding away.

In an instant, Bayanti was kneeling over his brother. He picked him up in his arms, moaning, "Oh, brother. Speak to me. Speak to me. Don't die. Please don't die."

Jagasti made a disgusting noise like he was trying to vomit, convulsed, was still.

The hall was frozen.

Bayanti let his brother's body down, stood, and, from nowhere, a gun was in his hand.

"Guards!" he shouted. "To me!"

Doors banged open and gray-uniformed soldiers ran toward him, blasters ready. The doors were secured, and a grim-faced line of men stood between Bayanti and the banquet guests.

"Murder," Bayanti breathed. "Foul murder. Poison! Someone in the kitchen is an assassin. You! *Maj!* Take a detail to the kitchen, and arrest everyone! Hold them in close arrest, ready for transport for interrogation!"

The officer saluted, and ordered men off. In seconds, from the kitchen, Njangu heard screams, shouts of fear.

"My brother . . . my brother is dead," Bayanti said, brokenly. "Now it is . . . now it must be . . . my task to carry on his duty. I shall try to fulfill his mission, though I am hardly worthy of standing in his boots.

"Yes, Jagasti. I promise, and everyone here promises, we shall restore the Confederation.

"And we shall not wait, we shall not delay, there shall be no more war games or sporting bouts that kill the best of us, but we shall move at once.

"I declare Operation Jagasti. First, my brother will be cremated, as he wished, and his ashes held, to be scattered over Centrum when we seize it.

"But first we must destroy the traitor Gegen, the one who ordered this vile murder.

"I order, within the week, all my armed forces ready to begin an attack on Gegen.

"He shall die for his fratricide, and any of his men who dare stand with him shall do the same.

"Now, I bid all of you, from soldier to statesman, yes . . ." and his eyes caught Njangu's ". . . even those who think they can give no more than a moment's laughter to ease the way of our warriors, now is the time.

"The battle is at hand.

"This is the beginning of the final war to bring back the Confederation, and I can only wish my dear brother Jagasti could be here to cheer and witness it!"

On the way out Maev leaned close to Njangu and lifted her eyebrow.

"Not bad," he said judiciously. "He could have used a little old-fashioned glycerin on his cheeks to make it perfect. Now, as soon as he has the body burned and all the cooks shot after somebody confesses, there'll be nothing to hold back Bayanti the Magnificent!"

A soldier heard the last part, missed the sarcasm, and nodded in approval, rubbing his red eyes, his tear-stained face.

"I suppose," Yoshitaro said, "this was *one* way to get matters up and running.

"I just don't think it's a very good one, and liable to get us all body-sacked."

CHAPTER
22

Bayanti, in the days that followed, put shame to the idea that younger brothers always follow in their elders' shadows. Dalet Eibar found time on her hands to report his doings, for Bayanti was in constant motion, from Protectorate world to world, fleet headquarters to shipping companies.

He had not been speaking emptily when he said everyone would be part of this battle. Training battalions were pronounced ready for battle as they stood, and fed into the battle roster. Merchant ships were given hasty armaments, often no more than a pair of missiles mag-clipped to the ship's hull and a simple computer and launch mechanism hung somewhere on the bridge.

To those who worried about losses in the invasion of Degasten costing them dear when they moved against Centrum, his answer was brief:

"The replacements, though they don't know it, now serve with Gegen. After we destroy my brother, his men and women will be given one chance to redeem themselves for their treason."

Garvin was mildly surprised when Bayanti summoned him, to give him his orders for the invasion.

"I chose to do this personally," he explained, "because you are aliens, and know little of our struggles.

"Also, to be personal," and he colored slightly, looking at Dalet Eibar, who sat primly beside him, "since your circus brought this woman to me, who appears to have luck with her, I feel I owe you a debt.''

"No, *Kuril,*" Garvin said. "You owe me nothing.'' Except to let *Big Bertha* go on her way, and he couldn't quite figure a way to put the request, and then it was too late.

"But I do, and so I will give you an opportunity to serve me, and to be present for my triumph, at which time you and your crew will be rewarded.

"I propose to keep you and your ship in our rear echelon during the landing on Degasten. When a landing zone has been cleared and is secure, we shall send for you.

"I envision your men, women, and animals being of great use in helping our wounded recover their morale before returning to battle, as part of our Retraining Force.''

There was nothing to do but bow, offer profuse thanks, and not look at Eibar, who was trying not to laugh.

There were fifty troops, under the command of a *Tain* Kaidu, assigned to *Big Bertha.* Kaidu, who looked to be a fairly competent soldier, if not a hardened warrior, explained that the soldiers were to ensure there was no hint of mutiny while the circus was with the military. "I know civilians, for some unknown reason, fear and hate serving under us. Think of me, Gaffer Jaansma, as your strong right arm.''

Garvin looked at him carefully, saw no trace of irony.

"Now what?" he asked Njangu.

"Now we deploy our people, to make very close friends with these guards, and wait for the time being right to haul ass away from these lunatics.

"Speaking of very close friends"—he sighed—"and of battlefield conversions, at least we won't have to worry about rescuing our Dalet. I got a message, through the means I set up before we chased her into Bayanti's bedroom.

"I saved and printed it.''

He passed a slip of paper across. All it read was:

He may be a son of a bitch, but right now he's my son of a bitch.

"Oh, grand," Garvin said sarcastically. "No worries about rescuing her now, and of course it'd never cross my mind that Eibar might really, really fall in love and start singing to Bayanti about everything, starting with us and what we're after."

" 'Course not," Njangu said. "That would be a good example of befouling one's own nest, also known as crappin' on the old mess plate, wouldn't it?"

But he held up crossed fingers.

"Twenty-seven seconds to lift, sir," the watch officer told Liskeard.

"Got it . . . somebody want to gimme a ship count of all those zoomies out there?" Liskeard asked.

It was just dusk, and the horizon was lit with ships taking off.

Garvin lost track at eighty-two.

Tain Kaidu, beside him, was starry-eyed, watching the might of the Protectorate move against Degasten.

"Ten seconds to takeoff," the bridge talker said.

Liskeard poised his hand over the sensor.

"Counting . . . four . . . three . . . two . . . one . . . lift!"

Big Bertha shuddered, came free of the ground, hovered tentatively, decided to keep on climbing.

"And so, the bountiful battlefleets of the proud Protectorate coolly climbed toward space, their glorious goal the degenerate dissolutes of the ghastly Gegen," Garvin said.

Liskeard snorted.

"Poetry," Kaidu breathed. "Real poetry. Damn, but I'm glad I lived to see this day."

N-space

"When," Kekri Katun asked Ben Dill, "will we take them?"

"Pardon?"

"Don't play innocent, Benjamin! Remember, I'm the spy that found out everything!"

"Not quite," Ben said. "There are secrets within secrets."

"Like what?"

"Like when we take them," Ben said. "Besides, nobody told me, either. Probably when they least expect it."

"How superbly analytical," Kekri said sarcastically. "I'm going to the gym. The least I can do is be in some kind of shape when we start hitting people."

"We?"

"Who else do I have to side with now that I've snitched off my employer?"

"Strong point," Dill said. "But can't we get in some kind of shape right here?"

"Doing what?"

Ben whispered in her ear, bit it, and Kekri yelped. "Later!"

"Later I might not have the steam for something that exotic," Dill muttered.

"Then that'll be your tough luck, won't it, mister?"

"I have decided," *Tain* Kaidu said, "to require the circus to turn in all firearms. We shall hold them safe until needed."

"Not sure if that's a good idea," Njangu said. "Although, of course, we'll cheerfully obey. But you've got to remember that most of the firearms . . . the handful that we do have . . . are required in the event any of the animals break free."

"If that happens," Kaidu said, "my soldiers will be able to respond within seconds."

"Morning, gentlemen," Dr. Froude said cheerfully as he, Fleam, and two other men wearing coveralls carried toolboxes and piping into the long bay assigned to the Protectorate's security detachment.

"Whazzat you're doing?" a noncom grumbled.

"You've got more people in here than the present conditioner can cycle," Froude said. "We're running an extra line."

"Well . . . that's damned thoughtful," the warrant said.

"Thought the smell was your feet," a soldier called to his mate, and the workmen set to.

By the end of the ship-day, the new line ran down both sides of the compartment, out, and down the corridor and into another, smaller compartment. There it was linked to a small pump, entirely separate from the ship's air-conditioning system.

Two dozen weapons were turned in to the Protectorates. Four of them were archaic, hand-worked projectile weapons, two were blank-only show weapons, and the rest were blasters Njangu said were normally handed out when *Big Bertha* made a landing on an unknown world.

Of course, many more, and the crew-served SSWs, were still hidden about the ship in search-proof hideys.

Kaidu, who said he was a reasonable man, told Njangu he had no interest, of course, in the missiles in the *aksai* or Nana boats.

"Just trying to keep myself and my men safe," he said.

"Couldn't agree with you more," Yoshitaro said heartily.

"I do not understand this about guns," Sunya Thanon said to Ben Dill. "I asked Alikhan, and he said an explanation might be more logical coming from a human, since all Musth are always armed."

"Ask," Ben said, who knew the two elephant handlers were trying to learn to be soldiers, and had laughed his ass off watching Alikhan learning to ride an elephant.

"These Protectorate men who took our guns," Thanon said, "now have power over us, is that not correct?"

"Correct."

"Then, is it not true that, in an equal society, all men ought to have guns, to keep from being downtrodden?"

"Uh . . ." Ben hesitated, remembering great heaps of people he knew were incompetent to have any weapon beyond a basic rock. "Sort of. Maybe."

"So then," Phraphas Phanon said, "anyone who tries to not permit you to have a gun is a budding tyrant, and should be killed."

"That's taking things a bit too far," Ben said. "Like, maybe several light-years. Tell you what. I'm just a common, ordinary weightlifter. Whyn't you ask somebody intelligent, like Dr. Froude?"

"Good," Thanon said brightly. "We shall do just that."

But Froude didn't have a good answer to the question either.

Felip Mand'l curled around the overhead duct, watch in hand, as the four Protectorates went by. They didn't look up, and if they had, wouldn't have thought to find a little person above them.

After they were out of sight, he made a note of the time, went down a doubled-knotted cord to the deck, and off to report to Maev Stiofan, who had the security watch.

The soldier held out a bit of fruit to Loti, the smaller of the two baby elephants. Loti, a polite sort, curled her trunk up as she'd been trained, came forward, daintily plucked the morsel, and swallowed it.

A second later she squealed in pain and then rage as the pepper-packed fruit went down her throat.

The soldier roared laughter as the elephant stumbled back toward her mother, moaning.

Still laughing, he turned, and met the eyes of Sunya Thanon.

His laughter died, and his slung blaster slipped off his shoulder.

But Thanon did nothing more than look at him.

The soldier backed down the corridor to a port, went through it hastily.

"The question is," Danfin Froude said to Njangu, "is what you plan on putting down the pipeline for our guests."

"Dunno," Njangu said, evading Froude's eyes. "Something that'll take 'em out quick."

"Logic would suggest a lethal gas," Froude prodded. "That will prevent future problems."

"Yeh," Njangu said. "And everybody in the circus, including half the Legion people aboard, will think that I'm a murderous bastard."

"Indeed," Froude agreed. "First, I can reassure you most of them already have that opinion, and, secondly, a sleep gas is a deal harder to synthesize than something that does a nice, clean job of killing."

"I dunno," Njangu said again.

"*Do* think about it," Froude said, smiling gently.

"You know," Sunya Thanon whispered to Phraphas Phanon, "I have had a terrible thought."

"Kiss me and it will go away."

Thanon obeyed. "But it is still here."

"Then tell me about it."

"Perhaps this Coando that we seek . . . the land where elephant and man are equal and friends . . . really does not exist."

"I know it does," Phraphas said firmly. "Just as I know we shall find it."

"Perhaps we are living in it," Thanon said. "Living in it here and now, on this *Big Bertha* ship and with the circus, not knowing our luck."

"Do not think that, my love."

"All right," Sunya said doubtfully. "At least I shall try not to."

"I've decided," Garvin announced, "this whole operation has become entirely too much of an adventure."

"Is 'oo ready to go home and hide under the bed?" Darod teased.

"Uh, no," Garvin said, as Jasith came to mind. "Not quite yet."

"What you've got, troop, is low morale."

"You think so?" Garvin asked.

"Yup," Darod said, sliding out of her nightgown. "All you need is to get your little lights screwed out, and you'll be perfectly 'kay."

"Couldn't hurt," Garvin agreed.

Emton, looking for one of his cats, hoping the little idiot hadn't wandered into this big-cat caging area, rounded a corner and froze in horror.

Tia, the missing cat, was crouched across a corridor from the leopard cage. One leopard, Emton thought that evil black bastard Muldoon, was lying very close to the bars.

Tia got up, and pranced close to the bars, and Muldoon swiped at her.

"Tia! Come here!" Emton almost shouted.

The black kitten looked at her supposed owner, made a sound like "prrt," danced toward Muldoon, and avoided another strike.

Emton darted forward and grabbed Tia.

"You are stupid, truly stupid," he scolded. "Big cats, wild cats absolutely hate little cats! What do you want, to be that monster's dinner? Thin-sliced kitten?"

Tia looked up at Emton and started purring.

"I think you might be able to use this," Ristori told Garvin, handing him a key.

"What is it?"

"The key to the contraband arms cabinet you gave *Tain* Kaidu."

"How'd you get your hands on it?"

"A simple plunge, with one hand, four straight phalanges to hook, and it was mine. That, by the way, is a copy. I returned the original to the *Tain,* and he never noticed.

"I thought, thought, thought those guns might be useful in the coming days."

"Well," Njangu told Maev, "I think we're as ready as we're going to be.

"Now all we need is a little external distraction for our guards.

"A good healthy space battle would do just fine."

CHAPTER
23

The old theory, before Man went into space, was that someone in a spaceship or satellite had an innate advantage over his planet-bound enemy. This was the "gravity well" belief—the fighter on the ground would have to overcome gravity to get his missiles or ships on an equal plane for combat.

The basis was from ancient wars, where the man on the clifftop or castle rampart could happily cock a snook and drop heavy things on the attacker below.

In fact, it didn't work out that way in space, since the "gravity well" proponents didn't bother to consider that any ship bombarding an object on the ground would be in a predictable orbit. All the defender had to do was launch a flock of missiles into the orbit of that ship or satellite overhead, and matters would take their course.

Sometimes, the old saw was true, just as sometimes the belief that "the bombers will always get through" was correct.

But not often, and certainly not for Bayanti's attack on Gegen's stronghold of Ogdai.

The fleet held about three AUs off Ogdai, and the elite first wave attacked.

Their intent was to take geosynchronous orbits and bombard Gegen's forces from space, especially his stronghold. Other ships were to orbit the world, taking targets of opportunity or assigned targets from Bayanti's Command and Control craft.

When everything was sufficiently pulverized, the troopships would land.

Of course, neither of the "Protectorates" worried about the original inhabitants of Ogdai, although no nuclear devices were used, since Bayanti wanted to occupy turf that wasn't gently glowing.

Gegen, not being stupid, had laid careful defensive plans—several species of unmanned satellites, down to the completely antique kinetic variety, were positioned in various orbits around Ogdai, plus bases on all three of the planet's moons.

A swarm of patrol ships launched as soon as Bayanti's fleet entered the Degasten system, plus Gegen already had about half his fleet offplanet.

Gegen waited until Bayanti's first wave was committed, and his computers could analyze their tracks. Then he struck. Well-emplaced missiles shot up from the planetary surface, and the waiting satellites were activated and went after their targets.

Inner space was a horror of explosions, ships exploding, tearing apart, going out of control and pinwheeling down into gravity's claws. Just out-atmosphere was a snarling dogfight of fighters, all control lost as they went after targets or tried to evade contact.

Half a planetary day later, and the remnants of Bayanti's first wave reeled back toward the fleet.

Gegen's ships dived back for their bases to rearm and wait.

Bayanti raged on the bridge of his flagship, threatened commanders with relief, with being shot, accusing them of cowardice and treason.

"Now?" Garvin murmured into Froude's ear. They were on the bridge of *Big Bertha*. *Tain* Kaidu watched the biggest screen worriedly, two of his soldiers behind him.

Lounging near the rear of the bridge were Lir, Njangu, Maev, and Ben Dill.

"Let's give it time to develop a little more confusion," Froude said.

Bayanti feinted with his second wave, drawing Gegen's forces offplanet. Then, escorted by three battleship squadrons, he sent in his attack transports. Ships slammed in, ramps dropped, and troops on foot and in Aerial Combat Vehicles got the hell away from the landing zone as ground-to-ground missiles hurtled in.

Next, the units should have formed up for the attack.

Instead, they just sat there, in tight defensive perimeters. Possibly their high commander had been killed and no one took charge, possibly that officer froze in place.

Bayanti's troops were getting hammered, slaughtered as they sat, while Bayanti fumed again on his bridge.

He fought for control, found it, studied his main tac screen, trying to figure what to do next.

It took a while—describing the battle from afar suggests there was coherency, analyzable movement, instead of swirling madness.

Bayanti made a decision, ordered all frequencies to all of his ships opened, and ordered all combat ships of any configuration to attack, repeat attack.

They were to swarm Ogdai, taking any target they could.

Most of Bayanti's warriors obeyed, and armed transports, light escorts, dived in-atmosphere, headed for the ground.

Gegen's antiaircraft systems broomed them from the skies, but there were more behind them.

Gegen's fortress was a mask of flame, the land around it fire and the shatter of crashed ships. But it seemed completely unharmed, its defenders still fighting hard.

*   *   *

"Now?" Garvin muttered again.

"I think so," Froude said.

Garvin snapped his fingers.

Tain Kaidu had an instant to turn, to see Njangu on his feet, two steps and in the air, feet together, lashing out.

His neck snapped, and he chicken-flopped to the deck.

One of his bodyguards had a pistol out, and Maev shot him. The other unslung his blaster, just as Lir's knife buried itself in his throat.

"Now, goddammit, why no fun for Ben Dill?" Ben asked plaintively.

"Shaddup," Garvin ordered. "Liskeard, get us out of here!"

The ship captain obeyed.

Just before the main screen blanked as *Big Bertha* jumped into hyperspace, Garvin saw a dot that was, in fact, a battleship, dive vertically into Gegen's fortress, at the center of the swarm.

"Shit!" Dill said, having seen the dive. "Wonder what happened? Wonder if they got Gegen?"

"Dunno," Garvin said, motioning to a talker, as the crazy blur of N-space surrounded them. "Don't care. Got other stuff to worry about."

CHAPTER
24

None of the dozen soldiers in their bay heard the quiet hissing begin. There should have been more off shift in the compartment, but the invasion wasn't a calming influence.

The gas was nonlethal. Later, Njangu was accused of getting softhearted or -headed, particularly by Ben Dill and Alikhan, especially considering, as Froude had suggested, how much simpler a killing gas like hydrogen cyanide was to manufacture.

Yoshitaro protested, vainly, that he wasn't getting sentimental, but was worried about the rather improvised piping springing a leak and killing people he cared about. "Although for somebody like you two, I'll cheerfully make an exception," he muttered.

Only one soldier heard the noise before she was overcome. After a few minutes, a suited member of the Legion checked the compartment, nodded in satisfaction, and left the sprawled bodies for a cleanup detail.

Two soldiers trotted down a corridor, blasters ready. They didn't look up, didn't see Lucky Felip crouched behind a pressuring unit overhead. Aiming carefully with the small-caliber projectile weapon his father's father had carried against the pranks of the biggers, he shot both of them in the head, then sneered at the memory of Lir's caution in not arming him, back on Cayle IV.

He jumped down onto one corpse, went looking for other targets.

The arms locker was open, and Running Bear was busily handing out weapons. He noticed, without much surprise, that more of the waiting people were from the circus than the Legion.

Seven Protectorates swept through one corridor in the animal caging. They whirled, hearing a growling, saw two bears charging them, huge-clawed paws sweeping the deck.

They fired . . . but the bolts smashed into the creatures without effect. Then the bears were among them, slashing, tearing with their fangs.

The sole survivor ran hard, put his back to a wall, and fired again.

The creature coming at him, blood dripping from its mouth, was unhurt.

The soldier went mad, spun his blaster and shoved the muzzle into his mouth, pulled the trigger.

Meters away, the robot bear's operator saw and threw up over her control panel.

Now the "Peace March" boomed through the ship, and the troupers went looking for weapons.

A soldier was backing down a corridor, blaster ready, his mate in front of him.

He didn't hear a hatch slide open. Then a soft voice said:

"Remember me?"

He spun, saw Sunya Thanon, a handler's billhook in his hand. The hook slashed in, took him in the eye, and smashed him to the ground. Thanon twisted the hook free, drove it deep into the man's throat.

"And how does *that* taste?" he asked.

The man's partner had his gun up as Phraphas Phanon shot him through the open hatch.

"I do not feel bad," Thanon said. "That was for all the cruelties we have taken."

Phraphas Phanon shook his head.

"That is not good, that is not the Way. But I do understand."

Somehow the horses' enclosure had been sprung, and animals galloped in panic back and forth across the huge show area.

Rudy Kweik and his wives were among them, trying to bring them under control.

A soldier saw a shot, fired at Kweik. He missed, but the bolt sent splinters up from the metal deck into Kweik's legs. He shouted, went down.

The soldier took aim to finish the man.

High overhead, in the rear of the control blister, Darod Montagna shot once, and the man spun back, fell dead.

She grinned humorlessly, looked for other targets.

Half a dozen Protectorates were crouched behind an improvised barricade. They heard growling, snarling, and saw Alikhan, flanked by Ben Dill.

One fired, and the two Legionnaires ducked for cover.

An overhead hatch opened, and Monique Lir dropped down onto the deck, Squad Support Weapon firing.

The soldiers tried to return fire, were too late.

One came into the open, and Alikhan dropped him with his acid-pistol, burning a head-size hole in his chest.

Ben Dill looked for a target, saw nothing but bodies.

"Aw, goddammit!" he growled. "You went and did it to me again!"

*   *   *

Erik Penwyth shot two soldiers down, thought they were both dead, trotted forward.

One rolled to his side, fired, and the round seared along Erik's side. He shouted in pain, went down, hand reflexively pulling a grenade from his weapons harness, thumbing it into life, and rolling it against the soldier.

The man reached for the grenade, didn't make it as it went off, tearing him almost in half.

"Medic," Penwyth moaned. "Goddamnit, medic!"

The soldier ran hard down the corridor, away from the nightmare that had killed three of his fellows, a man with his face and chest painted in black-and-white stripes, stripped to the waist, wearing only a leather diaper and leggings. The horror had shot down two of the soldier's companions with a pistol, hurled a small ax into the middle of the third's face.

The soldier had fled, hoping to find the exit from this ship, from these alien people.

Something moved ahead of him, something small and black. He fired, missed, and the animal darted around a corner.

He ran on behind it, away from that monster behind him.

The soldier saw the animal again, no bigger than his arm, running hard, close to a cage. He had his blaster ready to club it down when a black, clawed foreleg flashed out, caught his uniform, pulled him against the barred cage.

An instant later, Muldoon's hind leg tore at his neck, and blood gouted.

Tia came back around a corner, saw the body, and began purring loudly. An echoing purr came from Muldoon as he curled up, lifted his hind leg, and began cleaning it.

A soldier crouched in the center ring, behind a clown cart, trying to get a shot at Darod, high above.

He didn't see the *ra'felan*'s tentacle until it had him around the waist. He tried to turn, to shoot at the octopod, then the *ra'felan* smashed him against a bulkhead.

The *ra'felan* considered whether it bothered him to have killed, decided not, swung back up into the top of the hold, looking for another soldier.

The shouts echoed down the corridors, louder than the booming "Peace March."

"Rube!"

"Hey, Rube!"

The circus troupe, some with blasters, some with improvised weapons, combed their ship for the soldiers.

Two circus people were wounded, five died, but all of their panicked guards died.

"All right," Garvin said. "That's that. Dump the ones we gassed into a lifeboat and kick it out into normal space.

"Damned if I care where it ends up."

"Your orders, sir?" Liskeard asked.

"Make the first jump for Centrum," Garvin said, thinking that was probably as close to a historic statement as he'd ever make.

"Right," Liskeard said, then stopped. "Sir, could we hold for a second? I've got to check with my electronics people."

Garvin frowned, losing the historical moment.

"Go ahead."

Liskeard touched sensors, and a mike swung down. He spoke into it, listened, then nodded.

"Sorry I didn't report this before, sir. But our electronics people have picked up a stray transmission."

"From where?" Garvin asked.

"From us. They've tried to track it down, but sans results."

Garvin blinked.

"Going where?"

"We don't know that, either. But it happens as we jump, then again when we come out of hyperspace."

"I want to see that report," Garvin said. "Right away. And hold on the jump."

He waved the nearest talker over.

"Get Yoshitaro, Doctors Ristori and Froude to the bridge. Immediately."

"If it weren't highly unlikely," Froude said, "I'd suspect that someone put a bug on us back on Cayle IV."

"Somebody did plant a device," Njangu said, and told them about the transmitter Kekri Katun had. "But I checked its recorder, and there's been no transmission to or from her at all. Although I've got to remind you, Garvin, that she was told by Bertl, that Director she was hired by, that she would be picked up at the proper time. Maybe he wasn't lying."

"Most interesting, interesting," Ristori said. "Might I make a suggestion?"

"Of course."

"Let's make the assumption that we are, somehow, bugged. Would it not be possible to delay this jump closer to Centrum, and, instead, jump to some dead system where we can sweep the ship until we find whatever it is that's leaking, bleeding, transmitting?"

Garvin thought, saw Njangu nodding reflexively.

"Better safe," he decided, "than dead meat."

CHAPTER
25

Erik Penwyth stared morosely at the screen as *Big Bertha* settled for a landing.

"All green and nice, lots of water, and no population?"

"If there is," Garvin said, "they're keeping well under cover, and don't use any known frequency."

"Yeh," Penwyth said. "A no-doubt-goddamned Eden."

"Sure," Njangu said. "Since this whole system doesn't seem to have a name, why not? This'll be Eden IV, 'kay."

"Prob'ly monsters under every leaf," Erik said.

"Now, just 'cause this is the first time you went and got your plow shot off, don't get cranky," Njangu said. "Just to make you happy, we'll call the system Eden, and this planet Lonrod after your honey. Howzat sound?"

Penwyth considered. "Fine, I s'pose, assuming that Karo and I are going to be together for all eternity." He thought for a moment. "After due consideration, whyn't you go back to Scheme A, and go with Eden IV?"

No monsters appeared under any leaf, and so Garvin approved of letting the animals out for exercise and air, which was almost precisely E-normal, and anyone who wanted out for exercise, assuming they were armed and stayed within sight of the ship.

Meanwhile, he put every woman and man with any electronics experience looking for the source of that beep. The problem was that no one knew what triggered it, so there didn't appear to be any way of setting it off, short of making another jump.

Techs used signal projectors that broadcast up and down the spectrum of frequencies, but without result.

Njangu triggered Kekri Katun's transmitter twice, but that produced nothing, either.

His mood grew sourer as the hours passed, and then they'd been onplanet for four local days.

Nothing.

Like his charges, Emton was an early riser, and, again like them, once dawn was properly greeted, he went back to bed.

He led his six yawning cats through the animal area, Tia ducking a mock-lunge from Muldoon as she passed his cage, to the gangway. He'd taught one of the cats to rear onto her two legs and bring a paw up in mock-salute for the watch, who, grinning, returned it.

The troupe went down the gangplank, into the dewy grass, just as the sun's rim came above the horizon.

The cats were taken out to "stale," Emton's wonderfully archaic word.

Tia finished her business, tried to start a fight with another cat, was batted sharply twice.

She bounded through the grass, looking for trouble, finding none, and came to one of the ship's monstrous fins.

As she'd done for three days, she sniffed at the metal, found where it not only didn't smell right, but had exactly the right pliability.

Purring loudly, she began sharpening her claws, slowly at first, then, as they dug in, faster.

Emton came on her then.

"Ohmigawd . . . ohmigawd . . . Tia, get away from there! You're ruining our ship!"

Tia gave it another pull, just to remind Emton of who was in control, allowed herself to be picked up, and thumped on the flank with Emton's forefinger in punishment.

"Oh my God," Emton said, staring at the bare plas, and the narrow rip where things, unknown things, strange-looking electronic unknown things, showed through. "I'd better tell somebody. Oh my God."

"Well smack my ass and call me Sally," Garvin said in some astonishment. There was a crowd around *Big Bertha*'s fin.

"I'm sorry, sir. Tia didn't mean—"

Garvin became aware of Emton and the throng.

"Mister Emton," he said formally, "I think you may have done us the greatest service of any trouper, and you can, if the technicians are correct, count on a very, very large bonus when we jump for home."

Emton blinked in bewilderment. Garvin motioned to Njangu.

"Clear 'em out, if you would."

"Big rog, Gaffer." Njangu called his security people, ordered them to get rid of the gawkers.

"That's what I think it is, isn't it?" Garvin asked an electronics officer.

"Cats *shouldn't* be able to scratch through the skins of starships, sir."

"Careful, mister. Sooner or later you'll be putting the uniform back on, and wiseasseries will be remembered."

"Sorry, sir." The officer knelt, ran his finger around the tear. "See how it protrudes from the ship's skin just slightly? I'd guess maybe a mag-couple, maybe some kind of ultra-glue was used to stick it on."

"So somebody snuck up on us," Garvin mused. "Tied this can to our tail, and we've been banging away ever since."

Garvin took Froude and Ristori aside.

"You think that's what we've been looking for?"

"Might well be," Ristori said.

"So how would it get word back?"

"Possibly some kind of device like my Ohnce-Bohnce buoys," Froude said, "Or, another way that would work is for some sort of missile to be linked to the sender.

"Assuming Cayle IV as its origin, which is logical, when we jumped from there, the first missile was launched. It went into N-space after us, homed on that second signal, which makes it a pretty sophisticated piece of electronics right there, then jumped back out in whatever normal space we'd emerged in.

"Possibly another missile would then be launched to join it, and that one would leapfrog the first and jump with us when we left the next system. Or else the second missile would replace the first, but that would require the first's fuel and drive to be constantly in danger of being depleted.

"Each missile, probe, whatever they chose to call it, would signal back to its mate, then that in turn would 'cast a signal until it eventually reached this Bertl.

"Very sophisticated, beyond my Ohnce-Bohnce so much so that I would doubt the system is original with Cayle IV. Probably provided by the Confederation, or maybe one of the science worlds.

"In any event, it's something I plan to steal once we get back to Cumbre."

Njangu had come up and heard most of Froude's theorizing.

"So there'll be another probe jumping into this system in a time?"

"Precisely. Which will leave us the thrilling task of finding it, a metal toothpick, in a star system," Froude said. "That could take a while."

"Like forever," Ristori agreed.

"Or maybe not a probe," Njangu said. "Maybe a couple of battleships."

"Why?" Froude said.

"Let's just say a certain date . . . and a certain event . . . back on Cayle IV, have passed," Njangu said.

"Oh crud," Garvin said, remembering the bomb.

"I'd be expecting the worst . . . or else nothing, assuming we got the right people," Njangu said. "But I don't think it'd hurt to put out the Nana boats on the edge of atmosphere, with sensors all a-twinkle.

"Chaka and his flight suits need some exercise, anyway."

"Good idea," Garvin said. "Now, let's dissect this pimple and see what we've got, in reality.

"Make sure the techs work carefully.

"The bastards might have booby-trapped it, to discourage curiosity."

It was dusk, near the end of the first dogwatch, and Erik Penwyth was looking forward to his relief. His side hurt, still not healed, and he was hungry.

The troupers were all inside, most still in the mess tent, and the trampled field around *Big Bertha* was empty.

Penwyth caught a flicker out of the corner of his eye. Reflexively, in case this world did turn out to have fangs, he stepped back inside the lock. He picked up a pair of stabilized binocs, looked out again.

On the edge of the field, where low trees rose, were two figures. He had time enough to see that they were dark-skinned, very hairy, almost fur-bearing, and stood half-erect. He caught a flicker of something at one's neck—a bit of mineral on a thong?

Then they were gone.

Penwyth considered the name he'd given the system, the world, grinned wryly.

Perhaps.

Or perhaps not.

* * *

Five days later, one of the Nana boats reported something.

Or, rather, three somethings.

Not probes, but former Confederation battle cruisers.

Garvin ordered the boats to lie doggo out-atmosphere and wait for orders.

A few minutes later, Kekri's transceiver blurped into life. Njangu was all ready for that.

Several messages were already encoded—not quite the cipher built into the machine, but something just a bit off. The static machine also would confuse the issue. Plus the data being transmitted from Kekri's transceiver to the battle cruisers was the engineering specifications for *Big Bertha*'s primary drive, in excruciating detail.

That would slow the code technicians aboard the cruisers down for a while.

" 'Kay," Garvin reported to his war council. "Since this is the first time they've wanted data from this transceiver, plus something else that happened recently on Cayle IV, it's pretty obvious this is where the hand gets played out."

He smiled grimly.

"I'm very damned tired of being kicked around and running."

The three *aksai,* with Dill, Boursier, and Alikhan prone in the flight pods, floated out of *Big Bertha*'s cargo area, then slowly climbed, through drizzle and heavy clouds, toward space.

They didn't do their usual zooming because the secret armories on *Big Bertha* had been opened, and two ship-killing Goddard missiles, six meters long, 60cm in diameter, hung on the mounts set up back on D-Cumbre, under each wing of the *aksai.*

Liskeard hoped the watch aboard the three cruisers might be a little lazy, and, as long as the locator showed the circus ship hadn't moved, they might not be overeager on their radars. That was another reason for the *aksai* to lift at far less than full drive—the cruisers' proximity sets might be set to shrill if anything closed on them at too high a speed.

The warships hung in a geosynchronous orbit over *Big Bertha,* halfway between Eden IV and its single moon.

The *aksai* cleared atmosphere, held their orbit until Eden was between them and the cruisers, went to full drive for deep space.

Close to Eden's moon, they braked and reset their drives, to come back in a high-speed looping orbit directly at the ships.

Ben Dill watched them close on one of his screens.

"No challenge, no nothing, just sitting quackers, aw, poor babies," he said, then, into his mike, "Dill One . . . beginning attack pattern."

Two mike clicks came from the other *aksai,* indicating his 'cast had been received.

He was no more than a thousand kilometers from the cruisers when he activated the Goddard targeting systems. Minutes later, both beeped. Target acquired. He set both for the nearest cruiser.

"Dill One . . . closing," he 'cast. "On the high ship, targeted. Launch One . . . launch Two . . . breaking off."

"Alikhan . . . on the center ship. One is gone . . . two."

"Boursier, on the last scrap pile. One fired . . . the second's gone."

There was no sign of alarm or alert from the cruisers as the six missiles homed. All impacted, and there was nothing but three perfectly circular balls of flaming gas in space.

"*Big Bertha,* this is Mrs. Dill's favorite son. Coming home, with the broomstick tied to the mast . . . we've got a clean sweep here."

*   *   *

" 'Kay," Garvin said. "Now, if there's no more dicking around to be done, let's go on to Centrum."

"Takeoff within thirty seconds," Liskeard said.

The locator, and Kekri's transceiver, had been left behind, just in case they held any surprises.

The circus ship lifted away, vanished.

Two days later, the two primates Erik Penwyth had seen found the courage to approach these strange objects.

The one wearing a bit of mica on a string of gut chanced touching the transceiver.

It beeped at her.

She yelped, and, followed by her mate, ran for the trees, never again to come near this cursed place.

CHAPTER
26

Unknown System

The bridge was crowded as Njangu and Garvin slid in, finding a place away from the command console.

N-space still swirled about them.

Njangu saw a communications officer sniff the air. He could have told the man what the smell was—the stink of fear, waiting to see what would happen when *Big Bertha* entered this booby-trapped system, but didn't. The virgin would figure it out in a few moments all by himself.

Garvin caught Liskeard's eye, nodded a go-ahead.

"You have the security data from Cayle?" Liskeard asked an officer sitting in front of a screen.

"Affirm. Up and running."

Liskeard tapped a talker.

"All stations, battle ready," he ordered. "All compartments seal, report integrity."

Liskeard listened to the clatter of returns, and an officer said:

"All compartments sealed, sir."

"Stand by to exit hyperspace . . . on my signal . . . now!"

Screens unblurred, and *Big Bertha* was in normal space, hanging not far from a ringed planet.

"Receiving signal on watch frequency . . . N . . . N . . . N . . . origin one of two moons at two-A, main screen."

"Respond with R . . . R . . . R . . ."

"Receiving signal . . . C-nine-eight-A-R-two."

"Wait . . . wait . . . send challenge response of four-five-I-X-two-two."

"Signal sent . . . waiting . . . waiting . . . response of C . . . C . . . C . . ."

"That's clearance."

There was a moment of relaxation.

"Stand by for next jump," Liskeard ordered. "Twenty seconds . . ."

"I have activity from planetary surface."

"ID it!"

"Ships . . . several ships . . . taking off . . . correction. Missiles."

"Ship targeted."

"Activate ECM."

"Activated, sir. Trying to acquire control."

"Twelve seconds to hyperspace."

"Missiles will be in range in . . . thirty seconds. I have ten bogies homing. Correction. Four missiles jumped into N-space . . . no proximity report . . . six missiles remaining in normal space . . . proximity twenty-four seconds."

"Six seconds to hyperspace."

"Four missiles exited N-space . . . homing . . . homing . . ."

"Two missiles taken over . . . three . . . three diverted . . ."

"Three seconds to hyperspace."

"Single missile homing . . . impact in four seconds . . ."

"Jump!"

The world went swirly.

"Now, if that goddamned missile has lost us . . ."

Silence for some seconds.

"We lost it."

"Whew."

"Where the hell did that missile launch come from and why?" Liskeard demanded. "I thought we had all their security codes."

"I thought so, too," Garvin said.

"Maybe a system bought from another supplier?"

"Maybe . . . or maybe those goddamned missiles got a little rusty around the ears and got independent?"

"One more jump, and then Centrum."

"Let's get through that one more first."

"Silence on the bridge except for business!"

Njangu noticed the smell was stronger.

Unknown System

The screen showed a tight cluster of planets close to the sun, a scatter of ice giants on the fringes. The nav point had brought them out in a band of asteroids.

Eyes scanned screens, then, in a jumble:

"I have metallic objects homing on us!"

"Indicated asteroid has made a launch . . . count of twenty-seven missiles . . ."

"I have inbound ships from inner worlds . . . guesstimate robot interceptors . . ."

"Unknown objects homing on ship . . . ID as possible kinetic satellites . . . count thirty-five . . ."

"Metallic objects probably active mines . . . send countersignal three-four-Q-Q-Q-three . . ."

"Roger three-four-Q-Q-Q-three . . ."

Missile diversion send six-six-seven-eight-nine-nine-zero."

"Sending six-six-seven-eight-nine-nine-zero."

"Interceptors disappeared into N-space."

"Interceptor code single word WAVEN."

"Roger WAVEN, waiting for reappearance . . ."

"Mines have aborted, countersignal worked."

"Inbound missiles self-destructed."

"Interceptors returned to real space, sending WAVEN . . . WAVEN . . . no effect . . ."

"ECM attempt to lock on interceptors . . . no apparent effect."

"Countermissiles stand by for launch, on command," Liskeard ordered.

"Interceptors returned to N-space, sent signal of RAFET, I say again, RAFET."

"RAFET approved acknowledgment of challenge response. They've gone back home."

"Anything else out there trying to eat us alive?"

Silence, then a storm of negatives.

"Seven minutes to next launch," Liskeard said. "Don't relax."

Capella

"Stand by for reentry," Liskeard ordered. "If they've got anything that'll come after us, let's try to get a jump on 'em. That last was a little bit close for me.

"Four . . . two . . . we're out!"

They entered a system with a medium main sequence sun, five planets within habitable range, one too close in, three farther out.

"Capella," somebody breathed. Garvin thought it might be him.

"Anything?"

A string of negatives.

"There's got to be *something* out there standing guard," Liskeard said.

"Maybe they're saving their surprises for when we're on the ground," Njangu said.

His throat was very dry.

CHAPTER
27

Njangu's worries didn't last long.

As they closed on Centrum, the com officer made the standard arrival notice/request for landing instructions on one of the watch frequencies.

It was as if he provided a reveille call.

A slow reveille call, for it was on the third repetition that Centrum Control snorted awake and informed *Big Bertha* to take a parking orbit, and stand by for clearancing.

Froude shuddered a little.

"Clearancing, eh? Well, whatever happened, we can assume the teachers of Common were the first to go under."

"I think," Njangu said to Garvin, "you and I had best get flashed up."

They dressed in their conservative best, but could have taken their time, because it was three ship-hours before the watch frequency came alive, advising the ship *Bag Berna* to stand by for boarding and inspection.

The ship approaching them was identified by their *Jane's* fiche as unknown, which Njangu assumed meant built less than eight years ago, when their latest copy of *Jane's* had been sent off to the far frontiers.

"Destroyer class, it appears," Liskeard said. "Zoom me in closer if you can."

A tech brought up a screen with a realtime visual,

zoomed in until the destroyer appeared no more than half a kilometer distant.

"Interesting," Liskeard went on. "It's spent a lot of time in-atmosphere . . . not hangared . . . look at the corrosion on the outer hull. Not drydocked in a while. Not very shipshape, my friends."

He watched the ship's approach. The destroyer killed its secondary drive and braked into a parallel orbit two thousand meters away from *Big Bertha*. Mag-couples shot out. One missed, the other clanged against *Big Bertha*'s hull, and winches brought the two ships closer.

"Sloppy piloting," Liskeard assessed. "I would have horsewhipped myself for something that ground-pounder."

Space-suited figures swam across emptiness, into *Big Bertha*'s main lock, were cycled into the main hold.

There were a dozen of them, and, already waiting, were Garvin, Njangu, Monique Lir in spangles, Froude, not in his clown outfit, Alikhan, and Ben Dill in a muscle outfit, very picturesque and harmless.

The Confederation men and women didn't wait for anything like an atmosphere check, but evidently assumed since most of their greeters looked human, they must breathe something close to E-normal.

Helmets were doffed. A man, not much more than a boy, looked around. "Sheesh, what a goddamned big ship," he said, audibly.

Monique Lir started to frown at this indiscipline, hid her reaction.

A long-haired woman stepped forward.

"I'm *Haut* Fenfer, of the *Thermidor*. Welcome to the People's Confederation."

Garvin noted the change in the name.

"And I'm Garvin Jaansma of Circus Jaansma. These are my staff members."

"Your homeworld?"

Garvin decided to answer carefully, and make no mention of Cumbre.

"Garibaldi."

"I'm not familiar with that system," Fenfer said, and somebody in the ranks snickered.

"Your purpose in entering the Confederation?"

"To entertain the people of Centrum and this system's other worlds," Garvin said.

Fenfer hesitated. "You'll have to bear with me a bit . . . you're the first ship I've ever cleared."

Njangu kept his poker face firmly in place.

"Did you, uh, have any problems approaching Capella?" she asked.

"None," Garvin said.

Fenfer looked perplexed.

"That's good. Uh, do you have any contraband aboard?"

"This is the first time we've visited Capella," Garvin said. "What is contraband?"

Fenfer took a list from a pouch, began reading:

"Weapons-grade fissionable devices . . . subversive propaganda . . . narcotics not permitted by the Confederation . . ." The list went on. At its end, Garvin shook his head solemnly.

"None of the above. Except for dangerous animals, which are part of our show, and are always properly caged and watched."

"You're sure?"

"I'm sure."

"I guess the animals won't be a problem," Fenfer said. "Would you object to an inspection?"

"Of course not. My staff will be happy to escort your people around."

Fenfer turned to her team.

"Very well. You have your instructions."

"Assuming there are no problems," Fenfer said, "I have orders to escort you, Gaffer Jaansma, as commander of this ship, to *Dant* Romolo, on our fleet's flagship."

"I would be honored," Garvin said. "Shall we get

the inspection out of the way? I don't want to keep
Dant Romolo waiting."

Fenfer passed Monique Lir, gave her a meaning-
less smile.

Lir responded in kind, didn't wrinkle her nose.

Either Fenfer's suit needed decontamination, or else
the woman could use a bath.

Fenfer's ship, the *Thermidor,* wasn't that clean either, Garvin thought. The bulkheads and decks had
been mopped and swept, but here and there he spotted patches given a lick and a promise.

Similarly, the crew members were sloppily dressed,
some wearing bits of civilian clothes with their
uniforms.

They didn't have what the military called, in a word
Njangu always hated, "smartness."

Yoshitaro never gave a damn whether a trooper had
her/his nose spit-shined, but knew a well-trained grunt
moved with a certain snap, had an easy familiarity
with his/her duties.

Not the women and men of the *Thermidor*.

They behaved, Njangu decided, like sailors who
were two weeks or less short of discharge and simply
didn't give much of a tinker's damn.

Garvin thought it a bit odd that the *Thermidor*'s
Commanding Officer didn't bother to come down
from the bridge to the compartment he and Njangu
were held in, close to the airlock, out of curiosity if
no more.

He chanced asking their guard, a friendly-faced *Dec*
who'd told them he was one of the ship's quartermasters. As part of the "search" team, he'd been infinitely
curious about the circus and how it operated, and said,
wistfully, that he hoped he'd get ground leave before
they left.

Garvin scribbled out an Annie Oakley, said he
hoped to see him there and he'd personally give him
a tour of the midway, clown alley, and the tops.

He chanced asking why the quartermaster's CO hadn't come down and introduced himself.

The quartermaster looked up at the wall speaker, which Garvin thought interesting in itself, then said, in a low voice:

"He doesn't know what to think about you yet."

"Why doesn't he come down and get some input to make up his mind?" Njangu asked.

"No, no," the man said. "He hasn't been *told* what he thinks yet."

He refused to elaborate who would be the one who'd dictate opinion, and was relieved when the speaker beeped and announced they'd be closing on the *Corsica* in zero-seven minutes.

The *Corsica* was huge, a battleship more than two kilometers long, bristling with missile stations and chainguns for secondary armament.

It was also very smart, indeed, overheads, bulkheads, decks gleaming, uniforms spotless, their wearers moving with snap and panache, saluting officers with a greeting and a slogan that must have been changed regularly.

This one was "train hard, fight easy," one of the oldest and most deceptively false saws in the book. More realistic, Njangu thought, would be "train hard, fight hard; train easy, fight harder."

Njangu thought the ship and its crew were perhaps a little *too* nit and tiddy.

An aide, who didn't introduce himself, ushered them through an outer office with busy yeomen into *Dant* Lae Romolo's cabin, which was rather sparse, with computer projections hung haphazardly here and there on the walls. The only holo was that of a rather severe woman.

From Cumbre on, Garvin had the rather romantic dream that all this sneaking and subterfuge would end with him being able to stand at attention in front of

a high-ranking Confederation officer, salute him, and
report as he should:

"*Caud* Garvin Jaansma, Commanding Second In-
fantry Regiment, First Brigade, Strike Force Angara
from the Cumbre system, reporting in to the Confederation, sir."

But now he thought better of the idea.

Dan Romolo was a fairly small man, with a round
face, thinning hair he clearly didn't have the vanity to
have revitalized, and the beginnings of middle-ages
spread.

This did not mean Romolo was, in any way amiable-
looking or soft. His face was prematurely lined, comfortable with command, and his cold eyes stared hard.

Njangu was reminded of the late dictator Redruth,
and didn't like the hint at all.

"Welcome to the People's Confederation, and its
capital system," Romolo said, and there was a slight,
possibly sarcastic, emphasis on "People's."

"Your homeworld is Grimaldi."

"Yes, sir," Garvin said.

"My star charts show that as a barely colonized
world," Romolo said.

Garvin was surprised.

"It's been settled for at least four hundred years,
sir, as a base for traveling circuses like mine."

"Don't be surprised," Romolo said. "During the
course of . . . shall we say, change, in the Confederation, many records were either destroyed by accident
or mislaid and have yet to be recovered."

"Change, sir?" Garvin said. "All we know . . . all
the worlds we come from or landed on . . . is that the
Confederation has fallen out of contact with its
systems."

"Also, none of the military units we encountered
have been in contact with Centrum," Njangu chanced.
"Sir . . . what happened?"

He heard honest plaintiveness in his voice.

Romolo took a careful breath.

"The Confederation Parliament went through a sea change, very rapidly, after a long period of stress, a few years ago.

"The new members of Parliament have been forced to spend all their time rebuilding the homeworlds, bringing order, and unfortunately haven't been able to provide the Confederation with leadership or security.

"It's truly unfortunate, and all of us hope the situation corrects itself within the next few years."

Garvin knew he should have kept his mouth shut, but couldn't. This was, after all, the culmination of everything.

"Sir . . . what we've just gone through, getting here, which was always my dream . . . well, it's pretty close to pure chaos out there. We *need* the Confederation."

Romolo's lips thinned, and he nodded sharply.

"I'm not surprised. Let me ask you something . . . I believe you prefer the title of Gaffer . . . did you have any difficulties in reaching Capella?"

"We had to evade some people who called themselves the Confederation Protectorate a few jumps back," Garvin said. "And some of the worlds we attempted to perform on weren't that friendly."

"But nothing else?"

"Not really, sir," Garvin said. "What, specifically, did you have in mind?"

Romolo was silent, thinking.

"That's interesting. Very interesting. I think it might be valuable for us to examine your logbooks."

"With our pleasure, sir."

"That can be done later," Romolo said. "I'm sure you'd like to make planetfall as soon as possible."

"It's been a long series of jumps, sir," Garvin said.

"I'll happily give you a release to land where the People's Parliament allows, with my recommendation that you be permitted to perform as desired and given the full freedom of Centrum. You'll be assigned a pilot within the ship-day to ensure you make proper landing."

"Thank you, sir. I hope you'll find the time to be our guest."

"Unlikely," Romolo said. "I find that my duties here, away from the comforts of Centrum, take up all of my time."

He didn't sound like he was sorry about that.

"A circus," he said, pretending sociability. "I remember, as a boy, my mother taking me to a circus. That was in the old days, when there *were* things like circuses, and entertainment that wasn't always supposed to be good for you.

"There were monsters and animals and people doing amazing things. Amazing."

Then he dropped the effort, came back to the present.

"Very well. That's all."

"Sir?" Njangu asked.

"Would it be possible for me to inquire as to whether anything is known about one of the Frontier Worlds? I had a brother . . . I hope I still have him . . . serving with the Confederation forces . . ." Njangu tried to sound worried.

"My writers in the compartment outside have access to all Confederation records," Romolo said, a bit impatiently, too big a man to worry about small things like brothers. "You're welcome to ask one of them before you transship."

Garvin tried to keep from saluting, from doing a smart about-face, from looking like a military sort, and they went out.

"What was the name of this world again?" the yeoman asked.

"Cumbre," Njangu said. "D-Cumbre. All the worlds of the Cumbre system had letter-names, my brother said." He spelled Cumbre carefully.

The woman tapped sensors, shook her head.

"Nothing at all on Confederation Main Records or our star charts. What about the name of the unit, although it's unlikely there'd be anything under that listing."

"Uh, the last note I had from him said it was, uh, Strike Force Swift Lance. Its commander was named Williams."

Again, sensors were touched.

"I'm sorry. Perhaps you've got the unit name wrong, in which case you should check with Confederation Military Records once you're on Centrum."

"Son of a bitch," Garvin said, as *Big Bertha*'s lock cycled, and they pulled their helmets off.

"Son of a bitch indeed," Njangu said.

"I think we need a drink."

"Several. And get Froude and Ristori's asses for chasers and consultation."

"I'm making some very interesting, very tentative theories," Froude said. "You, Jabish?"

"I wouldn't use interesting so much as astounding, preposterous, absurd," Ristori said. "Perhaps I should pour this fine engine-room juice back in the snifter."

"Uh-uh," Njangu said. "I want you to keep up with us, and what you're coming up with can't be any weirder than what Garvin and I are probably thinking."

"Then talk to us, Gaffer Jaansma," Froude said. "You're the CO, so we'll let you be the first to dangle it out there."

" 'Kay," Garvin said. "This stress Romolo talked about. I'd guess that must've been the riots we heard about when we passed through Centrum as recruits."

"Maybe," Njangu allowed. "Or maybe the stress was worse. Like uprising, maybe. Or riots that never stopped."

Froude looked at Ristori, and both nodded tentative agreement.

"So when things fell apart, they really fell apart. I don't have any idea what this frigging People's Con-

federation is, or this People's Parliament," Njangu
went on. "But this thing about records being lost lets
me get very, very weird on what might've happened.

"Maybe," he went on, carefully not looking at the
other three, "in this period of stress somebody blew
up the Military Records Division."

"That's reaching," Ristori said.

"Besides," Garvin said, "there's always backups."

"Yeh," Njangu agreed. "And lemme stretch some
more. Not only were the central records blown all to
hooey, which I can see a mob doing who's been shot
up a few times by folks in uniform, but maybe the
backups are either on other worlds or some of those
sets of records nobody seems to have located.

"Shitfire, if they could lose any reference to Cumbre—"

"*And* have Grimaldi's records a few hundred years
out-of-date," Garvin interrupted.

"Why the hell couldn't they forget about a few
thousand grunts called Strike Force Swift Lance?"
Njangu finished.

"Not enough," Froude said, although Ristori, stroking his chin, was shaking his head in disagreement.
"Why haven't they sent anybody out to start touching bases?"

"I'll give you the easy answer," Njangu said. "And
the hard possibility.

"The easy one is that if everything turned to shit
on Centrum, everybody with any kind of authority was
busy trying to keep his own ass behind the firing squad
instead of in front.

"Think about it, Danfin. Everybody we know who
comes from one of the Confederation worlds who got
interested in politics has said they'd been sort of ignored for a long time before the bottom fell out. For
some worlds it was five years, for some twenty, some
even longer."

"True," Froude said. "I can remember trying to
communicate with colleagues in other systems who'd

done interesting papers, and never being able to make contact."

"As can I," Ristori said. "Even before I went on the road. It was a constant complaint at the conventions I used to attend, before terminal boredom struck, that whole segments of the Confederation were being lost, and valuable, long-term sociological studies would never be available."

Njangu nodded smugly.

"Let me tell you a little story. As soon as I finish what's in my glass, take the decanter away from Jaansma, then get some more of that chilled tea for a chaser."

Njangu did as he'd promised, drank deeply, then returned to his chair, slouched back in it.

"When I was very, very small," he said, "there was this group of tearaways a street or so over. I was far too young to join them, which was a good thing because they ended up getting nailed by the cops, given condit, and that was the end of that.

"Anyway, they were real dumb-birds, 'cause they were stealing from people around them, which of course guaranteed somebody would eventually snitch them off, which is what happened.

"Now, I lived in a shit-poor part of the world, and nobody could afford proper security devices, but they sure as hell didn't want to come home from work or a hard day's thieving and find their flats stripped barebones.

"So they started putting in iron bars. Over the windows, over the doors.

" 'Course, you can cut through iron fairly easy, but that takes time and work, and thieves don't fancy either.

"The point of the story is there was this one man, wife had left him with two kids, down two buildings. A fire started one night in his apartment, and he had all his ironwork neatly bolted in and locked.

"I guess he couldn't find the keys to the locks in time."

"The man burned?"

"To a crisp," Njangu said. "And the kids."

Garvin got it first.

"All those damned security devices we had to beep and burp and code our way through are like the iron bars?"

"Just that," Njangu said. "The goddamned Confederation went and built itself a fortress, and then forgot how to get out of it.

"That's why Romolo . . . and the boarding officer from that destroyer . . . were so curious about any difficulties we might have had coming into the Capella system, and why he wants to look at the logbooks, which I'll be falsifying as soon as tomorrow's hangover goes away."

"That's . . . well, not impossible," Froude said. "And I'll accept the codes were destroyed. But wouldn't they push their way through, very carefully?"

"Why? They had troubles here at home. And as for people from the outside . . . how many ships do you think it takes to vanish . . . blown all to hell by those frigging robots . . . before people quit trying?"

Garvin followed Njangu's lead, and poured himself a drink.

"I suspect," he said slowly, "if that's the explanation, or even just part of it, Centrum is going to be very goddamned interesting."

"Not to mention borderline lethal," Yoshitaro said.

CHAPTER
28

The guide pilot was a wizened woman named Chokio with very wise eyes. Liskeard told her that *Big Bertha* wasn't the strongest ship for gravitational stress, a complete lie, so he'd appreciate it if she'd approve a nice, quiet lowering approach that'd take them a while to reach ground.

"Cert'nly, Cap'n," she said. "Besides, gives you a good chance to have a look at Centrum. Y' been here before?"

"No," Liskeard said truthfully. Garvin came on the bridge, heard her question, shook his head untruthfully, figuring a flash visit as a bare-ass recruit in the rear rank wouldn't count for much.

"Give you a chance at th' glory what were Rome. See how things can get totally screwed . . ." and she caught herself. "Sorry. Meant how things can change in not ver' long."

As they closed on the planet, she grinned, and told Liskeard to open up a screen and gave an aim point.

It showed long ranks of starships, drifting aimlessly in orbit, loosely linked together with kilometer-long cables.

" 'At's th' Confederation Fleet . . . that which didn't get caught on the ground and tore up when things . . . changed, or was out Beyond, and never come back. Or left a'terward and never come back."

"What was it like when . . . well, the way you put it, things changed?" Garvin asked.

"It was shit-ugly for anyone wearin' a uniform,

didn't seem to matter if you were a soldier or a post-man," Chokio said. "I was very damned glad to be on th' moon as a girl operatin' a pushmepullme yard tug. Friends of mine on groundside said it got defi-nitely nasty out.

"Not that it wasn't warranted," she said hastily. "Damned Confederation bureaucrats and their thugs'd been pushin' folks around for too long. The people had enough, and so they started lashin' out in all directions.

"Sometimes they got the right direction, some-times . . ." She shrugged and pretended to consult a screen as *Big Bertha* entered atmosphere.

"Almost wish this ship of yours was like some of the oldies," Chokio said. "Thin-skinned enough so you could hear air whip, and have lousy enough heat exchangers so it'd redden up. That was back when there was romance in space travel.

"Brought one of those back to Centrum not long ago," she said. "It was some kind of old survey ship, and I guess they thought it'd have Confederation re-cords or something.

"Never heard anything more about it."

Big Bertha made a first orbit, shallowly descending as it went. Every viewscreen, every port was crowded, and as they got lower, it was easy to see the "changes."

Centrum was . . . had been . . . a carefully planned world, with huge islands of apartments near buildings that had to be governmental for their gray ugliness. In between stretched lakes and green belts.

In a closed compartment, Njangu and his Intel peo-ple were correlating what they saw with the map of Centrum they'd bought from Kuprin Freron, back on Tiborg Alpha Delta.

"See th' parks?" Chokio said. "Kinda shabbied up, aren't they? They were built not just for runnin' and playin', of course. Intended to cycle off CO_2, so folks could keep breathin'.

"When people got done rippin' and tearin', and realized th' heat wasn't on, some of th' fools decided to get in th' parks with saws, and *really* get back to th' land.

"The Cits . . . citizens . . . wouldn't listen to anybody telling 'em about oxygen regeneration, thought anybody who did were bigbrains, prob'ly part of the Old Order, and thought they'd make good targets.

"Finally, had to give orders to the People's Militia, made it a capital offense to cut down a tree.

"Not that anybody ever *considered* telling any Cit she didn't have the right to breed 'til we all have to breathe in alternate beats. Nawp, anything scientific was part of the old way of thinkin'."

She shook her head, said, almost under her breath, "People always seem hell-bent on makin' themselves into the worst damn' fools they can, don't they?"

Liskeard didn't answer, and *Big Bertha* closed on the ground, flying over a huge, burned-out ruin.

"That was Riot Troops' headquarters. Barracks, holding cells, landing platform on top. It went up like a torch, the first day of the rising. Heard there weren't any of 'em got through that night, which was at least one of the good things the change brought, and I think I'm talkin' a bit much.

"Got orders to bring you down at Mainport. I guess th' powers that be this week might want to see themselves a circus. Hell, I'm curious myself.

"Just hope the Mobiles approve of circuses, so everything goes smooth."

"What are the Mobiles?" Garvin asked.

"Th' Mobilization Party. They're the cuttin' edge, or at least they tell everybody they are, and seem to believe it, of th' change right now. They . . . and their leader . . . make sure everything's headed in the right direction."

"Who's leading them?" Garvin asked. "Might be a good idea to stay on his side."

"Things, they say, are changin'," Chokio said. "But then, they always are. A year or so ago, I would've mentioned the Freedom Party and Abia Cornovil, who's always interested in things new. Now, it's the Mobility. Next year . . ." she shrugged. "Who th' hell knows.

"Anyway, The Mobiles' current leader's a Fove Gadu.

"Gadu's one of those folks who knows better'n you what's best for you, and doesn't mind cuttin' a few throats or givin' a few lethal injections to those who disagree."

Abia Cornovil was a big man, middle-aged, naturally muscled, going a bit to pot, who dressed simply and wore his straight hair almost to his shoulders. If this were another planet than Centrum, Njangu would have thought him an ex-farmer. He found later that Cornovil had been a statistician, but the shovel and hoe must not have been too distant in his genealogy, for he was the one who'd taken charge of keeping the parks as intact as possible.

Strangely, he'd had a bad complexion as a boy, which he never had repaired, on a planet that would have had the best cosmetic medicos.

His voice was as burly as his presence, and his booming laugh could be heard throughout the ship.

Cornovil had insisted on seeing everything and meeting everyone, and was fascinated with every detail, from how horses handled N-space to how Sir Douglas cycled the pungent cat shit.

He appeared no more than a cheerful peasant, and both Yoshitaro and Froude had to keep reminding themselves that this man had ridden the crest of what appeared to be roiling anarchy for almost a generation, and had to be a great deal more than he appeared.

Cornovil insisted on having a drink with Garvin and his staff. Jaansma, rather maliciously, served him their own triply distilled engine-room swill.

He purpled a little, but kept from choking.

"Great gods," he said. "No wonder you're so eager to get out of space. Does this crap improve with age?"

"Yours or its?" Froude asked. "I've almost gotten to liking it."

"I'll send over some brandy imported from Second World," Cornovil promised. "If you people propose to keep the Mobiles entertained, you can't be poisoning yourselves."

"A question," Froude said. "Someone implied that this Mobilization Party has a great deal of power. Just how does the People's Confederation work, politically?"

"Quite frankly," Cornovil said, "we're still working things out, just as we've yet to be able to redeem the promise the Confederation made to other systems to provide peace and open trade.

"We have a Parliament of One Thousand, which supposedly is elected by the people. Anyone can run in the yearly race, at which one-third of the seats are at stake, and a simple majority qualifies you for admission. But in fact, there are a dozen parties. Since the Mobiles are now the strongest, you'd be advised to support their views if you wish a chance at election. My own, the Freedom League, is at least holding it's own. Others . . ." he shrugged, "come up, go back down, sometimes after being found out as secret supporters of the Old Confederation."

"How are the votes managed?" Njangu asked, and Cornovil looked at him warily.

"That's a pretty sophisticated question for somebody as young as you are," Cornovil said. "Does a circus require a political expert?"

"It's hard, visiting a dozen worlds a year, and wishing to keep on the good side of everyone," Froude said to get Njangu off the hook, "*not* to have an interest in politics."

"Ah," Cornovil said. "The votes are . . . handled, as you put it, somewhat carelessly. In the last three elections, in fact, there've been a number of accusations of fraud." He shrugged. "Unfortunately, the accusations were all against the Mobilization Party, which, being the most active and militant at the moment, responded strongly.

"*Very* strongly."

Njangu felt it wise not to inquire further, especially when Cornovil looked at him coldly, and Yoshitaro saw, once more, that slight gleam he'd seen before in the eyes of powerful men who'd gotten that power without any regard for honesty or legality.

But, three days later, two barrels of brandy arrived, as promised.

A man wearing a black sash, which made him an officer of the People's Militia, arrived, and informed Garvin that the circus was given permission to occupy the Central Stadium, both for quarters and performing, and he was ready to escort them there.

"I don't like this at all," Garvin told Njangu.

"Me either," Yoshitaro agreed. "This whole damned place feels shaky, and I'd surely like to stick close to the ship.

"You see any way we can get away with it?"

"Nope."

"Then let's line up the troops and parade on in. But let's give everybody who's in the know a gun. And we'll keep *Big Bertha* ready to lift and at standby. Plus we can maybe pray a little, if you remember any good gods' names."

The circus, elephants, cats, horses, clowns, little people, acrobats streamed toward the Central Stadium. The sidewalks on either side of them were packed.

But Garvin couldn't make a call. On some blocks the people were silent, staring, almost hostile. On others, they cheered wildly.

He decided he'd have to play things as they came.

He didn't find much comfort knowing the "possum bellies," the storage compartments under the lifters, were packed with weaponry.

The route had been hastily papered with flyers for Circus Jaansma. Garvin noted, with considerable amusement, that all of the flyers on one building had been posted upside down.

That had to have been done by an I&R sort, who'd also learned more than a bit about circus lore—the upside posters were traditionally put up for Home Sweet Home, the season's last play before they made for winter quarters.

Cumbre.

Garvin wondered if they'd make it.

They reached the Central Stadium. The best that could be said about the building was that it was huge, big enough for three or four circuses.

Fleam, the boss canvas man, was running around the arena, muttering, trying to determine where he'd put everything and everyone, trailing harried roustabouts in his wake.

Others explored the upper stories, found rooms for all.

The building smelled of decay, abandonment, and everyone, animals, people, felt uneasy.

But there was no other choice.

"I shall certainly try to appear for your opening show tonight," Fove Gadu said to Garvin and his staff.

If Abia Cornovil had a slight megalomaniacal gleam to his eye, Gadu broadcast it. He was thin, hair disheveled, and he'd missed a patch here and there when he'd depiled last. His clothes were indifferently clean, and it seemed as if he might not have bathed in the last day or so.

"I understand Abia Cornovil visited you," Gadu said, pretending to be casual. "What was your impression?"

"Why, he seemed quite in charge of things," Garvin said. "He wasn't really here long enough for me, at least, to make any stronger opinion."

"I see," Gadu said. "He made no mention of how

he saw what place you might have here on Centrum, then?"

"None, other than he wanted to see our performance, and was most interested in touring our facilities."

"Oh? Any comments?"

"None other than admiring."

Gadu changed the subject, asked many questions about *Big Bertha*'s passage to Centrum. It was obvious he knew well about Capella's self-imposed blockade. Finally, he seemed satisfied, quirked his lips in what he might have imagined to be a smile, and left.

"Whoo," Garvin said. "Cornovil gave me the chills; this bastard made my dick fall off."

"Mine just shriveled up and wrapped around my backbone," Njangu said. "What about you, Monique?"

"He reminded me of a couple of sorts I ran across over the years," Lir said. "Fortunately, both of 'em are dead now."

"By whose hand?"

Lir smiled, didn't answer.

Darod Montagna did a backflip off her horse as she came out the Back Way, landed easily on her feet.

Rudy Kweik, leg wounds still healing, limped toward her.

"Well?" he asked.

"Well what?" Darod said.

"What's your call on the townies? I can't get close enough to be sure."

Darod shivered, not from any cold, hugged herself.

"I can't make them out," she said slowly. "One section'll be cheering like bandits, the others look at you like they want to put a bomb in your shorts."

"I don't like this," Kweik said. "Sopi Midt says the midway's doing spotty business. Gambling booths do all right, but nobody's interested in the games of chance that pay off in stuffed animals."

"Maybe the gazoonies have figured out how fixed

everything is," Darod suggested, realizing how easily she'd started using circus jargon.

Kweik snorted.

"A gilly figure out a gaff? They know nanty, or they wouldn't be gillies, now would they?"

"That's one way to figure it," Montagna said.

"The only way I figure it is that we'll be damned lucky to make the run for home without a serious clem," Kweik said. "You might want to make sure you take care of yourself."

"I always do," Montagna said.

"Not with that whopping great boomer you saved my life with," Kweik said. He dug into a pocket of his baggy pants, took out a small pistol.

"Here. Midt's found a source for them. Twenty credits. They shoot projectiles, which makes me wonder if they come out of some museum. Tuck this away. A present for someone who might make a good horse rider in thirty or forty years."

"Where, exactly, am I supposed to stash this little toy?" Montagna said, grinning and doing a pirouette. Her costume didn't have room enough to hide a penknife.

"Find a place, Darod," Kweik said. "I know, feel in my bones, this clem coming on. And it won't be one fought with sticks and stones."

CHAPTER
29

The war council on the nearly deserted *Big Bertha* was particularly grim, and included two new members: Chaka and Liskeard. Not sure why they were invited, they held to the back of the small group: Garvin, Njangu, Lir, Froude, and Ristori.

Garvin looked very tired.

" 'Kay. Let's make this quick. We've got another show tomorrow, and I'd just as soon nobody wonders where we are.

"We came out here almost a year ago looking for what happened to the Confederaton, and hoping it was something simple we could help bandage up, and it would be back to something resembling business as before.

"And what a can of frigging worms we unsealed."

He nodded to Njangu, who took the floor.

"Probably we should've assumed there wasn't just one easy frigging problem with the Confederation. The first thing, which we knew going in, was that big chunks of the Confederation had been allowed to slip out of contact over the last twenty or more years.

"Troops were getting bounced back and forth and in and out, like our Legion, and those Protectorate fellows we just left cutting each others' nuts off out.

"I wouldn't guess there was much control on these units by the Confederation, to point out the obvious.

"So the Confederation, really, had to have been falling apart for a long time, a lot longer than anybody was willing to admit."

Froude and Ristori nodded unhappily.

"When Garvin and I were passed through seven years or so ago, there were already riots going on.

"Those, I guess, got worse and worse, and what happened was a general system collapse, ending up with this wonderful People's Confederation."

Froude stood.

"A little elaboration here, if I might. I've done some wandering about, trying to find any scholars that didn't get themselves shortened by a head during the collapse, or who aren't hiding deep in some hole somewhere.

"I found some bits and pieces. The initial fighting seems to have been spontaneous. Nobody knows for sure, but I'd guess an average riot got out of hand . . . or was successful, depending on your point of view.

"The Riot Troops, who were supposed to keep order, got massacred.

"A period of general anarchy came next. A lot of Confederation records, and their keepers, went under during this time, including the main Military Records Division and General Staff system.

"Then some people got together with a common cause—probably grabbing power for themselves—and enough others fell in behind for them to declare themselves a government.

"Then something interesting happened. That party, once it got power, got conservative and drew a line, saying that's enough of a revolution for us.

"But it wasn't enough for the people who'd been the original rioters. Another party got formed, to the left of the first, and they started screaming that the first party was nothing but Confederation lackeys, and it was time for their heads to roll.

"They *were* rolled, and that second party was on top, and said, enough of a revolution.

"But the people of the streets . . . they don't even seem to have a label . . . didn't have the power, and so here came a third gathering. They took out the second group, and were in charge for a while.

"That group, by the way, was the Freedom party, which Abia Cornovil, who most of you met, is the head of.

"Again, no satisfaction for the people on the bottom. They got involved with this Fove Gadu, who'd formed the Mobilization Party.

"It's interesting that it was formed to push for the People's Confederation to reach out for their old holdings, out to the stars.

"Some expeditions were sent out, found out their own booby traps backfired on them, since nobody had the records on how to defuse them, or couldn't find them if they did, and so the Mobilization Party looked for a new cause.

"It appears as if they're now grabbing for the center ring, and we arrived just a little short of what may be another coup."

He sat down heavily.

"That's about that," Garvin said. "So now the questions:

"Do we have a good idea of what happened?"

He got nods, agreement.

"Enough so so we can think about ending this recon mission, which has got to be the longest in history?"

Again, agreement.

"So we can . . . *if* we can . . . scurry on out of here for home, report to *Dant* Angara, and let him try to decide what the Strike Force is going to do next.

"Because, at least from my perspective, next is going to take some serious figuring and is way the hell beyond me at this point."

"The first question," Lir said, "is how do we break contact and get off Centrum?"

"I don't know."

"Let's say we can," Chaka said. "We still have that Romolo and his battleship sitting off Centrum, and he'd probably object to us just fading off stage right.

"I don't see us having enough *baraka* to take him on, let alone winning."

"The luck of Allah might not be required," Liskeard said. "I've got an idea that should shorten the odds with him. But I've got zero-burp about how the hell we rescue the circus and lift without all kinds of alarms going off."

"Nor do I," Garvin said. "Again, events sort of dictated what we'd have to do when we landed here, and we weren't given many choices."

"We might have no other option," Ristori said, "than to accept some losses in changing the order of things."

"*Soldiers* take losses," Froude said, trying to keep anger out of his voice. "Most of the people over in that stadium are civilians."

Ristori didn't answer, but held out his hands helplessly.

"We've got damned near every small arm aboard over at the stadium already," Lir said. "I just don't see any way to get the troupe back here . . . not even filtering people through a few at a time."

"And I know damned well," Njangu added glumly, "none of the animal folks will even think about abandoning their creatures, which doesn't make being sneaky any easier."

"Which leaves us stuck between the lid and the bottom of the shitter," Garvin said. "The bad guys have the first move. All of them.

" 'Kay. Now that we're all depressed, back to your posts, and we wait until we get an opening."

"There's one slight thing that Chaka and I can do that might help when the balloon goes up," Liskeard said.

"Which is?"

"Which starts with giving that dictator-in-the-making *Dant* Romolo exactly what he said he wanted."

CHAPTER
30

Four men hung in emptiness. Between them hung two Shadow antimissile missiles, with their bases inside a curved box and a Goddard shipkiller, with an unsightly bulge over its guidance area. A welding pencil flared, went out, flared again.

"That's that," the technician said, putting the pencil back in his belt pouch.

"And that," Chaka said, "is unquestionably the ugliest jury-rig I've ever seen, let alone had a hand in building."

"Don't be so modest," Liskeard said. "I think it's just plain gorgeous. Especially if it happens to work, which I doubt.

"Now, let's get our asses back to the scow and continue the mission, like they say. We're only halfway through."

Their suit jets spurted white, and they moved back toward the Nana boat floating thirty meters away.

About three kilometers away floated the mothballed remains of the Confederation fleet.

Dant Romolo received them personally on the bridge of the *Corsica,* rather eagerly accepted the package they'd brought.

"Is there anything else in your records that might be of use to me?" he asked.

"No offense, sir," Chaka said. "But not exactly knowing what you want from our logs, it'd be hard saying. But you've got all the data our instruments normally assemble and record."

"Good," Romolo said. "I'm sure it'll be of use to me . . . and to the People's Confederation."

Again there was that peculiar, half-mocking emphasis on the word "People's."

Chaka nodded, trying not to salute, and left the *Corsica*.

"Now we'll see if all your forgeries keep him happy," he said.

"They'll keep him quiet for a while," Liskeard said. "I hope.

"Meantime, we've got bigger worries. I got a canned 'cast bounced from *Big Bertha* an hour ago.

"That Gadu character they were telling us about has stood up in their Congress or Parliament or whatever the hell they call it, and has named Abia Cornovil a traitor to the People's Confederation, and said he's betraying them to foreign influences.

"Since we're the only foreigners to show up lately, it looks like the shit is starting to come down.

"There's another speech . . . a major address, according to what the 'cast said . . . that'll be made tomorrow.

"I think we better get on home so we're right in the middle of the X-ring."

CHAPTER
31

Garvin thought that forever after he'd associate politicians, and their rhetoric, with the rotting smell of the Central Stadium.

A holo was set up in the middle of the stadium's green room, which was packed, about half troupers, the other half Forcewomen and -men.

Fove Gadu's image stood in the middle of a chamber with wooden paneling, and old-fashioned desks and chairs. But any dignity ended there. Gadu was raving, and Garvin swore he could see spittle fly:

". . . this beast, this betrayer, the man who once was the best of us all, this traitor Abia Cornovil, now corrupted and betraying the People's Confederacy with these outlanders!

"My colleagues and I doubted our senses when we first had evidence of this betrayal, which would put all of the Capella system in the hands of foreign enemies, desperate animals and aliens who would shatter the centuries-old faith the people of the Confederation have had!

"But the evidence was irrefutable, and with great sorrow, yet determination, last night an emergency plenum of this Parliament ordered Abia Cornovil's immediate arrest, and for him to be brought before us, and, through us, all Centrum and its worlds, to be judged!

"Unfortunately, Abia Cornovil had made plans for his escape. In attempting to stop him, his lifter was brought down, and he died in the crash!

"So should all of Centrum's enemies perish!

"But our task is not yet over. For in the heart of Centrum these outsiders still linger, doing who knows what damage, who knows what damage has already been done in their insidious—"

"Screw this," Lir said, slapping the off switch.

"Yeh," Garvin said, getting to his feet.

"You heard what the bastard said.

"They'll be coming for us.

"Let's not disappoint them."

CHAPTER
32

It only took a couple of hours for the Mobiles to show up. While they were waiting, the troupers blocked all the exits they could find, although Garvin wasn't sure they'd caught them all, and Forcemen took up fighting positions.

Garvin and Njangu watched as the approach streets to the stadium slowly filled solid, the throng rolling slowly toward the stadium and the empty midway booths in front of it, chanting various slogans as they came.

Garvin keyed the stadium's PA system, which included outside speakers, on:

"Attention! This building will be defended if any attempts to enter are made. Do not approach, on danger of bodily harm or worse! Again, do not approach!"

The crowds hesitated. Garvin started to give another warning, and, from somewhere in a building down the street, what appeared to be four blasters fired in near unison, and the speakers scrawked into silence.

"Not bad shooting for basic rioters," Njangu observed.

"Not bad at all," Garvin agreed. "How much you want to bet there's some Pipple's Militia posted out there?"

"Hah. I've got better intentions than to die broke in a riot," Yoshitaro said.

* * *

Aboard *Big Bertha,* armorers swore as they unbolted missile pods from the three *aksai* and hoisted chaingun pods in their place.

"Leave a couple of Shrike tubes on each bird," their warrant advised. "These Centrum people might have a patrol ship around for the potting."

On the bridge, Liskeard looked again at a projection of the stadium, and also cursed. The people there would have to make their own escape. The closest landing point was at least five blocks from the stadium, in a tiny park he thought might be big enough for his ship to land in. Anything closer . . . he went over the ground centimeter by centimeter.

There *was* a razed building less than a block distant, but its ruins were reaching claws, and he dared not chance landing on top of them.

"Maroon all of us here," he muttered. "Hopeless. Frigging hopeless."

But he kept looking at the holo of that building.

Three volleys slammed into the stadium from gunmen in the front ranks of the Mobiles, sheltering behind the ruined midway. Darod Montagna had smashed a window, and set her sniper rifle up on a table, back far enough so there would be no reflection from her sights.

She saw someone with a blaster, and shot the gunman . . . no, she thought, it was a woman . . . down, looked for another target.

"You know," Ben Dill said thoughtfully to Kekri Katun, "there's always a chance that Ben isn't going to be able to save the day.

"Particularly stuck in this goddamned cement mausoleum instead of boomin' around in my *aksai*."

"Don't get gloomy on me," Katun said. She had a blaster cradled in her arms.

"I'm not," Ben said, "Just bein' realistic. And . . .

and, well, I want to know, in case anything happens,
that I, well, I sort of love you."

"Sort of?"

"Sorry. I love you."

Katun smiled at him.

"And I love *you.*"

Ben leaned over and kissed her, then looked
startled.

"You know, I can't remember anybody ever saying
that to me? Not lately, anyway."

Kekri whispered in his ear, and Dill's eyes were
wide.

"And I can't remember anybody, *ever,* telling me
they wanted me to do *that* to them."

"Stick around, big boy," Katun said. "There's *lots*
of things you've never done."

"Maybe that's the best incentive I ever heard for
not getting killed."

Njangu and Maev were going downstairs toward the
central floor when the speakers came alive again, and
"Peace March" boomed through the stadium.

"I think," Yoshitaro said, "I could learn to hate
that frigging song."

Jabish Ristori lay on his stomach, aiming a blaster
through a kicked-out floor window.

Danfin Froude sat next to him, back against the
wall, wishing that they'd moved faster and gotten a
blaster apiece.

Two stories below, the Mobiles seethed and
shouted, crashing through the midway booths. Rocks
sailed toward the stadium, and an occasional blaster
bolt or old-fashioned bullet whined off the cement.

"There," Froude said, pointing. "That man right
there, at the corner of the building. He's got some
sort of weapon. Kill him."

Ristori nodded nervously, found the man in his
sights, and put his finger on the trigger.

"Well?" Froude said.

Ristori was shaking uncontrollably.

Froude thought of saying something about Ristori's abstract bloodthirstiness, but kept silent. He pushed his friend away from the window and took the blaster from him.

He took careful aim, touched the trigger.

The round spanged off the building just above the gunman, who dived for cover.

"At least I got him worried," the scientist muttered.

Blaster fire chattered through the glass doors of the stadium, and the two Forcemen behind the tripod-mounted Squad Support Weapon spun away, lay moaning.

Felip Mand'l ran to the gun, squatted behind it. He'd been watching the gunners as they carefully fired single rounds at named targets.

"I think I've got it," he muttered to himself, sighted at a line of people, and let half a belt of caseless ammunition go. Bodies pinwheeled, there were screams, and people were running in panic.

"I *like* this," he said, and then there were two troupers beside him, both clowns in full makeup, with boxes of ammunition.

Lucky Felip found another knot of people trying to hide behind the midway's shooting gallery, sprayed the area with the rest of the belt.

A clown slammed a new belt into the gun, its barrel smoking hot.

"Hold down your shooting," he told Mand'l. "Don't want to burn out a barrel."

Lucky Felip grinned at him, nodded acknowledgment.

"The hell with pistols," he shouted. "I *love* this!" and more blaster bolts arced into the crowd outside.

"Screw all you buggers! In the ear and in the ass!"

*   *   *

The two men pushed at the door again, then again. It refused to yield.

A very big man with a very big hammer pushed his way to them, ordered them to stand back.

His hammer smashed again and again, and the door went down.

Whooping rage and excitement, the Mobiles were inside the stadium.

Njangu heard the shouts, knew what they meant, and shouted orders to Forcemen around him to spread out, get down, and not get taken from the rear.

Garvin, in his upper-floor observation room, also heard.

"Come," Alikhan said calmly. "There is work for us below."

The two grabbed their weapons and clattered downstairs toward the stadium's main arena.

A *ra'felan* tried to pull himself higher in the rigging as he saw gunmen spill into the arena. One man saw the movment, crouched, aimed.

Monique Lir, curled around the kingpost, blew him in half, grinned, found another man, killed him, and methodically continued her slaughter.

Sopi Midt scuttled from the circus's pay tent across the arena floor, a large red box under his arm.

He saw the woman with a pistol.

"No!" he shouted. "I'll share . . . don't . . . you can't . . ."

The woman, having no idea what Midt was screaming about, shot him in the chest, then again as he writhed in blood.

The box hit the floor, smashed open, and credits spilled out.

The woman dropped her pistol, scooped up money, and Lir killed her from above. Three others tried for the treasure, and Lir lobbed a grenade down.

After that, the circus's cashbox was left completely alone, bills and coins spread across the arena floor amid sprawled bodies.

"Come on, Ticonderoga," Emton coached. "Come on with the rest of us so we can find a place to hide, where we won't get hurt."

Ticonderoga, crouched under *Raf* Aterton's podium, lashed his tail, looked in another direction, pretending not to hear.

The other five animals were already huddled in a large, wheeled carrier.

"Come on, you horrible animal," Emton pleaded. He heard a noise, looked up, and saw two grinning Mobiles coming toward him, one with a club, the other with some sort of hook on a pole.

"Oh, go *away* you silly creatures," he said, pulling one of the small pocket pistols the late Sopi Midt had procured from an inner pocket. He pointed the pistol at the men, squinched his eyes closed, pulled the trigger twice.

He heard a scream, and a thud. Emton opened his eyes, saw one man laying motionless, the other writhing, clutching his stomach.

Emton got up, went to the wounded man, put the pistol to the man's head and, again with closed eyes, pulled the trigger.

By the time he got back to the podium, Ticonderoga was in the carrier, with the others.

Rudi Kweik's horses were surging against the ropes keeping them in the big room used for a cage. One gelding slammed into the rope netting, and it tore away, and the horses ran for freedom.

Kweik and his wives, shouting, waving their arms, were almost trampled.

A gunman saw Kweik hobbling into the arena after his *vrai*, shot him.

Jil Mahim saw Kweik go down, dropped the gunman, then darted out, grabbed Kweik by the neck of his voluminous shirt, dragged him back into an entryway where Fleam crouched, weapon ready.

"If any of the bastards get close . . . tie a knot in their tails," she said.

Fleam actually smiled. "They won't even get close."

She opened her aid pouch, tore Kweik's shirt open, winced as she saw the hole in his chest, close to his heart.

Shaking her head, she felt his back, found an exit wound. It wasn't a lung shot, she thought hopefully.

Kweik opened his eyes, smiled at her peacefully, then his body contorted, and he was dead.

Mahim pulled his shirt back in order, glanced at Kweik's wives as they began wailing, put them out of her mind as she scuttled along the wall toward another casualty.

A dozen men froze as Alikhan came out of a passage, a devourer-weapon in one upper paw, a wasp-grenade in his other. He shot two men, thumbed the wasp-grenade, and tossed it into the midst of the Mobiles.

They screamed as the grenade went off, and the pseudo-insects hummed out of the shattered box, stinging as they went.

Alikhan shot two more, and the others panicked, seeing the huge bullets strike, and then the maggotlike creatures inside spill out, expand, and begin eating.

None of them made it back down the passage to the stairs they'd come up.

Running Bear, sensibly clad in a coverall, ran at the head of fifteen troupers into the rear of the Mobiles.

He shot a woman with a bloodstained butcher knife, then realized he was shouting aloud.

To his eternal shame, it wasn't one of his people's half-remembered war cries, but the circus cry of "Hey, Rube."

* * *

Maev ran into the bear handlers' position, saw the two robots standing immobile, their handlers sprawled in death.

"Son of a bitch," she said, pulled one body out of the way, put a helmet on as she got behind the controls.

"I think I almost remember this," she muttered, and Li'l Doni came alive.

She steered him out of the position, toward a cluster of Mobiles bent over a couple of bodies.

One man turned, saw the shambling creature, and screamed. A woman shot the robot, saw her round impact, then Doni's claws ripped her throat away.

The Mobiles ran in all directions.

A few made it to safety.

"Now, let's go looking for somebody else to mess with," Maev muttered and, out on the arena floor, Li'l Doni shambled about at her bidding.

"The question is going to be," Sir Douglas said in a reasonable voice to Njangu, "whether we can put the pussies back where they belong, afterward."

"Yeh," Njangu agreed, keeping his blaster ready, again remembering Garvin's story, long ago on a burning rooftop, about why he'd joined the military, after setting a circus's cats on a crowd during a big clem.

"Well, nothing ventured," Sir Douglas sighed, and began opening the doors of the lifter-mounted cages.

The animals hesitated, and Sir Douglas went to the rear of the cages, began firing his blank pistol into the air.

"Come on," he said. "Help me."

Njangu obeyed, clanging his blaster barrel along the bars.

The cats reluctantly surged out of their cages and went down the passageway toward the arena floor.

"I'd suggest," Sir Douglas said, "you get in here for a few minutes, where it's safe."

Njangu thought that a very good idea.

The cats, angry, scared, came into the arena crouched, tails lashing.

Mobiles saw them, moaned in fear.

Possibly if they'd charged the cats, they might have frightened them back down the passage. Instead, people made one of two very fatal choices: they either stood frozen in fear or they ran, both perfectly familiar behavior of animals' prey.

Roaring, bounding, the beasts pounced, killing, killing again, and bloodlust built.

A few of the Mobiles had the courage to shoot at the cats, but only one hit, searing a bolt down one lion's side. A moment later, a smashing paw tore his head off.

The Mobiles were in full flight, back toward the side entrance they'd broken through.

"I guess," Sir Douglas said reluctantly, "we'd best go and tuck our friends back where they belong."

"I have one . . . three . . . five launches," an electronics officer reported. "Maybe more. Patrol ships of some sort. Medium-size."

Liskeard stood in the center of his bridge, considering his options.

There were none.

He waved to a talker.

"Is Boursier ready to launch?"

The talker asked.

"Sir, Boursier One is ready."

"Launch!" Liskeard ordered. "Try to give any close support you can at the stadium, and take out any of those patrol ships that get in your way."

The *aksai* in the hold dropped from its mag-couples, wobbled on its antigravs toward the open lock, was out into the open air.

Liskeard took a deep breath, made a decision.
"Close the lock and stand by to lift."

The stairwell to the exit was packed with pushing
Mobiles, trying to get out of this arena of horror.

Njangu appeared at a landing above. He held a sack
in one hand.

"Hey!" he shouted.

A few heard him through the din, looked up.

Njangu thumbed one of the grenades in the bag to
life, dropped the bag in the center of the throng
below.

He ducked back out the door he'd come in through,
deciding he didn't want to see what happened in
four . . . no, three seconds.

The Mobiles boiled out into the street, just as Jacqueline Boursier, swearing madly, fought the *aksai*,
never intended for low speed close air support, down
the avenue toward the stadium.

She saw people running, starting to shoot at her,
gawping in horror, and she toggled a sensor.

Her chaingun churned 35mm collapsed-uranium
bullets in a six-thousand-round stream into the street
below, red tracers, red death.

She lifted into an Immelmann at the end of the avenue, came back, trying not to notice the buildings just a
couple of meters below, very close to her wingtips.

Garvin was in a room, trying to help Knox keep
the showgirls from complete hysteria when his belt
com buzzed.

"Gaffer . . . this is *Big Bertha*. Stand by for pickup."

Garvin forgot about the women, ran hard for the
main entrance.

Big Bertha, bigger than the stadium, bigger than any
building in the city, banked overhead, then its nose
lifted.

"He can't do that," Danfin Froude said.

"But he is," Ristori said.

He was. Liskeard backed *Big Bertha* on secondary drive toward the sort of vacant lot. Its landing fins, then the ship's bulk itself, smashed down on the ruined building.

Smoke-blackened facing fell away, then the building's steel framing bent, broke, and *Big Bertha* was safely down, even if canted at a bit of an angle.

Some of the Mobiles chanced shooting at the transport, but a hidden port opened, and a pair of chainguns yammered, smashing buildings open as if they were cardboard.

"That's a good kitten," Sir Douglas soothed, as a tiger and two lions, growling, went past him back in the cages.

"Nice kitties," Njangu said nervously. A lioness bounded down the passageway, and into the cage.

"That's all but one," Sir Douglas said.

"And here he comes," Njangu said.

Muldoon, dark stains on his black coat, prowled down the passageway. He paused, eyed Njangu thoughtfully, licked bloodied jaws, went inside.

"All right," Sir Douglas said. "Now, let's get these cages in the air."

He banged the cage door shut, and Njangu started breathing again.

The stadium PA crackled on.

"*Big Bertha* is here! Everybody to the main exit for loading! Don't hurry, don't panic," Garvin's voice said. "We've got plenty of time, and nobody will get left."

Jiang Fong, his wife and child, the other acrobats trailing, were the first to reach *Big Bertha*, trotting up the ramp and through the lock.

"Names . . . quickly," Erik Penwyth called.

Fong answered, and Penwyth made check marks on a list.

Next came the horses, trotting together, Darod Montagna and Kweik's widows behind them, chivvying them up the ramp, back toward their safe houses.

Darod turned back, unslinging her blaster.

"You're supposed to stay aboard, once you make it," the officer told her.

"I'm still not through doing paybacks," Montagna snarled, and went back across to the stadium.

"Tails up! Tails up!" Sunya Thanon and Phraphas Phanon were chanting and, obediently, the elephants, in a long line, streamed out the main entrance toward the steps, following Sir Douglas's cat cages.

One brushed against the ticket booth, collapsing it.

Thanon and Phanon darted to the front, their blasters ready.

Thanon saw a man with a rifle, shot at him, missed. The man fired back, and Thanon screamed, went to his knees.

Phanon was beside him. Thanon stared at him, not recognizing Phanon for a moment.

"I wish," he tried. "I wish . . ."

He coughed blood.

"Perhaps I am now going to Coando," he said. "I will wait for you there."

Phanon's eyes were blurred as he heard his lover die.

He looked up, saw a bottle spewing fire spin toward him, smash down, and explode. The flames took him, and he screamed, tore at himself as his flesh blackened, fell across Thanon's body.

The elephants were milling, Imp screaming, close enough to the molotov to have gotten burned.

Two women with improvised spears ran toward the bulls. The spear was yanked away from the first by one raging bull, and the beast's rolled trunk shot out, smashing her skull.

The second tried to run, was taken, lifted, and hurled, almost casually, against a building.

Alikhan ran out of the stadium, eyes red in rage, a devourer-weapon in each paw, firing, and then there were no attackers left alive to shoot.

"Tails up! Tails up!" he called, and the elephants swayed back and forth, hesitating, then remembered the command, even if it came from an unfamiliar voice.

Obediently, once more in line, the elephants followed Alikhan, Imp and Loti close at his side, across the street and up the ramp into the starship.

Alikhan led the elephants back to their area, wished he had time to soothe and feed them, knew better.

He found a lift, went to the top of the starship, found Dill buckling himself into an *aksai*, Kekri Katun trying to help.

"Come on, partner," Dill said. "I want some blood."

"I alssso," Alikhan hissed, normally perfect Common lost a bit in his rage as he opened the canopy of his own ship. "In bucketsss and barrelsss."

In a holo studio halfway across the city, Fove Gadu was in mid-'cast:

"Oh no, we of the Mobilization Party have found Abia Cornovil was not the only one corrupted by the aliens. We have a list of over a hundred men and women, high-rankers all, who've leagued themselves with these monsters.

"Even now, as our fearless men and women are bringing down these offworlders, we have squads of the People's Militia out, tracking down these traitors, to bring them to People's Justice . . ."

Aboard *Big Bertha,* a com officer motioned to Liskeard. On an inset screen was the image of Gadu, pounding his fist on a podium.

"Sir, I've got a perfect fix on him."

"You're sure it's not an echo antenna?"

"Very sure. I've got all three of that station's antennae plotted, and this ain't none of them."

Liskeard smiled, motioned to a talker.

"Come, ladies," Knox said as he chivvied the showgirls toward *Big Bertha,* weaving through engine-revving lifters waiting to go up the ramp. "Don't panic, don't smear your makeup, and I guarantee I'll have the Gaffer issue a bonus for this whole day's silliness."

One of the women shrieked as two *aksai* floated out of the starship, not a meter overhead, then climbed for altitude.

Darod Montagna gunned down three Mobiles crouched safely—they thought—in an entranceway, then jerked sideways as rounds pinged off the sidewalk around her.

She rolled to her feet, dived for a solid-looking, only half-destroyed midway booth. The sniper's bolts slammed in around her.

"Pinned down, by all the hells," she growled. "What a goddamned amateur thing to do."

She heard a roar, and went even flatter as a strange-looking patrol ship, not twenty meters overhead, flashed past, cannon winking along its stub wings.

Gunfire chattered close, and she rolled over, blaster ready, as Garvin dived in beside her.

"Hey," she said.

"Hey," he managed. "What're you doing out here?"

"The same thing you are," Montagna said. "Being pinned down. You're about a hell of a rescuer."

"I'm sorry," Garvin said. "I saw you getting your ass in a jamb and thought I could help. I'm short a Zhukov . . . all I've got is me at the moment.

"Normally, enough. But now . . ."

The patrol ship came back by, but this time Boursier's *aksai* was on its tail. Someone on the ground put a burst through the *aksai*'s fuselage.

Boursier's ship fought for altitude, juddering, almost stalled, went inverted, corrected, managed to brake, and floated back inside *Big Bertha*.

"Hope to hell whoever's pushing that boat got that patrol ship," Darod said.

"Hadda be Jacqueline . . . and no, she didn't," Garvin said. "Here the bastard comes again, and I think we're his only goddamned target!"

"Go pick on somebody your own size, you bully!" Darod shouted.

Obediently the patrol ship lifted, and began an attack pass on *Big Bertha*.

A weapons officer aboard *Big Bertha* toggled two Shrikes, and they flashed out, struck the patrol craft, and blew it into fragments.

Flame and fragments clattered down around Garvin and Darod.

"Come on, you buttbreath Buddha," Montagna shouted. "No goddamned friendly-fire casualties allowed here!"

Garvin saw movement to his front, fired, and the movement stopped.

"Forget about incoming friendly rounds," he said. "There's enough folks out there on the ground trying to get us killed."

Five Centrum patrol ships drove toward the distant bulk of *Big Bertha*. None of them saw the two *aksai* and the pair of Nana boats until the first two patrol ships blew up.

The surviving three banked away, two holding wingmate discipline, the third going for the deck and full speed.

"Come on, come on," Ben Dill crooned, seeing one patrol ship dance in his sights. A Shrike beeped at him, and he let it go, switched his aim to the second patrol ship.

It suddenly rolled, went for the deck, Dill's *aksai* after it. He noted detachedly the first patrol ship bursting into flames, a ball of flame rolling down a wide avenue, flames spreading in its wake.

The second ship was weaving back and forth. Dill found it in his sights, fired without the Shrike telling it was ready.

The missile went off about ten meters from the patrol ship. The Centrum craft rolled and, still at full speed, crashed, tumbling, through a high-rise government-looking building.

Dill banked away, went for altitude, waited until his breathing slowed a little bit, keyed his mike.

"Uh . . . Alikhan One, this is Dill One. Need any help?"

"Alikhan . . . this is an elusive one. I think I might use some . . . no. He just flew into my missile.

"Do you see anything else to shoot at?"

Ben scanned his screen.

"Not really. Guess we go orbit Big Momma and strafe a little."

"I think I shall look for groups of people," Alikhan responded, "and perhaps lighten my ammunition load when I do."

Gunfire blasted above Garvin's and Darod's heads, and four Forcemen, Njangu at their head, doubled toward them, found shelter, waited.

No return fire came.

"I guess we went and killed the last brave Mobile," Njangu said.

"Now, if you two are through screwing around out here, would you like to dust yourselves off and get your asses back to where they should be?"

Garvin gingerly picked himself up, helped Darod to her feet.

"Yeh," he said. "But I gotta tell you, young Yoshi-

taro, you've got the shittiest rescuer's patter I've
ever heard."

"If you don't like it," Njangu said, "feel free to go
to my competition."

". . . the moment of victory can be only moments
away," Gadu went on. "I have instructed my friends
to be sure and take prisoners, hopefully the leaders
of this evil cabal, so they may testify at the trial of
our traitorous—"

He broke off, staring through the soundproof window at a very black, very ugly Nana class patrol ship
hovering no more than fifty meters away.

Chaka triggered his chaingun, and the rounds tore
the studio—and Fove Gadu—into shreds.

"I don't know if that contributed to peace in our
time," he said into his mike, "but it sure as hell made
me feel a lot better."

The band came out of the stadium proudly, still
blasting the "Peace March." Halfway across the avenue, Aterton shouted a number, and they changed
into the "Confederation Anthem."

A bit of shrapnel spanged off the concrete, took a
timpanist in the leg. His drum, held up by a dropper,
bounced away down the street, booming each time
it hit.

The band cascaded up the ramp, through the lock,
and was aboard.

Just behind them, the two *aksai* floated into the
ship.

"Is everyone accounted for?" Garvin asked.

"Checked and checked twice," Erik Penwyth said.
"Everybody's aboard, including all of our casualties."

"We're sure," Njangu said, sounded weary. "I made
two checks through that frigging stadium myself before I decided you needed some rescuing."

Garvin lifted his com.

" 'Kay. Take us upstairs."

"I have four ships closing," an electronics officer reported as *Big Bertha* lifted through the stratosphere. "ETA . . . guesstimate . . . four-three. Distance, maybe two parsecs."

"Can you make any of them?"

"Again, a guess, sir. But I'd try three destroyers escorting a very large ship. Probably the *Corsica*."

Liskeard turned to a weapons officer.

"How close is he to the baby we planted out by the mothballs?"

"Oh . . . one-five. Closing fast."

"At one-zero, launch the Goddard."

"Understood one-zero, sir."

The bridge was very silent except for the routine mumble of the watch talkers.

The weapons officer was staring into a radar screen.

"One-one . . . one-zero . . . on its way."

Half a system away, the modified Goddard stirred into life.

The *Corsica*, its three escorting ships in a vee in front of the battleship, drove at full power toward Centrum.

Dant Lae Romolo stared in some disbelief at the screens showing the chaos on the planet.

"*Damned* civilians," he said to himself. "They should never have allowed this situation to worsen!"

He scanned the huge bridge. Everything was as it should be, calm, proper. He saw, on a main screen, the symbols of the mothballed fleet "below" him, thought there would soon be reason to activate and man them.

"Sir," an electronics officer reported, "we have an unknown ship leaving Centrum."

"No doubt that's the invading circus ship," Romolo

said. "There should be no problem intercepting it before it tries for hyperspace."

The incoming Goddard was barely big enough to show up on-screen, an ignored dot until an electronics officer looked at a proximity screen.

"Sir," he said calmly to the officer of the deck, "I have an unknown object . . . coming in very fast . . . closing on us."

The OOD blinked.

"What is it?"

"No identification, sir."

The man hesitated, then: "ECM, can you acquire it?"

The woman tried, shook her head.

"Negative, sir. It's small . . . probably a missile . . . seems to be remote guided, but I can't grab the frequency."

"All compartments . . . seal ship."

"Sealing ship, sir."

Alarms screamed through the *Corsica*.

"All stations, report integrity."

A talker began reporting.

"Weapons, take out that incoming," Romolo said. His voice was calm, unworried.

"Yessir . . . acquiring . . . acquiring . . . launch one! Launch two!"

Two missiles spat from the *Corsica*'s tubes, while officers screamed at the escorts to wake up and do something.

The tricked-out Goddard "saw" the counterlaunch, and its controller aboard *Big Bertha* launched the two Shadows.

The four missiles intersected and exploded.

"Hit! Hit! . . . That's a negative . . . missile still closing . . . Intersect in five . . . four . . ."

"Counterlaunch, dammit!"

"Counterlaunching . . . waiting for target to—"

The Goddard slammed into the *Corsica*'s engine

area, and flame balled for an instant, was taken by vacuum.

Romolo was pitched headfirst over a console, landed sprawled across another as sirens screamed and alarms bonged.

He picked himself up, tried for broken bones, hoped that alien ship who'd so comfortably fooled them all had done as much damage on Centrum as he hoped.

Hoped and needed.

" 'Kay," Garvin said. "That's that.

"Captain Liskeard, would you like to take us on home?"

CHAPTER
33

Cumbre/D-Cumbre

"And how long has this been going on?" Garvin Jaansma said, staring at the holo of the rather handsome young man, listening to his words and wincing at the cliché.

"Five . . . maybe six months," Jasith Mellusin said, her voice shaking, afraid of Garvin's utter calm. "You were gone a *long* time. Over a year, you know."

"I know," Garvin said, thinking of Darod Montagna and then Kekri Katun. "Who is he?"

"One of my vice presidents," Jasith said. "We used to play together . . . when we were kids. I guess he was sort of my childhood sweetie. Please don't be mad at me."

"I'm not mad at anyone," Garvin said.

He felt very tired. All he wanted to do was leave this mansion, and go, by himself, without even Darod, to some island without any people, where all he'd have to do is sleep and eat.

"I'll send somebody to pick up my stuff," he said, going to the door.

"Garvin," Jasith said. "Will we still be able to be—"

The door clicked closed before her last words.

Garvin went swiftly down the huge steps, remembering this wasn't the first time he'd left this mansion. But this time, he realized, his heart didn't seem to be as broken.

He got in his lifter, started the drive, thought about their return.

Operation HOMEFALL was a success. *Big Bertha* had been given a hero's welcome, everyone aboard made a citizen of Cumbre. Some . . . a lot more than he would have thought . . . took advantage of the offer, and decided to put together a circus to work Cumbre, and other systems when it became possible. Among them was Fleam, who decided he'd finally found a career with ropes and canvas, and used his unexpected bonus to buy out of the Force.

Liskeard had been offered full redemption by *Dant* Angara, which he wasn't sure he wanted, and, while considering his options, had taken those troupers who wanted to go back to Grimaldi, all comfortably rich with their pay and surprise bonuses from Mellusin Mining.

As for Njangu . . . he and Maev had quietly separated, Maev having bought her way out of the Force and announcing plans to return to school.

Njangu had, quite strangely, told Garvin he was going fishing, for pity's sake, in some tiny village over on the coast. He's invited Jaansma to join him, saying, equally mysteriously, that "Deira probably had a friend or six to spare, if she's not married, and I bet that wouldn't make much difference if she is."

Garvin shrugged.

Maybe . . . or maybe not.

That solitary island sounded better and better.

He realized how much he'd changed, aged even, which was pretty melodramatic thinking for somebody not yet thirty. He'd walked into the military's trap, and now it appeared it had snapped closed on him.

He had no idea whether or not he liked the change.

Garvin looked up, through the lifter's canopy, at the night sky and the stars.

Beyond them, drawing him more strongly than anything he'd ever known, though, was the scattered jigsaw puzzle of the Confederation.